Brenda's Gift

A NOVEL BY

Cynthia Yates

BROADMAN
&HOLMAN
PUBLISHERS

Nashville, Tennessee

0-8054-2147-5

Published by Broadman & Holman Publishers, Nashville, Tennessee

Dewey Decimal Classification: 813
Subject Heading: ANGELS—FICTION
Library of Congress Card Catalog Number: 00-036001

All Scripture through chapter 8 is from the King James Version;
all Scripture after chapter 8, except for quotations from the
Book of Psalms, are from the NIV, the Holy Bible, New International
Version, copyright © 1973, 1978, 1984 by International Bible Society.

Published in association with the literary agency of Janet Kobobel Grant,
Books & Such, 3093 Maiden Lane, Altadena, CA 91001.

Library of Congress Cataloging-in-Publication Data

Yates, Cynthia, 1947–
    Brenda's gift / Cynthia Yates.
        p.   cm.
    ISBN 0-8054-2147-5 (pb)
    1. Angels—Fiction. I. Title.

PS3575.A76 B74 2000
813'.54—dc21

                                                        00-036001
                                                        CIP

1 2 3 4 5   04 03 02 01 00

To my son

Acknowledgments

Heartfelt thanks to the following people:
David Allen, Eloise Berg, Marion Berry, Lori Butcher, Al and Garene Cochrane, Helen Coker, Leslie Frazee, Patti Graham, Dr. Richard Kahler, Sheila Kahler, Pastor John Lukomski, Pastor Paul McKibben, Ellen O'Brien, Barbara Orazio, Debbie Pancoast, Marshall Pearson, Col. Ray Reed, Pastor Darold Reiner, Randall Snyder, Esq., Col. Terry P. Swanger, Ret. USMC, Kim Vincent, Paul Wilcoxen, and the men and women at the Swan Lake Ranger Station for putting up with my many interruptions and strange questions.

To my family, friends, editors, and agent, thank you for your confidence and encouragement.

To my son, Joshua, you are my hero and my inspiration.

And to my husband, Joseph, apart from the Lord, you are my life, darling. This could never happen—*would* never happen—without your devoted love and support.

A Note to the Reader

Who knows if angels have wings—or hands and feet—or if they dance or weep? The Bible offers little direct description of their form, but whispers allusion to their magnificent countenance . . . and we certainly know they sing.

Who knows if demons have claws—or carry the stench of hell or sneer or scratch the ground with dragging talons? We know that they are grotesque imitators of that which is good.

This book tries to deal with angels and demons within the realm of biblical witness, and though in fiction there is much truth, the actual nature ascribed to spirit beings has been sometimes subjected to human imagination as a means to make the story understandable. Though an angel emerges as an important character within these pages, the emphasis of *Brenda's Gift* is to incite the imagination of your heart—and, I hope, of your soul.

Prologue

There was nothing unusual about it. It was, if you'll excuse the simplicity of this statement, just a beat-up old book, and a skinny one at that. No hot-shot designer cover, no punchy name. Dust jacket long gone, it was worn in one corner, worn as if hit by a hammer straight on. And as odd as this sounds, the book looked as if it had been run over by a car. The hard cover was still sturdy, though, and dark with a well-traveled path of smudge and accumulated finger grime.

It was highly unusual for me to stray into the used-book section of our thrift store (usually a disheveled mess of corny romance paperbacks and old biology texts), yet I was drawn to the shelves in the corner, as if a hand was shoving me. If not for making myself a fool, I would have turned to see who was behind me, hurrying me toward the shelves. I spotted it immediately.

The title and the fact that it was an old book summoned me, along with the odd notion that it seemed to be making itself conspicuous. *A Resting Place,* it plainly said, followed by faded, flowing cursive, *The Book of Psalms.* The spine, not having to proclaim an author, I suppose, was left free: clean, empty space; rod straight and strong; still holding the contents tight within.

No shelf-sitter this book, I thought as I skipped through pages that had been dog-eared, ripped, marked, written on, underlined, smeared, and on one particular page, as best I could tell, violently—angrily—blacked out. There were crayon scribbles, too, and a faded red blotch that dried on the side so that thumbing through the book accordion-style, as I was doing, made

1

amusing animation for my eye as pages flicked quickly past me, like those booklets I bought for a dime when I was a kid.

What piqued my attention most, I suppose, was the inscription on the inside cover:

> *April, 1966*
> *Dear Will,*
> *This is a good book that has helped me a lot. Let me know what you think of it. We can write long letters! I wish I could be on the ship with you.*
> *With much, much love,*
> *Brenda*

It fascinated me that once upon a time Brenda had much, much love for Will. Was she a friend, a sister, a lover? Who was Brenda? And what was so special about the Book of Psalms? I decided to pay twenty-nine cents to find out and plopped the old thing on the thrift store counter, still fighting the urge to look over my shoulder.

It would be a curious twist for me to read this section of the Bible—a book I rejected outright. But I wanted to know how the Psalms had helped Brenda. Besides, I needed a resting place of my own. It wasn't until months later that I noticed an inscription on the inside back cover. It was written by Will.

> *1/5/68*
> *I want to be a gud son. I pray fore my mom and dad.*
> *Jesus is my rok.*
> *William Harwood*

* * *

Bashar-el was his Hebrew name. He was a simple creature, an angelic being, with a simple job: follow the book. He was the lowest of the angels, but rank mattered nothing to him or to the others. They had pledged to keep their focus on the Holy One, to bring Him glory. All the heavenly host had free will, and Bashar's was set on serving his Lord, whose honor he kept in the forefront of all thought. To Bashar, there was no question in following the One who was love, not since he'd seen His face. This was his clear choice: to follow the Logos, the eternal Word of God; to guard it was of greatest importance. Therefore, Bashar-el, the angelic being who followed the book, was simply known as Chosen.

Chapter

One

Sometime in 1955

The slamming door made the walls tremble, as if the power of his father's fury had found its way into veins of board and joist and hemorrhaged violently throughout the house. Will bolted for bed. Tangling with the quilt, he kicked it loose from the fold-and-tuck tightly anchored by his mom. The seven-year-old was a veteran of countless arguments and knew the thunderous shudder would turn to dull, dead space when Mama rushed upstairs.

Will pulled the covers to his chin and closed his eyes so hard his lids fluttered. Tonight, he would pretend to be asleep. The door to his room opened as the settled silence pushed his mother in. Choking on her sorrow, she lay down beside Will and cradled him and cried. The scene was so familiar, so bewildering.

At first Will pretended sleep as his mother rocked and wept, the smell of Old Gold cigarettes strong in her hair, the sense of her pain so deep, too deep for the boy. Surrendering to his heart, he murmured, "Don't cry, Mama," confusion overwhelming the little boy. The stupid little boy.

Imbecile

"Pay attention, William!" his father commanded. "This is not hard! Read!"

Lost in a terrifying world of confusing letters and words, paralyzed by fear of his father, Will stammered, "E . . . esss h . . . h . . . ttt g . . . ooo . . . dd . . . nn . . . u . . . rr."

"You are going to sit here until you get this right!" bellowed his father. "Read!"

Tears painted salty streaks on the little boy's cheeks and collected in the corners of his mouth with a dribble. Will was utterly, utterly lost.

"Read!!"

Heaving sobs now, adrenaline laced his body with hysteria and the boy soiled himself. His father's hand came down, and Will fell to the floor. He collected himself into a tight ball and pulled away from the torment. "You filthy little imbecile!" raged his father as he threw the beginning reader on his son.

It would be the stuff of novels to say his mother came to the rescue, but there was no rescue from Will's father, not for mother or son. Professor Edward P. Harwood, whose public demeanor skillfully projected a proper "man of letters" ruled his household with wrath. And his outbursts of anger were becoming routine as Will's limitations became clear. Patty Harwood lived in as much fear as her son but found comfort in her husband's prolonged absences from home, which often followed the slamming door.

Will adored his mother, who patiently helped him with workbook assignments. "Sound out these letters, Willie, and make a word. Listen to Mama . . . d - o - gg." She always pronounced the last letter of words with great definition, as if last letters were very, very important. *C - a - tt. R - u - nn.* Will tried; oh, how he tried! "No, Will, *not* God!" she was fairly mortified. "Dog!"

"Dog . . . g" Will would repeat, and she would smile and relieve him of further after-school duties, the unspoken rule to finish homework before Professor Harwood returned, a goal becoming easier and easier to meet.

In spite of the anxiety his father caused, Will would gladly face him to avoid one dreaded place, one place that meant nothing but pain, shame, and sorrow. That place was school. His hatred of school would someday cause truancy and early delinquency (as delinquency went in the sixties when Will became a teen). Will, you see, was emerging as an embarrassment, an ignoramus. The class dummy.

Brenda

Brenda smiled at Will as she took her place beside him. Her smile was real. It spoke of a sweet and sincere spirit, and it made Will blush. Brand-new to his second-grade class, she was assigned to the empty seat, back when school desks were big enough for two and had hinged lids with holes that once held ink.

Brenda and Will shared space that first year, a space filled with close, abiding trust and etched with a bond that would last forever. As his clear and present advocate, Brenda's friendship became a safety net for the beleaguered boy. Brenda was popular in her own right. Others left Will to his own oddity when Brenda was around.

As Will grew older he grew tall. Being backward should have been enough for the boy, but now his mere physical appearance made him distinct. And he wasn't spared the adolescent rush of hormones and awkward behavior. Other students deliberately hazed him, knocked books off his desk, tripped him, and demanded submission when they spoke.

Day after day, Wacko Will faced humiliation as the class idiot. Tears were long gone. Defeated, Will accepted the designation. He *was* stupid. He didn't need other kids to remind him. He didn't even like other kids. Just Brenda. She was always kind to him.

"Hey, Stupid Oaf!" came the derisive jab. It was from John, the leader of the pack, the promising athlete, the wise guy with the duck haircut. "Carry my lunch tray to the table." It was a regular trick as other boys, clan members with John, waited in ambush to trip or shove. And then came the taunts and the laughter.

"Ignore them, Will," said Brenda as she bent to retrieve the tray and gave John a glance that meant business.

"They tripped me, Brenda," Will wailed.

"I know," said the girl, putting her hand on top of his to still the growing pressure in his gut. "They are the ones who are ignorant."

"Here, Brenda, this is for you." Will reached into his pocket and pulled out a note he'd worked on for days. "It's a note for you, Brenda."

Brenda slipped the note into her bulging loose-leaf binder and squeezed his hand. "Why thank you, Will!" She knew how hard Will worked to express his feelings of love for her and repaid him with grace—and with notes of her own, notes deliberately simple for the boy to read. He saved every one in his special box.

How a wooden cigar box had found itself into the Harwood home was a mystery. In keeping with his image, Will's father was a pipe man, the smell of cherry tobacco evident the second you stepped inside. Nonetheless, a cigar box had found its way there and was Will's prized possession. Trinkets from carnivals, a Canadian coin, colored pebbles from creeks, and a used casing of a .22-caliber bullet were carefully stored in the box. Yet no treasure was as meaningful as Brenda's notes, which were held together with a fat rubber band that had "Busy Bee Dry Cleaning" stamped on in white print. At night Will struggled to read Brenda's straight, plump, cursive, and, in time, was able to ignore the slamming door. It seemed the house itself grew weary of response as slams were now met with indifferent yawns; even the stairs remained still.

And so was life for young Will Harwood: torment by day, notes by night, until the end of his sophomore year in high school, when Brenda suddenly left town, and the boy's world caved in.

Delinquency

"Mrs. Harwood, I'm calling to report that William hasn't been in school for nearly one week. Can you tell me, is he ill?"

"Yes . . . ah . . . he's been sick lately. Ah, I am sure he will be back in school next Monday."

Patty Harwood put down the receiver and cradled her stomach with both arms as she leaned against a wall. There was nothing to hold, barely skin and bones, yet the thin woman reached for her stomach, like she always did when she was anxious. Except for nicotine stain on two fingers, her hands were red and angry from a nervous rash and incessant nail-biting.

"Where are you, Will?" she asked the wall, the boards, the joists, her question as much a part of this house as the empty air. This was their tomb, their cocoon, their prison, their sanctuary. This was thunder and silence.

Patty took her place alongside a picture window and watched the street. She was stationed at her post. From this spot she had watched the years go by, hidden beside a drape, concealed from the outside; an ever-present watchman keeping guard. From this spot she had seen her smiling little boy peddle up to his father. From this spot she had seen him climb off the bus alone, so alone. From this spot she had watched the last time Will greeted his dad, when he had run to his room. What had Ed said to him? Where had the smiles gone? What had happened to change everything?

Medical reports had insisted that Will was a normal, healthy boy. Lazy, Ed had called him, and good for nothing. Yet her baby, her precious baby, was anything but worthless! She *knew* Will was smart . . . but . . .

Patty gripped the drape, her bony fingers white, yellow, red, as her gaze shifted toward the flower pattern on the rug. She followed the outline of a rose, the stem so clear and strong, branching toward another but never connecting. She was losing touch with Will. The comfort they had once found in each other was gone, and now Patty was alone. Once they were each other's hiding place, each other's security, but Will's rebellion began to fray the tight cord that connected even them.

An outside movement startled her. She held her stomach tightly and turned ashen. Professor Harwood pulled into the drive. "Where are you, Will?" she said to the drape in desperation.

* * *

Will was in the company of an extremely agitated policeman. Officer Newton made no effort to hide his disgust. He had chased the boy and caught him, the chase an unpleasant reminder of his increasing girth and lack of fitness for duty. It was a winded run through an orchard, over a fence, and into the traffic that had brought Will to a halt. A fleshy hand came down and pushed Will hard onto the chair.

Pants ripped from barbed wire and his hand cut badly, Will fought back tears. A fire teeter-tottered inside and teased him with rage, then panic.

"What's your name, boy?" snarled the policeman.

"Will Harwood."

"What were you doing in Wilkinson's garage?"

"Nothing."

Booked on vandalism, Will met with Officer Newton for the first—and not the last—time. He began his career as a delinquent, as calls from school and the early arrival home of Professor Ed Harwood became routine. Alienated now from his mother, Wacko Will was on his way to becoming the town oddity. A striking boy once he grew into himself, he was nonetheless regarded with jest, and not a little fear. And he was a continual embarrassment to his father.

Teachers had passed Will along for want of what to do. Some teachers had helped Will learn enough to get by but were unfamiliar with learning disabilities; special education was still years away. Through their motivational coaching, along with his mother's faithful night duty, Will was reasonably literate. (His understanding of math added to his peculiarity and was dismissed as proof that he was living on some inexplicable edge.) Actually, after years of practice, Will was able to work his way through certain words with ease. (How simple life would be if all words spelled the same backwards as frontwards! Like *Mom* . . . or *Dad*.) Will had developed his own system of reading that put him at fifth-grade level if anyone had taken the time to check.

Brenda Returns

It was the summer before Will's senior year when something wonderful happened, and it all began with a call. Patty immediately corrected the young woman on the phone (for she was not the first young woman to call for Ed). "You must mean *Ed* Harwood."

"No. This is Brenda Martin. I'm calling to talk with Will."

If it has ever happened that your heart, your very heart, has nearly burst with a tingly, excruciatingly happy explosion, then you will understand how Will felt when he heard Brenda's voice. A lump played leap-frog from chest to throat, and his entire body turned into gooey marshmallow. She was coming over, and they would take a walk!

Patty jumped aside as Will blasted upstairs. The boy became atomized, bouncing off everything in his way, into the bathroom, bounding to his dresser, clothes flying, water running, Will . . . whistling?!

Brenda was as kind and gentle as ever, yet there seemed to be a sorrow about her that bothered Will. This would be the first of several long walks during hot, leftover summer afternoons and in the comfort of solid friendship. Will wanted desperately to touch the hand of his doe-like friend and tell her she was nice. Old, faraway feelings built inside of him during their walks, feelings he used to have when Daddy came home . . . before he got stupid.

Will knew Brenda did not like his rebellion, and so he tried to overcome his anger. And because of Brenda, he was determined to try harder during this last year of school. But it was not to be, and in the second week of September the predictable happened, when Will let loose his anger.

Three boys were huddled near Brenda's locker. One was John. John had taken Brenda to the sophomore Valentine's dance, an occasion that had caused much conflict within Will. But that was a long time ago. As Will approached from behind, he could tell the boys were taunting Brenda: he knew the look, the body language, the cryptic sounds well. "Slut," said John, in chorus with the jeers of the others. Crying, Brenda looked up and saw Will explode. "No!" she yelled.

Will Leaves

Officer Newton sat in the living room of the Harwood home. Professor Edward P. Harwood and his wife Patricia sat apart. Will was in jail.

"I spoke with the recruiter this morning," Newton said. "There should be no problem. You just have to sign the form since he's not eighteen yet."

"Gladly," said Ed Harwood. And with the stroke of his pen, the little suburb outside of Chicago was finally free of its local idiot, of Wacko Will, of their embarrassment. The year was 1965. Will was on his way to Vietnam.

The Marines were good for Will. Once and for all rid of the stigma that pestered him nearly all of his life, he was just another jarhead, a blond head shorn to nubbins, who found himself on equal footing: *every* recruit in basic training was stupid.

Testing proved him borderline literate, but Will was capable in other areas. The United States Marine Corps was not concerned and assigned Will to its infantry division. After basic training, he was to board one of four ships headed for Vietnam. Patty was there to see him off.

* * *

Patricia Harwood looked breakable as she waited on the unusually cold, windy dockside. She held a box of Will's favorite cookie bars and a gift from Brenda. This her first trip alone, Patty had traveled by bus to be there. She was weary from dodging a heavy, smelly man who shifted and snored, adding to other night sounds as the bus cruised its way along a southwestern route. Yet for all the smell and discomfort and cold, she was glad to be away: home was hell. Her only solace came standing next to the window every day, keeping watch and holding her stomach with reddened hands, hands that were cold now in spite of gloves.

Choppy ocean waves slapped the side of the ship. *How in the world can something that big float?* Patty wondered, her wondering mixed with fear. She had to be there to say good-bye to her baby. She would have *stolen* the money if Ed hadn't agreed to let her go.

Ed had been visibly relieved when Will left home and had made it clear he would not be welcomed back. Closing her eyes, as if to close off thought, Patty shivered in overwhelming sorrow when she remembered home without Will. Will, on the other hand, was doing well. His first, tentative steps into the world carried him toward integration with himself. He missed his mother and Brenda, but he liked it out here.

His calls home were so infrequent that Patty never left her post at the window. When the phone did bring him near, she could not stop the searing pain in her belly, the red-hot poker that branded her as Wacko Will's mother . . . and Ed Harwood's wife. "No, Willie, he's not home. I'm not sure where he is."

"Mama!" came the call. She looked frantically. Will stepped out of a mass of shouts and tears. He was carrying a sea bag. Patty nearly swooned: so much about him was different, and he was smiling. She disappeared in his hug.

Sirens were sounding, bells were insistent, and the throng about Patricia Harwood and her boy was filled with hugs and clamor. The frail woman, the woman who was old before she was young, braced against the cold as anguished words forced their way out, pushing to be heard above the wind and the noise of others: "I love you, Willie!"

More than ever her words hit home. They landed indelibly on his heart and found a resting place in his soul. Her tears were burning and frantic; the sound of her words could never *ever* leave his memory: "I *love* you!"

Their eyes locked. He had heard her. "I love you too," he said, for the first time in years. It made the tears fall harder. "Don't cry, Mama," said Will tenderly, as he picked up his duffel and was gone.

Chosen

Chosen had seen war before. The Chaldeans, the Assyrians, the Egyptians—so many others along the way. It was chronicled in the old Book, and the scenario never changed. *Why must the heart of man harbor such wickedness?* he wondered. *Why couldn't man submit to the Holy One? After all, the teaching of the Master was in the Book for all to read.* But philosophizing wasn't part of Chosen's work as he followed Will down the narrow steel staircase to the bunk that would be home for his first six-month tour with the Marine Amphibious Unit.

Huston

"Is that present from your sweetie-pie?"

Will looked down and saw Huston, a fellow from basic training and now his bunkmate. Even after all these weeks it was hard for Will to adjust to normal conversation.

Will held the gift and let memories sweep him back to summer walks and easy feelings. The look and feel of the package—unmistakably a *book*—brought some alarm. It didn't matter. The bright wrapping was covered in one corner by a card with familiar, plump cursive. "To Will," said the card, which was decorated with a hand-drawn heart.

Oh, if they all had a heart like Brenda, thought Chosen, *how different this world would be!*

"Sort of," Will finally answered, flushed in his face, as he ripped the paper.

Chosen watched closely as Will worked through the book's title. Huston, who was as tall as Will and more imposing, was drawn to the book in Will's hand. He reached over (actually he felt as if he were *shoved* over), and blushed at his forward behavior. *"A Resting Place: The Book of Psalms"* read Huston, relieving Will greatly.

"I know Psalm 23 by heart; learnt it in Sunday school," boasted Huston. "You want to hear it?"

"Sure," said Will, uncertain about what a psalm was, but not about to tip anyone to his ignorance. Will knew about Sunday school because Brenda went there. He figured a psalm had something to do with the Bible. His father got mad when people talked about the Bible.

"'The Lord is my shepherd; I shall not want,'" began Huston.

As Huston recited the precious Word, Chosen felt a thrill pass through him. The Word brought such peace and joy to this angelic being. He knew its truth, its strength, its power. Chosen smiled as Will opened the cover, saw Brenda's inscription, and quickly closed it for another time, for a time when he would be alone to work through the words and find meaning.

"'. . . and I will dwell in the house of the Lord for ever,'" beamed Huston, as the great ship lurched and the journey began. Will, Huston, and other Marines of the MAU were on a ship that would maneuver around Vietnam and send troops to land for special patrol.

Huston, who complained regularly about the length of his bunk, soon learned Will's secret. But Huston was kind. Theirs was an unusual bond, created by close quarters and the shared intimacy of facing death each time they stepped into swirling sea and waded ashore or were dropped from helicopters like rocks off a steam shovel.

Will hauled the book everywhere, wearing the corners of its dust jacket thin. He stuck it in the center of his pack to protect it from sweat and rain. The book was his heart; it was Brenda herself.

"Let me see that thang," said Huston in his Kentucky drawl. Will's heart jumped every time Huston asked for the book. For some reason, Huston liked to read out loud. And he was such an impressive and friendly fellow, it didn't seem to bother others. Will gladly reached over the side of his bunk and handed the book to Huston.

"Let's see whare this thang opens up to today!" proclaimed the young man.

"Howdy-doody! This thang opened right up at the beginning, Willie Boy!" And Huston read, and William Harwood listened, and Chosen prayed.

Something was starting to churn inside the boy. Chosen could see it in his eyes. Will was hearing the mighty Word, the Word that would not return void, the Word that brings life. It was more than Will's heart that was beginning to listen; it was his spirit, and there was a battle going on.

"'Blessed is the man . . .'" Huston's voice turned to drone as Will stared at the steel ceiling and thought. He wished he knew what box he had checked on the personal information forms. The words had been too hard for him to read in such a short time: he knew they had something to do with God. His dog tags said "Protestant." To Will it looked like "tantestorP." He was too embarrassed to ask Huston what *tantestorP* meant.

"'Not so the wicked! They are like chaff' . . . you know what chaff is, Willie? Hey! Listen up!"

Chosen prayed hard. Will's mind was piecing together words, a different word-puzzle than usual: *one nation under God; for god's sake, Patricia!; No, Will! Not God!; God bless America; God bless you; religion is for idiots . . .*

"Willie-boy? You listenin' to me or you daydreamin'?"

"Hey, dumbbell!" came a call from another bunk. "Answer his question!"

Chosen sank to his knees. A snarl came from behind. *"You will never get him, Bashar. Never!"*

"Tell him what chaff is, you stupid oaf!"

Will's belly tightened. Like bullets in the dark jungle night, two emotions clashed inside him. Charging toward their mark, shame and anger collided and fought hand-to-hand. Chosen shoved Huston to his feet as Will hit the floor, positioning Huston as a barrier from the taunt.

"Ooh, look who's all worked up, it's the dummy! Be quiet now while his mommy reads him to sleep!"

Will lunged at the heckler. Huston blocked his charge and wrestled with him. Huston and Will and Chosen crashed to the floor in a heap. The snarl turned to stench and hideous satisfaction.

Huston gathered his friend and gave warning to the others in the room, particularly to the tormentor: there would be no more talk like that. How naive of the strong Kentucky boy! The ridicule might stop in front of him, but Will's secret was out. Old patterns of shame surfaced, as did anger. It was the last time Will let Huston read out loud. He shoved the book under his mattress, ripping the dust jacket to shreds.

The Battle

Huston continued to befriend Will and to shield him from abuse, but through the next several weeks Will became increasingly withdrawn. This did not matter much to the others. The war in Vietnam was not the stuff of movies. Friendships were important, but the all-for-one, one-for-all camaraderie of the John Wayne era was gone. One man followed another, and, like one foot followed another through the mud, one man replaced another.

Will was with his unit on ground patrol in the Mekong Delta. As dusk began to settle on the third day, his feet rubbed raw against wet boots. Leeches and insects covered his hands and neck. Heat pierced his helmet like a spear, driving madness deeper and deeper into his skull. His brain melted to a little puddle of searing lava. A high pitch, a whine—or was it a snarl?—reverberated through his head.

"You better pop a salt pill, Willie-boy," called Huston.

Chosen walked alongside the boy and held him steady. Will's legs were giving out, and the shaking was starting; heat exhaustion was claiming its victim. Will struggled to move forward, one foot following the next through the sucking mire. It was July 12, his eighteenth birthday, but even he forgot.

The first shot they heard sounded like a pop. It was a dull, small sound, but enough to throw these battle-wise Marines to the ground and to pump adrenaline through every sweaty muscle. Following instinct, following training, following each other, they dropped. But one was already down.

"Willie!" came the scream of panic. Will turned and saw Huston on his back. The bullet had pierced his neck, and blood pumped freely from a ragged hole. Will clawed his way through mud and screams, like crawling through lard. Chosen rushed to Huston. It was a time of great emotion for the angel; he knew Huston was going home. Eternity faced this young, brave Kentucky boy who held the Word in his heart. Chosen saw the escort arrive to take Huston home and smiled in the midst of terror and death.

Will could tell Huston was dying. "Get your stupid head down!" barked a command from behind. Will leaned over Huston and could not stop the tears, volcanic, erupting tears that came from his core, mixing with the lake of blood on his friend's chest.

The flow of blood was waning. Chosen held Huston's head as a mother cradles her newborn. Chosen praised and glorified the Almighty for this young man's life and prayed that moment for Will. Huston, following his Master, had faced the last enemy, death. In moments—as mortals track time—he would be held in the arms of Jesus. But Will was left behind.

Through eyes clouded with blood, Huston could see his friend. He was not in pain, but weak. He braced himself and reached inside for one last push of strength; his words had to hit right at Will's heart.

"You read that book, Willie-boy," he mustered. And he was dead.

"Get your head down!" yelled another voice. "Hey idiot! Get your stupid head down!" the voice taunted again.

Will lay alongside his friend and aimed his rifle into the thick, matted jungle. Explosive noise, heat, and filth seemed far away. He lay there with his rifle aimed, alone. So alone.

Chosen knelt beside Will and continued to shield him from enemy attack. Something was happening inside of the boy, and Chosen was worried; horrible snarls came from behind. A squadron of demons oozed from the sludge, repugnant with rancor, their purulent discharge a rancid film that covered the bog. Chosen and Will were surrounded.

"The Lord rebuke you!" screamed the angel, posturing for battle.

Squeals of laughter mimicked the angel. *"Oooh, the Lord rebuke us! This is our turf down here, Bashar, this boy is ours! . . . Will, Will . . . Do not let the man taunt you anymore. You have the power to stop him right in your hands. Do it! Do it! No one will ever know. Silence him and end your torment!"*

Will snapped. Emotion detonated inside his gut, rose through clenched jaw, and escaped in primal scream. A lifetime of confusion, anguish, and rejection surfaced with maddening power. His anger—his vicious anger—wanted, *demanded*, retribution. With stealth and purpose, Will turned himself around and pointed his rifle again. He would be taunted no more. Under cover of falling night, jungle brush, and enemy fire, Will pulled the trigger. And the demons danced.

Guilt

No one would ever know. His tormentor gone, Will adjusted to life without Huston and with bedeviling guilt. Shame was a familiar feeling for Will, but *guilt* became a new and agonizing companion. To make matters worse, Brenda's last letter caused a stir inside him that compounded his misery.

At first Will stuffed Brenda's letter in his pack, crushing it like old trash, but now it became irresistible and he worked through the wrinkled words, reading and rereading with surgical precision. Brenda would be heading to nursing college soon. She told Will about her plans, that she prayed for him every day (twice every day!), and she wrote, like she always did, about Jesus. This disturbed Will. Huston had talked about Jesus.

"See this Psalm 40 here, Willie-boy? Talks about bein' in miry clay— sounds like us, don't it? Says He puts our feet on a rock. You know who our rock is, Willie? It's JE-sus. That's a fact, Willie, that's a fact."

As Will thought, Chosen worked . . . just a few more inches, and . . . it would finally . . . there!

"Hey!" came a call from Huston's bunk. "What the . . . ?"

The book landed on the new man, the marine who filled the space of the empty bunk, the replacement.

"Hey, Willie! This your book?" A hand held the book up and Will reached down and grasped it.

"Yeah," he said. Chosen knocked it from his hand, and it fell open on his chest to Psalm 1. *Blessed is the man . . .* his thoughts flashed to a bloody, bug-infested field. *Howdy-doody . . . you know what chaff is . . . read the book, Willie.*

Will knew chaff all right. Chaff was fighting your way free and ending up in chains. Chaff was hating yourself for being stupid, hating yourself for being smart. Chaff was no escape. Will's jaw tightened with stinging pain as guilt, in a thunderous shudder, coursed through his body. Chosen held Will much like he cradled Huston. He stroked Will's forehead, and as Will forced himself to work through Psalm 1, he felt a distant promise of peace, as Chosen prayed.

The Missionary

Will had been to Saigon before. Alone this time, he wandered through storefronts killing time. Dutifully—most likely to prove his sameness—he bought his mother a Buddha, a teapot, and chopsticks. With three days to spend, Will searched for the place where he and Huston had rented a room. He took a wrong turn, not at all by accident, as Chosen beamed with high hopes and rushed ahead.

Joe Kauffman was a Yank dressed comfortably in Asian clothes. Old and tired, Joe was headed to church to prepare for evening service. A Mennonite, Brother Joe grieved over the conflict in Southeast Asia and found himself at odds with his own pacifist beliefs. Joe knew firsthand the atrocities in Vietnam as well as Laos and Cambodia. He could not shake his feeling of failure (in himself, in mankind) as thoughts of this war closed in on him. Deep in prayer, anguish, and confusion, he rounded a corner and slammed into the tall marine. They were both surprised. Chosen was delighted.

"Watch it!" yelled Will.

"Sorry, son," said Joe, who was picking up the books he dropped. "Sometimes old men get lost in their thoughts."

"You an American?" asked Will, almost too eagerly, for he was more lonely than he knew—and this man called him "son."

"Well . . . yes . . . I haven't been to the States in many years, though. I've been here since after the war."

Will looked confused.

"After World War II," said Joe. "I'm a missionary."

Will stared intently and watched the old man retrieve another book. He had no idea what a missionary was, but knew it had something to do with God.

"That a Bible?" he asked.

Chosen helped Brother Joe straighten his arthritic back and look the boy in the eye.

"Yes it is," said Joe, with growing interest in this young soldier.

"Somebody gave me the book of Psalms," said Will. "I had a friend who knew one by heart."

Joe softened toward the boy in spite of his aversion to the uniform. He offered his hand. "Joseph Kauffman," he said with a smile.

Will hesitated, but his hand shot out almost on its own. "Will Harwood," said the lonely boy. And they shook hands and parted.

Joe continued his walk to church, every step heavier, more effort than the next. He chastened himself for not opening up to the boy, for being too focused on his private battle, for . . .

"Hey, Mr. Kauffman!" came the voice from behind. "You think you could take me to Sunday school?"

Joe took Will to church, to dinner, to his home, and, because of the timing of Will's visit, to what Brother Joe called Thursday, Friday, and Saturday school. Will—carried by the wings of an angel—was immersed in brotherly love, unconditional acceptance, white rice . . . and Jesus. Joe reveled in the boy (could he even *think* this without offense to Will . . . the *simple* boy), a young man oddly isolated from the world happening around him. Joe answered questions, prayed, and talked. And on the night before Will left, Joe listened.

As for Will, he'd never felt such security and trust. He was losing his heart to something bigger than he, something more powerful, something provoking him to new feelings. He was hearing about Jesus. Jesus, who was mocked, who was ridiculed, who was scorned, who did not fight back, but who died. God, according to Brother Joe, very God.

Conversion

Back in his bunk, before the next patrol, Will steadied the book on bent legs. Thanks to Joe Kauffman, he had a whole Bible now, but he kept going back to Brenda's gift. He read the inscription (he knew it by heart), and turned to Psalm 1. Her crumbled letter his bookmark, he ran his finger under every word, smudging the page as he sounded each carefully (though he was learning them by heart too).

"For the Lord . . . k . . . nowth the way of the . . . rigg . . . hatas: but the way of the un . . . dog, no! . . . *god* . . . ly sh . . . all peer . . . no! pear . . . ish."

"Knock it off!" came the reprimand and hard poke from Huston's bunk. The replacement had learned Will's secret in no time and was not kind like Huston.

Will caught himself. He must have been reading aloud. Chosen held his breath.

"Sorry," answered Will. A sigh and a snarl.

"Religion is for losers!" came back from below. Will didn't answer. Again, the taunt: "You're stupid, man, to believe that junk!"

Will tensed. He swung off the bunk and headed down the aisle. Chosen trembled and ran after him.

There was one place on ship where Will could find privacy. He stepped into the tiny space and closed the door. Chosen unfolded his wings as an iron shield around the toilet. Will clutched the book in his hands, pressing it against his chest, as he awkwardly knelt and fit his big body around the commode.

"I'm sorry, God," cried Will. "I'm sorry, I'm sorry!" Over and over came the repentant plea.

Chosen wept for the moment, a celestial chant began to build in the background, and the presence of the Holy One filled Will's heart and soul. Stench and snarl faded to whimper and to the faint sound of claws scratching steel in hasty retreat.

"Jesus," uttered Will, "Jesus, be my rock. Jesus, help me!"

The presence and power of the Holy One brought Chosen to ecstasy. The angel bowed in humble adoration as Will was infused with God the

Holy Spirit. Will slumped in exhaustion, his head in his arms, sobbing away years of torment, rebellion, and pain. His heart right, that night the boy fell into deep sleep, the sleep of a newborn, as Chosen rocked him with a lullaby—and the angels danced.

Chapter
Two

January 1968

An electric cord came straight down, hit the blackboard, and disappeared from sight, giving the old clock the appearance of a lollipop hanging over Professor Janoff's head. Big, with black trim, the clock was generally ignored until the end of class neared (save its annoying tick during the quiet of exams), when eyes furtively glanced as if to hurry it along, especially on Fridays. Today was Friday, and in five minutes the lollipop over Janoff's bald head would make a strike for liberty, when the bell signaled freedom.

Brenda turned from her professor's boring recapitulation of bowel resection and gazed out the window. Anatomy could wait until library time tomorrow. All she had on her mind was tonight: Stephen was taking her to a James Bond movie. And it was raining.

She touched her hair for the hundredth time. Thanks to the girls in the dorm—who were determined to turn their wallflower into a rose—she'd slept the night in curlers. That morning she had sat passively as friends teased and lacquered her head with hair spray. Indestructible as it felt, it did look pretty for a first date, her first since the dance so many years ago. Brenda was anxious and worried about the rain; a whole case of hair spray would be no defense against this downpour.

The bell startled her.

"You sure were off in never-never land!"

Brenda's roommate for the past two years, her closest friend at nursing school in North Carolina, stood clutching an assortment of tablets and textbooks. Amy waited for Brenda to collect her gear before the two of them wandered into the hall. Water pipes running up the walls rumbled and hissed, adding a damp feel to match the weather outside. The sound of rain pounding the roof dimmed as Brenda and Amy worked their way down expansive wooden stairs to the main floor. Brenda hesitated at the door.

"I'm definitely not wearing that madras blouse of yours tonight! Can you see it? Wet hair and all the colors of the rainbow dripping down my arms! Think he'd ask me out again?"

The girls giggled, gathered their loads close to their bodies with one arm, tried to shield their heads with the other, and set out at a dash. They ran alongside shrubs heavy with rain, buds just beginning to burst from stick to bush. They walked hurriedly single-file under the eaves of the administration building, passing a cluster of antiwar protesters with posters that hung like huge, limp curls on boards. In spite of the weather, the rally would go on, as the more ardent demonstrators gathered to shout slogans. The girls splashed their way by. Amy shrieked when a raindrop landed on her neck and tunneled itself under her dress.

"Maybe I'll call Rich and ask him to pick us up by ark!" she yelled toward her friend. More laughter.

No rainstorm was going to douse Amy's excitement for Brenda, for it was Amy who had campaigned these past two years to get her roommate to date, chipping away at her friend's firm resolve to keep away—safely away—from any young man who showed more than platonic interest. And there had been many. Brenda's sweet spirit and gentle manner attracted others and turned the eye of more than one medical student.

Brenda sprinted off the curb and landed ankle-deep in a puddle, splashing water up her legs, making long, flesh-colored streaks on her white nylon stockings. She knew Amy was perplexed by her resistance to dating, and knew full well her conniving roommate was certain that Stephen would bring her spinster days to an end. The fact that he was Rich's best friend made the arrangement perfect: for Amy, this was the stuff of dreams.

Brenda sidestepped another puddle as she thought about Amy's grand plans: she and Brenda would be in each other's wedding; she would be Aunt Amy to Brenda's kids; Rich and Stephen would do guy things, they would go into practice together, no—join the Peace Corps first, and travel to distant countries and help the poor—such was the strategy her eager roommate had detailed over a hasty lunch that day. Brenda kept the lead as the girls dashed up the sidewalk, actually relieved she was finally breaking free from her fears. Besides, she secretly dreamed the same dreams as her roomie.

"You go decide what you're going to wear. I'll get the mail," said Amy when they reached the dorm.

Once under cover, Brenda touched her hair with both hands. She felt the shape of a sleek bouffant and worried whether her French twist would hold through the evening. Thanks to the hair spray, the rain hadn't done much damage. She walked down the hall to their room.

No clanging water pipes here, Brenda and Amy were spending their second year in a brand-new dorm and had ranked a first-floor room. Brenda piled books on her corner desk and opened the burnt orange curtains that covered expansive windows. The Vietnam protesters were still near the administration building, huddled in a steamy mass, the soggy posters now held over their heads as shields. Brenda looked at the sidewalk leading to the dorm, and her stomach knotted with fear: in a few hours Rich and Stephen would come down that walk.

It was no secret that Stephen was attracted to her. She thought of the times he had come along with Rich to visit Amy, bringing him into her little world long enough to feel the pull, the inside blush. And yet masterfully she had kept her space, keeping Stephen in his place. At the slightest hint of interest, Brenda's instincts went on full-scale red alert as she fought demons of despair and pushed Stephen away. If it hadn't been for Amy's prodding, along with a dorm full of others whom Amy had acquisitioned for her campaign, Brenda would be facing yet another Friday night in front of the rec room TV. "Dear Lord," she prayed, "protect me."

"Fat letter from your mom!" Amy plopped her books on her bed and went straight to Brenda's closet.

"I think you should wear your peach cardigan. You'd never get a regular sweater over your head. Anyway, they always keep the heat too high at the theater, and if you wear that white sleeveless blouse of yours—the one you wear with your wraparound, that one—then you can unbutton the sweater if you are too hot, anyway . . ." Amy rattled on while Brenda opened her mail. Brenda hadn't had someone fuss over her so much since Mom and Granny fussed over her the . . .

Brenda's hand shot to her mouth, as if to cover a scream. Her other hand held a newspaper clipping up close to her face, which she read through trembling lips and tears that would not be stopped. It was an obituary.

Hand still attached to a hanger in the closet, Amy froze. "Bren . . . WHAT?!"

"It's Will—he's been killed in action."

There would be no James Bond that night. As rain hit the window and streaked rivulets down the sill to race to the ground, Brenda sank to her knees and buried her head in her arms while she leaned against her bed and wept. News of her friend's death triggered an emotional commotion in the young woman that had been working its way to the surface since she accepted Stephen's invitation. Her friendship with Will linked her to the past, his death a strange incentive toward release from private hell. It was time to tell her story.

* * *

It wasn't rain but snow that had worried Brenda four years ago, standing obediently as her mother and grandmother circled her in the fashion by which older women size up their progeny. Betraying her Irish roots, the grandmother spoke first.

"You are lovely as red clover in the meadow, lass," she cooed. Brenda was the love of her life. Many was the time she rocked back and forth in her squeaky chair and told Brenda about the joy she'd brought the old woman. Back she would rock as her feet lifted off the floor, then down, the balls of her feet in sync with the rhythm, pushing up and back again. Back and forth. A lilting, hypnotic trance would come over the little girl as her grandmother held her and sang lullabies and taught the child to pray.

"I think John is going to have to fight off the other boys!" gushed her mother.

"Oh, Mom!" laughed Brenda, stealing a glance at the clock radio next to her bed. John would be coming up the walk in less than an hour. John! *The* most popular boy in school, and she was his choice for the Sweetheart Dance! Brenda's palms felt clammy as she ran them down her dress, trying to smooth the layers of red lace that billowed over the satin bodice.

"Are you sure this dress isn't too old-fashioned?"

"Oh, Brenda! How can you ask that?! Your cousin Cheryl wore this to her senior ball!"

"But that was two years ago . . ."

Charmed by her granddaughter's innocence, the old lady smiled broadly. "Lassie, you're a wee bit fidgety!"

Brenda didn't need the doorbell, the predictable barking of their dog Scooter, or her father's call to tell her John had arrived; she'd been watching from her window (when she wasn't fussing at the mirror), swallowing hard, and trying to stay calm. This was her first big date; would she remember the dance steps her girlfriends had taught her? What if he wanted to kiss her? How would she fit with John's crowd— for John traveled in a different group than Brenda, who kept company with the college-bound, academic types. John was a jock from the word *go*. He was also a year older than his classmates, held back in primary grades because of performance. He wasn't slow, like Will; John was a rebel—he didn't care, he didn't try, and as the budding star athlete, he didn't have to. He was soon and future king to students and teachers alike. John could be overbearing at times—and she certainly hated how he treated Will—but he held a certain power that left the girls defense-less. To be his date was nothing short of highest honor. As far as Brenda was concerned, it was nothing short of a *miracle!*

After posing for customary pictures, making a fuss over the token wrist bouquet of red and white carnations, and listening to her father's lecture about curfew, winter driving, and speed (the school gym was so close they could walk), Brenda and John were off.

Brenda noticed something strange from the start. The friendly—almost gushy—manner that John had shown during the past few weeks seemed strained. John was aloof. Complete silence crashed down on Brenda and sent her into a miserable state of self-doubt. *It's my dress!* she thought. *I look hideous in my cousin's formal. He's embarrassed to be seen with me!* John parked his car against a snow bank and left the girl to slog her way through rutted tracks to get to the gym.

The dance was a disaster. John left Brenda alone, dancing with her only once. Fighting tears, she stood near the punch bowl, trying to smile and make small talk with curious couples. The disc jockey played *Sugar Shack* by Jimmy Gilmer and the Fireballs, as bodies twisted and jerked around her. When slow numbers interspersed she wanted to die, and retreated into a corner as sweethearts swayed in slow, back-and-forth movements, locked in eternal embrace. It was during one such slow dance that she saw John approach her. The hapless girl smiled valiantly.

"Let's go," he said.

She never questioned him. Glad that her public humiliation would soon be over, Brenda followed John to the coat rack, found her coat under a heap on the floor, and dutifully followed him to his car. Just a few more minutes before she would be home . . . quite a bit earlier than planned. John turned the car in the opposite direction. Before Brenda could open her mouth, he reached over and pulled her toward him.

"Come next to me, baby," he said, with sudden attentiveness.

Confused, but suddenly tickly inside, Brenda dutifully sat next to John as he drove farther and farther from school—and from her house. He pulled into an alley behind an old apartment building in the seedy part of town. This time John opened the car door for her and helped her out.

"My friend has a little place here," he said.

A jolt of panic raced through Brenda as she followed him up a stairway that smelled of rotted trash. Careful to hold her dress away from dust in the hall, anxiety built inside Brenda as she tried to pick her way in the dimly lit building. She sensed she was in danger and was confused why John would bring her to visit his friend. He opened the door to the apartment and switched on a light. Brenda had never seen anything like it before.

An old couch sat in the middle of a room, its cushions so worn that cotton stuffing pushed its way free of confinement. Clothes were scattered everywhere. Dishes and food wrappers competed with clothes for floor space. The windows were covered with filthy shades and ripped curtains that had given up the ghost long ago. There was a strange odor in the apartment. And there was no friend in sight.

John headed for the kitchen and returned with two sodas. Brenda stood nailed to the floor near the door.

"Come sit down," said John, as he spread himself on the couch. "My friend should be here any minute."

Brenda walked toward John, instincts telling her to flee. She'd never been alone with a boy like this. Was he going to kiss her? She wanted to go home.

"John, I'd like to you to take me home, please."

"You're not afraid to be alone with me, are you, Brenda?"

"No. Of course not. It's just that . . ."

"Come over here and have a soda. We'll leave after my friend gets here."

Still buttoned in her coat, Brenda sat on the couch. She sipped the soda and grimaced.

"This doesn't taste right!" she cried.

"Oh, it's a new brand of soda my friend has. Sip it again—the taste kind of grows on you."

Brenda took another sip. She was beginning to shiver from fear. John reached over and held her hand.

"I'm sorry I wasn't more attentive at the dance, Brenda. One of my friends was having a hard time with his girl and I needed to talk to him. You understand."

"It's just that I felt so embarrassed . . ." Brenda began to say.

"Let me make it up to you," said John, as he leaned over and kissed her. Her first kiss. The flutter kick inside her belly nearly knocked her backwards.

They kissed again. Brenda began to feel warm. He kissed her again, this time pushing her back on the couch. Balancing her glass of soda in the air, wanting to be kissed, but . . . unsure, Brenda began to protest.

"John, stop!"

"It's OK, baby, relax. Nothing is going to happen."

Completely naïve to his advances, Brenda felt suffocated as the wool collar of her coat rubbed against her neck. John was making his move. Certain she was in peril, she began to cry. "Stop! I want to go home!"

It was too late. There was no stopping John.

The News

A meeting was scheduled that evening with John's parents. Eyes red and puffy from unremitting tears, Brenda sat at the kitchen table flanked by her father and mother. Oh, for this to be a bad dream! But how to dream dreams of such things as you don't know? "Bonny lass" was now the stuff of dreams, as the anguish of her secret torment had changed Brenda forever, troubling her parents, who discounted her strange new behavior as teen turmoil. Granny knew, though; she knew something terrible had come over her precious grandchild, and prayed fervently that Brenda would be blessed with grace to cope with whatever had befallen her. Granny soon changed her plea to mercy. Brenda was pregnant.

The news had rocked the small Martin family off its foundations. Brenda was loved and trusted by godly parents who listened with horror as she sobbed heaving sobs and shared the ordeal that had gripped her since the dance. Now her parents understood: they remembered thinking it odd that night when Brenda hurried to her upstairs room, odd that she spent so long in the shower, odd that her wrist bouquet had been tossed in the trash, odd that Brenda was in bed "sick" the next morning and stayed home from church, odd that she would not talk about the dance. Odd, but the way of teens, thought her mom and dad. What was worrisome, however, was that she hadn't smiled since that night. Now they knew why.

As Brenda finished her story, her father stormed from the room. Jack Martin slammed the door to the garage and stood dazed. He wanted blood.

He wanted to kill John. Blinded by tears, he let out a scream as he sent a pail across the floor with his foot. He slammed his fist against the wall. Thoughts of that boy with his daughter ran through his mind, flaming to the intensity of rage until he was breathless, sinking to his knees broken, angry, hurt, and scared. He buried his head in his hands and wept. His baby girl, his baby girl.

"Jack, we must pray," came his wife's voice as she put her hands on his shoulders.

"PRAY?!" he bellowed.

"Yes, Jack, pray. Brenda needs us to be strong for her. We can't get through this on our own."

"Did you leave her alone?"

"No. Mother is with her. Jack, you are usually the first to say we must pray . . ."

The man looked like a helpless, lost little boy. "Edna, what are we going to do?"

"The Lord will lead us, Jack." She knelt down on the cement floor next to him. "Take my hand. Be strong for your daughter."

It was prayer alone that got Jack and Edna Martin through their meeting with John's parents. That, and Pastor Crismore, who had arranged the meeting. John was excused from this unnecessary encounter by his parents, who came ready to fight. After all, their son was being falsely accused.

Brenda sat motionless as John's parents relieved their son of any responsibility.

"Of *course* John denies this! Your daughter made a play for him and he had to restrain her. He was so disturbed by her insinuations for sexual encounter that he had to avoid her during most of the dance. Anyway, even if it was true, which it isn't, why would a *decent* young girl go to an empty apartment with a young man? Your daughter is lying. You would do well to ask her who she really took up with—it was probably that idiot Will Harwood—and send her away before she influences good girls. And we'd better not be bothered with this issue again or we will hire a lawyer." That was the meeting in a nutshell.

Within a week Brenda was, indeed, on her way out of town. She would stay at a home for unwed mothers in Albany, New York, until the baby was born. Afterwards, she would live with an aunt and uncle until she finished her junior year. Pastor Crismore, a kindly man who had known the Martins for years—and had baptized Brenda when she was ten—made the arrangements. The little family fought hard to stay together through the shock. The prayer of Jack and Edna Martin that early spring afternoon on the cement floor of their garage was to be the first of many petitions to the throne of God, begging for mercy and strength for the family and for Brenda. Their prayers were heard.

The Appointment

Bashar-el had not been to Earth for centuries. His most recent assignment (if that is what one calls the duty to which angels are called) had been to join the company of angels in continuous praise and adoration of the Holy One. And now he was instructed to follow and guard the Word. His job was to follow the book and to help where possible (without interfering with human will, of course) as it traveled through time and became instrumental in the lives of several people. That the Holy One would choose him for this task was no small honor: the Word of God, from the smallest jot or tittle, was revered. That he would be assigned to the book of Psalms was a particular joy, for he was there when David and the others had penned the beautiful prayers. The book was about to start its journey; Bashar-el was eager to obey and to please. His name on earth would be Chosen.

* * *

Granny reached for the book with the colorful cover. *A Resting Place,* it said, *The Book of Psalms.* She had been searching all afternoon in the cramped bookstore, desperate to find a special treasure to send with her granddaughter. She was pleased with her find. Brenda had a Bible, but a book dedicated to just the Psalms would have special meaning to her since Granny had read them to her bonny lass since she was a baby. "Read me the one about the birds again, Granny!" the little girl would plead, and Granny would turn to Psalm 84: "Even the sparrow has found a home, and the swallow a nest for herself, where she may have her young." Granny closed her eyes and swallowed hard. She bought the book, and Chosen was thrilled, for his earthly tenure was about to begin, and he hooked a ride on top of Granny's sedan as she headed toward the Martin house.

The Home

Brenda had never been around nuns before. She'd seen them from time to time and understood that they had chosen to spend a cloistered life apart from the world, but that was all she knew. She was met at the train by a rotund, jolly face, framed with starched, white headgear. It was Sister Barbara who took her hand that day and Sister Barbara who would introduce her to a strange new world of institutionalized rigor and discipline. Brenda would live out the remainder of her pregnancy at St. Catherine's home for unwed mothers. She would join a sorority of sorts, the initiation a price too great to bear alone. For the most part the home was a haven, a barrier between the young girls and an evolving society that still cast off and castigated misfits.

Brenda's room was sparse and dull, much like a cell: a single bed lined one wall, a sink was in one corner, a desk in another, a wooden chair and a small closet completing the picture. The window to her fourth-floor room offered an industrial panorama of the roof of the building next door. A radiator sat prominently under the window. There was no carpet, only flooring worn so thin it had lost its pattern to time.

Chosen stood in the corner and surveyed the room. The friendly nun had just left and would be back in one hour to guide her new charge around the home. Brenda was exhausted and alone. She had never been alone before. She had never been away from home. She had never been . . . pregnant. She felt her stomach, sat on the bed, and studied the space that was to be home for the next seven months. "Dear Jesus," the girl whispered, "help me. I am so scared. Please help me."

Chosen, who probably had been selected for this mission because of his empathetic nature, walked to Brenda and wrapped his wings around her. He'd been with her since Granny had given her the book. He'd watched her every move and was deeply hurt for the pain this dear child would have to endure.

Yet he felt his work with Brenda was extra special, for she was carrying a child. This was much like the time he had helped to guard another young mother and child, the One who would redeem the world from sin. Chosen held the girl tight and hated sin with all his might.

Sister Barbara

When you are expected to be up early for chapel, perform your assigned chores, attend class, complete homework, attend chapel once again, and adjust to a strange new world, the days fly by. Especially when a character named Barbara is watching over you.

Sister Barbara was not the head nun. That was Sister Patience, which Brenda felt was a poor choice of names indeed, once she had a chance to observe the no-nonsense woman. She and the other girls—some who could match Brenda's experience with John word for word—assigned the rather dubious title of Sister Im-Patience to the nun and shared war stories of their encounters with her rigid demeanor. Barbara, on the other hand, was their friend and advocate. It was Sister Barbara who "smuggled" them out to the local Tastee Freeze, Sister Barbara who winked at them when they giggled during assemblies, Sister Barbara who held them when they cried in the night or when they clutched a toilet with morning sickness. It was the jovial, fat nun with her enormous rosary clanking against her stride who put up with chants of Sis . . . sis . . . sis . . . Sister Barb . . . barb . . . barb! It was also Sister Barbara who comforted them like a flock of frenzied lambs the night one of them committed suicide, and who prayed with each girl when her baby was taken away.

And it was Sister Barbara who loved the Psalms as much as Granny! Soon after Brenda's arrival, she and Barbara developed a friendly rivalry. Barb would leave Brenda's book open to a particular psalm (for it was Barb's job to inspect the girls' rooms each week), and the challenge was on to see who could memorize the longest part. Brenda looked forward to Thursday afternoons when she returned from class to see what psalm Sister had selected for the week. Chosen loved Thursdays, too, and always rushed into the room ahead of Brenda. It was at the beginning of Brenda's third trimester that

Barbara chose Psalm 139. Chosen wondered how Brenda would react to David's words and watched the girl as she sat on the side of the bed and read.

O Lord, you have searched me and you know me . . . you have laid your hand upon me . . . if I settle on the far side of the sea, even there your hand will guide me.

The angel watched the girl closely, her stomach full on her lap. Brenda's lips moved as she read:

For you created my inmost being, you knit me together in my mother's womb. I praise you because I am fearfully and wonderfully made, your works are wonderful, I know that full well. My frame was not hidden from you when I was made in the secret place.

Brenda stared intently at the book and then shifted her eyes to the window, fixing a blank stare on the roof. Chosen could see she was troubled. He'd grown so fond of this dear girl! How was she responding to this song of David? Chosen remembered the exact moment David had written these words, how David was overwhelmed by the might and mystery of God when he suddenly realized how impossible it was to flee from the Almighty. Would Brenda have a similar revelation? The words of the psalmist worked on Brenda's heart. Her face hardened. Chosen ran for help.

"I thought you might want to talk before dinner."

The voice came ahead of the large woman who peeked around the door. Chosen gently pushed Sister Barbara into the room. Brenda kept her eyes on the roof.

"Sister, it says 'my frame was not hidden from you when I was made in the secret place.' Can it be possible that God was there when I was raped?"

Tears, so long ago dried up, began to slide down her face.

"Why didn't He stop it? He could have, you know. Why didn't He protect me?"

Chosen prayed and glanced with hope at the imposing nun. This was a critical moment for Brenda. How Sister Barbara responded was so important. *Tell her that all of heaven weeps for her!* yelled the impassioned angel. *Tell her how He hates sin!*

Barbara sat down next to Brenda. She wiped the girl's cheek with a hand that continued up the girl's face to push hair off her brow. Sister Barbara looked at Brenda with tenderness. She had wondered earlier if it was wise to leave the book open to that particular psalm but felt . . . convicted . . . to do so.

"Brenda," she began, "I don't really know if He was there. We know that He is everywhere. The psalm you read today tells us that. We also know that He is holy, and because He is holy, He cannot be in the presence of sin. That is why we say sin separates us from God. When John raped you he was sinning. Did the Lord know what was happening? I believe He did because He knows all. Could He have stopped it? He could, Brenda, but He wouldn't."

The young girl looked bewildered. "Why?!" The sound of her question was pitiful, weak, and filled with pain.

Chosen prayed that Brenda would understand.

"Brenda," Sister Barbara continued, "When God created mankind He gave us free will. He gave us the freedom to believe or not to believe, to obey or not to obey. If He interfered with our free will, then we would not be free, would we?"

"But He is my Father, and He is supposed to love me and protect me. How could He let me go through that . . . this . . . how?!"

"Do you think He does not weep for you, Brenda? This may be hard for you to hear, but He also weeps for John, who is lost to Him right now. He died for John. Over and over we have read in the psalms that He is faithful and His love endures forever. We are also reminded that His ways are not our ways, Brenda. What happened to you was awful. But blessing will come from this, I promise you."

Barbara told Brenda she would bring her a tray for dinner and then left the girl alone. Brenda felt the baby kick . . . and suddenly, in spite of herself, felt the touch of peace. She thought of the child inside her, her child, and reached for the book again.

Your eyes saw my unformed body. All the days ordained for me were written in your book before one of them came to be.

This child belonged to God. Her baby had a destiny. She lay on her side as Chosen knelt, and she prayed for the baby in her womb. She prayed that the baby would never go through such pain as she; she prayed that the baby would grow to be strong and godly. She prayed for her mother and father and Granny, whom she missed desperately. She prayed for Will. And she prayed for John. That night Brenda underlined all of Psalm 139 and wrote "I forgive John" in the margin. She slept the sleep of one whose heart was searched and found pure.

The Birth

As Brenda's pregnancy neared its end, she suffered from bouts of depression. Pastor Crismore had found an adoptive family for the child, and Brenda was informed. All he would reveal was that the baby would be living with a family in the Midwest. Her prayers for the baby were constant, as were Chosen's, as Brenda's body became bulky and full of child. Her parents made plans to be with her for the birth of the baby and were supportive in every way. But the thought of keeping the child was not an option. As good and godly as the Martins were, they were not able to cope with the publicity of a bastard grandchild and felt the baby would be best served with an adoptive couple. Brenda began to have second thoughts, but ever obedient, she met with a lawyer in Sister Patience's office and signed papers releasing claim to the child in any way.

Her parents drove to Albany in early November. The reunion was joyful, if a bit uncomfortable. They struggled to act normal about their daughter's condition, which was a very real reminder of the tragedy that had befallen their family, and gave them an unsettling notion that their little girl had changed forever. The doctor said that Brenda could deliver anytime.

Conversation with her parents drifted from news of home to Granny's health, but one taboo topic was never broached: talk of the baby was obviously, and tragically, avoided, as if by not talking about the impending birth the pain of separation would be less. Edna and Jack were good people. They were simply uncertain how to behave at this moment. There was no mulling over names, no excited anticipation, no baby clothes. Brenda asked her mother to take her to a department store and insisted on buying a small Bible to be sent with the child.

Chosen fretted over Brenda. He could tell that her moment was near. He paced in her room, back and forth, watching her sleep, listening to her breathing. If he had his way, she would be at the hospital now. He fluttered his wings in a nervous twitch, as someone would drum fingers on a desktop. Not able to stand it any longer—after all, he'd attended many births throughout the ages—he nudged Brenda awake. She tried to sit upright and was knocked flat by a contraction. Holding her stomach, she waddled down the hall to get Sister Barbara, who had curiously awakened just moments before. Chosen hurried Barbara out of bed.

Another wave of contractions hit. Chosen was absolutely in a dither. But not Sister Barbara, who could do the routine in her sleep, which was not so preposterous a thought since babies seemed to have a proclivity for middle-of-the-night arrivals. Other girls began to waken, and words of encouragement followed Brenda as she and Sister Barbara—who donned her habit in record time—headed down the hall. They would take the service elevator to the ground floor and walk across the street to the hospital. Chosen ran ahead of them, rushing to the emergency room, where he pushed an orderly to be in place when the women arrived. He flew back and forth between the maternity ward and the hall where Brenda was wheeled along, rousing everyone from their desks, knocking over coffee cups—the baby was coming!

Sister Barbara left Brenda while she tended to paperwork. *Don't be scared, don't be scared, little one,* sang Chosen, wishing she could hear. Another contraction. Where were the nurses?! Chosen flew to the nurses' station and pushed the alarm for Brenda's room. Nothing. He pushed again. Finally, a nurse responded.

"Can I sit up?" implored Brenda.

"You just lay there. This is what you get for fooling around!" snapped the nurse.

"But it hurts!" Brenda cried.

"You should have thought about that before you got pregnant. Girls like you deserve to hurt."

Chosen was outraged. He wanted to deck the nurse right then and there. A cackle came from behind.

"So, Bashar, you thought we'd stay away for long?"

"Dark One!"

"It is I, Bashar . . . or should I say Chosen? And I am many."

"Be gone, Dark One, this child belongs to the Lord!"

"It is the baby we want, Bashar. And we will have it!"

Chosen erupted in rage and stormed toward the demon, but it was too late. All that was left was a hideous stench. On high alert, Chosen turned to check Brenda, who was begging the nurse for help.

"You'll get no help from me. You deserve to be in pain, you little tramp!" said the nurse.

"Sister Barbara!" wailed Brenda. But Sister Barbara could not hear. She was down the hall trying to reach Brenda's parents.

Brenda was writhing in agony and drenching the bed with sweat.

"I gave her something for pain," the nurse told the nun, who was still on the phone. "She is starting to say the strangest things. You'd think I was holding back her medicine! You can take your time, Sister, she will probably rest some now."

The nun held her hand over the receiver. "Did you call the doctor?"

"He's on his way!" came the lie. Barb looked up when she thought she heard a little cackle.

Brenda's pain was too great. Something was wrong. Chosen flew back and forth to the door of her room, afraid to leave her alone, but frightened for her condition. *Where was the doctor? Where was Sister Barbara? Where was help?*

Barbara patiently tried to dial the motel one more time. For the life of her, she could not understand why she was unable to get through. She wanted to check on Brenda, but the on-duty nurse assured her that all was well, and it might be several hours yet. "Hello? Hello? I'm trying to connect with the Martins . . . hello?" A scream ripped through the air. It was Brenda. Barb turned white. She dropped the phone and ran, the big rosary tangling with her belted rope and smashing against her legs. She gasped when she entered Brenda's room. Brenda was hemorrhaging and blood soaked the bed. "Nurse!!"

Chosen prayed feverishly. He sensed evil and turned to face his enemy.

"Be gone!"

"Not until we're finished, Bashar!"

Brenda screamed. Seeing the trouble in the room, the nurse ran to her station. In a panic, she fumbled with the phone to call Emergency—

and Brenda's doctor. The big angel exploded toward the demon. Brenda and the baby were his charge. Shrieks and sickening sounds came from the brawl. Talons grabbed above Chosen's right eye and twisted with fury. He beat his wings and dragged the beast across the floor. The battle raged between spirit beings as Sister Barbara lifted her voice in prayer and tried to calm the girl.

"This child is sanctified unto the Lord!" yelled Chosen above the din. *"The Lord rebuke you! In the name of Jesus, I command you to be gone!"*

A baby boy slipped onto the bed, blue and strangled from the umbilical cord. Brenda shuddered and went limp. Two nurses and a young doctor charged into the room.

"Suction!" yelled the doctor. "Oxygen!"

Chosen lay in a heap in the corner, breathing hard. The stench was gone. The sound of a baby began to emanate from within the frantic crowd, a feeble sound at first, followed by a hearty wail. Brenda was sped into surgery to stem the hemorrhage. Sister Barbara slumped into a chair and then to her knees. The girl's life was in peril; the battle wasn't over yet.

Saying Good-Bye

Brenda awoke with a headache. She instinctively reached to her belly and felt soft skin where once a little life formed a taut belly. She closed her eyes to clear her head, trying to remember what had happened. The baby! She had the baby! Where was the baby?! She opened her eyes again and her mother came into focus.

"Mom, the baby . . ."

"He is fine, Brenda," said the relieved mother, making reference to the child for the first time since she'd come to Albany. "You had us pretty scared . . ."

"A little boy? Can I see him?"

Perhaps understanding for the first time, Edna lowered her eyes. "No, Brenda. His parents have already come for him."

His parents . . . No! thought Brenda. *I am his parent!*

"It is for the best, Brenda. Now we need you to get well."

Chosen knew his reaction was strange since Brenda's name was written in the Book of Life, and, for the believer, to die is Christ. But he was elated when Brenda awoke. It brought to mind a time when the Master had brought a young girl back from death. Yet his joy was mingled with sorrow for his charge. There must be *something* he could do . . .

Brenda stared at the ceiling of the hospital room. The light over-head seemed to pulse: bright, dim, bright, dim. Dim. She turned her head away from her mother as tears dripped onto the pillow. "Bless my little boy, Father God," she prayed. "And maybe someday, please God, please, can I meet him?" Back from a brief jaunt into the parking lot, Chosen beamed.

Sister Barbara came into the room.

"Brenda," she said softly, "there is something I have to ask you. The couple who adopted your baby do not want to leave until they meet you. They are a little more modern than most others, and they feel it is important to talk with you. The decision, of course, is yours. Would you like that?"

This was quite different from what Brenda was prepared for. She had been coached from the start that she would know nothing of the adoptive parents. This was more than she could ask for.

"Yes."

Brenda sat in bed as best she could. Tubes connected to her arm pre-vented her from smoothing her hair. She watched Sister Barbara leave the room and then return. A young couple followed her. They were fine looking and gave an immediate impression of goodness. The woman was carrying the baby. Brenda's throat began to burn as she battled hysteria.

"I know we are breaking all the rules, but we've been told your story, Brenda. We wanted you to know that we will love this baby with all of our hearts and we will tell him about you when he is old enough to understand. That is, if you will permit us."

Brenda could only nod, her eyes and nose beginning to drip tears that came straight from her heart. All she had wanted was to see the baby! The woman was holding her baby!

"We've named him Danny. I hope that's OK?"

Another nod.

"We will be sure he knows this Bible is from you and will teach him to treasure the Word of God."

Halleluia! Chosen danced and fluttered his wings in praise.

The woman approached Brenda. "Would you like to hold him?"

Tears collected at the corners of Brenda's lips and dripped off her chin. The woman placed Danny in her arms. She looked at his pink face and touched his mouth with her finger. A happy laugh bubbled up from her throat when he opened his eyes. She looked in his face. This wasn't a child of sin, this wasn't a product of rape, but a child of God, her child, whose face she would etch on her heart for all of time.

"Tell him," said Brenda, her voice hoarse with emotion, "tell him that I will pray for him every day."

"We will, Brenda, we will." And they took the baby and were gone.

*   *   *

Amy sat spellbound. It was after midnight and the rain had stopped. Brenda stood near the window and peered into darkness. "Danny is a little over three right now."

"Bren, I am so sorry. I had no idea."

"I'm glad I finally told someone. I think about him every day, and I am determined to meet him again some day, but I find peace knowing he is with a good family. That keeps me going."

Both girls slept fitfully that night: Amy with the startling revelation running through her head, Brenda with the freshness of recounting a sorrowful tale. The next morning Brenda skipped study at the library so she could write a letter to Patricia Harwood.

Chapter
Three

Late February 1968

    Twenty years ago she had been vibrant, popular, and happy. Content with a waitress job after graduating high school, Patty had been on a roll with the rest of postwar America; it would be a long time before political or social issues mattered—and divided. For then, Patty Smith had been as generic as her name, dressed in a crisp, white uniform with black apron for the evening shift at Charlottesville's first all-night diner. Patty would count her tips, gab on the phone, and wait with the certainty of one who lived in perfect agreement with the norm of the times, for the inevitable day she would marry and start a family. It had made no sense to spend time or money on college, not for a young woman whose singular intent in life was to keep house and rear children. That is the way it had been twenty years ago, when the expectations of an eighteen-year-old waitress with strawberry blonde hair and a mask of pale, fading freckles turned toward fulfillment when a handsome graduate student sat at one of her tables. Fate had been sealed that night when Patricia Smith, working girl, met Edward P. Harwood, erstwhile scholar.

In the fashion of a young woman out to land her man, Patty spent hours plotting with friends about how to land the "professor." She managed to wrestle important information from him while waiting his table: what his studies were (English Literature, emphasis on the Classics—but with a secret yen to become the next Faulkner); which building at the University of Virginia he emerged from at 11 A.M. each Tuesday (Cabell Hall); what his favorite cookie was (oatmeal raisin) so she could surprise him when he stepped out onto the famous lawn of Thomas Jefferson's pet project, now a small, elite southern school for boys from wealthy families. She even learned his address so she could send him notes that revealed her infatuation for the dashing, pipe-smoking pedant. (Patty's notes, by the way, were written in perfect penmanship and demonstrated a good mind and a wit— for Patty was an intelligent young woman, trapped, though she was, in class distinction and static social mores.) Patty had carefully crafted each missive as a glowing testimony of Ed's intellectual prowess and of his unlimited potential. "Why, you could become president of the United States!" she'd once gushed. She had flirted with Ed for three months before he finally asked her out.

It took the determined young woman nearly two years, but a victory sign had flashed between girlfriends when Patty was led down the aisle by her electrician father in the fall of 1948. Patty had her man, a man too full of himself and too emotionally immature from a life of indulgence to possibly relate to another human being on an intimate and cherished level. Trouble brewed from that day forward, when a startled maid of honor was groped by the brand-new groom, and Ed had berated Patty for the "cheap and vulgar" wedding reception her parents provided at the church hall. Patty dismissed his outbursts and set her face to a happy and prosperous future of keeping house and rearing children. Many children.

And so it was that with two years of study ahead for Ed, Patty ceremonially traded her white nylon uniform for maternity clothes as she settled into their tiny apartment and grew bigger and bigger with the baby boy born nine months to the day of their wedding. But that had been twenty years ago. Things were different now. Patty was different, too, in a most tragic way.

News of Will's Death

Professor Harwood steeled his heart for the blow. The voice on the phone was cordial, but succinct. A chaplain and a commissioned marine officer from the Great Lakes Naval Station would be by at seven. He put the receiver in its cradle and tightened his jaw, chin jutting, lips pressed together. Ed knew. And, for just a moment, his gut churned and jumped as adrenaline rushed into his cells, furtively, furiously, fanning embers. He knew.

Patty looked up as he returned to the kitchen and resumed his meal. His eyes caught hers, and real contact was made for the first time in years. The pipe-smoking, good-looking professor let himself lapse back to a different time, a time when life held promise and a bright outlook: a son—a son named after his brilliant and successful grandfather. Hah! The town imbecile! Anger spilled into the space between man and woman and quenched cold any flicker of familiarity. Ed hated Patty and Will for ruining his life. To him, Patty was an embarrassment: a weak, whimpering, uneducated trollop. He'd outgrown her years ago. He'd left her emotionally as well and continued to comfort himself in the arms of students, faculty wives, and still, even now, an occasional waitress at an all-night diner.

Ed stiffened his back against the yellow Naugahyde chair. He would not allow the briefest, not the tiniest, not the smallest iota of compassion to actualize. He knew why the men were coming. Yet as he processed his thoughts, he began to find relief again, the relief he had felt when Will was sent from home. He reached for the potatoes and never said a word.

Patty watched out the window as the government car pulled into the driveway. Two men got out. Electricity jackknifed through her chest as a groan pushed its way into the dusty drapes. She grabbed hold of a pleat with such power that her red, chapped hand turned white. A gasp hurdled up from the base of her gut, up through bronchial tubes, up through windpipe, larynx, and into space, its final exit a sound of pain—deep, unstoppable pain. "G . . . gaa." The blood drained from her face.

Ed met the men at the car. The one with the cross on his uniform shook Ed's hand first. Then the other. They appeared to be speaking solemnly, attempts to head toward the house blocked by Ed, who was determined to have this business finished and done with. They handed Ed an envelope. He turned abruptly and walked toward the house, jaw set in stone. Patty closed her eyes. *Willie! Willie! Oh, how Mama loves you!* Car doors slammed, screen door slammed; Ed stood in the archway to the living room. "Will is dead," he said. She watched the government car until all that was left were distant brake lights and a turn signal as it disappeared from sight.

* * *

The end of 1967 and all of 1968 were particularly bad for American marines in Vietnam. It was the time of the TET Offensive, and it was a decisive time for the base at Khesanh. Originally established to train mountain tribesmen, Khesanh was chosen by General Westmoreland to become a strong and vital foothold in his march against communist insurgents in Laos. Khesanh was also a matter of prestige. Some military brass grumbled openly against the wisdom of Westmoreland's plan, but, in strict adherence to military code, obeyed orders and plopped a contingent of marines into that stronghold that was saturated with Vietcong. Khesanh was to be a test case, blood-red litmus, as tens of thousands of the enemy swarmed through surrounding hills. We would make a stand at Khesanh, and *how Khesanh went, so went the war.* Khesanh did not go well.

Chosen hated everything about Khesanh and Vietnam—he had always hated war: just, reasoned, necessary, ordained, sanctioned, voted for, vindictive, hateful, heart-of-man—Chosen didn't care. He hated man's inhumanity to other men. His reaction to such events as Vietnam was like intense spiritual nausea. But his feelings had to be put aside. Chosen had to focus his attention on Will, who was living in physical, emotional, and spiritual torment. The angel had grown so fond of Will, it was all he could do to keep from interfering. He interceded for his charge almost fitfully as the poor boy struggled along with others to survive constant battering from the enemy. The men fought bugs, they fought the fear of near-certain death (as Khesanh became a blood bath for both sides), and they fought each other.

As before, when Will was onboard ship, friendships were guarded and rare, each man counting the days—the *seconds*—until his replacement would take over his bunk and carry on. But it was different here. Far too many men left Khesanh in body bags, shoved into the demanding maw of C-130 planes brought in by courageous pilots who flew into the base to make deliveries. The big planes would shudder and paw the primitive airstrip impatiently as men hurried under the blast of engine idle. Food, water, and supplies were hurled onto the ground, human cargo shoved aboard. Once in a while, a mail sack landed with a dusty thud.

Will had been reassigned to the Third Marine Amphibious Force in late 1967 and, as the marines were wont to be at the forefront of any hot spot, was airlifted twenty minutes west of DaNang to this area landlocked by enemy forces. Westmoreland wanted Khesanh upgraded to a firebase, an artillery stronghold . . . a test. "We are not, repeat *not,* going to be defeated at Khesanh," said the General. "I will tolerate no talking or even thinking to the contrary."

Khesanh would become an embarrassment to the proud and mighty marines, who hunkered down and dodged bullets, fire-throwers, mortar, insects, monotony, fear, noise, and depression every way they could.

The marines lived under constant pressure of assault in an underground maze of tunnels—like rats in miserable holes—with a stifling, blood-soaked film that seemed to hang in the air, heat and filth, trips to the latrine a run for your life: life itself was a latrine. The valiant men were part of a patch test: military rats, political pawns, pawns always expendable when bigger pieces are the prize.

Will had one possession to his name in Khesanh. Everything else was in his footlocker at DaNang. (Unbeknownst to Will, the footlocker had recently gone up in smoke and flames during a mortar attack.) It was Brenda's gift he kept with him and that remained close to his heart. Will kept the book under his shirt, using a sling of muslin that was black from perspiration and dirt.

Chosen followed Will faithfully, wishing the boy would read again, wishing he would take refuge in the Word of the Almighty, wishing he would drift away from this hell through the majestic poetry of David and the other psalmists. *He was young like you, Will! And he fought in battles. Will, Will.* Chosen closed his eyes in the anguish of angels who face frustration in their work. *Holy One,* he prayed, *why won't you stop this?!* He pleaded for the time when men would lay down their swords—their rockets and artillery and hatred—and live in peace. War was an acrid stench—a stench, to Chosen, accompanied by heinous laughter and haughty proclamation: *"Bashar! Save your friend now! Save everyone, oh mighty angel of God!"*

Will did not waver in his faith, simple as it was. He clung—privately—to his clumsy understanding of the Cross. But he never quite grasped the grace that Brother Joe spoke about, and in spite of Brother Joe's assurance of God's mercy and forgiveness, the young man was still beset with guilt. Besides, Will and the others had a more urgent matter to contend with—hold the base.

The tall boy called Wacko Will was gaunt now, worn out, his eyes crusted with the glaze of war, of having seen too much, too much. And he was tired, sometimes too tired to run for cover when the mortar pounded the base, coming like snow whipped by wind that frosted water into flakes and raced from Lake Michigan to cover Chicago and home.

Chosen could tell by watching the boy that the Holy Spirit was at work. . . . and that Will was struggling with compliance. Late one afternoon the angel sensed impending crisis . . . urgency . . . doom . . . fear. He watched as Will lay on top of his sleeping bag on the dirt floor, hands behind his head, eyes closed in thought. His lips seemed to move—in prayer? He tightened his jaw, jutted his chin, and pressed his lips together in firm resolve. Hoisting himself, he approached another marine, one least likely to reject him. And then he spoke.

"Do you have some paper?" he said, with an edge to his voice that sounded like urgency.

Chosen watched with such tenderness as to cause the big, bold angel to sigh: Will was writing a confession. The crooked table he leaned against was made of an ammunition box supported by two-by-four scraps. Will whittled a stub of pencil and smoothed the paper with his grimy, bug-bitten hand. He was writing on the back side of a blank requisition order.

Dere Sur:
I kild one of us on Makawg. I em sary.
      Pvt. Will Harwood

Will folded the paper and slipped it between the pages of Brenda's gift. This was Chosen's chance, while the book lay on the dusty, makeshift table.

"Harwood!" came a no-nonsense call.

Chosen frowned.

"Yes, sir."

"A drop is coming in. You and Krause pick it up."

"Yes, sir."

Every man on base dreaded parachute drops; not only were they unpredictable, turning the men into targets (*Step right up! See if you can shoot the little soldiers and win a Kewpie doll for your lady!*), retrieving the supplies in the dimming light of day—for drops were often made at dusk— was equally dangerous. Chosen continued to sense impending crisis. He began to feel fidgety and desperate—and desperate angels can sometimes resort to desperate actions. He grabbed Will's hand and shoved it on top of the book. *Read the book, Will!* the angel screamed. And as if his words echoed from one dimension into another, Will looked down at Brenda's gift. The hard glaze in his eyes softened; thoughts of Brenda always brought him joy.

Will had received one letter from Brenda since he'd been at Khesanh, a letter that gave him his only happy moment on the base. Finally able to somewhat understand Brenda's joy for Jesus now, Will was surprisingly pleased when he deciphered other news from his friend. In that predictable round cursive style of hers, Brenda told Will about Stephen, a word Will struggled with for days until he settled at Step Hen.

How Will had treasured that letter, which was stolen one day by a frantic man on his way to the latrine. Had Will discovered the thief or known the outcome, the tension in his hovel might have made a trip outside a picnic in the park. Holding Brenda's letter—and her book—connected him to her and took him home, home to Mama. How he missed Mama!

His discernment level hitting *Tilt!*, Chosen pushed against the boy's shoulder. Will mechanically responded with a swat, then reached down and opened the book. Chosen fluttered his wings and praised God. Will read Psalm 1 with the recollection of one who knows something by heart, yet still follows the words, like following a worn path to a pleasant stop in the wood, or like following words in a hymnal, words to a hymn that you had memorized before you could walk.

Chosen suddenly sensed another presence in the room. He turned and saw his friend Zepha. Chosen looked at the other angel with pleading, questioning eyes. Zepha nodded. *It is time.*

Will sat staring at Brenda's gift. He had no thoughts, no consuming emotion. He had only peace. Peace like he'd had the night he wrapped his big body around a latrine on the ship and surrendered himself to Jesus. Peace that seemed to become elusive and vague during the long months afterward, there in the shadows as Will boxed with demons of incrimination and despair and guilt. Turning to the end of the book, he reached for his pencil and began to write on the back cover:

> *1/5/68*
> *I want to be a gud son. I pray fore my mom and dad. Jesus is my rok.*
> *William Harwood*

And in the manner of those who are somewhat simple, he carefully printed his address in Wheaton, Illinois, and included his phone number.

"Harwood!"

"Yes, sir!"

Will closed the book and reached for his makeshift sling. It was gone. He leaned alongside the ammunition crate and groped on the dirt floor in the dim light that filtered down from the canvas roof. An angel toe pushed the dirty rag out of sight.

"Harwood!"

"Coming, sir!" In a fit of frustration, Will tossed Brenda's gift on his sleeping bag and ran through a maze that brought him to the airstrip. There he met the big plane and mortar attack all at once. Chutes were dropped, and the plane banked sharply for its speedy escape. Chosen ran after Will; Zepha was already in place. Will was dead from an explosion before a big chute brought its cargo to the ground. Will would now know the fullness of agape love. The angel knew that all the company of heaven was welcoming this pilgrim to eternal peace. Yet, in spite of happiness for his young charge, the angel screamed. He screamed for all the Wills, all the Hustons, all the savagery. He screamed at pain and suffering, he screamed at sin, he screamed at death. And he—keeper of the book, chosen of God, Bashar-el—felt alone and disconsolate for the first time in his being.

* * *

The special delivery driver knew, even though this time it was a small box and not the standard military footlocker. The middle-aged man in the gray uniform had delivered dozens of lockers since the conflict in Vietnam began and hated this part of his job. He hated the military for consigning this duty to others—let the brass ring doorbells and see how it feels to awkwardly place these lockers at the feet of families torn to shreds like the men in the papers every night. He hated walking to the door with what was left of sons and husbands, averting his eyes from other eyes that were swollen or empty from grief. He hated bringing to the "home of record" all that was left: khaki-colored lockers, rickrack, ticky-tack, all in a row, like miniature coffins, labeled "Deliver To." Deliver to the parents of the valedictorian of his high school class. Deliver to the wife who is pregnant with this man's first child. Deliver more pain, deliver, deliver. And even though this time it was just a box with the familiar government seal, the driver knew, as he eased his truck alongside the sidewalk and forced his feet to march to the door—step, step, step—one step closer to pain. "How do you do? I am bringing all that was left. Please sign your name on line number 19." Will was nineteen. Was. Except in Patty's mind, where Will was still alive.

Patty greeted the uniform with unusual cheeriness, causing the driver to reckon he was mistaken about the package. After all, other than the closed drapes, he saw nothing unusual about the home. Some homes—yes, the buildings themselves—were gripped in a death clutch, the air around them heavy and dull, the sidewalk screaming in rage for the loss of the boy who bounced his ball, the dread door that opened onto pieces of people trying to fit together again. But this house, long ago silenced, gave no indication that a patriotic son once lived here. The driver doffed his cap in deference to the frail woman and jogged back to his truck. He felt lighter now, glad to be wrong, whistling as he hoisted himself into the cab, one strong hand pulling against the dull blue steering wheel with the big plastic knob attached to make turning—and leaving—easier.

Smiling the open-mouthed, giddy smile of a child, Patty held the package against her stomach and headed into the kitchen, first certain to polish the handle to the front door, since, after all, she'd touched it. She muttered to herself and admonished her little boy for sending more presents—why, she hardly had room anymore for the cards and letters and rice bowls and kimonos and medals of honor her hero son kept sending her. She carefully laid the package on the yellow kitchen table, the Formica and chrome polished so severely it reflected light from any source, and if the aluminum canisters could talk—or the toaster or the Farberware coffeepot—they would tell the same story. The past weeks had seen a crazed woman cleaning, cleaning at night when sleeplessness tormented and prodded until its victim obediently rose to pace, to stand by the window and watch, to scrub (quietly, of course, on the nights that Ed came home). Cleaning all for the day—one day soon!—when Will was coming home! Patty worked to remove staples from the box, one by one, putting them on a salad plate rimmed with blue willows: ordered, lined like little soldiers, straight as pins. Her little marine had sent something home—you see? He did! She scolded an imaginary friend: "I *told* you he sends me presents, you just wouldn't belive me. Look! Here is a whole *box* from my son!"

A box with a letter from Will! A letter with an official imprint. "Oh, no, we don't need to read that! It's probably news about another award he's won. My Will is a marine, you know. Let's just look at the present!"

Will's dog tags hit the table with a muffled sound, as metal would that was wrapped in a cellophane envelope. Part of the chain protruded, and in the way of those things, the entire chain seemed to follow, slinking its way free until only the tags were sealed from sight. Patty's hideously red-raw, nail-bitten finger stroked the chain, followed a route along its loopy pile, traced it round and round. Suddenly stone-faced, her eyes drifted: eyes that would not return the compassionate gaze of the delivery man, but would watch him drive away as they guarded from their post; eyes that saw disarray and dirt everywhere and that signaled a command to clean the house for Will's return; eyes that hadn't seen Ed for three days; eyes that suddenly grew large with revelation from some inner place that only the delusional go; eyes that pressed furiously to the task at hand—the nice necklace must be protected from harm. Careful not to wrinkle the cellophane, she pushed the chain back through the opening and carried the dog tags upstairs to Will's room. Bereft and aghast by Patty's appearance and condition, Chosen followed.

It had been a long trip, as humans count time, and Chosen was weary. He was weary from emotion and weary from battle—for he had joined the fray as the escort was engaged in combat over Will's lifeless body, his soul immediately in the presence of God. What the enemy had wanted with the body puzzled Chosen, but all ended well, and Will's mangled corpse had been sent to a mortuary at DaNang where it was placed in an aluminum container for shipment home, a journey that had ended in a military cemetery when Ed Harwood, Will's father, instructed the marines to "Do what you want with it." And now, because of the book, Chosen found *himself* in Will's home—a home chilled by its emptiness apart from God.

Will's room was impeccable; Patty made it so. Sheets washed and ironed every Monday, every clothes hanger exactly three inches apart from the other, Will's clothes pressed and folded again and again, Patty waited for her baby. Will's room was her womb, her hiding place, where she would curl on the floor (the bedspread might get wrinkled) and hum lullabies and hold her stomach and rock. "Mama loves you, Willie!" she would pronounce over and over. "Mama loves you!" Today, with her pressing matter at hand, she opened the door to Will's closet and reached toward the shelf, brushing against hangers that clattered to the floor. But Patty didn't notice. She pulled a rubber band marked Busy Bee Dry Cleaners off of a worn box and placed Will's dog tags next to an unopened letter from Brenda Martin. Chosen lit up when he recognized the familiar cursive style and wished he could see that dear, sweet girl again. He studied Patty's face and felt profound anguish for the troubled woman. Unfurling his great wings, the angel was about to tenderly comfort Patty when they both jumped at the sound of a slamming door. Ed was home. Suddenly lucid, jolted back from the drift and safety of delusion, Patty panicked. More hangers crashed to the closet floor as she fumbled with the rubber band and shoved the box out of sight. She raced downstairs, the angel behind her. She was too late. An enraged Ed stood in the kitchen, the letter with the government seal in his hands. He looked at her as she raced in and stumbled against a chair to stop. He tore the letter in half and crushed it in his fist before he threw it on the floor.

"Is there anything else?" Ed demanded.

"No, Ed . . . I haven't even seen what else . . . I mean . . . what is even in the box."

Ed dumped the contents on the table. Chosen gasped as Brenda's gift slapped against the gleaming yellow Formica.

"What is this?! A book?! He leaves behind a book?! What a joke!" bellowed Ed.

Patty reached forward, wanting to touch it, touch her son, hold him, dear God! Ed pushed her aside.

"Give me the book!" she yelled, adrenaline and panic leapfrogging through every cell that had fight left in it. She was fighting for her son. She butted her head against Ed, trying to keep him away from her baby. He held her back easily with one arm.

"A book!" he was laughing now. There was other laughter in the room. Chosen bristled. He wanted to intervene, to protect Patty, to protect the book, to stop Ed. *No Bashar,* came a voice, *you cannot interfere.*

Oh Bashaa-arrr, came a singsong call, turned nasty. *You lose! He is one of ours! Look at his repulsion as he reads the title. Stand back, righteous angel of your God! Fool! Watch what we do to your precious book!*

Patty sank to the floor sobbing. "It's a present from Will!" she kept repeating.

"You stupid imbecile, Patricia! Your stupid imbecile baby is dead! He is dead, dead, dead, dead! And so is his stupid God!" And with that Ed Harwood stormed out of the house, taking a skinny book of Psalms with him. Patty crawled on the floor to the door and watched Ed drive away. She curled into a fetal position and wept as winds heralding the coming March pushed the storm door of Will's childhood home against the shivering body of his mother. It was dark when Patty composed herself, pushed her thinning, matted hair from off of her face, and struggled to her knees. She pulled herself up by a chair and walked to a drawer in the kitchen. Her mind was fighting against constant attack, struggling to survive, surrounded by hissing, dizzy sounds and faceless, bloody images. She held her head with both hands and whimpered. Finally, with a last gasp of determination and resolve, she became resolute, fixed on a mission. She had to have order in her life; she had to have control. She reached in the drawer and grabbed the scotch tape, and began to put the letter with the government seal back together.

Tossed Away

Chosen flew fast as Ed gunned his car down the expressway, knuckles white, his neck bulging in thick, veiny ropes. He cursed his wife, he cursed his son, he cursed God. They had ruined his life. He, a man of letters, stuck at a miserable junior college, consigned to the fringes of academia. The gifted Edward P. Harwood (he had been told many times he was gifted), only son of the Harwoods of Richmond, marginalized, groping students in stolen clutches in supply closets, hating, hating. And married to that weak, sniveling creature, that ignorant, classless scourge of his life. And his imbecile son gets religion?! He needed a drink.

Ed drove to Chicago's seamy side, to a hiding place of his own, where esteemed colleagues would not dream of venturing, where Ed could nurse his burning anger and disappointment with life and where he could satisfy the demanding demon of alcoholism, a demon that consumed and liberated. Drinking was one of many demons that Ed Harwood entertained awares, demons that do not live on the spiritual plane, but come from the nature within, demons that grow grotesque and uncontrollable. Ed was haunted by the ghost of a handsome, pipe-smoking intellectual—who could even one day become president.

Ed pulled his car alongside a curb on a blue-collar street; parking lots weren't necessary for the neighborhood bar. Men—and some women—would be inside where the musty, stale smell of booze and cigarettes mingled and stank. It was the stench of darkness, of hopelessness, yet it was a place where Ed would pay to stay. The cluster of real demons that accompanied him shivered with delight as Professor Harwood, man of letters, grasped the handle to a door with filthy gingham curtains on its window, and stepped inside. Before he went into the bar, though, he walked to the side of the building and threw the book in the trash.

Chapter

Four

March 1968

Chosen positioned himself on top of the trash barrel. The barrel's rusty color reminded him of the dusty floor of Galilee, a deep red-brown that changed the soles of sandaled feet to umber. A big metal barrel was not very different from an earthen pot, he thought. There was a time when every home from Galilee to Judea had several large earthen pots, some to hold oil, some to hold new wine, but most especially to catch and hold rainwater, such a precious commodity in that arid land. The big pots had been covered with fine cloth to keep drinking water clean. *You blind guides! You strain out a gnat but swallow a camel.* Chosen's lips separated in a melancholy smile, his thoughts far away.

Chosen remembered a particular event when there was water *and* wine. Not the wine of discarded bottles cluttering the barrel beneath him, but the wine of times before, wine from fresh grapes, wine from water. He remembered the sunshine, the music, and the merriment, and when remembrance brought him to the happy face of his Master, Bashar-el caught his breath. Oh, to see His face again! The angel was homesick. He longed for the company of the heavenly host, for the fellowship of saints, and for the indescribable ecstasy of absolute immersion in praise and adoration.

Wind tunneled alongside the neighborhood bar, and Chosen lowered himself closer to the book to keep it safe. He had warmed himself in the glow of Jesus' smile on that special day in Cana, still distinct in the big angel's recollection: how the Master loved weddings!

The wedding feast at Cana had been a jubilant and colorful ceremony, everyone there attired in festive clothing and an equally festive mood. Colors always seemed more vivid on the Lord—or so the angels thought—as if the creator of color was celebrated and worshiped by color itself, the decorative bands on Jesus' garment cascading like music from shoulder to hem, His long tunic tasseled and cloaked.

Jesus and His followers joined their voices in acclamation as the groom was ushered to the wedding canopy by the bridesmaids. And then the bride arrived amid a shout. The Lord's joy had been a foreshadowing of the great wedding feast to come, of that the angel was certain. Every angelic being awaited the moment when Christ would be united with His Bride and drink of the wine again. The expectation of that soon and coming day consumed and energized everything celestial, even a big angel roosting on a pile of garbage alongside a neighborhood bar in Chicago.

And so it was that Chosen, lulled by wistful reverie and sighs of impatience for his coming King, huddled on top a rusty barrel and began to pray fervently for Ed and Patty Harwood and for a quick retrieval of Brenda's book by the next favored soul.

Joshua

Joshua prayed. And when Joshua prayed, he connected. Big white teeth with gold caps flashed as his lips moved, first slowly. Every eye in the dim and stale storefront church was on him. Joshua's short, thick arms lay motionless on his lap. His eyes closed in dream, his mouth whispered sound, sound that everybody leaned into, ankle deep in still water. It was quiet in the church when Joshua prayed.

A rhythm began to build. Joshua stood and walked to a platform. Slits of sunlight pushed through cracks in a boarded window and caught the floor just right, turning him into a sundial, casting shadow on the twelve o'clock hour. High noon at the Freedom and Grace Tabernacle. It was time to preach. And Joshua didn't have a pulpit. Joshua had a room.

The milky blur of his eyes flashed, so white that veins stood out like red rivers flowing from black stone. "Are you with me?" he asked the crowd, barely above a hint of sound. *"I'm whispering a secret in your ear."*

"Go on."

"You know what that secret is?"

"Go on."

"You belong to Him. You belong to Him and He belong to you. He your brother. He your brother, Halleluia. He your brother."

"Halleluia!"

"And your brother tell you, you gotta love like He loved. Love your enemy. That's right. That's what He say, that's right."

The pace began to quicken, his hands began to move.

"Things ain't good in Chicago-land, uh-uh, but we got a good God anyhow."

"Preach, Brother."

"Trouble is brewing all over the land; sisters and brothers are fightin'— oh, yeah—sisters and brothers thinkin' they should rise up and demand—and DEMAND—equality. Fightin'. Fightin'. But we got a good God anyhow."

"Yesss, go on an' preach!"

"Dr. King had a dream; that ain't no secret. He had a dream that we *is* equal, we equal, we equal, we equal cuz we got a good God anyhow. Oh Jesus, save Your people, bring justice and peace to this land . . ." His arms went into the air, his hands shook. "Deliver us, deliver us, make the pain go away. You know pain, Jesus!"

"Yes, yes . . ."

"You know pain. You been lifted on the tree. You know pain. We know pain too."

The crowd was on its feet.

"We gonna suffer, too, Jesus, suffer some more. But how long? Set our people free!"

Shouts and clapping.

"We know You gonna set us free—You already set us free from that nasty old clawfoot . . ."

"Halleluia! Preach on, Brother!"

"We don't need worry 'bout the devil no more, oh no. He be a defeated foe, and we know YOU A GOOD GOD ANYHOW!" he boomed.

"Anyhow!" All hands raised, hundreds of fingers waved, lemmings waving and pointing and wiggling in the sand.

"Anyhow!" It was thunder in the church when Joshua preached.

An hour later Joshua sat down, hands on his lap. He wore a neatly pressed smile, pressed like the old suit he wore, like his white shirt with the frayed collar and monogrammed pocket, and like the perfectly ironed hankie that he used to wipe his brow. His smile looked like laughter; his veiny eyes gazed at the cross on the wall with unconditional praise and adoration. Others in the room began to pray, following the lead of a large woman named Mattie.

"Brudda Joshua speak da truth, we knows, we don' gotta worry no mo."

"That's right, Sistah."

"No, we got Jesus on our side. Nuttin' gonna stan' in de way a JE-sus. Halleluia, JE-sus!" shouted Mattie, turning her gaze on the preacher with unconditional praise and adoration.

"Halleluia, Jesus," shouted the flock.

"Halleluia, Halleluia," said the old black preacher, averting his eyes from Mattie and smiling at the crowd as the sun strained through weathered boards and marked the one o'clock hour.

In the Trash

The sun strained through the slit of an alley and marked an angel as well, as he kept vigil on a trash barrel. It had been two days since Ed had flipped Brenda's gift onto the top of an already full garbage pail, two days since Chosen saw him stumble into his car and speed away. And if not for a poor, wretched scavenger, Brenda's book (and Chosen) would have stayed put until the city sanitation department rolled its massive truck into the neighborhood for early Monday morning collection.

Chosen saw the man—no! the *woman*—approach the trash cans. She was layered in clothes: parka, vest, sweatshirt, sweater. Her hair fell ratted alongside her nose and covered her face as she rummaged through the filth. Fingernails dirty and ragged, the wretched woman mumbled continuously. "Beethoven with a burr," she kept repeating, a hoarse cackle after every pronouncement. "Beethoven with a burr." She pushed trash off the top of one barrel and dug for bottles, looking for a leftover drop. "Beethoven with a burr," she announced with authority. Chosen's heart crashed to the ground. He stood in shock as the woman held a beer bottle up high, into the sun, and swallowed, the flat brew leaking off her chin. He saw her face now. *The face of someone's daughter, a face once cradled and sung to.* "Holy One!" he groaned. *"This is Your daughter! How can this be?!"* He had seen other women in such impoverished states throughout time, but this woman touched him to his core. *Pick up the book!* he pleaded. *Let me help you.*

The woman reached for the book, read the title, cackled "Beethoven with a burr," and threw the book in the alley.

"Psiakrew, kobieta, odejsc! Odejsc!" Chet Godlewski, the bar's Polish proprietor, didn't have the heart of an angel. He exploded from the back door of his tavern, waving his apron, and chased the woman away. She left mumbling, teetering away with cackle and murmur, off to the next stop on her daily rounds. Chosen was flustered. Torn between running after the woman and whacking a bar owner, his attention suddenly turned to a loud, whining sound in the alley. The angel froze, uncharacteristically bewildered. Too late. He stood helplessly as a young man on a moped bore down on his precious charge. Squinting in the sun, the driver barely noticed the bump as he gunned his scooter onto the street and vanished in a white puff of exhaust. The book would have to wait until the next day, when a large woman named Mattie would come down the alley and when the good pleasure of the Lord would be fulfilled.

Mattie

Mattie wheezed when she walked—or waddled, depending on your take, for Mattie was not of delicate bone nor was she diminutive of size; the ground fairly ducked as she marched along her route on Monday morning. Marched and wheezed, marched and wheezed, and sang her favorite song. Mattie was a deeply spiritual woman, "cuz grace receeved, 'twas grace that saved her soul—somehow." A beautiful, lilting Jamaican accent punctuated Mattie's words and song. She was on her way to the Pleasant Valley Tavern, pushing an old baby carriage that held repast for bar patrons: kapusta, pierogi, ksan (that torrid horseradish that burnt the linings of red, bulbous Polish noses) and, her specialty, stuffed cabbage. How a black woman came to make the best stuffed cabbage in Chicago was no mystery: Mattie once worked for Polish people in New Jersey and was taught the finer nuances of Polish cooking by the family's "Babci." *No cook too long the onion. Lotsa caraway. No use too big the cabbage.*

"'Twas grace that bought my heart thu . . . far . . ." Mattie's rendition went, "an' grace my soul re . . . ceeve!"

She marched over a diminishing berm of rotted snow, laughed, and sharply jerked the buggy to the left. But this was not just any left turn. It was a turn, a single step among countless steps, that caused the heart to skip an extra beat, to fire off-key, to clutch the gut with a hint of adrenaline—*no put too much the salt*—to even clutch the gut of a big, happy woman like Mattie. The turn, the step, headed her across another street among countless streets— and across the line.

There is a Mattie in every city, and there is also a line. In fact, there are many lines, especially in big cities where people are wont to gather along ethnic, religious, or cultural sympathies: a clear distinction of turf. Invisible walls, barriers, signs, flags, standards, fences, boundaries, and warnings surround each comfy little niche. It is the same everywhere. *Don't you dare to enter our space, keep your place, especially—and we really mean this—especially if you're a nigger.* The lines create a jigsaw puzzle of different shapes and colors. And the puzzle pieces have names: Uptown. Downtown. Hoagietown. Chinatown. Hymietown. Central Park. Ghetto. Slum. Put the puzzle together and what do you have:

Chicago. Detroit. Los Angeles. Perth Amboy. Tacoma. New York. Raleigh. Study the pieces by color, especially by color: this color matches up with this one, that piece doesn't belong here, here is the missing piece! Separate the pieces by color and shape. Crooked lines, straight lines, streets, boulevards. Mattie crossed the line, Chicago's Mason-Dixon Line, as she stepped off the cold, gray curb and left behind a part of the puzzle that still didn't fit and was still warm to the touch from last year's riots, when streets were turned to scars. Scars on the city, scars on the nation, scars on the back of a black woman pushing a baby buggy. Main Scar. Maple Scar. Front Scar. Scar Ain't Healed Yet. Scar In Your Own Backyard: because anger erupts right where you live; it's personal. When rage finally pushes its way through steel and smashes every lock to smithereens; when it holds a pillow over all self-control until it is lifeless and can no longer resist; when anger comes, it's not "out there," on the other side of the line, it's here. Right here. It lives in your gut, bubbles in your blood, festers into bile, and shoves its way into your neighborhood. When it detonates, you smash and throw and hit and break, right where you live. But Mattie was leaving all that behind for now, as she jerked the buggy to the left and stepped off the edge of the chalky gray sidewalk.

Though it might have been with a bit more urgency to her step, or with the tiniest shrill in her voice, Mattie marched on, on to the Pleasant Valley Tavern. And she was not alone; Monday mornings were always good pickings for a pooch named Pup.

Pup

There was no other way to describe Pup than to simply call him a dog. He was generic mutt, pound hound, Heinz 57, quintessential dog. Medium size, a merle color infused with brown, black, gray, and tan, he was the dog found sketched inside of caves, found in art, and found in our minds when we think *dog*. His hair was short and his body one continuous mass of muscle. His ears flopped over like envelope flaps; his pointy tail moved in permanent motion, windshield-wiper thin and wagging.

And, as common lore expects dogs to share the characteristics of their masters, Pup obliged, his square jaw set in a permanent smile that looked like laughter, for Pup belonged to a kindly old black preacher named Joshua. Joshua had fashioned a collar for his dog out of an old leather belt, not that the dog had use for such adornment, but city code required a rabies tag and license. Pup, therefore, smiled and waggled and jingled when he walked. And he walked with his friend Mattie every time she delivered sauerkraut and stuffed cabbage to his other friend Mr. Godlewski, who greeted the dog with a piece of Polish sausage. Pup did not see color. And the guttural sounds from Mr. Godlewski did not matter one bit. There were no lines in Pup's world as he gaily walked and sniffed along the way.

Things were not so gay for an upset angel, however, who fitfully paced alongside Brenda's gift as it lay in the hard-packed, damp alleyway alongside the tavern. Under a clear command to leave the book where it lay, Chosen was miffed (patience not as strong a virtue as obedience—for Chosen would *never* disobey). How could he stand still and just *wait* for someone to find the book?! After all, he was still trembling from the close call with the garbage truck.

The early morning commotion of a truck working its way down the street had put the angel on alert. Certain the book was safe from the greasy, cavernous pit in the back of the truck, he watched as pickup men worked their way toward the bar. Two men fetched assorted garbage pails, emptied them in the back, and pushed a hydraulic lever that brought down a steel plate to crush the cans and bottles and paper destined for the dump. One man would bang the side of the truck with his fist: *Move on!*, and the routine began again.

Methodically, without much talk (for talk was impossible amidst the roar and scrape and crushing sound), the men two-stepped their way toward Chosen, who never reckoned on the truck backing into the alley. Eyes wide in alarm, utterly panicked over his dilemma, Chosen flew fast circles around the shuddering and squealing mass of steel, while the driver maneuvered its big steering wheel, bringing the nose of the truck into the middle of the street, and began his backward pass. The men on the ground were already reaching for the trash barrels alongside the bar. Chosen saw the truck bearing down on the book, the left wheels in perfect alignment, inches away. He had to act fast. And so he did.

The truck bucked and hiccuped forward. The reverse gear, it seemed, would no longer engage. Try as he might to wrench the lever into gear, the veteran driver with forearms that had the strength of pistons was no match for an angel. Up in the cab on the worn Naugahyde seat, Chosen held the floor shift easily, as the frustrated man rammed the clutch hard against the floorboard and used both hands to force the gear into place. It would not budge. The angel had done his job. The disgusted driver shifted into first gear and pulled onto the street, the men on the ground already at the next stop. Brenda's gift had been spared. Yet look where it was!

Chosen blamed himself for the condition of the book. He was weary, and though he knew better (he was an angel, after all), he seriously doubted the merit of letting the book lie on the ground in an alley next to . . . what was the name of the place? . . . the Pleasant Valley Tavern—this was too much. Too much. He scanned the sidewalk and the alley for someone to appear. If he could just get someone within his sights, the angel was sure he could maneuver circumstances so the book was found. He never *ever* expected the Lord to send a dog.

His treat right around the next corner, Pup accelerated ahead of Mattie. Knowing the route (and reward) by heart, he loped toward the back door of the bar.

It would be hard to say who was more startled, the angel or the dog, for as Pup excitedly galloped into the alley, he sensed the angel's presence and came to an immediate, comical halt, as both front legs locked, his rear half crashed into his front. Pup tumbled and came up growling. Chosen's heart gladdened at the sight of the dog, for Chosen (just as Pup had found himself a moment before) was head-over-heels crazy about animals. He had great and tender fondness for this special part of Creation. And how he liked dogs! *What a great gift to man,* Chosen thought, *for God to have provided such a devoted and uncomplicated companion for His children.* He stared at the growling, then cowering, creature and knew at once that he was to endear himself to the animal. It would be his great pleasure.

At first, Pup had different ideas. Tail between his legs, he crouched low and whimpered. The dog sensed Chosen, and what began as fear slowly turned to guarded acceptance. The dog sniffed the ground, the air. Chosen approached. The confused dog cried, and though he could not physically feel Chosen's touch, he became calm as the angel stroked his head and cooed. Well, not calm, actually—Pup became energized! He lowered his chest to the ground, his hind end in the air punctuated by his pointy windshield wiper on "maximum." Pup wanted to play. Lost in the innocence of the creature, Chosen laughed, then turned serious when Pup grabbed the book with his teeth and began to shake his head violently. *Play with me!* he was saying. Chosen retrieved the book from the dog's mouth. *Spit that out!* the angel yelled. What fun for the dog! This time he grabbed the book and raced in a tight circle, like a puppy chasing its tail. Chosen took the book from the dog's mouth again. Before Chosen could get the dog to stop the game, Pup was off and running, delighted to have the prize clenched between his teeth. He ran right into the baby carriage, causing Mattie to react a little faster than usual to save the sauerkraut from spilling.

"Gitta way, crazy dawg! Gitta way! Now . . . wha' you got dere, Pup?" Mattie reached over, revealing her rolled cotton stockings and heavy legs as her dress lifted in the back. She pulled the book from between the axles of the carriage. The dog ran back to the alley and twirled in dizzy circles.

"Crazy dawg!" she laughed and looked at the book. "A Restin' Pla . . . The Book o' Psalms, wal ah'll be . . ." whistled Mattie as she examined the contents (to be sure the inside collaborated with the out).

"Where dat dog git dis book? Dis book don' belong in no dog's mout!" She placed it reverently in the carriage and continued to her appointed meeting. Chosen was elated. The book was off the ground, it was in the hands of someone who obviously knew its value, and when he flew along with the lumbering woman as she retraced her steps home, he joined her in song . . . and played "catch me if you can" with a quintessential dog.

Back over the Line

The little entourage walked down streets lined with simple brick homes, some with a one-car garage, most with a worn parking space where lawn might have been. Some yards were surrounded by chain-link fence, probably to confine the barking dogs running back and forth, back and forth, chopping at the air with bared teeth; that is, until they sensed the angel—when they would whimper in fear or submission. Being a part of this tiny threesome—one invisible, one impervious, one running in happy circles—was ministering to Chosen, who had seen much evil and pain since assigned to the book. He reveled in Mattie's interpretation of "Amazing Grace" and closed his eyes for a while to drift on her song. Oh, how he needed this!

"When we been dere temousnot tears, be shinin' like de sun!"

I've been there thousands and thousands of years, and there are no tears. Just wait, dear one, just wait! Yet as they crossed back over the line, as they came closer and closer to Mattie's world, Chosen began to feel oppression and doom. He needed wait only a few more blocks to *see* what he felt. It could have been Vietnam.

Not much to begin with, the "Negro" section of town had finally settled down after a long summer of ghetto violence. Anger had begat racial unrest. It was during the summer riots of 1967 that police began to stockpile an arsenal for all-out war, and a black militant wing under such men as Elijah Muhammad and Malcolm X became impatient with the feeble liberal mantra of integration ("We don't *want* to be integrated into the system that's killing us. We want separation and freedom.") and began to demand a separate state of their own ("Give us equality and justice or leave us be.").

Chosen's spirit drooped as he followed Mattie's march. Past small mountains of decay and rot, past boarded and charred buildings, past clusters of black men now sporting the "natural" Afro in defiance of white projection into their culture. *Black Power!* The two words were hastily sprayed on every empty space: on walls, street signs, sidewalks, telephone poles, across broken windows, on benches, and etched onto the face of every young black in the neighborhood.

"Go back to the cotton patch, Jemimah!" came a sneer. Mattie shot back. "You mind yo'self, you don' talk that way to yo Sistah!" Chosen bristled. Pup trotted up to the offender for a rough tickle behind his ear. Mattie marched on, pushing the buggy around a whiskered man lying on a cardboard pallet. She kept on singing. "I once wa' loss but now I be foun', 'twas grace that made me me." She stopped in front of the Freedom and Grace

Tabernacle, opened one of the two windowless doors, and stepped inside. Pup squeezed in and joyfully ran to a door at the end of the room.

"Brudda Joshua!" Mattie giggled. "Brudda Joshua! Ah gots a present fo' you!"

Joshua Gets the Book

Joshua Jericho Jefferson emerged from the back room, his short-sleeved white shirt pressed, as always, to perfection. He had been working on a leaky sink in the women's bathroom when Mattie arrived. Joshua tried not to betray his irritation, for Mattie had a penchant for long conversation—and a loud and clear claim on the widowed preacher, much to Joshua's extreme consternation. The widowed Mattie, on the other hand, was delighted to have reason to pay a call on the man of her dreams and presented the book with aplomb.

"It fell rite from heaven, Brudda Joshua, ah swear! Landed rite on top my black cookin' pot, rite dere in de buggy, ah knowed it's fo' you, ah knowed it right off, and ah sez to de Almatty, sen yo angels to protect me so's ah can brin' dis to Brudda Joshua, an ahm here to tell you dis be a special book, a special book, Brudda Joshua, you mind me now, dis be a *special book*."

Joshua thanked Mattie and took the book. Peace flooded Chosen. In spite of the physical condition of the building and the unlikely chain of events leading to this moment, Chosen sighed a great, heaving, shuddering sigh and tears formed in his eyes for the serenity that overcame him; he, who was so bereft a few hours ago. *My ways are not your ways, says the Lord God Almighty.*

Joshua studied the book, saw Brenda's inscription to Will, and read Will's primitive confession. He then opened the book to a certain page, direct in his manner, as if he knew by heart where it was—like putting your hand directly on a light switch in the dark—and he paused for a long time while he read Psalm 77. There seemed to be a hint of faraway in his eyes. He turned the book over and over in his hands. "Seems to me we might want to clean this up a bit!" he said. This pleased the angel—and the woman—immensely.

"Ah was thinkin' dat very thin', Brudda! Now you gets back to yo work an ah'll go clean dis up good. Ah'll make us up a pot o' greens too," Mattie laughed. "No sense me bein' here witout fixin' my pastor some good food, nosiree." She was off past the restrooms and disappeared into Joshua's small living quarters before the man could protest. Pup thumped his tail on the wood floor. Joshua Jericho Jefferson shook his head in annoyance and wandered back into the women's bathroom.

The next few weeks were a touch of home for Chosen as he settled into blissful routine with Joshua and his dog, Pup. Pup did manage to *break* routine and confuse his owner, however, when he abandoned his usual sleeping spot next to the bed in favor of Joshua's favorite easy chair. Joshua covered his pet on those nights when the last cold gasp of winter rode on every gust of wind, but lately Pup slept the sleep of one nestled in the lap of an angel.

Joshua spent much time in prayer, and prayer meant one thing to the devout man: reading his Bible. The preacher sat at his desk (an old card table with one wobbly leg) and read, his mouth in constant motion. Chosen relished the fact—reveled in it, really—that he knew what was in store for this saintly man when he entered glory. He envisioned the happy commotion and the heraldry that would greet Joshua when he went into eternity. The glimmer of the angel's excitement sent just a hint of extra light for the old man to read, the dog stretching and sighing at his feet. For two weeks, a tail thumped the wooden floor, an angel rested, and an old man prayed and tended to his flock.

Ministry

Chosen tagged along as Joshua ministered to others: to the infirm (*Brotha Joshua, I knewed you'd come today!*); to widows (*Brotha Joshua, lets me make you dinna.*); to children (*Brotha Joshua! Brotha Joshua! Tell us about the chariot!*); to the men on the street (*You got no call with us, you a Uncle Tom. Get away with you white man's Jesus.*).

It frustrated the angel that *anyone* could possibly reject Christ. *Hadn't they heard? Didn't they know?* But the kindly Joshua held his peace. He held his peace with such dignity and with such a gentle spirit that most members of the burgeoning Muslim movement held respect for the man, in spite of their barbs. The young men who heckled him had cut their teeth in the faith,

Joshua's faith. The young men (and young women too) were grandchildren of people who had migrated from the South, people who would never dream of separating faith from culture—seeming to give them a submissive and passive manner, when in fact they were modeling patience and long-suffering—people who insisted that civil leadership come from the pulpit, and who went to church all Sunday long.

Sunday! How like heaven Sunday at the Freedom and Grace Tabernacle could be! So much activity, so much color, so much clamor; sound coming together all at once, sound that lifted floorboards and ceiling joists as voices boomed "Amen." Amen again and again. Sunday without end. Swaying. Crying. Pleading. Praising. Mattie supervising and becoming more bold about her "rightful" place beside the minister; men and women forgetting the tension that coursed through the community, forgetting the poverty that hit them hard, fast, and continuously, forgetting the epithets, forgetting the gray, chalky curb; body heat collecting like a scirocco gathers mass to meet the arctic wind head on. All the day long: singing, playing tambourines (there were only tambourines and mouth harps in Joshua's church, the old player piano—that someone had painted lime green—sat crippled in a corner, having long since given up its last, miserable chord), and preaching. Good preaching. It was Sunday. And on Sunday, Joshua, their beloved Joshua, didn't need a pulpit. Joshua only needed a room.

Week after week, Joshua took his flock from the edge of despair; he grabbed hold of all of them by the scruff of their necks and pulled them back. *You come back here. You got no call being sad like that. You a child of the King!* He flashed his veiny eyes and smiled and told them everything would be all right, no matter what, *cuz they had a good God anyhow.* And they believed him. Joshua reached inside and touched every man, woman, and child with his trembling hands, sending hope like a current, charging out from every heart into every distant land, till whole bodies fell spent on a bench from the sheer exhaustion of blessed assurance and from surging, living faith. The Freedom and Grace Tabernacle on Sunday was prime-time, full-tilt, all-out rapture for Chosen. He understood, and already felt himself, the love every person in the room held for the pastor, for the unimposing man who appeared out of nowhere and started preaching on a street corner of Chicago twenty years ago, who kept his past locked in a vaulted chamber of his heart, who cherished and proclaimed the Word of God, and who always wore a perfectly pressed smile.

Omen

There was one incident that marred Chosen's two-week idyll. It happened late one night when the winds didn't blow but when the smell of spring was teasing people's sensibilities. Joshua was asleep and unusually still, odd for the preacher who never smiled in his sleep and often cried, like Pup might cry when giving chase to rabbits in a dream.

That night, Pup growled. Instantly alert, Chosen's discernment went into overdrive. The enemy! He glanced at Joshua, who didn't stir. Pup became agitated, pulling his lips back repeatedly, showing teeth that meant business, his tail out straight and still. The dog's eyes turned toward a high window, the scruff on his neck raised to double him in size. Chosen didn't have to look. He heard the thuds on the roof. One. Two. Three. There was no other sound, just a frigid chill that descended on the room, as Joshua pulled his heavy quilt closer around his neck and turned on his side with a snort. Chosen settled down next to Joshua and prayed for protection. *"Righteous Father, deliver this man from the evil one, I beseech you."* And as quickly as the evil came, it was gone. In short order, Pup whimpered, turned in tight circles on Joshua's chair, and fell resolutely to resume his sleep. Chosen was left to wonder. Had this been a harbinger? A warning? Whatever the reason for the demonic appearance, Chosen cautioned himself not to let down his guard. *Be self-controlled and alert. Your enemy the devil prowls around like a roaring lion looking for someone to devour.*

Bible Study

Joshua poured a glass of milk and sat at his desk. He reached alongside three neat stacks of tracts—*Will You Be Ready? Do You Know Jesus? Who Is Jesus of Nazareth?*—and grabbed *A Resting Place,* catching the edge of Billy Graham's *Decision* magazine, which went fluttering to the floor and landed on top of Pup, who had just settled down near Joshua's feet.

Joshua had read from the spruced-up little book often. "this is as good as it gits, Brudda." He seemed to like the compact, easy maneuvering of the slim book, not that he ever turned to any other psalm but one. Today, however, he did something different. He pulled his own Bible across the table and opened to Psalm 77, without a doubt his favorite text. He removed a faded envelope (Chosen figured it to be a bookmark) and proceeded to place it in the exact spot in Brenda's book. And performing his customary ritual, Joshua placed his hands on the open pages, closed his eyes, and prayed before he began to prepare for Sunday's sermon. He reached over to his easy chair and hoisted a brilliantly colored afghan (made by Mattie—who else?) and wrapped himself tight. Joshua hated the cold. He was glad he'd soon see the last of March. "What this month good for anyhow?" he muttered to himself. "No good for nothin' month, good for nothin' but wind. We got enough wind, Lord! We can do without this *March*." He said the last word forcefully, making a point. "Maybe it called *March*," he was having fun now, "maybe it called *March*, Pup, cuz we be *marching* to keep warm!" He laughed.

Hearing his name, Pup jumped to attention and scanned Joshua's every move for the slightest chance of a handout. The old man pet the dog's head, which was now flat and drooling on his lap. "You go on, now. I got work to do." Pup turned languidly and hoisted himself into Joshua's easy chair, and Chosen beamed.

Knowing Joshua was rightfully handling the Word of God, Chosen prayed for him to be guided by the Holy Spirit and began to chant in praise. After a time, the black man (and it could be said that Joshua was the color of darkest ebony) pushed away from the card table and paced. *"Lord, I know somethin' comin', I can feel it Lord, from the bottom of my heart, from the bottom of my feet, I can feel it. Now, Lord, You know I don' question You no more, no sir, no sir, but Lord, You gots to help me. Your work gettin' mighty heavy for this old man. I know it's time, Jesus, I know I gotta speak the truth. I'll prepare my talk, and You prepare their hearts. I ain't ready, I ain't ready for all this rememberin', it's been a long time, I guess I'm ready. If this be what You want. Now I ain't complainin', no sir, but I'm thinkin' You gotta send me a little help."*

Chosen radiated. He wrapped his arms and wings around the dear man and held him in a grip so tight that Joshua felt weightless, as if lifted off the floor on angel's wings (that is what he would have *said* at the moment); he felt safe. He felt so safe that a lone tear welled, and welled, and then, pulled by gravity, set off on a journey down Joshua's nose and landed on the floor. "Thank you, Jesus," whispered the old preacher as he sat down and began, once again, to fashion a sermon from Psalm 77.

The Sermon

The air felt . . . dare it be said . . . sanctified. It felt peculiar, different, somewhat uncommon as people took their seats in hushed reverence the last Sunday in March. There were no signs, no bulletins (for Joshua's church was much too poor for bulletins), no announcements in the newspaper: Preacher at Freedom and Grace Tabernacle to Bare His Soul on Sunday. It was in the air, it felt right, and folks knew—they knew—they were in the presence of the power of the Almighty.

A quiet settled over the room, just like Joshua's quilt on a cold night, a quiet that drove some to want to hide in shame. So it is in the presence of God: a feeling of highest perfection, of never needing to eat, sleep, breathe, live, work, play, dance, skip, sing—but only to be in the Presence, just to be. You are so . . . whole; everything is so . . . right; nothing is wrong, nothing matters. You only want to be there, and you want to be there forever. And yet there also comes a feeling of lowest imperfection, of shame. When you sense the presence of the Holy you want to crawl beneath the floor, to prostrate yourself in awe, to turn aside your face. And the two feelings, the highest and the lowest, don't collide. They fit comfortably inside each other. Really. That's how it is when you lower your eyes and Almighty God cups your face in His hands to pull your gaze upward.

Mattie turned around to whisper to a friend. "Ah feel the *presence* of th' Lord!" she uttered, wide-eyed, nervous, swiveling back to watch the door to Joshua's apartment. Everyone watched the door.

So unlike him not to greet the people that morning, not to be on the sidewalk to tease the children, to shake the hands of his brothers, to artfully dodge a heavy woman in her latest wide-brimmed hat. Not today; Joshua was alongside his bed, on his knees. Chosen was right beside him. He appeared troubled but was otherwise prepared—and well-pressed.

It was to be an important sermon—that he knew, that was *all* he knew. He knew in the way that the still and certain voice of God speaks to your spirit and you are left to simple obedience. That's what it comes down to. It matters not that you walk in a fog; it matters not that the voice makes sense, it matters not that it twists your gut like a wrung-out mop. You must obey.

Why must he preach on this—on this! "Give me strength, oh Lord, give me strength," cried the old black man. "You know how bad it hurts." But reading the psalm from that book—*Dear Will: This is a good book that helped me a lot*—reading something for the millionth time, had triggered an urgent need in Joshua to tiptoe into his past—*not too far!*—and preach an important sermon. Besides, he would be able to keep the hurt pressed down, nice and neat. He always had.

Chosen wrapped one wing around the man's shoulders, imbuing him with the calm and strength he would need. The old man uttered "Amen" and rose to his feet. He straightened his tie, picked up his Bible—no, he picked up Brenda's gift, and headed out the door. Chosen, immediately aware of the Presence, bowed in deep adoration. Other angels filled the room, suffusing it in a sun-gold glow that could not have come from the west-facing boarded windows at ten o'clock in the morning.

"We ain't gonna sing just yet," said Joshua. "We ain't gonna pray just yet, no, cuz I done prayed all night anyhow. I got some preachin' to do, then we sing and then we pray."

Not a peep. Mattie turned to scan the crowd and shush any offender, for naught. She saw her son Monroe in the back of the room. *Monroe!* Her heart somersaulted to see her boy back in church. "Neber mine dat Nation o' Islam bussness, nosiree, you know JE-sus, Monroe, why you goin' do dat falz re'gion?" *My name is now Monroe X. I reject the name imposed on me by some slave master!*

Halleluia! thought Mattie. Monroe X was back in church! She finally turned around—and faced Joshua's glare. She wiped her sweaty palm on her flower print dress (it was called a muumuu back then), and smiled demurely.

Joshua began.

"Long time ago—long time ago—I said no to the Lord. That's right, I turned my back and said 'No, You ain't a good God anyhow. No, You ain't.' But the Lord, He stuck by me no madda what. He say, 'Joshua, I show you, you don't see now, but I show you I am a good God.' An' He did."

One cautious "Amen" from the crowd.

"He showed me again and again."

"Yes."

"And then he give me a prayer. He say, 'Joshua, this be *your* prayer, you keep this prayer in your heart, this be our little con-ver-sation.' And now He say to this ole man, He say, 'Joshua, open your heart cuz you gonna preach that prayer.' And I say, 'Lord, it PERSONAL!' and He say, 'Son . . .'"

"Yes . . ."

"He say, 'Son, I be with you all the way.'"

"Preach, Brotha Joshua."

And Joshua began to preach.

"Once I was an angry man. I yelled, 'I don' think You there, You ain't there, You a lie! If You was there none of this woulda happen, if You was there You woulda helped. I say You can't help me cuz You ain't there anyhow, nohow. And now look; I got nothin' but hurt.' People say, they say, 'Joshua, it gonna be all right,' and I had nothin' but hurt. I hurt so bad I want to kill. There ain't no peace—you listen now, I *know*—there ain't no peace when you gotta kill cuz you hurt so bad."

Dead silence.

The presence of God the Holy Spirit was so strong, Chosen folded his wings close to his body and lay prone on the floor.

"There ain't no sleep, neither, no sleep, no peace. Just hurt an' hate. It all broken into pieces. Everythin'. I shook my fist—'You ain't no good God anyhow, if You was . . . if You was You wouldn't leave me for no good.' Cuz I wanted to kill. I wanted to kill God."

Mattie's eyeballs fairly popped out of her head and landed on her lap.

"Where be this big love-God anyhow? He not there for me. No . . ." Joshua's voice momentarily drifted off. "He not there for me." Long pause. Long enough for Joshua to rewind a tape in his mind, splice out detail, to relive a little, ankle deep in memory. "Then I had time, I had a lot of time—

the Lord, I know now, He gave me time. I had time to think. I think about the Cross; my mind keep goin' back to the Cross. When I don't even *want* to think about the Cross, I think about the Cross."

A tentative, "Go on."

And Joshua preached for an hour on the Cross. He came alive, his arms raised and his hands waved and everyone in the room let out one huge held breath. Mattie was fairly blue. He was back. They would sing. They would pray, and they would walk out into the darkened street that night, every one of them listening to their preacher's words again and again. *Did he really want to kill God?*

"He a good God, he a GREAT God anyhow! He holy, He can do anythin'—anythin'—listen to me, He can do anythin' He want, but He *went to the Cross,* He already been killed! I can't kill no God already been killed, how I gonna do that? He already been killed . . . but . . . He . . . ain't . . . dead."

The crowd was electrified.

"HE A GREAT GOD ANYHOW! He gonna deliver us, He gonna take away our hurt, He gonna give us the dream, He just givin' us a little more time."

The tambourines began to play, songs were sung, and prayers were prayed. And Joshua, obedient Joshua, felt greatly relieved. It was over, and it wasn't so bad. If only that evening's service had gone as well.

Confrontation

The unforgiving month of March was going out with a roar; the first thunderstorm of the season pelted the storefront church that evening with fistfuls of rain. Children ran throughout the room during the midday meal. People balanced plates and pulled coffee cups out of the way in the nick of time during earnest games of tag. Mattie shrugged off Monroe's departure, hoping his morning appearance might raise her stock with Joshua. Pup, allowed in the big meeting room because church was not in session, begged with saucer eyes and drool from every person in the room. "Don' gib dat dawg no chicken boan!" ordered Mattie, practicing for the day when she would be the dog's rightful owner along with Joshua.

Later in the day as people took their seats, an a cappella choir took a shot at "On the Cross," and Joshua emerged from his quarters in a fresh white shirt. Songs sung and prayers prayed, it was time for the evening teaching.

Weary from the emotion of the past twenty-four hours, Joshua had planned a short exhortation. He started to talk about Christian virtue in a believer's life when Monroe X, Mattie's son, stood.

"You a fool, Joshua. We don't listen to no fool!"

"Monroe!" yelled a mortified Mattie.

"Monroe *X*, Monroe *X!* I am no slave owner's property. And I don't want to listen to no slave owner's religion. I got my own religion. You got a white Jesus. You preaching white nationalism. I don't want to be no whitey. I want to be black. I am black. You see my skin? You see your skin? You black. You gotta start thinking black."

Chosen watched Joshua closely. The man was tired. Why couldn't this young man leave him alone? Suddenly there was a shrill laugh that only Chosen could hear. Thud, thud, thud, thud. Like the pelting rain, the thuds came on the roof. The wind outside collected the sound of hell and swirled it round and round the block. Chosen braced himself and extended his wings fully to protect the old man from behind.

Joshua faced down the heckler.

"Son . . . ." he began to say.

"I ain't your son, and you ain't my daddy, handkerchief head!"

One of the men bore down on Monroe.

"No!" said Joshua. "Let him speak."

"The white man is the enemy." Monroe was now addressing the crowd. His passion undeterred, he shouted—spat—words that wouldn't be stopped. "You wouldn't be in this country if some white man hadn't kidnapped you and brought you here. They wronged us! They stole us!"

A teenage girl defiantly shouted, "Amen!" Mattie shot her a look the size of a cannonball.

Joshua was drained. "Sit down, Monroe."

"A coward can sit, a chump can sit; we been sittin' long enough, Joshua. You talk about a dream. You're a fool and King's a fool. Look at them—" Monroe swept his arms over the people. "They don't dream. There ain't no dreamin' here, old man, and when you can't dream, you can't hope, and when you can't hope, you wake up dead every day—they ain't livin', they dead."

Now the man did grab the boy, who managed to fire a parting shot that zeroed in to the center of Joshua's heart like a laser, blasting off a lock to a chamber that had been closed so very long ago, knocking Joshua off his careful tiptoes and sending him, flat-footed, to a rendezvous with his past.

"If you're not willing to pay the price, Joshua, don't you talk to us about no freedom! Freedom and Grace Tabernacle! You don't know what you're talking about! You a white man's nigger." And with that, Monroe X was evicted from the storefront church.

Remarkably, Joshua managed to complete his little sermon that night, somehow overruling emotions that were playing snap-the-whip in his body. He implored the troubled people (some of whom were mulling Monroe's words in their minds) to show God's goodness through their words and their works; he reassured them that God would work for good in the black man's life.

"You be people of the *Good* Book, is that right?"

"That's right," said one woman; not a peep came from Mattie.

"Then you got to be good, Brotha and Sistah . . . or," he tried to jest with them, to lighten the evening, to bring them back, "you be up to no good!" The old man was scraping bottom. It was grit alone that kept him on his feet. The best they could do was smile. *I want to kill God. When you can't hope, you wake up dead. Handkerchief head.* They'd had enough. It was time to go home.

"Now what you gonna do with the Good Book if all you do is say what it say but don' DO what it say? You know what you do with it? You drop it on the floor like this . . ."

It was lost on them. There was no shock left in the room as Brenda's gift slapped against the floor.

"And then you just go about your business," he said with a vaudeville voice, shuffling off to Buffalo, working them as hard as he could. "What you gonna do with the good book, what you gonna DO?" The old man was near tears, desperate to do his job, to care for his people, unable to stuff back the ragged piece of glass that was working its way free of his heart.

Talons scratched against the roof as one by one the demons left. Chosen heard them go. He scanned the room. He saw a dazed congregation staring back at its pastor.

"It been a long day today, a long day. Let's us thank the good Lord for what He worked in us today," whispered Joshua.

"Yes." Let's get this over with.

"Let us thank Him for bein' with us today."

That got a rise—some affirmation, some clapping, a little tambourine. Joshua paused.

"And let us thank Him for Brother Monroe."

Silence.

"Come on, now. Monroe, he just a boy, he our boy, ain't that so? We got to pray for him, we got to love him."

Mattie was too embarrassed to move and looked down into her ample lap.

"Sistah Mattie, why don't you pray for your boy?"

This was too much. Mattie looked up at Joshua, her eyes begging, pleading: *Not now! Please, not now!* Joshua returned her gaze.

"It's OK, Sistah, maybe someone else will pray for Monroe now, it's OK." Joshua's heart, filled with the ganglia of pain and emotion that it was, found room enough for the misery of a large woman in a wide-brimmed hat.

The Dream

It *had* been a long day, yet in spite of fatigue that turned his every movement to lead, Joshua didn't retire. He sat at his desk, absentmindedly stroking Pup's head.

This is what dogs do best, thought Chosen as Pup glued himself to his master's side and offered sensitive, knowing eyes. *I am here. Touch me and see. I will never leave your side. I will make you smile again. See? I'm wagging my tail for you.*

What was happening to the old man? Chosen fretted and petitioned for counsel; what should the angel do? This fine man, this good man, seemed suddenly broken. What was going on in Joshua's mind as he stared the empty stare of despair? The angel eyed Brenda's gift on the desk. What was the connection? Why was the Book of Psalms—and Psalm 77—suddenly a prop in the drama of this man's life?

Joshua closed his eyes in defeat. He was yielding to exhaustion, the flame of his spirit flickering a final warning before falling headlong into the dark. Chosen did not know (and Joshua was too weary to fight any longer), but that deeply embedded, ragged sliver of glass was working its way out, painfully tearing at tissue as it went. It forced its way toward a neatly pressed surface that showed no signs of wear, that had been ironed shut so long ago that memory was only surface play. Not anymore—and this a gift from God. The shard was coming, once and for all, ripping away from the recess of Joshua's heart and inching, inching, finally free. This was why the book. This was why the Presence. This was why, yes, this was why even Monroe. All for Joshua. *And grace my soul released.* Chosen began to understand. It all had something to do with Joshua, who at the moment was gulping hard, swallowing, pushing air against the tearing in his gut, his black hands forming tight fists. He would punch it back if he had to.

Not if a big old angel had anything to do with the situation. For Chosen knew that healing cannot come until the shard, the sliver, the memory, is released. Maybe, thought the angel, there was something he could do to break the stronghold of Joshua's resistance. He looked at Pup: the Lord had used a dog and so could he!

Joshua felt a poke on his leg. From out of the blue, Pup wanted some fun. Into the play posture he went, front legs flat on the floor, windshield wiper sky high. "Not now, Pup—go—shoo!" Not a chance.

A dizzy circle, a bark, a jump onto Joshua's easy chair, and—unbelievably—a flying leap toward his master, belly-flopping smack in the middle of Joshua's desk. The wobbly leg collapsed, sending everything to the floor on top of a suddenly penitent and very worried dog.

The book lay in the heap, the envelope/bookmark on top of a glossy tract. *What Does It Take to Follow Christ?* This was not quite what Chosen had orchestrated, and while he regrouped, and winced at the scolding Pup would receive, he saw that he'd achieved his goal.

Joshua reached into the heap, grabbed the bookmark, righted the table, and with trembling hands, opened the envelope. There was no glue holding it shut—no glue would have held its strength for forty-nine years. The flap was merely folded in on itself and never once had been disturbed; there was no need to read the newspaper clipping ever again. Once had been enough.

Other than the yellow tint of age, the clipping was surprisingly intact. If the news article had been longer, more precise—*Dear God in heaven it was precise enough!*—then it would have folds; creases blurring print. No, it was a short piece, short enough to fit snugly in its little paper vault, locked away, like a shard of ragged glass embedded in a black man's heart.

Joshua put the piece of paper on the table, cleared his throat, and despite the protest thundering in his head, began to read out loud.

The Chicago Defender, August 2, 1919

> . . . In all parts of the city, white mobs dragged from sur-
> face cars black passengers, wholly ignorant of any trouble,
> and set upon them. An unidentified young woman and a
> three-month-old baby were found dead on the street at
> the intersection of 47th Street and Wentworth Avenue.
> She had attempted to board a surface car there when the
> mob seized her, beat her, slashed her body into ribbons
> and beat the baby's . . .

Joshua struggled for air, he could not go on. His chest heaved as one who has run for his life, who has scratched and clawed and screamed to push the suffocating pillow off his face to live, after all, to live with a sliver the size of Calvary. The angel knelt against the old man's legs and raised his arms to heaven while Joshua sobbed, a plaintive, screaming sob, "SARAH! SARAH!" Joshua sobbed and screamed for the first time in forty-nine years. He cried himself into stuporous sleep.

In what may have been breach of protocol, but certainly an act of mercy, the strong angel lifted the old man onto his bed and covered him reverently with his quilt, as the long day faded into a long night filled with dream. Not the liberating dream of black men, but the frightening dream of one black man: lucid, real, in never-never land, never-again land.

If you're not willing to pay the price, Joshua, don't you talk to us about no freedom!

Joshua, we gots sorrowful somethin' to tell you. Maybe you betta sit, son. Sarah and the baby boy. We bad sorry for you, Joshua, bad sorry.

The hatred and anger that drove him crazed through the streets of Chicago, attacking every white face.

For crimes committed against the State of Illinois, I sentence you to thirty years in the penitentiary.

. . . the baby's brains against a telephone pole.

The old man was damp and hot to the touch, hot pus coming with the scraping sliver, fever pitch in sleep. Chosen held him close.

I'll kill you! I'll kill anything white! Solitary confinement. We got ways to deal with niggers.

My name is Charles. I'm here to talk with you about the Lord.

They killed my wife and my baby; there ain't no God.

They killed his only begotten Son, Joshua. He knows your pain.

You got no call reading the Bible, nigger.

Joshua, I think you should find a psalm that you can call your own—sort of your own special prayer with God.

The quilt flapped up and down with every jerk of Joshua's legs. Chosen held more tightly.

Not satisfied with this, one of the rioters severed her breasts, and a white young-ster bore them aloft on a pole, triumphantly, while a crowd hooted gleefully. All the time this was happening, several policemen were in the crowd . . .

I cried out to God for help; When I was in distress; I was too troubled to speak . . .

You sure do know your Bible, Joshua.

You say you goin' back to Chicago? What you gonna do, Joshua? You say you gonna preach? Hoo, boy! You come a long way!

I will appeal; the years of the right hand of the Most High, I will remember the deeds of the Lord . . .

Here, cousin, I safe dis for you in dis env'lope. I thoughts you might like to . . . uh . . . have it.

If you're not willing to pay the price, Joshua, don't you talk to us about no freedom!

It was late in the night when all became still. The troubled man finally, mercifully, slept, too exhausted to dream. Chosen never let go his grip. He was still reeling from the account of the murders. It seemed to the angel as if the very sound of evil crashed down on the room. Reading about Joshua's baby brought him back to Bethlehem long ago, to sounds he would never forget, so lucid in his mind was the sound of slaughter.

How could man, created in the image of God, foster such malignancy and hatred in his heart? HOW COULD HE??? Every sound of that wicked event in the holy city played in Chosen's head: the hoofbeats, the rattling swords, the mothers' pleas and shrieks, the screams, the shrill sound of death. Sound pounded and pounded, driving the silence of the room into an ear-splitting wail as the old man lay corpse-still and his devoted dog held vigil next to his bed. *The evil, the evil, Lord God, the evil!* The angel—the ministering angel whose job it was to help God's greatest creation—struggled under the weight of evil. *So great a gift as man will never ever understand,* mused Chosen, *that God Himself bore the full weight of evil on the cross. Eloi, eloi, lama sabachthani?* No. Why has man forsaken God? The week was about to bring more evil and struggle.

The Riot

It was a dark and quiet week. One small light shone over his sink, otherwise Joshua sat in his chair in the dark. He could barely stand the light of day when he let his dog in and out the back door of the Freedom and Grace Tabernacle. The man sat stone still, coping, dealing, processing, allowing himself to remember, calling out in anguish as the shard of broken glass continued on its journey.

Pup tended to his needs outside and raced back to the door, signaling his return with a single bark. *Bark!* yelled Pup. *It's time to let me in.* The door would open, the dog would squeeze inside, the door would close, and the dog would resume his vigil. *I will never leave you, master. Never.*

Mattie turned away from the locked front door of her church for the third time that week, muttering. She knew Joshua was all right because she'd seen Pup in the street. Pup, who had refused to walk with her on Monday to the Pleasant Valley Tavern. Pup, who had been able to resist the handouts of rib bones and leftover corncobs from his friends along his neighborhood route. Pup, who suddenly seemed as reclusive as his master. She would get the courage to go around to the back door, she would . . .

If dat door be locked tomorra' fo' sure ah goes to de back door . . . and she wad-dled away.

There was nothing left of Joshua but shell. And the shell was in danger of caving in on itself; there was no smile to hold his face together; there was no neatly pressed shirt to keep up appearances; there was not even a pair of shoes to keep him on his feet. Just shell. Shells don't have brains to think or hearts to feel. Shells don't have stomachs to feed, teeth to clean, eyes to see, ears to hear, mouth to speak. Eyes to see. *Those who have eyes, let them see. Mine eyes have seen the glory of the coming of the Lord. Lift up your eyes.* Nope, no eyes.

The newspaper clipping had been placed in the envelope and returned to its resting place, marking Psalm 77 in Brenda's gift. The book was on the card table, the pile of magazines and tracts . . . and Joshua's Bible . . . still on the floor. Mouth to speak: he'd said her name. If only he hadn't said her name; names make people real. *A woman and a three-month-old baby.* No! *Sarah Anne Jefferson and her baby Joshua, Jr.* Say it! Say it! *I'll hit you with this billy club, nigger, till you say it!* Admit you attacked the man in the store, the man in the street, the man in the park. But they weren't real, see? They had no names.

Thankful the old man at least had to care for his dog, Chosen grimaced at the smell when Joshua finally opened the fridge and poured sour milk down the drain. Pup was relieved, too, for who knows what Joshua would stick in his bowl these days? Pickings were getting slim, and Pup looked from bowl to master to bowl again when Joshua filled it with dry Rice Krispies. *Snap, crackle, pop.* Thud, thud, thud. Chosen went on alert. The dog's hair bris-tled. Joshua drank a glass of water. Chosen wondered if this time they would stay. He didn't have to wait long for his answer. Thud, thud—*thump thump thump!* Someone was pounding on the back door.

"Joshua, ah knows you in dere, Joshua! You gots to open up, Brudda Joshua, pleeze open up, I got powerful bad news fo you." *Maybe you betta sit down, Son, we gots sorrowful somethin' to tell you.* Thump thump thump. The back door opened, and Mattie poured into the dark apartment. She had been crying. She was still crying.

"Oh, Brudda Joshua, wha' we gonna do? Dey kilt Dr. King! He ded, Dr. King be ded! Wha' we gonna do?!"

Joshua reeled. He stared through the big woman, beyond time and space, his head nodding up and down, up and down, like a carnival prize on the dashboard of a car; bob, bob, bob, went his head, buzz and whine filling the empty shell. He looked down at the floor. "Som'body kilt him ded. De whole cou'try goin' bad, Brudda Joshua, *Brudda* Joshua!"

Loud banging came from the front doors. Others needed their pastor. There was fear in the air, a dread that settled in the hearts of every older Negro behind the line, a rush of bravado and revenge in the hearts of the young. Dr. King was dead. There was a once king, but there ain't no future king. The dream was over. In an instant, on April 4, 1968, every single black person in America woke up.

Mattie grabbed Joshua's arms and shook. "Brudda Joshua, we gots to git out an stop the young uns, they goin' crazy!" The pounding at the front door became more insistent, Pup began to bark. Chosen clamped his wings around Joshua and shook him a little himself. *Come on, dear one, I will go with you. Come on.* Joshua looked Mattie square in the face. He grabbed a jacket, slipped on a pair of shoes, and started his run to the front door, Mattie, the dog, and a very apprehensive angel bringing up the rear.

No sooner did Joshua step onto the street than he heard distant sirens—and was hit in the leg by a bottle. The two strong black men who had been banging at the door were a surprise for Chosen—and put him on instant alert that things were about to get messy. The angels recognized each other at once. The two extra had been sent to help protect the man and woman; danger would be great that night. The enemy was having a heyday with the assassination of King and the tumultuous pain and anger it would cause people of color. The little group worked its way down the street. Looting and rioting was reaching proportions that exceeded anything Joshua had yet seen. Joshua tried to enter the fray but was restrained by the two men several times as waves of hatred washed over the little niche behind the line that colored folk called their own.

"Whitey ain't no good!" yelled a twelve-year-old from Joshua's church, who seemed lost in a rage of destruction. "The war won't be over till they kill all of us!"

"Stop throwing rocks! Stop!" yelled Joshua, reaching for the boy's arm.

"I'm throwing rocks, and you should too, Brotha, till white man stops treatin' us like slaves." This from a child who sat in church—his church—who could recite Scripture, who had been taught the love of Jesus . . .

Fires began to break out. People raced in several directions at once, atomized, exploding like the bomb in Hiroshima, sending up a cloud of smoke. Smoke signals. SOS. See Our Skin! It is black. See Our Sty. We live like hogs in a pen. Stop Our Slavery. You stole us.

Guns, Molotov cocktails, rocks, bottles; Mattie was hit in the head and went down, landing on top of a fire hydrant. "Sistah Mattie!" It took the two men (angels or not) and Joshua to pull her into a doorway and out of harm's way. The gash over her eyebrow was nasty and deep. Joshua ripped the sleeve off his jacket to use as dressing. Sirens seemed so close, yet so far. Where were the police? A mob worked its way down the street, led by a young man in an Afro, spitting hatred and revenge. Joshua broke away from his protectors and ran to meet the man head on.

"Monroe, you got to stop this! You hurtin' your own people, Monroe! Listen to me!" Joshua shrieked.

Monroe pushed Joshua's chest, sending the old man back against a cohort, who was quickly jerked away from the preacher by his two protectors, Pup left with the bleeding Mattie. Monroe raised his hand to push Joshua again but thought the better of it as he faced the glare of the two strangers.

"You get out of our way, old man. Your dream is dead. I told you, but you wouldn't listen. It's dead like you gonna be dead if you mess with us. Nobody gonna mess with us no more."

"Monroe, your mother, she been hurt bad."

A hint of shock in the young man's eyes, he quickly collected himself. "Let Dr. King take care of my motha!" said Monroe X as he shoved his way past a terrified old man and led his wild band down the street.

"Come on, now, Brotha Joshua, we betta get you someplace safe," said one of the protectors.

Mattie's bleeding was profuse; she would need medical attention. "We best get her back to my place," said Joshua, "it's close by." Close enough for the heat to hit the little band as they rounded the corner. The Freedom and Grace Tabernacle was ablaze.

"Call the fire department!" came the urgent plea from the old preacher, who forgot that fire trucks seldom entered burning ghettos. It was policy: "Refuse entry to fire, fearing safety of firemen." Where were the police? Joshua broke into a dash, pushing through mobs of people everywhere, like a fullback plowing through heavy defense, Chosen running block. He ran into the building, the angels right behind.

"Brudda! NO!"

Mattie's weakened voice was picked up by demonic spirits lighting the night like fireflies. "Brudda! NO!" they mimicked. "Brudda! NO!" bounced off, wicked laughter through the night.

Straight into the heat and smoke, Joshua had a mission. He stumbled over a stack of folding chairs, anvil-hot to the touch, and passed the lime green piano, its paint shriveling into tight curls before detonating into flame. All the while he was protected by the strong men who yelled at him to go back. No, Joshua was on a mission worth dying for. He groped his way past the restrooms and reached the door to his quarters. The sound of the fire—of the inferno—was deafening. "Joshua, get out!" yelled one man as he effortlessly shielded Joshua from a falling roof joist.

The preacher man would not be stopped. The doorknob branded his flesh to the bone. The door exploded open from a blast of heat behind it, whirlwinds of molten air making a weather system of its own. *It will be windier than usual in Chicago tonight.* Joshua slammed against a wall and fell to his knees. Chosen created a cocoon of safety for them as the other two helped Joshua to his feet. Sounds of falling timber, a chilling sound of piano wires snapping, and, as Joshua groped on top of his desk, the sound of a faithful dog. Pup had followed valiantly into the building and was coming to his aid. "Joshua, the back door!" yelled one of the men. Clutching Brenda's book, Joshua heard the call of his pet. "Pup!" he screamed. The men were ushering him toward the door; even the supernatural intervention of angels beginning to be little help in this inferno. "Pup!" Joshua heard his dog bark again and then a yelp. The men pushed the preacher outside to safety.

Chosen flew at lightening speed to save the dog. He found his body under the corner of the smoking piano, hair singed, blood trickling from his mouth. Pup sensed the presence of the angel and tried to wag his tail. Chosen carried the beast to the back door. And in the manner of dogs, in the manner of one of God's greatest gifts to His children, Pup managed a few steps before he collapsed. Joshua and the men ran to him and pulled him away from the heat. And all of time stood still. For a frozen moment the sounds of despair and violence stopped as if a finger had pushed mute on a sky-switch far away, the blaze just before their eyes became as insignificant as a yawning campfire, the searing pain in the old man's hand vanquished. Joshua knelt beside a quintessential dog the color of merle, and gazed into his face. In that moment he saw a puppy that fit into his jacket pocket, saw a bundle of energy running in front of him during walks, felt the slobbery breath of a devoted animal who gave him wet kisses and begged for handouts. The two protectors stood aside as a dying dog and an anguished man formed a universe of their own in the midst of the bedlam, a skinny book of psalms on the ground next to them. It was a final treachery, a final injustice, a calamity that would knock the sensibilities of the old man flat. Pup looked adoringly at Joshua and thumped his tail once. And then he closed his laughing eyes. And an angel cried.

Lips trembling, the old man put his burnt hand on his dog's head and passed out.

Closure

Tires beating pavement, squeaking brakes, the uproar of rusting tailpipes and belching trucks: the incessant sound of traffic created a continuous drone. It was the sound of hurry up and wait, bumper-to-bumper blaring, on Chicago's Dan Ryan Expressway. To dare to stop the flow would be tantamount to a breach against some traffic god's code of proper driving behavior: Keep moving. Loco motion. And so the airport shuttles and busses and delivery vans, the taxis and limos and motorcycles, the sedans and semis and potato chip trucks all blasted their way back and forth in a dash on a conveyor belt gone mad. Zip. Zip. Zip. They flung themselves by, not noticing anything but their white-knuckle clutch on the steering wheel. Zoom! *Did you see that old man?* Zoom! *What old man?*

The man had been sitting alongside the highway on the damp ground since morning, caught in the drippy early fog that reaches out from a big lake like a mitt. He never noticed the disruption of the sun (his bones did) as it burnt away haze and filled all space with power and promise. It was into this bright promise that a bee flew, a sure and certain sign that May was on its way. The man sat amidst litter that marked the edge of every highway: discarded aluminum cans, broken glass, paper of every type and sort: newsprint, candy wrappers, assorted crumbled sacks. He sat amidst last year's weeds, dead-brown and brittle, leftovers not yet rotted into earth. *The Lord God formed the man from the dust of the ground and breathed into his nostrils the breath of life and the man became a living being. Then the Lord God made a woman from the rib he had taken out of the man, and he brought her to the man.* He sat amidst oil-stained dirt and bush stubble. He could have been a bum, a vagabond, a tramp (for this was before the more civilized term *homeless*); he could have been, but for the fact that he was cleanly shaven and wore neatly pressed clothes. He raised his bandaged hand to swat the bee.

The old man came to this spot near the highway that morning on a personal pilgrimage. This was holy ground. This was where, long ago—before a swath of progress leveled block after block of niche—there stood an intersection called 47th and Wentworth. He was as close as he could get.

Excusing himself that morning from the company and care of the two men who had come to his rescue the night of the riots, Joshua set off on his grave mission. The kind men offered no resistance and helped him dress, as they had helped him dress the past few weeks. They wished him a good day. Little did Joshua know that he would never see his benefactors again, the two strangers who had brought him to shelter in their rented room, who nursed him and tended to his every need. Little did he know that he would return to a farewell note, along with enough cash to get him on his feet. Little did he know, as he set out with a big, invisible angel beside him, that he would return to a newer and even happier life in the service of his Lord. But just then, that morning, Joshua needed a little more time.

Joshua reached into his shirt pocket and pulled out the envelope. He removed the newspaper clipping and stared hard. The gears of a bus groaned. *Is a bus a modern-day surface car?* It was time to let go. Hanging onto that slip of paper had cost too much: a lifetime of pain; a lifetime of denial; the life of his dog. Clinging to the past, clinging to Sarah and the baby, had pushed the jagged glass deeper, made it more painful to release, brought him to the brink of despair: *I can't let it out now; it's been so long, it will hurt too much, can't You just let it be? It's not hurting anyone.* Only me. Only me. How wrong he was. Time's up! Time to step boldly away from the past and heal his damaged heart. Time to say their names out loud: "Sarah! Little Joshua!" And time to say good-bye.

Chosen sat alongside Joshua and prayed. He knew his time with the dear old man was about to end and wanted to do his angel-best to intercede and protect. Joshua took a deep breath, steeled himself, and ripped the newspaper article into pieces. He threw it into the sunny space in front of him like confetti on a parade. *"I offer this up to You, Lord. I don't want to hurt no more. I accept Your promise of freedom and grace, Lord. I do. I do."* And the ragged sliver of glass fell to his side like so much litter. The old man was bathed in love, carried that moment on a sun bubble through time and space and held in the arms of God. Chosen smiled. *Dear one,* he uttered softly, *dear one.*

After a time Joshua arose, wiped off the seat of his pants, and headed in the direction of the Robert Taylor Housing Project on Chicago's south side.

"Brudda Joshua!" gushed Mattie, the stitch marks over her eye beginning to form a shiny, tight scar. "Brudda Joshua! We all been so worry 'bout you!"

"May I come in?"

"Ooh, Brudda Joshua!" swooned Mattie as she stepped back to make way for Mr. Right. Bug-eyed with the opportunity presenting itself, Mattie raced to her kitchen to fetch a treat, mumbling disgust for not having home-made goodies on hand. She nearly ripped a cabinet door off its hinges, knocking over cans of tomato soup and tuna as she swept everything out of the cupboard looking for something to give her man.

"Ah be rights dere, Brudda!" giggled Mattie as she dumped a box of Lorna Doone cookies onto a plate with one hand and tried to put water in her kettle with the other. "Ah gots inst' coffee, Brudda, inst' coffee. Here, you hafa cookie! Haf two!"

Joshua visited with Mattie over instant coffee and Lorna Doone cookies before he got to the point. "I know Monroe is in jail, Sistah Mattie, and I would be happy to accompany you to visit him."

"Oh, Brudda! Dey won' led nobod' go in an' see him, nosiree, no dey won', I try. Brudda Joshua, I try, but dey sey I gots to leef. Dey gots no bail fo' him neder."

"Let's give it a try, Sistah Mattie. Let's go there tomorrow."

Mattie was beside herself: should she dress for a date or for a visit to the clink? Love won out. *Dat Monroe X gonna go get mess up wid dat Nation o' Islam, serve him right!* When Joshua stopped by to get Mattie the next day, she was dressed for the kill.

Chosen stepped off the bus with the natty couple. As they headed up the broad stone steps of the precinct jail, the angel's eyes pinched back tears. He knew he would not see these two dear saints again, not in this plane, for when they walked through the big wooden door it would be time for Chosen to leave. He would not be needed for a while and was being called home. Step, step, step. Chosen flew backwards in front of the two, slowed by Mattie's lumbering climb. Step, step, step. Chosen was desperate to mark their faces in his mind, to touch them, to let them feel his love. Step, step, step. Just before they reached the door, when they paused on the landing for Mattie to catch her breath, two little white feathers drifted on the breath of an angel and landed at their feet.

"Lookit, dere, Brudda! Dese mus' be from a dof! Dese be a sign from God! A sign from God!" Chosen chuckled. Oh, how he would miss Mattie!

"I do believe you is right, Miz' Mattie," said Joshua, who picked up the feathers, their quills strong enough to be pushed inside a perfectly pressed lapel and rammed into the band of a wide-brimmed bonnet. And with the loving and whispered good-bye of an angel, the two walked through the heavy door.

Chapter
Five

December 1970

"Looks like a mama and her little boy in that Ford, Gear Shift. Let's say we put her in a rocking chair for a while. Come back."

"Gotcha, Teddy Bear."

With that a shiny red Kenworth shot past an aging blue-and-white van on the Pennsylvania Turnpike. The truck driver maneuvered his semi into a lane ahead of the unsuspecting woman and tucked her between himself and his friend; chivalry was an active and satisfying part of a line-haul driver. The two truckers escorted the woman and her child until she turned into a rest area, the blast of their horns bidding farewell.

Over-the-road truckers were a special breed: men, and a few women, who needed the freedom of the open road and thrived on the challenge and adventure of travel. These were not desk people, especially not the veterans who eschewed the local delivery routes that were normally rewarded to experienced drivers. These were vagabonds, nomads, pilgrims, and explorers, navigating seaways called turnpikes and highways and byways. They knew their country intimately, interstates connected by trade hubs like caravan stops on the Sahara. Some chose the trucking life to escape, caught nonetheless in a web of highways that somehow brought them full circle, no matter how far they traveled, no matter how fast they went. Not Carl. Carl Montgomery, a sweet, single man who needed escape from nothing, was simply created for the road, for the smell of oil and diesel, and for endless kibitzing with buddies as he crisscrossed America. He was made for the slippery-smooth leather on his worn seat, now covered with a matted sheepskin pad, and for coffee that tasted like last week's socks. For winter, summer, spring, and fall, and everything in between, Carl rode the road. Trucking was his life, visits to his mother's home—his childhood home—a chance to plug into family and friends, pay a few bills, play pinochle with neighbors, and get his truck serviced.

"Looks like we might get weathered in, Teddy Bear. Hope Mama didn't have far to go. Over."

"New York plates. If she was headed home, we better pray she has someplace to stop. Mr. Weatherman says it's getting nasty."

"This is Dead Eye, come in."

"Hey, Dead Eye! What's your twenty?"

"Lollipop 53. Just come down from Canada. There's a bad one right behind me, that cold and snow is riding me piggyback. Over."

"Thanks, Buddy. I'm covered. Hey, Gear Shift, come in."

"Gear Shift, go on."

"I got a room at Trudy's. Meet you for dinner? Come back."

"Gear Shift going to shoot for home tonight; my Sweet Lips gonna keep me warm. Over."

Carl laughed. "You two still honeymooning! Merry Christmas, Gear Shift. Be safe now. See you later."

"Wish your mom a Merry Christmas for me, Teddy Bear."

"Roger."

"Teddy Bear, this is Dead Eye. Come in."

"This is Teddy Bear."

"You all have a good Christmas. Keep on truckin'. Over."

"You too, Dead Eye. And don't forget what it's all about."

Chosen leaned back and rested his head against the top of the slippery leather seat. The cab of the truck was cozy, with pine scent coming from a cardboard evergreen swinging lazily off the rearview mirror, as Carl drove straight into sky that was blacker than usual, even if it was winter solstice. The expansive view from the truck began to diminish as Carl Montgomery and his companion Bashar-el, recently returned from some heavenly R & R, turned on headlights and charged headlong into the year's darkest hour.

Carl reached into a plastic case and pulled out an eight-track tape. He chuckled as "A Boy Named Sue" reverberated through his cab, even though the throaty bass of Johnny Cash sounded thin and tired on the tape he had played nearly to disintegration. "How do you do!" Carl bellowed and slapped the steering wheel with fresh laughter. Johnny Cash never grew tiresome for Carl. *My name is Sue!* Chosen tapped his knee with his hand, the man in black began a doleful song about Folsum Prison, and the red Kenworth hurtled through increasingly heavy, horizontal snow.

Brenda's gift rattled and bounced beneath the big metal springs in the truck's seat, a gift to Carl from his pinochle partner. The book of Psalms was now on the road, nesting under an aptly nicknamed teddy bear of a fellow who loved trucking, Johnny Cash, and a man who once traveled the roads of Galilee and Judea. Chosen, propped for adventure, was glad to follow the book once again—now that it was finally out of jail.

Bailed Out

Nearly two years earlier, on a sunny spring day, a black preacher named Joshua and his ladyfriend Mattie had walked into a precinct jail on Chicago's south side. With Mattie whispering, "Ah tole you so, Brudda, ah tole you so!" the two had been refused admittance and had been sent away. Their visitation to Mattie's son Monroe had been denied. Before leaving, Joshua had handed the small book to a policeman.

"Would you see that Monroe, um, Monroe X, gets this book? Tell him, would you, that it is from his pastor."

The policeman had affixed a note to the book and placed it on the counter. What had happened next was predictable in a busy office, especially in the midst of a shift change: the book was moved to another spot, and yet another, and yet another, until it was finally buried under a pile of *Modern Detective* magazines in a corner of the room. It had stayed there until a can of Coca-Cola, temporarily propped atop the pile by a file clerk, had tipped, sending the carbonated, sticky black contents flowing over the stack. During mop-up the clerk had discovered Brenda's gift—the note and Monroe X long gone—and had placed it in the personal mail slot of a cop named Jerry. Jerry, well known and respected as a Christian man, would certainly appreciate a religious book. Best friends for life with his buddy next door, Jerry had decided to give Carl the book for use during his quiet time along the road.

* * *

Chosen had been thrilled to be back in service, his joy mingling with sorrow for leaving the throne of God. He'd watched the pinochle game with interest and enjoyed the good camaraderie between Carl and Jerry.

"I thought you might like to have this for your quiet time."

"Well, thank you, Jer. You know, I've been meaning to delve into the Psalms a bit more—going to be one of my resolutions!"

Chosen and Carl would hit the road the next morning, a thermos and a mother-packed box of goodies in hand. This was to be a short trip for Carl, who planned to be back in time for Christmas Eve. Weather permitting.

The Storm

Just at that moment, though, with Johnny Cash crooning—some would say croaking—in the background, it was beginning to look more like weather *forbidding*. The wretched *n-* word, *nor'easter*, started to hiss over the CB as truckers all over the northeast began to shift into lower gear, turn up their defrosters, and think about shelter from the storm. Every trucker alive had memories of being stranded in snow, of jackknifed trailers out of control, of numbing cold and hunger as highways became crowded and blocked with traffic that could not budge. Or worse, the fatal pileup. This was red-alert time for everyone on the road.

"Hoo-Boy, this is a bad one!"

"They gonna be jammed like sardines in a can at Trudy's tonight!"

"Glad I've got a room. This cramped sleeper is hard on these old bones!" chortled Carl as he placed the mike back into its clip without so much as a blink of his eyes from the road—he might as well have been driving in Braille. Visibility was close to whiteout as he slowed the big rig and literally inched his way down the familiar route, watchful for passenger cars with terrified drivers at the wheel. "Dear Lord," prayed Carl, "please get these people to safety." Chosen breathed an *Amen,* letting loose a breath he didn't realize he'd been holding. This was harrowing. Carl's expertise and experience worked clutch and gears and brought the big semi closer to the truck stop. It was slow going. He nearly hit a white Ford Falcon that crept along, half on the road, half off, dangerously close to plowing into a berm of snow made by the monster plow that had shot past them some time ago. Chosen could not shake the look on the young driver's face as Carl's big truck came within a whisker of scraping the side of the car. The angel had to help.

Chosen touched the terrified student's shoulders, the muscles as tight as the rubber band on the fat stack of Christmas cards resting on the passenger seat. The young man was ashen with fear and near tears, yet with the big angel's touch, he steeled himself. He had a sudden wave of confidence, and was, as he would later say to his parents, suddenly, *miraculously,* able to see the side of the highway and gingerly drive to the all-night truck stop. "I was praying real hard, Mom, and it's just like my prayers were answered. It was bad, Mom. I'm not kidding. It was the worst weather I was ever in, even worse than when we all went skiing up in Vermont, remember? Worse than that! And then, it was just like my car was on *radar.* Boom! Right into the parking lot. And boy, was it crowded! I had to sleep in the car under my laundry. I'm not kidding, Mom; it's a miracle I'm even here. A miracle. Would you pass the potatoes?"

Trudy's

It was crowded at the truck stop, and a relief to the veteran truck driver that he had a room reservation. Snow and wind—it was the wind in a
northeaster that was the real culprit—slapped Carl silly as he examined his
big truck, front to back. He hoped Trudy had enough supplies on hand, aware
that holiday travelers would put a real strain on the food, the restrooms, and
the nerves of normally friendly waitresses. Indomitable human spirit and
enterprise seem to follow blizzards into crowded truck stops, though, and
people were usually pretty cooperative in a situation like this, he mused as he
inventoried his box of goodies. The cookies and jerky and chips could spend
a night below freezing; the tangerines and bananas should move inside. Carl
stuffed fruit into his coat pockets, grabbed his overnight bag and thermos, and
climbed down to the pavement already compacted with snow. Loud lights
from Trudy's signs were hazy and surreal behind the wall of weather. Carl
waved to a driver who eased a semi alongside the Kenworth as he tromped
his way toward Trudy's. Chosen smiled in the direction of a college student
in a white Falcon as he walked next to Carl.

Trudy's was exactly as Carl predicted: wall-to-wall people. Babies crying; bedraggled parents; students still dazed from finals week; salesmen dressed
in the boisterous fashion of the early seventies, each with a wide, garish tie
hanging like a loose noose around his neck as he indignantly waited his turn
at the phones. People sat slumped against walls, occupied every available spot
of space, and sipped from thick white coffee cups. The air already had the
smell of packed bodies, the floor a slushy mess of snow, road salt, and pea
gravel. Just four days before Christmas, the radio played carols when not
interrupted by weather reports. One small TV hung on a platform over the
café counter, the screen as snowy as the sky. The evening news concerned
itself with one thing: the big blizzard coming from Canada by way of special
delivery. *Ho Ho Ho, do* not *return to sender.* The restaurant was full, but not
crammed like the expansive lobby and gift shop; waitresses policed counter
seats and booths and made short shrift of malingerers.

Carl looked toward a cluster of three booths way in the back corner and
saw a hand shoot into the air. He waved back and excused himself through a

gaggle of anxious travelers; the brotherhood of truckers looked out for one another. Carl never doubted that a warm dinner and good company awaited him. Trudy herself walked over, order pad in hand.

"The others can have the frozen burgers," she gestured toward the hapless travelers. "We saved the stew for you fellows."

Trudy wasn't being mean. This was more than good business: this was family. These familiar faces clutching their stainless-steel thermos bottles were no different from cousins, brothers, uncles, and friends. They ranked high here and were treated as returning heroes every time they pulled into the vast parking area especially for them. Chosen looked at the assembly of men and cocked his head: they nearly all looked alike. They could be brothers: XL flannel shirts straining to cover expanding bellies, short-cropped hair, calloused hands with fingernails as big as quarters, furrowed foreheads from squinting through massive, sun-splotched windshields, and arms with the strength of pistons.

"Want to get together for some cards?"

"You know," said Carl, as he pushed the side of his fork through a piece of banana cream pie as thick as a tire, "I'm beat. Too much pinochle last night! Tomorrow for sure if this hangs on." And with that he headed toward the narrow stairs that would lead him to a small room with a single bed. It was a cubicle, really, with a community bath, but Carl was grateful Trudy installed the cramped quarters a few years back. Lying down and straightening the spine was a real necessity—and treat—for men who spent their lives bent over a steering wheel. Carl was glad to get away from the mass of people downstairs, prepared himself for a noisy night, and slipped between the sheets. After punching pillow feathers into submission, he was sound asleep.

Chosen looked out the window at the congestion of cars, vans, and trucks. The snow showed no mercy. He remembered a time when the Master used weather as a faith lesson for the twelve. The men were utterly terrified . . . more terrified, chuckled Chosen, by the power Christ had over the wind and waves. *Why are you still afraid? Do you still have no faith?*

The aluminum frame on the window developed a crust of frost, and the glass began to fog. Glad that Carl didn't have to spend the night in his truck, Chosen fretted over the poor people stranded at this truck stop and prayed for those still caught on the road. Every now and then he saw the circling light of a snow plow or a highway patrol car as it led yet another car to safety. After a time, Carl awoke.

The Girl

Carl was not a night person and was particularly testy when he awoke soon after drifting into deep, comfortable sleep. Mumbling under his breath about "too much coffee," he slipped on his pants and stepped out of his room, headed to a toilet down the hall. He was doubly irritated to have to wait his turn, for travelers had found the stairs that led to the narrow hall and bathroom facilities. He was heading back to his room when he encountered a very stoned young girl.

Lysergic acid diethylamide (LSD) had pretty much run its course in the turbulent sixties, but still held some appeal to acidheads and impressionable college students. Carl had seen the effects of drugs (there is much more to see than scenic byways when a man spends his life on the road) and regretted that some truckers used drugs to keep awake, go to sleep, or to enhance a night of play at an all-night truck stop. Yet truckers who did mess with drugs avoided LSD because of its unpredictability: an acid trip peaked after an hour or so, but could last several hours. Or longer. Rumor had it that for some it could last a lifetime. Reduced muscle control and reduced coordination made the drug very unappealing to anyone who blasted down the road dragging several tons of steel along.

The young woman weaved down the hall, tripping over tired bodies that were trying to endure this horrible night and to find an agreeable position for sleep. She was perspiring, short of breath, and shivering from cold, her thin coat drooping off her shoulders, the string tie next to the zipper banging into her knees. She was near hysteria, tears and laughter mixed into slurred speech.

"Bug off!" yelled a pile of bodies along the wall, curled onto themselves like snakes in a den.

"S'cuse me," mumbled the girl as she tripped into more bodies and careened off a door marked with the number 3. Carl watched the girl, bothered that he had to pass her to get to his room.

"Mister," she said to a man on the floor, "can you make me warm?" Her lips were purple. The man on the floor turned away from her. "Get lost!" She stumbled into Carl and Chosen. The man was annoyed; the angel, filled with compassion.

"Mister, can you make me warm?" Her teeth were chattering.

Carl looked into her dilated eyes. Her long hair was uncombed and ratty. Chosen immediately thought of the woman at the Pleasant Valley Tavern: *Beethoven with a burr.* He reached to touch her face, fever hot in spite of her violent shaking. The angel began to press his wings around her. The man grabbed each of her arms as they reached up to his neck and pushed her away firmly, embarrassed by the encounter.

"I can warm cold make," she murmured as she tripped her way into the next person and Carl entered his room. Chosen zoomed down the hall and stomped the groping hand of one man as the girl stumbled by. The angel returned to Carl, who was getting into bed. This would not do. Not at all. Not one little bit. The child must be rescued. The angel would see to it.

Carl could not get comfortable. The people in the hall added to his misery by adding their groans of discomfort to other night sounds. He pulled the blanket over his head and punched the pillow into a ball. He curled into a ball himself, his back hard against the wall. Nothing he could do would help his sleeplessness or fight against the chill that seemed to be filling the room. Unaware of the big agitated angel who pushed the window open and snored loudly in his ear—a noise he attributed to the man outside his door—Carl squinted his eyes in consternation; he had never been cold in this room before. And if the truth be known, he could not get the girl out of his head. She could not have been more than fifteen years old, too young for college. She looked too young to drive. How did she get there?

Chosen could not forget that dear child, either, and did whatever he could to prod the big trucker to action. Carl threw back his covers and walked to the window, which he discovered open. He pushed it shut with a bit of temper as he fought guilt over his lack of compassion toward the teenager. The snow was as thick as ninety-weight gear oil. The parking lot seemed still, the cars looking like rows of igloos: Igloo City. He pulled on his pants again, put on shirt and shoes, emptied fruit from his coat pockets, and headed out the door. The restaurant and lobby seemed less crowded, the vertical thrust of bodies settled now, on the floor. Some people braved the night in tight clusters in their cars.

Rescued

Carl found two friends playing cribbage. He slid alongside one man and watched the game. Somewhere near the souvenir shop a baby cried. Outside, a snow plow headed to the gas pump, its chains making muffled sound on the newly carpeted parking lot, leaving link impressions in the snow. Chain angels. Thwack, thwack, thwack went the sound of the chains as the tires came to a crunchy stop. Carl got up and walked to a side window to look toward his truck. He scraped the window with the hard edge of a menu and rubbed it clear with his sleeve. Chosen practically pushed his nose against the pane.

Carl saw an unsteady figure walking from truck to truck. Packed with snow, long hair flopped like wet, matted cotton. It was the girl. She banged on the fender of a Peterbilt sleeper. A door opened, and she began her climb inside. Chosen breathed on the window to clear the pane as Carl watched her struggle up the side of the truck. *You're a good man, Carl! Rescue her!* The big angel could only think of Mary of Magdala, of the circumstance that led her to a life of prostitution, of the woman's shame and suffering. *Come on, Carl!* The angel was half out the door as Carl shot back to the booth, grabbed his coat, and headed out at a run.

Carl hurried through snow up to his knees. He banged loudly on the door of the truck. A light went on.

"What?!" came an interrupted and irked voice.

Carl thought fast. "My girl's in there, and you best send her out." He didn't know if this would work: he didn't recognize the rig, didn't know the driver.

"Free country, mister."

"Free to get your head caved in if you mess with my woman."

Chosen was shadow boxing against the truck: *Let me at him, let me at him!*

"She ain't worth it. You can have her." And with that, the girl was pushed through the door and slid onto the ground. Her jacket was left behind, her blouse open. Carl reached down and placed his coat around the dazed and confused teen. "I'm s-s-s-so c-c-c-cold," she said, as the mid-day hit of acid began to show signs of waning. The angel held her hands to warm them, two limp, dead fish, hanging off her arms. Carl ushered his bundle into the restaurant, raising the eyes of some who had sidestepped the crazed teenager earlier. He guided her to the booth.

"Keep an eye on her," he commanded his startled friends as he went to fetch hot chocolate. The men looked at the girl, then at Carl as he negotiated with an exhausted waitress for canned soup and toast. This was not a smart thing to do, and they all knew it. Kids like this were a dime a dozen on the highways—runaways, druggies, prostitutes; it was best to let them be. The radio played "Away in a Manger," the cribbage players packed their game and walked off, and the waitress brought the food Carl had ordered. *No crib for his bed, the little Lord Jesus lay down His sweet head.* A state trooper sat at the counter and looked their way suspiciously. Chosen diverted the policeman's attention with a well-placed kick against a postcard rack, provoking the baby to wail.

The girl ate the toast, her long hair shielding her face from view. She was too shaky to spoon the soup into her mouth, so Carl filled an empty coffee cup with the broth and encouraged her to drink. Her trembling and filthy fingers lifted the cup to her lips. She huddled against the corner of the booth, a tiny thing, thought Carl, who should be home in clean pajamas dreaming of Christmas presents and family and friends. They sat there for a long time in silence, the girl refusing to make eye contact, the man completely baffled at what to do next. He did the only logical thing he could think of: he bought more toast.

"My name is Carl," the gentle man finally said, embarrassed by his uncertainty. She gripped the mug with both hands and continued to look down.

"I . . . um . . . do you want more to eat?" She shook her head no. Yes. Carl poked his neck toward her to watch more closely. A hesitant nod again, yes. This time a grilled cheese sandwich. The waif nibbled at the crust until the full aroma of the melted cheese fully reached her senses and she polished off the sandwich with a few well-placed bites. Hiccup. Hiccup. *That's what happens when you eat too fast, Nancy.* Hiccup.

"Excuse me."

"What?" The trucker leaned closer to hear the faint squeak from the waif.

"Excuse me." Good parenting overruled her determination to remain mute and sullen.

"Oh, sure," said Carl as nonchalantly as he could muster. Hiccup. "Here, take some water."

"Thank you."

Chosen was glowing. Her feet becoming tingly, the girl was warming up and calming down. The angel cooed to her. "Jingle Bells" played in the background. *Laughing all the way.* It looked like she would cry. Carl reached for a fistful of napkins.

"Do you want to talk?" he asked.

Her head shook no.

"You want to at least tell me your name?"

"Nancy."

"Well, Nancy! I'm glad to meet you! My name is Carl. Oh, I already told you that, didn't I?" *My name is Sue, how do you do?* They sat a long while more. He figured her to be a runaway and tried to keep communication open.

"You on your way home from college?" Nothing.

Carl tapped his foot. Chosen did what he did best: he prayed. The state trooper wandered toward their booth. Nancy saw him approach as she wiped her dripping nose. She panicked.

"Mister . . . Carl . . . please . . . please don't let him get me, please."

Carl looked into the eyes of a child. His mind went into high gear. The trooper was closing in for a good look. The trucker had never been in this position before; he knew he was playing with lit dynamite, but her pleading eyes did him in. Besides, he reckoned, he could always call the cops later. In a moment of decidedly bad judgment, Carl cleared his throat and spoke.

"Now you listen to me, young lady. When we get home your mother is going to have a fit over that hair of yours. Send you off to college, and you turn into a hippie. I have half a mind to ground you for your entire break."

Had he left his good sense back in the truck with the jerky and chips?!

"Just what do you think your little sister is going to think when she sees you? You know she looks up to you. You look like a bum!"

He was really getting into it. The policeman lingered by the coffeepot near their booth.

"All the other kids dress like this . . . Daddy!" came the emboldened response from Nancy. "And anyway, I'll be sure to be a good role model"— she was sounding sarcastic—"for darling little Sissy."

Carl locked eyes with the trooper. He should call the man to the table and tell him the facts. He locked eyes with the girl. Her begging glance over- ruled all sensibility.

"Listen, daughter," (maybe the *daughter* was a bit much), "I will not let you spoil Christmas for the rest of the family just because you got some crazy ideas in college."

"Daddy, I *WON'T*! Don't be so uptight!" Nancy nearly yelled.

The trooper shook his head and walked toward the door.

Carl was trembling now. What had he done? Could he be arrested? Was he harboring an underage girl? Nancy giggled. Carl looked at her incredu- lously. Such a sweet face, it didn't make sense . . . adrenaline pushed so far into his throat, he couldn't swallow.

"You were pretty good . . . Daddy."

"Well, thank you . . . daughter . . . um . . . Nancy." Awkward silence again. "Say, would you like a piece of pie?"

Hesitation. Chosen whacked her on the back. Hiccups again. More giggles.

"*Hic* . . . sure . . . *cup.*"

Nancy pushed her long hair behind her ears in order to eat the pump- kin pie. *Hey, Nance! What kind of pies should we make this year? Let's surprise Grandma and make divinity fudge. Sissy really misses you now that you have your own room. Nancy, honey, is there anything you need to talk about to me and your mother?*

"Do you want to talk?" asked Carl again as he looked up at the clock and resigned himself to a sleepless night. Nancy shook her head no. The trucker got bold.

"You a runaway?"

The girl looked at him. There was such innocence behind her eyes, confusing Carl even more. She still seemed unspoiled, pure, but the drugs, the bare facts . . .

"Sort of. Well, I guess. Yeah. I mean, yes." This girl belonged to a loving family someplace. And the big man could see that she was dead tired.

"Well, there is time for talk later. That is, if you want. I think you need some sleep now." She looked at him, fear suddenly etched across her face.

"Don't worry, Nancy. I'll sleep in my truck."

Carl escorted the girl up the stairs, evoking stares from the few sleep-deprived travelers lining the walls. Stepping over a snoring heap of a man, he opened the door with his key. "You go in there and sleep. Don't let anyone in, Nancy, not even me. I won't pull out tomorrow until I know you are all right. OK?" The girl stepped over the sleeping man, and, once she was safe on the other side of the door, held onto the knob with both hands, ready to slam it shut in defense. "OK."

"And Nancy . . ."

She could barely stand from exhaustion.

"Don't go taking any more acid."

She closed the door. As she tripped into Carl's bed she murmured, "They gave it to me." And she curled up on the bed and fell into deep sleep.

Prayers in the Night

Chosen had his work cut out for him. He followed Carl out to his truck, through the snow—it was still snowing!—and up into the cab. A snow cocoon. Carl sighed. No sense clearing his bunk and burrowing in for the few hours left of the night. He might as well head back inside. He reached under the seat and grabbed a Bible so worn it appeared shredded, groped around some more, and put his big fingers on a skinny book of psalms. The night felt eerie as he stood next to his truck, the distant, urgent scrape of a snowplow intruding on the unearthly quiet that rests on a world capped with snow, its pristine beauty tinted by the haze of blinking neon light.

Carl headed for the trucker's back booths, which were kept clear of haggard travelers by a combative waitress. There the veteran truck driver, the teddy bear of a man, opened his Bible and prayed through the night for a waif of a girl. Chosen divided the waning hours between the bedside of the sleeping girl and the hulk of a man who finally dozed off in a booth in Trudy's truck stop.

Daylight came much too soon for Carl. His neck screamed protest every time he turned his head; his body punished him with every move. He walked to the window. A mauve-pink hue replaced black sky, and the snow slowed. Plows continued their back-and-forth assault, the crews working overtime through the night while their wives gleefully planned an extravagant Christmas. Travelers shoveled each car from its snow-white sarcophagus, unkinking body parts like stick men and women. Pioneers sailing across the continent in Conestoga wagons, they boarded up and headed out. Carl fretted a bit over his deadline, certain the storm would provide alibi for tardy arrival. He looked toward the narrow stairs, wondered how wise it was to push the little book under the door of his room, and rubbed his burning neck. Actually, he felt *driven* to take the book upstairs, to hastily scribble a note on a napkin.

Nancy: Please read Psalm 25. Your friend, Carl.

Of course, he wasn't aware of the enormous angel who did everything but announce over the speaker, "Carl Montgomery report to door of your room with book of psalms. Be sure to put marker at Psalm 25."

Getting involved with that girl was the most foolish thing he'd ever done; nonetheless, Carl continued to pray through the early morning. *"Bring her back to her family, Lord. She's just a kid. She's not nobody's girl, is she, Lord?"*

No, she wasn't. And Chosen was going to be sure that *somebody's* girl would be home for Christmas—if he had to fly her there, wherever *there* was, himself.

Runaway

Nancy had slept in stupor. The effects of the LSD had finally worn off, leaving her with a splitting headache. She sat cross-legged on the bed, clutching the pillow, holding it against her chest like a shield. She thought hard, shaking her head to clear her mind only once, when stabbing pain stopped her cold. What had happened? Those older boys, the ones at her new friend's house. How they had begun to pay attention to her. How they had started to touch her. She closed her eyes. *Nancy, are you feeling well? Are you having trouble at school? Nance, your mother and I are becoming alarmed. It's nothing, Daddy. I'm old enough to think for myself. I can pick my own friends, thank you.*

What had happened? She twisted her mouth in troubled recollection. The parties. Those same boys. The touching, the kissing. Beer. Lots of beer. And then the trip. She was invited to go along. Just a few days. What difference did it matter if her parents wouldn't consent? She should just go. She was old enough to think for herself, wasn't she? Just a few days. She'd be back in school on Monday morning.

How grown-up the newly defiant fifteen-year-old had felt when she left with her friends; beer, rum and Coke, and cigarettes her newly acquired tastes. Onward they had traveled for a week, stopping at gas station restrooms, sleeping piled in a heap in cheap hotel rooms, eating doughnuts and hamburgers, the car radio so loud it cut a trail for them, like a machete on a jungle path. They were free, free as birds. *But the very hairs of your head are numbered . . . ye are of more value than many sparrows.* Soon into the trip, Nancy had panicked. She'd wanted to go home. They would turn back tomorrow. The next day. The next. They had filled her with booze. But the young girl was becoming a liability. It was getting too much to have their little mascot along.

It was an acid-laced sugar cube that had gotten Nancy into trouble. She had never touched drugs before, was too innocent to know a drug if it had pounced on her. In a fit of anxiety over her situation, Nancy had hiccupped. "Here, kid, suck on this sugar. My old lady says it will get rid of hiccups."

Too much to handle once she was high, the boys had deliberately left her at Trudy's truck stop earlier in the day before heading down the highway. And now there she was, cross-legged on a strange man's bed with a pillow and a pounding head, unaware that a ministering spirit was planning his next move. He had to get the girl to read the book that lay on the ruby-red shag carpet just inside the door. Nobody said an angel can't knock! Thinking three raps would be quite appropriate, Chosen tapped on the door. Nancy looked and saw a book skid across the floor.

Psalm 25

Carl's every step made crunching sounds in the snow. Thanks to the heroic work of the plowing crew the snowfall was now controlled, carved into well-packed tunnels to guide travelers home, down the road, to grandmother's house they'd go. The big man busied himself clearing the truck of as much snow as he could reach with a borrowed broom. He watched a white Falcon rock back and forth, back and forth, tires spinning until with the help of some men—and a happy angel—it broke free of its fetters and whirred off into the early sun. Carl headed back to his station in the booth. He wondered where this situation with the girl was headed. Now it was his turn to grasp a warm cup in both hands and look down.

"Here, Mister . . . Carl . . . here's your book. I read that page. Um . . . thank you."

Unto Thee, oh Lord, do I lift my soul. Remember not the sins of my youth, nor my transgressions: according to thy mercy remember thou me for thy goodness' sake, oh Lord. Turn thee unto me, and have mercy upon me; for I am desolate and afflicted. The troubles of my heart are enlarged: oh bring thou me out of my distresses.

The transformation in the young girl was so dramatic as to cause the man to sit straight in his seat. Thanks to the use of Carl's shaving kit, Nancy's hair was combed back, her face clean—and freckled!—her blouse tucked into her jeans, her body clean. The big trucker and the girl looked at each other across the table, she turning her eyes away in shame and innocence, he diverting his awkward stare. A big old angel sat on the edge of the table, his legs crossed, swinging one foot merrily while he sang Christmas carols in thanksgiving. The girl told the trucker her story. The trucker cried. Trudy was enlisted to care for the child until her parents made arrangements for her return. Arrangements!! They were running to their car and headed for the Pennsylvania Turnpike before the phone lines were cold.

Carl wanted to stay for their reunion, but his load had to be delivered and another one loaded for the trip back to Chicago. Besides, he had a reunion of his own in a few days: he and his mother would walk, as they did year after year, to midnight service to sing some carols of their own.

Chapter

Six

May 1970

Fresh on the heels of the counterculture scream of the sixties, Americans seemed to grope in a dark abyss made by the rip of revolution. Dazed people suddenly needed resolution and reasonableness as they stepped away from the upside-down decade, as if throwing off dirty clothes. It was a time of waning confidence in government, media, and establishment. There was no place to turn, no one to trust but self. And so it was that as the big Kenworth crisscrossed a visibly tired and shaken nation, homes turned into temples of self-discovery, front yards began to display individual expression (*I am me and I live here!*), and backyards suddenly felt the prick of spade and hoe as people turned to such solitary pursuits as gardening. "Mi, mi, mi, mi" emerged not as a warm-up for a croaky populist country singer who still thrilled a stocky truck driver, but as a theme song for the emerging Me Generation. America was weary.

None of this escaped Carl Montgomery: years of observation, experience, and outright engagement gave an over-the-road trucker a remarkable opportunity to take the pulse of the nation. The attitude of other drivers, the type of freight hauled, the clothes people wore, even the music coming over the radio turned every truck driver into a budding sociologist as he watched and mused and listened from his perch high above the highway. Like the country, Carl was weary. He longed for the state of well-being before all the radical language and crazy activity hit the nightly news; he felt uncomfortable with public protests and demonstrations. And though he struggled with weightier matters such as Vietnam and race relations, there were some issues, frankly, that Carl wished would just go away. He might have been a bit hasty, though, to align himself with his sloganeering buddies in his own protest against the rebellious free-thinkers of the time—"America: Love It or Leave It" was prominently displayed on his bumper, and a small American flag whipped in the wind off his CB antenna.

Carl didn't care that the freedom and self-discovery now occupying everyone's mind was a direct result of the turmoil of the sixties. He just wanted everything to be nice again, everyone to be content, people to be civil and friendly, even if it was all surface play. Ignoring cultural trends, the sweet, decent man resolved to muster as much virtue as possible toward everyone he met.

So while the rest of the country began its earnest search for meaning and personal excellence, Carl continued to bring his big truck to a stop when he saw motorists in distress, and to honk and wave for little children in backs of station wagons. He maneuvered his rig wide to keep from splattering mud into windshields, was careful not to crowd motorcycles off the road, and winked his headlights in greetings. He offered words of encouragement over Citizen's Band airwaves and policed his behavior at truck stops. Carl tipped his hat when he met women, petted dogs, held doors for strangers. He did chores around the house for his mom, played cards with Jerry, and entertained an angel unawares. And true to his New Year's resolution, Carl reached under his truck seat every day and pulled out Brenda's gift along with his tattered Bible. Today was May 26, exactly 146 days from January 1, and Carl was about to read the first of five psalms of praise.

Bible Study

It was a splendid day. Traveling to Cleveland from Atlanta, Carl hit the road early and drove with the shadow of his big truck keeping pace alongside. He liked this southern route, in spite of the heat, and planned his midday stop at a favorite rest area where he would nap on a blanket in the shade before he commandeered a picnic table for Bible study. Chosen particularly enjoyed these stops, for while the big man rested, the angel patrolled the grounds. True to his credentials as a ministering spirit, Chosen was able to offer a little help at nearly every stop. Overheated cars suddenly started, overheated emotions were mysteriously overruled, miserable and bored children were amused, car keys were found, motion sickness abated, spirits soared. Chosen thrilled when Carl pulled into each stop, and when the Word was opened every day, the angel burst into song, song that was beginning to bear the twang of Country-Western as the angel boomed every tune from *Johnny Cash: A Believer Sings the Truth*. The truth be known, Chosen had never heard the truth *sung* this way before; his favorite song, of course, was "Oh Come, Angel Band," which played right after "Gospel Boogie."

Yes, May 26 was a day of praise. *How can you not praise He who is so good, Carl? He who is so faithful to all generations! See the family near the other picnic table? He is faithful to them! See the elderly couple pulling the travel trailer? He is faithful to them!* Songbirds and butterflies joined the angel in acclamation.

Now here *is social commentary,* thought Carl. *All the commentary and virtue a man ever needs is right here in this skinny book of Psalms.* Certainly he could study the psalms from his tattered Bible, but he rather enjoyed using the separate book, it being from Jerry making it both separate and special. He studied Psalm 146, whispering key words as he read:

*Happy is he . . . whose hope is in the L*ORD *his God; . . .*

Which executeth judgment for the oppressed; which giveth food to the hungry.

The LORD *openeth the eyes of the blind: the* LORD *raiseth them that are bowed down: the* LORD *loveth the righteous:*

The LORD *preserveth the strangers; he relieveth the fatherless and widow.*

That should be reported on the nightly news, never mind the "God is dead stuff"—nope, *it's men who die and stay dead, says so right here*—*it's God who remains faithful forever.* Carl beamed as one enlightened. Somewhat smug and *very* proud he understood the text, he reached behind his ear for a fat-pointed, stubby pencil. This was too good to leave alone; he must underline some important words, words like *giveth,* and *openeth,* and *raiseth,* and *loveth,* and *preserv* . . . The pencil shot up over the page in a nasty gash as a thick hand came down hard on Carl's back. Carl's body splayed forward on top of his books, and his chin skidded on the coarse, wooden picnic table. Chosen went on immediate alert but sensed no danger.

"I see you're reading the Good Book!" came the voice behind the hand.

And with that, Buckminster Berry dropped his pack on the ground and sat purposely on the bench opposite Carl, who at that moment was collecting his wits, eyeing the heavy-handed stranger, and fretting over the deep black stripe across Psalm 146.

"Good to see a man read the Good Book. Memorize much?"

Chosen liked the man at once. Carl, in a snit over his eraserless pencil, did not share the angel's gracious opinion.

"Memorize much what?"

"The Good Book!" Buckminster Berry seemed, oh, impatient . . . in a friendly sort of way.

"No."

"Why not?"

Carl was digging deep for nice . . . and virtue . . . and friendly. Chosen sensed a special anointing on the stranger, who was in the process of pouring water from a canteen into a collapsible tin cup.

"Look . . ." said Carl, as he prepared to take leave.

Buck put the cup on the table. "What are you reading?"

"Where?"

"In the Good Book!" Buck thrust a pointing finger and knocked over his water. "What are you reading in the Good Book?"

Carl scooped his Bible and Brenda's gift as a puddle spread watery fingers across the table. "Psalm 146."

"A praise psalm! Great social commentary for today, don't you think?" Carl was flustered and flabbergasted all at once. The stranger went on:

> Praise ye the LORD. Praise the LORD, O my soul. While I live will I praise the LORD; I will sing praises unto my God while I have any being. Put not your trust in princes, nor in the son of man, in whom there is no help. His breath goeth forth, he returneth to his earth; in that very day his thoughts perish. Happy is he that hath the God of Jacob for his help, whose hope is in the LORD his God: Which made heaven, and earth, the sea, and all that therein is: which keepeth truth for ever: Which executeth judgment for the oppressed: Which giveth food to the hungry. The LORD looseth the prisoners: The LORD openeth the eyes of the blind: The LORD raiseth them that are bowed down: The LORD loveth the righteous: The LORD preserveth the strangers: he relieveth the fatherless and widow: but the way of the wicked he turneth upside down. The LORD shall reign for ever, even thy God, O Zion, unto all generations. Praise ye the LORD.

Throughout the recitation, the stranger's arms talked as fast as his mouth, expansive karate chops punctuating syllables, words, sentences. Chosen recited the words along with the stranger, while Carl whistled low in amazement.

"Where you headed?" asked the stranger without pause, as if Psalm 146 ended with "Praise ye the Lord, where you headed?"

"Cleveland."

"That will do," said the man as he collected his pack and a worn banjo case and looked at Carl expectantly. After all, it was time to hit the road.

Chosen burst into laughter at the man's forward behavior. And having the discernment of angels, Chosen had an advantage over Carl, who remained flustered and uncertain about the stranger who talked faster than the speed limit as they headed toward Carl's truck.

"Sure nice of you to give me a lift you know I've been to Cleveland once before I'm thinking about maybe buying a new water bottle they make sturdy plastic bottles now so much lighter than a canteen also need to get a haircut one of these days wish I looked good in a crew cut like you do."

Carl eyed the man sideways as they walked across dry grass toward the parking lot. Though he gave an appearance of disarray, he was not typical of the bums who hitched their way to urban decay across America. Carl made

the man to be in his late thirties, his khaki pants and earth shoes a dead giveaway for a northeast—and probably academic—background. He could not
tell if the man was ruddy or just well tanned, as his muscular legs kept pace
and his arms continued to talk, his gear hanging off both shoulders. Pale, curly
hair fought to be free from beneath a Boston Red Sox ball cap; his eyebrows
were thick and bleached from too much sun. One crooked tooth stood out
alongside neat, clean rows of others, well-kept and flossed.

Carl slowed his pace as they neared his truck, wondering furiously how
to ditch this presumptuous fellow, who was probably some kind of religious
kook, what with knowing the Bible like that. The stranger excused himself
when they neared the restrooms. This his chance, Carl made a dash for his big
rig and hopped inside. He would do well to make a clean getaway. For the
life of him, he could not understand why his truck wouldn't start. *Rrr . . . rrr . . .
rrr* came the sound, an angel holding his finger over the air intake. *Rrr . . . rrr . . .
rrr.* Carl stomped the throttle. *Rrr . . . rrr . . . rrr.*

"Want me to try?" The infuriating call came from the stranger as his
face appeared, framed by the passenger window. "I'll just put my gear here,"
said the man as he shoved it onto the sleeping pad behind Carl, clunking the
bewildered trucker in the head with the bottom of his banjo case.

"It should start now," said the stranger confidently, as he shut the door,
adjusted his ball cap, and settled back for his trip to Cleveland. "Let me know
if you want me to drive."

The Trip to Cleveland

Carl moved the big rig out of its parking spot and ignored the plaintive
"HONK!" of a little boy as he pointed the truck north and pouted over his
dilemma. Particularly energized, Chosen opted for the open air and positioned himself on top of the hood as every valve and piston worked flawlessly
to propel the Kenworth up the highway.

"So what's your shtick?" came the question above the sound of air
whooshing into the cab.

"My shtick?" Carl was rehearsing a plot to rid himself of this man. What
was he talking, "shtick"?

"You married?"

"No."

"You live on the road?"

"Some."

"So you just drive a truck?"

"Yes," spoken through gritted teeth.

"So, that's your shtick. You drive a truck and you read the Good Book. You must be a good man."

Carl softened.

"You running from something?"

Carl bristled. "No, I'm not running from something. I just like to drive a truck, OK?"

Static announced a greeting over the CB.

"See you got company, Teddy Bear, over."

"Hey! I'll get that for you!" said Buck as he reached for the handset.

"Teddy Bear, this is V-8, come in."

"Hello, Mr. V-8. Hello . . . Lost him."

Carl pulled the truck onto the shoulder to evict the stranger on the spot. Buck anchored the mike in its holder and looked at Carl.

"So! I'm traveling with a good man named Teddy Bear!"

In spite of his aggravation, and probably because a big old angel placed a calm hand on his shoulder, Carl glared out his rearview mirror and shifted back onto the road. It took only a few short miles to learn that neither nature nor Buckminster Berry could stand a vacuum, and the stranger began to talk.

"My name's Buck, by the way. Real name's Buckminster, but even my mother wouldn't call me that. Called me Bucky. Some call me BB—last name Berry—but I just like Buck. Wished I had a name like John or Tom or Pete or Bill, you know, but we get what we get." Did Carl detect a hint of New England in the man's voice? "Your name's Carl, isn't it? Saw it on the door. Carl's good. I would settle for Carl. But it could be short for Carlton. Is it short for Carlton?"

"Just Carl."

"Carl's good."

If there was any doubt that Carl would drive clear through to his destination that day, it vanished when Buck came aboard. The trucker would deposit the man in Cleveland and be done with him. All he had to do was drive a familiar route for the next six hours and do his level best to keep the man's hands off every knob and control on the dash.

"What's this knob for?"

"That is the air brake lock . . . *don't* touch it!"

Buck reached for the CB once again. "Do I need a special name to use this thing? I know! You could call me Buckaroo! 'Hello. Hello. How do you do? My name is Buckaroo, and I'm on my way to Cleveland with my good buddy Carl; just wanted to wish everyone a pleasant day. Um. Good-bye. Um. I'm over now.'"

"You've got to push the button on the side when you talk," instructed Carl. Big mistake. For the next hour Buck reveled in the good nature and camaraderie of the truckers and managed to throw in a little preaching to boot.

"Walk in the Spirit, and ye shall not fulfill the lust of the flesh. For the flesh lusteth against the Spirit, and the Spirit against the flesh, and these are contrary the one to the other, so that ye cannot do the things that ye would."

"Cut that out," said a red-faced Carl.

"Cut what out?"

"Stop preaching. The boys don't like anyone telling them what to do. You keep your ideas to yourself."

"Those aren't my ideas. Apostle Paul. Galatians 5, actually. No sense telling anyone my ideas when I can tell them what God has to say, is there?"

Carl gripped the steering wheel and kept quiet. Cleveland could not come too soon. He reached for his favorite eight-track and plugged it in. No sooner did Buck hear the music than he reached back and grabbed his banjo case, nearly smacking Carl in the head as he swung it from the backseat.

"John R. Cash was born in Kingsland, Arkansas, on February 26, 1932. Are we going to drive through Arkansas? Did you know he wrote about the flood that took out the family home in '35? Didn't even write music till he was in the Air Force. Won six awards just last year. Yep." Now he was fiddling with his banjo. "We don't need that scratchy old thing," he announced grandly as he jerked the eight-track from the built-in tape deck in such a manner that part of the tape caught on the hinged opening, a long, thin, brown noodle hanging in a loop. "I'll fix that later."

Carl was ready to kill. His foot came down with a little more force on the accelerator, the arm of the banjo banging his shoulder. Buck began to play and sing:

Chicken in the bread bowl peckin' out dough.

Granny, won't your dog bite? No, chile, no.

No, chile, no.

Chicken in the bread bowl peckin' out dough.

Granny, won't your dog bite? No, chile, no.

No, chile, no. No, chile, no.

Buck laughed. His fingers danced all along the neck, up and down frets, nimbly tightening the fifth string, fingernails peckin' some soul from his old banjo. In spite of himself, Carl tapped his fingers on the wheel. Buck played country, he played bluegrass, he played Cash and Dylan and Haggard. His rendition of "Kiss an Angel Good Morning" caused an angel to blush, and when Buck strummed and sang "The Old Rugged Cross," there was a noticeable tear in Carl's eye.

"Sorry about your tape." Buck spoke after he managed to slip his instrument in the back without hitting Carl. "I think you can wind these things up with a screwdriver. You got a screwdriver?"

"NO!" yelled Carl, trying to gather the ganglia of broken eight-track toward him. "It's old. Been meaning to replace it anyway." So help him, he was going to swat the man if he reached his way.

"You going to stop for dinner?" asked Buck, dinner hour passing as fast as each mile marker as they sped toward Cleveland.

"Going all the way through," answered Carl.

"Oh. You got anything to eat?"

Carl frowned. "There's a cooler down behind your seat."

The headlights from the big Kenworth seemed to jump and jerk as the truck hurtled down the highway, while Buck leaned over the seat and tried to pry a cooler from under a sleeping perch. With a shout of victory, and with Carl plastered against the steering wheel, the cooler came loose, spilling pop cans, fruit, and Hermit cookie bars all over the front seat. An opened bag of corn chips added a festive, party-like appearance to the passengers. Chosen steadied the big trucker as Buck picked chips off the seat. "You know, you really should eat something more wholesome," he announced as he thrust his thumb into a juicy orange and squirted the near-insane truck driver in the face.

"Always wondered if we should pray before we eat junk food," said Buck as he crammed his mouth with the crunch of the chips. "Probably we should pray to be protected from what we eat, what do you say, Carl?" Buck was laughing so hard he didn't hear Carl's insensitive and biting remark.

Cleveland was settling down for the night, and quiet. Carl drove his semi along back streets and came alongside the curb next to a row of warehouses. The huge yard was surrounded by fence with outward-leaning strands of barbed wire at the top. He let the truck idle. Buck didn't budge.

"End of the road!" Carl announced with marshaled authority. Buck sat in the darkened cab. "Nice meeting you!" Carl announced again, and wanting to get this ordeal over with, he turned to gather Buck's gear. Chosen was crestfallen as Carl nearly shoved Buck and his banjo out the door. "There's a cheap motel up the block." Carl was trying to assuage his guilt.

"Where you going to stay?" asked an equally crestfallen Buck.

"Oh, I'll stay in the yard in my truck tonight," said Carl, who was at that moment planning to shake corn chips off his bedroll.

Chosen stood on the darkened sidewalk next to Buck, his pack, and his banjo. Carl shifted into gear and moved his truck toward a guard station at the gate to the compound, made a right turn, and headed into an inky black backside of a building. Wings drooping and looking over his shoulder at the unconventional Buckaroo Berry, the angel followed the Kenworth.

Going to Kansas City

The next day Carl was fairly festive, jubilant to be rid of the man. Chosen moped and wondered about the whereabouts of Buck. Carl shared muddy coffee and a little gossip with the friendly dispatcher and hooked onto a load destined for Kansas City. If he made all his connections, he would haul out of Kansas City to Nashville. Nashville meant the Grand Ole Opry— and a couple of days of downtime before going on to Atlanta again.

The big truck shuddered and rumbled as it was held to slow motion through the yard toward the guard station. Carl waved, turned the big wheel hand over hand onto the street, and began to whistle. Chosen sat dutifully alongside. Kansas City would be a long day, but Carl would be there before his favorite rib joint closed. The Kenworth wound its way toward the truck route that would lead them out of town. In no time the truck would be chasing its own shadow as the early sun cast a golden ray on the road before it. Carl was clearly captain of his ship and set sail for smooth traveling, unaware that he was in a direct path to adventure. For looming just ahead, just around the corner, was Buckminster—Buck—Buckaroo—Berry.

Chosen saw him first. Carl might have missed him had the angel not caused a flash of light to slow him down. The truck protested against the downshift as Carl regained his bearings—and saw the man on the street. The pack and banjo case were unmistakable. Buck walked with the same vigor of yesterday, his gear swinging from both shoulders, oblivious to the semi creeping up behind. Chosen's heart leapt, so glad to see the irrepressible man again. Carl winced. And even though he was too high for the man to see, tried to scrunch down to avoid eye contact as he passed the man. This was foolish. Why should he feel guilty about that bum? He should just gun the truck and zip by and get to whistling again. His foot, however, felt restrained and heavy.

He's a good man like you are, Carl! There is something special about him in spite of his absentminded behavior! Remember your resolve to be virtuous! The angel implored. *You can't just leave him here!*

"Oh, yes I can," said Carl out loud, as if responding to a finger-wagging complaint. And with that he accelerated past an irrepressible man who at that moment was reciting, of all things, the Magna Carta.

The Lord preserveth strangers . . .

The driver sighed, the truck pulled neatly alongside a curb, and the angel hooted, *Hooray!*

Buck's face appeared, framed by the passenger window as he pulled himself up to make inquiry. "Where you headed?"

"Kansas City."

"That will do."

It will do nicely! thought an excited angel. This time Carl ducked when the gear was stashed. Buck adjusted his ball cap and settled back for his trip to Kansas City . . . and beyond.

An unusual silence settled over the two men as the big truck raced earnestly to catch its shadow. The cab filled with peace and grace; the men needn't think, plot, plan, fret, talk—or even pray. The air was already filled with prayer, and it was palpable. The angel saw to it as he joined his voice with the company of heaven in thanksgiving for these two men, in supplication for their well-being, and in praise for the One who is faithful and true. Carl noticed that Buck closed his eyes, his head nodding with the easy rhythm of the motor, contentment carved into his face like a mustache on Rushmore. In spite of himself, this pleased the trucker, who acknowledged the silence with a smile of his own. Long after the big truck caught its shadow, Carl spoke, "So, Buck. What's your stick?"

"My what?"

"Your stick. You know, I drive a truck and read the Good Book."

"You mean my *shtick;* I think it's a Jewish term. Oh, I just go where the Lord leads."

See? I knew he was a religious kook! "Where is He leading you now?"

"Here."

"Where, here?"

"Here. In this truck. With you. You got any food?"

They pulled into an unpaved parking lot and headed through a revolving diner door for breakfast—praying, of course, before commencing to eat. Carl would soon learn that they'd need all the prayer they could get: it was in Nashville that their adventures would truly begin.

Grand Ole Opry

Lucky for them—in spite of Memorial Day Weekend mobs, they were able to buy tickets to a matinee. Carl had been to the Grand Ole Opry several times, but this was a first for Buck. The two men found their seats in the grand theater, and the show began. A man in loud Western wear and cowboy hat approached the microphone and began to sing.

Buck leaned toward Carl and announced matter-of-factly. "That's not the way it goes."

"That's not how what goes?"

"The song! He's changed the lyrics, even changed the music. That's not right."

"Shhhh!"

Carl turned and smiled politely at the glaring people behind them.

"It really goes like this," announced Buck, who began to sing into Carl's ear in a loud whisper while he kept beat on the shoulders of a man in front, who jerked forward and slammed his nose into a women's bouffant hairdo.

"Shhhh!!!"

"It's just his style," whispered Carl through clenched jaws. He pushed Buck's hands onto his lap and told him to be quiet.

"No reason to change something that was fine to begin with. There's nothing original about stealing lyrics," came Buck's rather noisy complaint before he settled down for the next act.

"See? There they go again! *That is not what the original artist had in mind.* She's ruining the song."

Carl cringed.

"Will you shut up?" The collective voice came from all sides. Buck pulled the bill of his ball cap toward his nose and burrowed into his seat, his arms crossed tightly across his chest. "No reason whatsoever to ruin a good thing," he muttered.

Carl leaned so far away from Buck that a heavy, perspiring woman gave him the evil eye. His respite was short-lived. On autopilot, Buck was keeping his own time to the music. He was aggravated that most of what he heard was poached from original artists, that original intent had been nuanced away, that the pure, sweet sound of country music was unrecognizable in the new hip/pop, outlaw sounds. Bad enough the *country* was in flux—but this too? It was like reproducing the Mona Lisa with finger paint.

A hand clamped down on Buck's shoulder. "Would you come with me, please?" It was an usher, carrying a flashlight as big as a billy club. The man turned to Carl. "You gonna make trouble?" A shake of the head: unh unh. "You can stay; your friend will be outside."

Chosen watched the usher deposit Buck on the sidewalk. "If you can't keep quiet, you've got to keep out." The big trucker and the heavy woman both returned to an upright position. Carl tried to regain his composure. And the performers managed to finish their matinee without the critique and direction of a man in a Red Sox ball cap.

The Derelict

Caught in the crowd as it funneled its way outside and into the hazy mix of light when day turns into night, Carl strained to see Buck. Not that he held any responsibility for the man, mind you, but they had come together, and besides, Buck's gear was stashed in the motel room they shared. Clusters of people wandered off, showing particular interest in a gathering crowd down the street. From a distance, Carl heard polite applause, and was certain he heard—carried on the edge of a late spring breeze—the voice of a man that had just a hint of New England.

Using an upturned trash can, the backrest of a bench, and his legs, Buck beat a rhythm and belted out a song . . . the way it was meant to be sung. His big teeth laughed and his eyes welcomed everyone to join in. Some did. A bum—a real bum—filled a discarded pop can with pebbles. Now Buck's one-man band had mariachi backup. Carl stood behind the crowd and shook his head in grudging respect for the unusual man. He watched as two children twirled in the gay sound, and joined his own hands in applause when the music was over. The bum lingered as the crowd disbursed, his presence disturbing to Carl.

"Hey, Carl! Come and meet our new friend."

Oh, no, Buck, don't be doing this, thought Carl as he sized up the mendicant. Befriending street people like this was not a good idea. Chosen sized up the man as well and felt an uncomfortable tug in his spirit.

"What's your name?" asked Buck, his bleached, bushy eyebrows lowered for serious discussion.

"Name's George."

"Glad to meet you, George. My name's Buck. Carl, this is George the musician. George, this is my good buddy Carl." Buck offered his hand. Hesitant at first, George offered his hand in return. Long fingernails, cracked and caked with dirt, punctuated slim fingers that stuck out from a tattered woolen glove that was reduced to palm and wristpiece. Filthy hair hung in wavy clumps and sprawled down George's back on top of the heavy canvas coat he wore in spite of the heat. His hair was white, abrupt with yellow-blonde streaks. A flat-topped, flat-brimmed black hat topped his head, its band replete with feathers, assorted pins, and fishhooks. He wore leather shoes without socks or laces. And he smelled.

"Carl and I were just about to study the Good Book, and we'd like you to join us," announced Buck, bringing Carl to instant attention. He shook his head in protest and jerked Buck to the side.

"A," said Carl, pointing to his fingers as he counted off his reasons for protest, "we don't even have a Bible. B: We are in the middle of Nashville. C: This guy is bad news, I can feel it! D: It's getting late." He came to his pinkie. "And E . . . E: You are completely, beyond a shadow of a doubt, certifiably NUTS!"

Buck put his hand on Carl's arm. "This man needs the Lord, Carl. And I can just recite . . . what are we up to . . . Psalm 149? And then we'll pray. We can sit on this bench. It will only take a few minutes. It's OK."

"It's *not* OK, Buck," insisted Carl as he looked over his shoulder at the derelict. "Look, the guy is plastered. He's a tramp, Buck; he's no good. Now let's get out of here." No use.

"All the more reason to tell him about the Lord, Carl. 'For I am not ashamed of the gospel of Christ; for it is the power of God unto salvation to every one that believeth; to the Jew first, and also to the Greek.'"

"Yeah, I know, I know, but this dude ain't no Jew and he ain't no Greek. Besides, doesn't the Bible say something about throwing pearls or something to the dogs?"

"Give not that which is holy unto the dogs, neither cast ye your pearls before swine, lest they trample them under their feet, and turn again and rend you," replied Buck.

Chosen remembered well: How people had sat mesmerized when the Master preached His most famous sermon! This teaching had brought smug smiles to the faces of Pharisees: teach only according to the spiritual capacity of those listening, said the Master, don't share the holy Word with people in such low esteem as a dog in the street. Of course, the angel mused, the Pharisees heard what they wanted to hear, they never really seemed to *listen . . .* what an irony that, in a sense, Jesus had included them in His indictment.

George stared at the two men, blood-red rimmed eyes, his pupils swimming in a mix of whiskey and wine. Chosen stared at George. In spite of his pity, Chosen sensed deception and fraud. As did Carl. Buck clung stubbornly to his mission: Save the bum! Rehabilitate the man! Bring him to Jesus! Halleluia!

George tipped sideways against a building.

"This guy doesn't need no Bible study, Buck. For crying out loud, if he needs *anything* it's strong, black coffee!"

Buck slapped his leg and ran up to George. Coffee it would be. And food! "George, you hungry?"

"If you could give me a couple dollars for some food . . ."

Oh sure, thought Carl. *What you really want is another bottle of Thunderbird.* Knowing he was losing his argument, and with a trace of mean-spirited determination to foil George's attempt to solicit cash, Carl interrupted. "You two stay here, and I'll get George something to eat." George wobbled some more and watched with cunning and relief as his obvious opponent walked away.

Buck put his arm around the stinking man and led him to the bench. "George, let me tell you about Jesus Christ . . ."

Chosen watched as Carl disappeared down the street in search of hot, black coffee.

In the meantime, the angel stood with Buck and his mission. With a sincerity and love that could come only from years of dedication to the One who is love, Buck showered the man with kindness. He unreservedly called him "brother" (George smirked) and tried to ease any embarrassment the man might have over his condition (none). He demonstrated respect toward the derelict and tried valiantly to infuse dignity and value into the man's worth. *Imago Dei.* Buck was carried away by his determination to do good and did not notice as pearls dropped and scattered on the hard-packed earth in front of the street bench. But the angel noticed as he watched the derelict work the impassioned man with the skill of a master puppeteer: His wife and children were killed in a car wreck (a lie), he had lost his interest in life and lost his job (a lie), his mother needed medical attention (a lie), he was trying to get on his feet (a lie), and—oh, yes, Halleluia!—he would give his life to Jesus on the spot.

Buck breathed deeply and put his arms around the man's shoulders. This was what it was all about, to be right where the Lord wanted him, to be showing agape love. *But a certain Samaritan, as he journeyed, came where he was: and when he saw him, he had compassion on him.* And as dark began to fall over the bench, a tear ran down Buck's cheek as he led the poor, wayward man in the sinner's prayer.

Carl shifted his weight to his other leg as his toes impatiently tapped the floor of the restaurant. Finally next to be served, he fought rising turbulence inside his gut as a family of five (not counting Grandma) argued over hamburgers or hot dogs and changed their order repeatedly.

Chosen—who should have been rejoicing for the soul of a sinner now joined in eternal security—remained guarded. The angel simply could not believe the sincerity of this sudden conversion. Uncomfortable with the moment and with the growing isolation of the surroundings, he scanned the distance for Carl.

"If I just had bus money to get back to Kentucky, see, then I could move in with my ma and get back on my feet."

Carried by the thrill of ushering a lost soul into the kingdom, Buck reached for his wallet, for, as Carl had already learned, Buck had plenty of capital to finance his wayfaring ways. George saw the cash in Buck's wallet and steadied himself to control his wicked grin. Chosen was becoming highly agitated and with relief saw Carl in the distance, who at that moment was balancing a flimsy paper tray with an increasingly soggy coffee bottom. The angel raced to hurry the trucker back to the street corner—just as a nearby overhead light bounced off a flash of steel.

The Attack

The tray steadied by Chosen, Carl turned his gaze toward the distant bench, squinted to adjust his bearings, threw the tray on the ground and broke into a run, a wild-eyed angel shooting past him in a blur. A man in a Red Sox ball cap lay slumped on the ground.

"It hurts, Carl," said Buck, his hand pressing against the stab wound in his side. Carl knelt next to his friend. The angel prayed desperately and pressed his hand over the wound to slow the flow of blood.

"You just be still, partner," said a terrified Carl. "We'll get you to the hospital real quick."

The emergency room doctor shook his head in amazement and cautioned himself against using the term *miracle* too loosely. He emphasized Buck's good fortune, though—if there is such a thing as good fortune when you are robbed by a knife-wielding convert—and puzzled at the nearly superficial wound without serious internal damage that required only surface suture.

"His ribs are going to be mighty sore, and he should probably see his doctor in a week to check on those stitches, but otherwise, I don't think it's necessary to hold him for the night. I'll give him a couple of pills for pain. He's a lucky man."

Carl thanked the doctor, took his turn with the police, and then headed to the front desk.

"Look, um, my friend just got robbed. I want to pay his hospital bill."

"Name?"

"His name is Buck . . . Buckminster Berry."

"That will be taken care of by his insurance, sir. We will file the claim from here. Your friend is free to go."

Buck had insurance? Carl stroked the back of his neck and shook his head as he followed the glossy floors to the cubicle that held his friend. The curtain parted and two policemen emerged. Carl thanked them for their help and turned to his pale . . . partner. A tearful angel stuck to Buck's side like some kind of superglue; it was his fault that Buck was stabbed; he should never have left him. Waves of uncertainty and doubt swept over Bashar-el as a voice instructed him. *The heart of man harbors much evil. You cannot war against the flesh, Bashar. Only I can change the heart. I have placed you there because you are worthy. My grace and peace I give to you. It is sufficient.*

Carl helped Buck into a cab. The quiet ride to their motel reminded the tender trucker of a quiet Cleveland Street just three days before, three days that seemed forever ago. It was already hard to think of life without this impossibly quirky man.

"Carl?"

"Yeah?"

"What time is it?"

Carl twisted his body to hold his wrist near the overhead light. "Eleven forty-five."

Wincing with each breath, Buckminster Buck Buckaroo Berry opened his mouth and tearfully recited the fourth in a line of five praise psalms:

> Praise ye the LORD, Sing unto the LORD a new song, and his praise
>> in the congregation of saints.
> Let Israel rejoice in him that made him, let the children of Zion be
>> joyful in their King.
> Let them praise his name in the dance; let them sing praises unto him
>> with the timbrel and harp.
> For the LORD taketh pleasure in his people; he will beautify the
>> meek with salvation.
> Let the saints be joyful in glory; let them sing aloud upon their beds.
> Let the high praises of God be in their mouth, and a two-edged sword
> in their hand.
> To execute vengeance upon the heathen and punishments upon the people;
> To bind their kings with chains, and their nobles with fetters of iron;
> To execute upon them the judgment written; this honour have all his
>> saints. Praise ye the LORD.

As the cab pulled into the dark motel parking lot and another day dawned, the driver, the trucker, the angel, and the quirky man with a stab wound all uttered, "Amen."

More Adventure

An enduring bond grew between the two men. Over the next several weeks Buck learned to speak the language of truckers, and Carl learned to duck. Trips to Chicago turned into grand homecomings as Carl's mother, charmed by Buck's gregarious nature, prepared meals with special emphasis on his favorites: clam chowder thick with potatoes and crispy rice treats. Carl reveled in Buck's stories as they rode the road, stories so nonsensical that they must be true. *There was this man up in the hills of Georgia, Carl, he filed his teeth—they do that, you know. Had a trained skunk for a pet. Kept his knife pointy but deliberately dull. Said it did more damage that way. Dull like a slab of bacon.* Talk of knives brought sorrow to both men—Buck, because old George (who was still loose, probably "passing through," said the cops) was lost to sin; Carl, because he knew better than to tangle with a fellow like that. After Carl's doctor declared Buck fit—with a special emphasis on *lucky*—the two of them left the episode in Nashville behind them.

Buck kept his past behind him, as well. And Carl never pried. From time to time the irrepressible man would visit a bank to replenish his funds, and he once let slip "One of my students . . ." Other than that, the two friends kept their close, personal bond impersonal, their developing trust and allegiance separate from anything but here and now. On the road they shared motel rooms or slept under stars, guarded by an angel who still felt responsible for Buck's attack.

Buck concluded the words of Psalm 103 as they sped along the highway. They were "back" to 103, Buck agreeing it a great idea to study a psalm each day . . . but this time going backwards.

> But the mercy of the LORD is from everlasting to everlasting upon them
> that fear him, and his righteousness unto children's children.
> To such as keep his covenant, and to those that remember his com-
> mandments to do them.
> The LORD hath prepared his throne in the heavens: and his kingdom
> ruleth over all.
> Bless the LORD, ye his angels, that excel in strength, that do his com-
> mandments, hearkening unto the voice of his word.
> Bless ye the LORD, all ye his hosts; ye ministers of his, that do his pleasure;
> Bless the LORD, all his works in all places of his dominion: bless the
> LORD, O my soul.

"Carl, do you believe in angels?"

Chosen smiled broadly and leaned toward the trucker to hear his answer.

"Never thought about it. Do you?"

"Sure do. Not so sure about *guardian* angels, but I do believe there are spirits. Can't read the Good Book and not know that."

"No, I guess not."

"The Good Book says, 'Be not forgetful to entertain strangers; for thereby some have entertained angels unawares.'"

"You sure had a guardian angel that night in Nashville."

"Yes, I guess maybe I did. But I think *that* angel's name was Carl."

Carl blushed. And hit his brakes with the mastery of the seasoned veteran that he was, holding his big rig steady, steady, bringing it to a stop along the shoulder of the road. Minutes behind an accident, Carl and Buck jumped from the rig and ran into a field. There lay a pickup truck on its side, tires still spinning. Others ran to the aide of the young woman behind the wheel, who emerged bruised but shaken, hysterical for what lay behind her truck: the twisted wreck of a horse trailer, its top ripped off, a flailing and equally hysterical animal trapped inside.

The woman screamed. "Star! Oh, Star! Oh, Star!" She shook violently as a man from a sedan tried to wrap her in a blanket. The situation was dire; the life of a frantic golden horse most certainly at stake. Bewildered people began to collect around the accident as Star screamed in pain and fright.

"Help me, please, please," shrieked the woman. Pushing away from attempts to calm her, she ran in circles around the trailer. "Please, please, oh, please help me! Save him!"

Carl and Buck ran to the wreck. The horse continued to kick violently, trying to loose himself from his prison. A ragged piece of metal cut deeper into his rump every time he thrust his leg.

His love for animals so profound, Chosen raced to the injured palomino while men at the scene convened, and Carl shot back to his truck to call for help on the CB.

White with fright, the horse's eyes flashed in frenzy. Chosen reached back and effortlessly bent the twisted metal edge away from the animal's body. He wrapped his strong arms around the horse's head and spoke into his ear. *Whoa, now, whoa Star. Shhh, be calm now. Shhh.* The horse jerked his body but was no match for the angel, who soothed him with power and authority. *Whoa, now, steady. That a boy. Shhh.*

The horse had to be extracted. A power company truck was volunteered to pull the trailer upright. Cables were on hand. Yet every time anyone approached, the terrified animal became confused and frightened again. Calming the horse became most critical, and all were in agreement the animal faced certain destruction if the situation were not promptly resolved. *If only his eyes were closed,* thought the angel.

Buck grabbed the discarded blanket and walked slowly toward Star's head. Chosen held on tight.

"Careful, Buck!" yelled Carl, just returned from contacting the highway patrol.

"Easy, fellow, easy," came the soft words as Buck threw the blanket over the animal's head, sucked in his breath, and grabbed hold for dear life. The horse became still, comforted by angel and man. Carl whistled low in amazement as Buckaroo Berry spoke soothing words and pressed his body close to the horse in a white-knuckled clutch, his nose up against an angel's, unawares. Others sprang to work, cables were attached, the utility truck found traction in slippery grass, and the trailer was righted with a dusty thud. Star slipped out in a shudder. Clearly the hero of the day, Buck raced to the animal and grabbed his halter. The young woman flung herself at the animal. "Star! Star!"

Star remained calm as Buck ran his expert hand over his body. The gash on his hind end was deep, but would heal. Star would be fine, Buck assured the young woman, and as the horse accepted a handful of grass, a roar came from the crowd.

Chosen stroked the black velvet nose of the animal and felt his warm breath come in snorts. He whispered into his ear one last time, and the horse whinnied as the angel turned to follow two men up a bank to a waiting truck.

Carl would tell this story many times, of the horse and his friend Buck, and of the tragedy that was averted. "*You* were like a guardian angel to that horse, Buck," said the trucker in earnest.

"Just call me Buckaroo Berry."

Revival

One day, Buckaroo Berry and Carl Montgomery came across a revival in Alabama. Cars lined up for entrance to an old farm, an endless train of faithful come to be delivered. A huge, white tent sat tethered alongside the barn, as people of every description traipsed through brittle weeds and settled in for a night of gospel truth. That's what the sign said: "The Gospel Truth Revival."

"Let's stop!" said an excited Buck.

"Buck, you don't want to go to one of them things. Bunch of people rolling all over the place, people falling down, lots of yelling."

"I've always wanted to attend one of these. Come on!" He could be irresistible. Carl shook his head and maneuvered the semi to the side of the highway; if Buck wanted to go, he'd have to hike back to the farm.

The two men worked themselves into the sweaty crowd. Babies, children, men, women, young and old: people kept coming. Chosen thought back to the crowds that came long ago, streams of people coming to hear the Rabbi, people who carried infants in slings, the old, the lame; people came.

As is characteristic of human nature—even in a revival meeting—crowds settle toward the back, the few seats remaining in the front row. A burly man in bib overalls, who could best be described as a huge callous with feet, cut a swath through the milling throng and told Carl and Buck to "Sit heer." Carl did not like this one bit. He hated emotional shows of religion, felt it was degrading. Buck, on the other hand, was buoyed by the fact he was attending his first revival. This, he reasoned, *must* be different from a Billy Graham Crusade. It certainly was.

The singing started. Carl felt uncomfortable—captive, actually—stuck way up front, impossible to make a quiet slip out the back flap. He stood and sat and stood and sat without so much as a peep, while Buck happily joined the clapping and swaying, his bright teeth flashing smiles all along.

There were two preachers, more like a team: Preacher #1 and his faithful sidekick, Preacher #2. *Tag-team preaching,* thought Carl. *This ought to be good.* The preachers stood on a raised platform in front of the faithful. A wobbly table sat to the side, a large wooden box resting on top. One of the preachers held his arms in the air to still the crowd. Chosen remembered the apostles raising their arms just the same way as they walked among the gathering flock along the shores of Galilee.

"You all come to hear the gospel truth?" yelled Preacher #1.

"Yes!" came the roar, the people primed from the delirium of song.

"The gospel truth, so help you die?"

"Yes! Amen!"

And the preaching began. But it was all wrong.

"The Bible says to go into the world and preach the gospel truth to the chosen."

Buck lowered his eyebrows in thought.

"You know who's the chosen? Not the Jews, not the Japs, not the niggers—who's the chosen?"

"We are!"

"That's right, and that's the gospel truth!"

Carl looked at Buck. Buck looked at Carl. Chosen smelled danger.

"Only the white man will be saved; all others will be condemned. This is the gospel truth, right here in the sixteenth chapter of Mark."

"That's not true," uttered Buck, who immediately felt the jab of Carl's elbow.

"We are the rightful children of God. We are His pure heirs. We are the anointed, the blessed; no other man can touch us, no sickness can stop us— you know who brings sickness into the world, don't you?"

Preacher #2 danced on his toes. "It's the devil Jew, it's the devil kike." He waved a fat black Bible. "The Bible says in Romans that the Jew is damned because he is ignorant, the Jew is the devil because he killed Christ, the Jew bankers spit on His grave."

"That's just not true—that's not in the Bible," said Buck, a little too loud for Carl's comfort. Preacher #2 shot a scowl at the two men.

"We are the superhuman race!"

Clapping, stomping, and yelling.

"We are the anointed. Nothing can touch us. You know we got snakes here tonight, don't you?"

Electricity coursed through the crowd.

"You think snakes can hurt us?"

"NO!"

"Not snakes, not poison, and no devil Jew!"

"And that's the gospel truth," called Preacher #2.

"The gospel truth!"

"Oh no it's not!" came the call from the front row seat. "That is *not* in the Bible!" This time he was loud enough to get the attention of the dynamic duo . . . and everyone else at the meeting.

Noise—threatening noise—came from the crowd. Carl began to entreat Buck to stop. Chosen braced for certain trouble. Danger hung on every tent peg. And there they were: Chosen saw the demons everywhere. The place stunk of demons. *Holy One, help us!* An army of angels appeared. Relieved, Chosen took his place behind the two men.

Arms went into the air to quiet the crowd. Preacher #1 spoke, his every word accented by hate. "Suppose you come up here and tell us what the Bible does say." *That should shut him up,* he thought as he gave a nod to the man in the overalls at the back of the tent. Think again.

Carl reached for Buck's sleeve, but he would not be stopped. It was the Grand Ole Opry all over again. Buck stepped onto the platform, shielded by sword-wielding angels. Chosen stayed with Carl.

Buck was at ease in front of a crowd and seemed unperturbed by the man in the overalls who was now holding a baseball bat.

"For one thing," Buck said to the two preachers, "you were quoting Romans 10 out of context." He turned to the crowd. "It's called Scripture twisting. The apostle Paul was not condemning the Jews, he was *praying* for them. And nowhere does the Bible say the Jew is the devil—matter of fact, right in Romans 10," he turned to the men to make his point, "the chapter you were citing—it says 'for there is *no difference* between the Jew and the Greek; for the same Lord over all is rich unto all that call upon him.'"

"You are of the devil! You are straight from hell!" The preachers turned to the crowd. "Do you hear this man! This man does not know the gospel truth; he is a Jew lover!"

Insults hurled, both preachers lunged toward Buck, who fell backwards against the table, spilling a crate of angry rattlers. The crowd detonated into frenzy to escape the snakes. Spiritual warfare engaged in earnest. Carl grabbed Buck; Chosen threw snakes into the furor and protected his wards with blinding light as they ducked under a tent flap and ran for the Kenworth like a couple of jackrabbits in a race. To ensure their escape, Chosen blasted around the tent, pulling stakes as he went.

The Kenworth jumped to attention, and for the first time in his entire career on the road, Carl Montgomery burned rubber as the big truck lurched off in a flash of supernatural light.

"I wish you wouldn't do that," whined Carl as they sped away.

"Everything they said was a lie, Carl."

"But you don't mess with people like that, Buck!"

A long stretch of road passed before Buck replied. "Someone's got to."

The truck driver sighed.

Good-Bye

A few weeks after their close call at the revival—and long enough that each time they relived the moment a bit more humor was added to soften its troubling seriousness—it became apparent to both that their time together would soon end. There was no reason: just a sense, a premonition, a feeling that hung over them until Buck finally broke the tension; it was Buck's prerogative, after all, to end this wonderful adventure. Carl dreaded the announcement, which came in typical Buckaroo style, after Buck spilled a bowl of chili on the lap of another trucker as he tried to squeeze through a mob at Carl's favorite stop in Kansas City.

"Sorry," yelled Buck above the din then he made matters worse by smearing the mess with a handful of paper napkins.

The man cursed, taking God's name in vain.

"Bless His holy name," replied Buck.

"What?!" spewed the man as he shoved Buck away.

"Bless His holy name. You blasphemed the Lord's name in your anger. I just said, 'Bless His holy name.'"

The enraged man was about to pop Buck in the nose when an arm caught his fist. Carl was taller, and heavier by at least fifty pounds. He glared holes into the man.

"He said, 'Bless His holy name.' And I say it too!" said the teddy bear of a man as an angel smiled in triumph. The antagonist sat down and turned away. Carl bought Buck another bowl of chili. They sat at a corner table covered with worn, red-checked oilcloth. Buck ate slowly and deliberately. Carl poked his straw at lumps of ice in his tea.

"Thanks . . . partner," said Buck, showing his big white teeth in a smile that quickly turned downward. He cleared his throat. "Remember back when I said I went where the Lord sends me?" he began.

Don't do this, thought Carl. *You're like a brother to me . . . don't.*

"Well, hard to say why, but I guess I've got to stay here for a while."

"Kansas City?"

Buck poked his chili with a spoon and nodded his head yes. "Probably you should shove off without me in the morning." A rare silence came over both men, Buck's arms resting on the table, not a muscle to be moved. Chosen wept for the two of them.

P.S.

A note was stuck under his windshield wiper. Carl could not bring himself to reach for it, certain it would bear a message of farewell from his friend . . . his brother. For the first time, Carl could understand the meaning and impact of words that had meant nothing before he met Buck: brother in Christ. *What the heck was that supposed to mean?* he used to say. *After all, we're all sort of connected anyway, aren't we?* No, not like this. Not like a quirky stranger worming his way into your heart—right into the muscle that made it work, that pumped life to your body all day long. Not like the bumps on your head from a banjo case, spilled coffee, Bible by heart. Not like the man who knew the "Good Book" and lived it. Buck was different. Special. Close. Gone. Carl didn't even try to stop the tears.

Finally reaching, he held the folded note in his hands.

> *Dear Carl,*
>
> *Though friends for a season, there is a coming day when we will be united in glory. I will miss you, my friend, and pledge to pray for you every single day as I go backwards and forwards through the book of Psalms. I hope you will remember me in prayer as well. May God richly bless you and your mother, and may he protect you as you travel blue highways.*
>
> *Your brother in Christ,*
>
> *Buckaroo Berry*

How lonely it was without him! The truck itself seemed to feel the loss as it reluctantly worked its way through the early morning haze of fall. Chosen sat in Buck's spot, praying for both men and longing for the day when they would all be face to face.

This time the trucker saw him first. Carl noticed a small crowd of commuters file from a bus and gather momentarily around a man with a banjo. He parked the truck down an alley and walked hurriedly toward the crowd. Just before turning the corner he stopped and leaned against the cool brick of a building to listen to the voice of a man that had just a hint of New England:

"Unto thee, O God, do we give thanks, unto thee do we give thanks; for that thy name is near thy wondrous works declare. . . ." Carl smiled and choked back a tear. Without a doubt, he was listening to #75, the next psalm in the backwards journey he'd been on since his world turned upside down that splendid day in May.

"May God richly bless you, too, my brother," whispered Carl as he turned and headed back to the truck.

Chapter
Seven

April 1973

As sure as morning comes, as sure as today follows yesterday and tomorrow follows today, the postcard came, the third year in a row. Carl was waiting this time and met the postman with a nod. Nearly noon, Carl and his mother would maintain silence for the next three hours, a solid Montgomery tradition. It was Good Friday, and other than the predictable postcard and the expectation of Easter, there was nothing good about this day. Carl had hated Good Friday ever since he had been old enough to read about the crucifixion. It still pained him to read an account of Christ's death. He headed toward their kitchen, still rich with the aroma of imported cinnamon. As ever, the burly trucker and his mother baked hot-cross buns to distribute to neighbors when they headed to church for quiet meditation.

As sure as Saturday follows Friday, tomorrow the house would reek of vinegar, and his mother would plead for help with egg detail, to his absolutely enormous annoyance. Carl felt foolish every time he grabbed the translucent crayon and scribbled names across a white shell, invariably running out of room. Add to that the concern Buck had voiced about the accoutrements of Easter.

"Folks no more celebrate Christ at Easter than they do at Christmas, Carl. It's not the same anymore. Just a family get-together, that's all."

The postcard was from Buck.

Carl showed it to his mother who smiled broadly: it was still a celebration when Buck came home, if only on a postcard from Sacramento. Last year it was Anchorage; the year before, Tallahassee. And as certain as his card arriving on Good Friday was its message: always a quote from Thomas Jefferson, followed by wishes for God's blessing on the two of them, and signed "Your Brother in Christ, Buck."

Carl and his mother read this year's quote in silence: *Error of opinion may be tolerated where reason is left free to combat it.*

Where does he come up with all of this? wondered Carl, who placed the card on the bird's-eye maple buffet in the dining room. Tomorrow an egg would be placed alongside, one marked "Buck." Within a few days the postcard would join the other two within the pages of a skinny book of Psalms.

From Tallahassee: *I tremble for my country when I reflect that God is just; that His justice cannot sleep forever.*

From Anchorage: *I have sworn upon the altar of God, eternal hostility against every form of tyranny over the mind of man.*

Where are you, Buck? wondered Carl, who still scanned every street he drove for a man with pack and banjo. It seemed at first as if Kansas City had swallowed Buck whole; Carl would linger and cruise streets on his way out of town, hoping to hear just a hint of New England. True to Buck's request, Carl prayed for his friend every day—backwards and forwards.

Deliveries in hand, Carl, his mom, and an angel stepped into an early spring sun that momentarily obscured the gloom of the day. First stop: Jerry, who answered their knock with a hug, a handshake, and a respectful silence. Others would do the same, some passing a bag of their own to Carl's mother: *chrusciki* from Mrs. Rybicki, *lefse* from the Svare's, scones from Mrs. Sutton.

Mr. Sanchez had passed away last year; there would be no stopping there; the Johnsons had moved; the Schwalls were out of state visiting their daughter; ritual stops were decreasing exponentially. Soon there would be no one left to give hot-cross buns, as time-worn traditions were dismissed by the Me Generation one by one.

Chosen hated Good Friday too. If ever an event challenged the obedience of the angelic host, that was it, when every beneficent spirit struggled under suffocating, blinding horror as it watched the crashing climax of history and could not intervene. The import of that moment multiplied the magnitude of the Fall by eternity. The angels' hatred of the terribleness of sin—and of the influence of Lucifer, once one of their own—was surpassed only by their grief as the Holy One, the One they worshiped and adored, now screamed in pain with each hammer blow. And they, they who could destroy Roman legions, they who could obliterate the Sanhedrin and all of Christ's enemies in a flash, a blink, in an instant, were under the sharp command of God the Father not to interfere. They had to obey. Scripture had to be fulfilled. The God many mocked, the great I AM, so loved, so loved, that He gave Himself as payment, as reparation. The cosmos shuddered under the explosive power of endless blasts of rage, and angels sobbed in protest as incarnate God became the sacrificial lamb.

For crimes committed I sentence you to prison, said the Judge and Father, who then stepped down from the bench, removed His robe, and announced, *But I will go on your behalf. You are free.* Go and sin no more.

Yes, on Resurrection morning there would be jubilation; it was, after all, the most loved day of the year. But to face the memory of the moment so many years ago—just yesterday—NOW! to the timeless being, was agony.

Easter

Easter Day was festive for the Montgomerys, who stayed dressed in their church finest to walk next door for brunch, balancing cole slaw, sweet potatoes, coconut cream pie, and the ubiquitous eggs, one each for Jerry, his wife, his kids, and for a young German student named Dieter.

In the tradition of Jerry's family, major holidays were complete only if they included those who would otherwise be alone. This year no exception, Jerry and his wife invited the young tourist to stay with them for a few days before continuing his exploration of the United States. And with the confidence that comes from knowing an answer before it is spoken, Jerry asked Carl to take Dieter with him on his run to Minneapolis the next day.

Camped around the groaning Easter buffet, family and friends laughed and loved and shared the accustomed comfort that comes from a lifetime of living next door. The German boy thoroughly enjoyed their show of affection.

Other than his thick accent, Dieter Stahlberg seemed the same as all of the American students Carl had seen: lanky, bushy brown hair, bell-bottomed jeans. He seemed a bright boy, if not a tad aloof, which Carl and Jerry both attributed to culture. But to hear him speak! Carl was charmed by Dieter's accent and graded him a "B" for English.

"Would you pass zuh vater."

"Zuh meal taste goot."

"Tank you for hospitality."

The language of angels knowing no bounds, Chosen prayed for this latest stranger as both houses settled into nighttime routine and sleep: *Himmliecher Vater, bitte segne diesen jungen Mann mit Deiner unvorstellbaren Gnade, schuetze ihn und moege er Freude und Hoffnung finden durch die Weidergeburte Deines Sohnes. (Father, send this young man abundant grace, protect him as he goes, and may he find lasting joy and hope in the Resurrection of Your Son, I pray.)*

On the Road

"Well, Dieter," said a still-stuffed Carl as he stashed the boy's backpack on the bunk, "do you have a special destination?"

"I am go to Portland, Oregoan." He pulled a worn paper from his pocket, weak with crease, an address written in old-country script. He showed the paper to Carl. "Do you know?"

Carl politely studied the paper and shook his head. "No, can't say I know where that is."

After a final trip into the house to retrieve his bulging bag of goodies, and after one last hug and a "See you next week," Carl climbed into the cab. Dieter was already waiting, hands thrust into his down vest to escape the morning chill. An angel called Chosen ("Besonderes" to Dieter) and a skinny book of Psalms sat in the middle.

"OK, Dieter, let's hit the road."

"Super," said Dieter, sounding like "Zuppah," the boy a bit unsure about the efficacy of "hitting" the road—probably an American custom.

Vorwaerts! said the happy angel. Onward.

Chosen was always glad when Carl had someone on board, reveling in the bold new expression of the trucker's love for Jesus and of his impressive understanding of the "Good Book." The mighty Kenworth carried Carl and occasional others over hill and dale as the teddy bear of a man told stories about a fellow named Buck and the impact he'd had on his life, the most important being a closer walk with Jesus. *For I am not ashamed of the gospel of Christ; for it is the power of God unto salvation to every one that believeth; to the Jew first, and also to the Greek.* When others were not on board, Brenda's gift sat prominently on the passenger seat; maybe it was a little corny, but it was Carl's way to stay close to a quirky man in a Red Sox baseball cap.

After Carl hooked onto his load, the semi eased out of town, headed west. Traffic was heavier than usual, noticeably more dense due to the Easter holiday and a recent end to the oil embargo. Americans had been "hitting the road" in droves, glad to be rid of long lines at gas stations and of rationing. Gas prices remained high, though, and with the economy in shambles, over-the-river-and-through-the-woods-to-Grandma's-for-Easter-dinner required a lot more planning and thought than before.

"So, what grade are you in, Dieter?"

"I am third-year economics at Goettingen."

"Are you on spring break?"

"What is the meaning of 'break'?"

Carl smiled broadly. "Did the school give you a holiday?"

"Ach!" Now Dieter smiled. "Das is break. No, I take off time to come to America."

Carl nodded his head and settled in to the rhythm of the road. He'd never been to Germany, but was certain the rich dairy country they'd soon traverse would comfort the boy. They listened to a little bit of a brand-new Johnny Cash tape, listened to gossip and greetings on the CB, and listened to the news, which was filled, as always, with the dire situation in Vietnam and the dastardly doings of Watergate. They stopped at a rest area for a mid-morning snack, Dieter perplexed when Carl handed him a hard-boiled egg and a pastry without fork or plate.

Back on the road, Carl was in the mood for conversation. The spring sun had put a bounce in his spirit, his most favorite day in the world still causing a residual glow.

"Are you going to be an economist?"

"Yes, but much study before das can be. Much study."

"Did you come to America to explore?"

"Yes, but also I have purpose to go to Portland, Oregoan."

"How do you like our country?"

"America is nice."

"Anything surprise you?"

"Before I come I tink everyone having gun, like television. Also I tink everyone eating hamburger and French fries."

They both laughed.

"It is big. Much space. I cannot understand space like das until here. Too much space: hard to travel!"

"You have a lot of trains in Europe, don't you?"

"And bicycles and bus, and we valking very much. Too far to valk here!"

This must be the new generation, thought Carl as Dieter destroyed a few stereotypes he had about Germans: that they are not friendly, that they have no sense of humor. He shifted his weight—sigh, his ever-increasing weight—and ran the windshield wiper to wash away bugs.

"Dieter, OK with you if I take a little break after lunch? I like to do a little Bible study." Carl acted nonchalant but watched the German student for response. There was none. Dieter continued to look out the window, unmoved by Carl's announcement. Or was he? After a time, he spoke.

"Man does not need Bible, Carl."

Uh oh.

"Is foolish myt." Was he testing Carl? Taunting him? Was this the sound of challenge, or was there the slightest hesitation in the boy's voice?

Carl had heard the arguments about myth before—and, as before, still panicked when faced with antagonism. Buck would have jumped right in. Buck would have known what to say, would have said it well, and then clapped the man on the back. Carl just kept quiet as he pulled the Kenworth into the rest area and nosed it up against a grove of trees.

Lunch Break

The trucker grabbed his cooler, his tattered Bible, and the skinny book that filled the space between man and boy—a space as wide as a chasm, the Grand Canyon, the Atlantic and the Pacific, the cosmos filled with infinity. An infinity that faced all. Where would it be spent? In the presence of the One who is sovereign? Suspended on a link in time and space, connected to nothing, going nowhere? In desperation and sorrow when irretrievable loss is suddenly real? *The rich man also died, and was buried; and in hell he lifted up his eyes, being in torments . . .*

The big angel stuck with Carl and Dieter during their lunch stop, much more concerned about the boy's soul than assisting motorists. This attitude of his—this belief, for those who proclaimed unbelief were certainly believers in their unbelief—this attitude was prevalent in the halls of learning. Bible As Myth: the humanities course in many schools.

Dieter walked the grounds while Carl studied his Bible. Sad that the boy curtly declined participation and derided the Book before wandering off, Carl finished the fourth chapter of Luke and closed his Bible. The front and back covers were barely connected to the text, old gates hung on broken hinge—even the tape he'd used was brittle and useless. Carl reached for Brenda's gift. He was partway into a study of Psalm 119. Because of Buck he now allowed sufficient time for the longer psalms—119, by the way, taking exactly three weeks and a day.

And take not the word of truth utterly out of my mouth . . .

I will speak of thy testimonies also before kings, and will not be ashamed.

I will not be ashamed.

It never failed. The big trucker could have predicted that the Word would, as he would say, "nail him:" he'd been ashamed—at least insecure—and had not offered an answer for the hope that lay within him. It just never failed: Be talking about a certain subject, open your Bible, and boom! Certain subject. Do something you shouldn't have, open your Bible, and boom! A clear accusation. Backslide just a little, open your Bible, and boom! A gentle nudge that feels like you've just gone a round with Mohammed Ali.

The angel knew what Carl felt and offered supplication for a little extra boldness to settle on his dear companion. Carl underlined *And take not the word of truth utterly out of my mouth,* shut the book, and scanned the area for Dieter, who was sprawled on his back in a patch of sun.

The Conversation

"Please, Lord, let my words be Your words," whispered Carl as he wheeled his truck back onto the highway.

There was a noticeable, though slight, strain between the two, as if squared-off in opposite corners, both uncomfortable with talk; the man troubled by his failure to contend for the faith, the boy clearly agitated by mention of the Bible. Carl broke the impasse.

"Tell me, Dieter, what is the source of your religious knowledge?"

"I do not believe in religion; it is opiate of zuh people."

"So you're an atheist?"

"Wit humans, not God; Wit nature, not deity."

Carl held the steering wheel with both hands and moved his jaw back and forth, his lips in a pucker. To Chosen, it was eighteenth-century France all over again: man, the measure of all things. *Come on, Carl! Keep the talk going!*

"So human beings are the source of your religious knowledge." Carl was very nervous. "You must believe, then, that humans are trustworthy."

Fresh from university, Dieter filtered the works of Sartre, Camus, and Kafka through his mind. Trustworthy? He'd never thought about that before. But *he*, Dieter, *he* could be trustworthy; he could be the source of his religious knowledge, and why not? "Life has no ultimate meaning; how I believe or tink makes no difference, only here and now," he said with confidence.

"Well, Dieter, as a Christian my source of religious knowledge is the Bible, and the Bible says it makes a big difference how I believe or think."

"Ach, Carl, I tell you Bible is myt!"

Dieter was unequivocal: this uneducated American was not aware of the abundant scholarship that called the Bible into question, that compared the claims of early Christians to the myth and tradition of mystery religions, that cited historical inaccuracies and textual contradictions. But *Dieter* knew all of this: he had learned it all at university—and would certainly defend it as trustworthy. Yes, probably. At least, until Molly came along.

As Dieter watched the passing farmland, a tender feeling bubbled in his heart for the graduate student from California now studying at Goettingen. Molly had all the credentials for becoming his soul mate, if not for that confounded nonsense about Jesus Christ . . . and the Bible. *Dieter, for everything you are learning about the Bible, there is much more scholarship—sound scholarship I might add—* (Molly had a way of pointing her finger at him) *that discredits the claims of your professors. These teachings are not trustworthy, Dieter.*

Trustworthy.

Dieter missed Molly and hoped to see her in a few weeks when she returned to the States. He'd had his route, his plan, his mission, mapped for months before he took this sabbatical. California would be his last stop.

Carl spoke.

"Do you really believe that millions and millions of people—many people a whole lot smarter than me—cling to myth, Dieter?" (*Than* I, thought Dieter, *smarter than* I.) "That must mean that history is filled with gullible people." Carl shook his head. "Man, that must mean that I am gullible!"

And Molly . . .

No protest from the boy.

Hoping it would do some good, *wishing* he could be heard, Chosen eagerly coached Carl. The big man brightened.

"You know, Dieter, nobody forces me to believe any of this. That's the thing about God, He gives us free will and a brain. My friend Buck used to say something about not parking your brain in the garage when you picked up the 'Good Book.'"

Molly's words bounced through Dieter's thoughts. *That's what's so neat about Jesus, Dieter. He is a gentleman. He stands at the door to your heart and knocks, but He will never force His way in.*

"Das means nutting, free will, das can easily be coming from man. Man makes choices, so vat?" Dieter felt smug.

Carl shot back. "Tell me about East Germany."

Chosen crowed: score one for the big guy!

"Das is different. Das is government!"

"That is man, Dieter."

Carl was on a roll—jumping all over the place, but, hey, he was no Buck; he was gathering all the ammunition he could muster. Shotgun approach.

"The people in East Germany aren't allowed to think for themselves, are they, Dieter? God doesn't treat His children that way. He gave us brains, and the Bible tells us to use them."

To drive home the point (OK . . . and to show off a little), Carl quoted Thomas Jefferson, hoping to impress the German boy. He did.

"See this little book here?" Brenda's gift lay on the seat between them. "It's part of the Bible." Dieter perked up. "I've got a whole Bible too, but this is just the Book of Psalms, kind of like prayers and poetry."

Where are you going with this, Carl? wondered Chosen.

"And you know what it says in the Book of Psalms? It says that only a fool says in his heart that there is no God."

"You quote zuh Bible to prove zuh Bible, to prove your God: das is meaningless." Score one for the German who barely broke a smile, the emotion of his thoughts on Molly and not on his victory in this skirmish . . . he did wonder, though, if the man would be as smart as Molly and counter with her same arresting comment. Not to be: Carl was stumped.

Tell him it's more than one book! yelled an impassioned angel. *Tell him it was written over hundreds and hundreds of years by dozens of authors, all superintended by God the Holy Spirit! Tell him it all testifies to one unified message!* No use.

Milepost after milepost flew by as Carl twisted his jaw and puckered his lips. He finally spoke again.

"Have you ever read the Bible, Dieter? I mean, cover to cover?"

This was getting dangerously close to Molly's glaring indictment.

"Nein."

"Well, excuse me for being a little harsh, son, but how can you pass judgment on something you've never read yourself?"

Touchdown! Chosen was hooting and hollering: *Good job, Carl!*

This is intellectual dishonesty, Dieter, to call the text myth or groundless if you've never personally examined it, read it, and studied it. Judgment cannot be rendered with honesty until the evidence is heard, Dieter (she had a way of saying *Dee*-eh-tuhr). *Go read the Bible—that will take you about a year—*(she was pointing at him) *and then come back to me with your arguments!* Molly's feisty personality drew him like a magnet.

"And let me say just one more thing, Dieter." Carl was on a roll. "I have a good friend who says the only way you can know for sure that there is no God is if you are God yourself. I didn't know what he meant until he put it this way: a man would have to know everything about everything that ever is, was, or was gonna be, and he'd have to know about everything here on earth and in the entire universe in order to know for sure that there was no such thing as God, so, he'd have to *be* God. Get it?"

Not on your life.

The rest of the day was spent in polite banter, the tension softened a bit, but the boy—could it be?—pouted since the talk. The trucker drove on, unaware he'd been an instrument in the sovereign will and purpose of God, or that he'd ripped a scab off the hole left by Molly's pointy finger. Carl could tell that the boy was dealing with deeper issues, issues he chose not to share— issues that the boy dare not share.

L'Abri

Dieter had happily traveled to Switzerland to visit Molly over the Christmas holiday. Spending a few days in her company had been reason enough to go, the Alps a bonus to the young man who had cut his teeth on the gnarly, wind-ravaged stumps that cluttered every mountain trail and bowed down low in greeting as he and his family spent holiday time skiing or hiking, drawn to the giant monoliths like mountain goats. A place called L'Abri—*It's a great place,* Dee-*eh-tuhr, sort of like a Christian commune*—could be endured as long as he had Molly and the mountains. He never planned on enjoying himself.

Once at L'Abri, Dieter had felt at home with others his age and had reveled in the different ethnic backgrounds: Molly and a few others from America, a man from India, several other Germans, a girl from England, and a Swiss couple who seemed to be in charge. Days had been spent preparing meals, chopping wood, milking goats, and skiing. The evening meal had been one of great camaraderie and gusto, Dieter laughing at the antics of the Americans, who had entertained the group with jokes and teases and folk songs, Molly very much the ring-leader of the bunch. Dieter had tucked his smiles away, however, and listened from a corner when nightly discussions began. The Swiss man, the leader, the one who galvanized everyone with his demeanor and clear, unmistakable intellect, had spoken at length. He had spoken of God, of Christ, of redemption. He had spoken of creation and evolution, of the dangers of waning morality. And he had spoken with authority. Dieter had been impressed, yet had remained cynical, protecting his unbelief with all of his might. He had listened to questions from skeptics, and answers from the bearded man in lederhosen as he dazzled everyone with his response. But not Dieter. No way. *How can such an intelligent man—such intelligent people—believe such myth and nonsense?* The young German boy had been troubled that he, only he, could prevail against such folly. If Molly had thought he would suddenly convert to her foolish belief in Christianity by bringing him there, she was wrong. It was a good opportunity, however, for him to share his plan with her. And so one night, in the quiet corner of a Swiss chalet, warmed by a wood fire and illuminated by moonswept snow that pushed against the window, they had had a talk.

"Then you should go at Easter. It's a time of reconciliation, Dieter. It is when we remember Christ's death for us."

"I need no one to die for me, Molly."

"Oh, Dieter!" Molly had said with an irrepressible hug around his stiff upper body. "He loves you so much!"

Minneapolis

Minneapolis loomed ahead. Completely oblivious to his backup angel band, Carl rehearsed his next words.

"I've got a challenge for you, Dieter."

"Wat is das . . . challenge?"

"When you go to bed tonight, just for the heck of it, I want you to make believe there really is a God."

"Ja."

"And when you close your eyes to sleep, I want you to have a little conversation with Him."

Big, green signs announced their arrival in Minneapolis. Leftover piles of dead snow dotted the roadside; the north-facing slopes looked like glaciers left behind from a different time, a time called winter that came early and left late in a country called Minnesota.

Carl went well off his route and brought the young German close to the downtown area. "I don't know about youth hostels here, Dieter, but you should be able to find someplace to hang your hat tonight."

"Hang your hat," *a strange comment, indeed,* thought Dieter, who wore no hat. He thanked Carl profusely for his zuppah kindness, for sharing his food, and for the conversation. Grabbing his backpack, he jumped from the truck, waved good-bye, and disappeared down a street as Carl worked his big rig through traffic. Chosen, under an abrupt command not to interfere, took one last look at the Kenworth, and in desperation raced back to the cab to whisper "I will miss you" into his "good buddy's" ear. And then he turned to follow a German student with bushy hair.

It was not until Carl hoisted himself into his truck after dollying down his freight that he noticed it was gone. There on the spot where Brenda's gift had been was a five-dollar bill. At first angry, and then heartsick, Carl felt the power of the Holy Spirit surge through him in assurance that the book was where it belonged. He leaned over his steering wheel and closed his eyes in prayer for young Dieter, begging the very throne of God that the words in that skinny book of Psalms would not return void.

Chapter

Eight

April 1973, continued

Chosen had never been on a train before. But the German boy had . . .
plenty. And so, with the deft skill of a practiced traveler, Dieter followed internal radar to the Minneapolis train station. His neck cranked back, he studied
the expansive schedule and smiled; the train to Portland departed at 11 P.M.
If luck continued, this train would deliver him to Portland in two days—still
within reach of the end of the Easter holiday. Dieter's smile was justified;
everything was going according to plan. He glanced at the long ticket line
filled with families clustered like grapes on an invisible conveyor belt, the end
of the holiday crush.

Chosen felt at home in the grand architecture of the train station, which
reminded him of cathedrals in Europe and of the Temple. *God that made the
world and all things therein, seeing that he is Lord of heaven and earth, dwelleth not
in temples made with hands.* The reminder of the Temple made him homesick

and aggravated his already low spirits, for Chosen's heart was still in a Kenworth that was bedded down for the night, and he yearned for his friend Carl.

The angel knew Carl would spend tonight in a favorite trucker's motel, that he would play cribbage with his CB buddy V-8, that he would call home to check on his mom, who was beginning to show signs of senility. He knew that tomorrow there would be good-natured banter when Carl backed into a trailer and hooked onto his load, that he would fill his thermos at a café with tile floors worn into grooves, that he would listen to the morning news before singing along with Johnny Cash. And he despaired that Carl would be alone. Chosen could barely stem his tears, and struggled to turn full attention to this German boy who held Brenda's gift hostage in his backpack.

Thieves

The backpack skidded along the floor next to the boy as the line advanced toward the ticket counter. In the manner of practiced travelers (and maybe a tad careless, though the boy was not accustomed to petty larceny), Dieter pushed the pack with his foot as he moved ahead, muttering in German about the absurdity of no student fares. All the while, the pack was closely eyed by a couple of thieves who worked public gathering spots for their daily bread.

Theirs was an old trick, and any unattended luggage was prey: create a disturbance nearby, grab the bag, and be out the door in a snap. The patch on the pack flap a dead giveaway *(Deutschland),* it could hold nice surprises, for certain the guarantee of a good camera. Chosen's discernment went on high alert. He watched the men. Dieter advanced again—*Simon says take two giant steps*—just as one of the men "spilled" coffee on the man in the front of the line. The small commotion a perfect accomplice, the other man grabbed Dieter's pack with a clean yank and took off at a lope. Odd, really, that he would trip over his own feet and splatter across the highly polished marble floor in a sprawling swan dive.

"Halt!" yelled Dieter, who caught up with his pack as the thief ran. A few Samaritans gathered around the shaken boy and ushered him back in line. "Mean Joe Green"—having spent entirely too much time watching football with Carl—sported a smile as wide as his wingspan.

The Train to Portland

The Empire Builder sliced through the moonlit darkness that settled over Minnesota. Dieter roamed the aisles until he found a vacant double seat at the front of one car. This would give him legroom and the chance to sprawl on top of his pack, which was now under careful watch on the seat beside him. A veteran of rail travel, he was asleep in no time. Chosen stood next to Dieter and studied him, contrite over his lackluster interest in this charge. It was one thing to work in tandem with Carl and cry to the Holy One for the soul of this unsuspecting boy; it was one thing to become so accustomed to a roly-poly trucker nicknamed Teddy Bear that you forgot your assignment and thought of yourself as part of a team; it was one thing to grow complacent and comfortable with the routine of an over-the-road trucker and his mom. But to be on a train with this stranger so suddenly . . . so abruptly. At least with the others there was some warning, some notice, some feeling or sense that their time was coming to an end. But this. Ripped away. And now this sleeping lad, overshadowed by a humbled linebacker angel, unawares.

Train sound mesmerized passengers, dulled their senses, cradled them in a steady *clip, clip, clip* against the iron ribbon. Soon every overhead light was off as eyelids closed and heads cuddled into crevices between seat backs or nodded forward in final surrender to the night. Farther west, the train slid unnoticed over the vast North Dakota countryside, the sound of its wheels conjoined by snores and the occasional cry of a baby.

Montana and morning hit at the same time. Here was Big Sky Country. Dieter sat transfixed by endless wheat fields and prairie. The train followed the highline highway through once-in-a-while towns, past countless grain elevators, and pierced the heart of the Sioux Indian Reservation. Dieter concentrated on the view—not so much on perfectly patchworked quilts of just-turned earth or newly emerging winter wheat, or on distant buttes that stood square-jawed and jutting from the earth.

Dieter, rather, watched with all of his might when the train slowed for each stop: Wolf Point, Glasgow, Havre, Shelby, or when it flew fast past homes on the prairie. He was startled by the bleakness that looked back: rusted cars left behind homes like yesterday's trash; old tires piled atop trailers to hold the roof against mighty winds charging willy-nilly across unlimited, uninterrupted space . . . holding down the fort. He saw endless barbed-wire fence, adorned with paper boxes, newsprint, rags, all caught in the grip of the wind and flung against each barb, caught like a floppy fish on a string, left to wave hello as the Empire Builder sped by. A startling contrast to the immaculate hamlets and burgs of Germany, where time allied itself with progress in a gentlemen's agreement of sorts, Dieter stared at the hardscrabble existence carved by pioneers on a barren, dryland patch of earth called Eastern Montana. Dieter desperately searched for Indians, staring with intensity and purpose through the train windows. All he saw were people in trucks. People in pickups muddy with gumbo; in pickups dusty from sand that scraped away paint like steel wool; in pickups with missing tailgates, skinny dogs in the back; people with wind-tempered faces clustered four to a bunch as they paced the train in their GMC.

Boy

Backpack in tow, Dieter twisted his way up the aisle, rocking with the clip of the rails, and passed over a bridge that linked car to car. Into the dining car, he evoked the ire of stewards as he and pack filled one side of a booth. Onward to the observation car, he sat in a swivel chair and faced the outside world. Here he nibbled on his last hard-boiled egg, one marked "Aunt Lil," and sipped a Coke. Here he finally reached for the skinny book of Psalms. And here Chosen's heart picked up an extra beat. Knowing this boy's mind was closed to things spiritual, Chosen prayed especially hard—for without the illumination of God the Holy Spirit, he would be merely reading words. Chosen sighed. Just words. Dieter read the book with methodical examination, not a bit different from his hostile professors. Page after page, the German boy scanned each psalm with chilling precision, as if on a quest. A

quest, but not—by no means!—for the Holy Grail. No emotion. No illumination. Just words. Dieter split his time between examining Brenda's gift and
watching the distant Rocky Mountains inch into place.

It was four o'clock in the afternoon when the train pulled out of
Browning, smack in the middle of the Blackfeet Indian Reservation, yet too
far from the inside stuff of town for Dieter to see. It was a town ravaged by
weather, by geography, by white man's insistence on compliance to white
man's standards . . . and by alcoholism. Had he seen the belly of Browning,
Dieter would have been shocked, for there the faces stared back in hopelessness. Dieter would have seen a forsaken people. He would have seen his
Indians.

The call of the emerging mountains magnetic, he let the book lay open
on his lap. The winds between Browning and East Glacier pushed against the
side of the train in sudden bursts, letting out deep breaths in pattern, the
heaving, lumpy foothills like so many pregnant bumps. Dieter Stahlberg was
about to enter fairyland, a place so majestic that the contrast between it and
the desolate prairie was too much for the human soul to comprehend . . . too
glaring. Glacier National Park boomed into the heavens. Still smothered with
snow, the peaks exploded into a big sky, the end-of-day sun oozing into
cracks between them, looking blood-red-orange-yellow. Up and up the train
inched, toward sturdy avalanche sheds, toward a geography that shut off air to
lungs and reduced one to primal senses that were ultimately worthless, no
match for the enormous display of sights, sounds, and color.

Dieter sat entranced, his spell broken by a lurch in the train that spilled
the book onto the floor. Mid-retrieval, he came nose to nose with the pointy
tips of cowboy boots. Cowboy boots! Dieter's heart jumped. He was going
to meet a cowboy! Upward coursed his gaze, up past faded dungarees, to the
purple-and-white braided cord of a belt, to the pearl snaps of a wild print
shirt, to the chin that looked like a prairie butte . . . to the black braids.
Magnificent in build, the huge man flashed friendly eyes and pushed at the
brim of his misshapen Stetson. Dieter had found his Indian.

"I see you're reading the Good Book," said the red man.

"Vat is Good Book?" asked Dieter, betraying his roots. Friendly eyes
penetrated the boy.

"Mind if I join you?"

"Bitte. Nein. I mean no . . . please . . . sit." He could not take his eyes off the braids. A hand shot out.

"My name's Boy."

Dieter stammered, his mind turning gears and wheels. He extended his hand. "Boy?" *Zis vas zuh name? Junge?* "Dieter," he said, with a bit of misgiving when the perfectly formed man grasped his hand in a vise. Completely rattled, he continued, "Dieter Stahlberg."

"Boy Walks-At-Night," came the utterly confusing response, as Boy settled himself in a swivel chair next to Dieter with a polite thud. The angel with the man stayed by his side.

Chosen was thrilled to see Shoham, and the angels acknowledged each other with a show of affection. *"This one lives amid great darkness. He requires special protection. He preaches the gospel fearlessly. There is much demonic oppression here. I am his guard,"* announced Shoham-el.

Chosen and Shoham rejoiced in each other's company. How excellent to be with another as you, one who spoke the same language of praise and prayer, one in perfect harmony with your very existence. Shoham knew of Chosen's mission. *"Boy is fulfilling the Master's perfect will right now. Dieter is greatly loved."* Chosen nodded relief and joy to learn that the Word would not, indeed, return void.

"This is Glacier National Park. They call it the Crown Jewel of America. It must remind you of your mountains at home. They big as this?" There was an odd, sing-song inflection to the Indian's voice.

Dieter pried open his throat. *"Ja,"* was all he could muster. The boots, the braids, the skin . . .

The Empire Builder chugged deeper into the massive mountains, past forests of poker-straight lodgepole pines, packed hundreds to a bunch and clinging to the sides of the track, skyscraper high.

"My ancestors hunted these lands. Can't hunt now in a national park. You hunt?"

"Nein."

"Look close now, might see a grizzly. Had a grain spill near here last summer, and it caused quite a stir. Those grizzlies will be leaving their dens about now." He whooped. "Doggone if there isn't one with a cub! Lookit, Detour!" Boy became animated. As did the entire train.

Excited passengers pasted themselves against the windows for a closer look, as a hint of evening fell softly over the golden bears and the postcard-perfect mountains. Dieter was euphoric: an Indian and a grizzly bear—the stuff of myth!

Myth.

Needless to say, Chosen found the sow and cub irresistible and raced to them in a split-second dash. The cub grunted like a pig; the sow wheeled in the direction of the angel, confused. She calmed and continued rooting for corn while an animal-loving angel and a grizzly cub tumbled in the snow—to the delight of every lucky traveler on a train that crept and climbed, climbed, reaching ever higher toward the Continental Divide. Energized by his romp, Chosen returned to his charge, to conversation that had just begun, and to a disapproving scowl from Shoham-el.

"I am go to Portland, Oregoan."

"Got relatives there?"

Dieter blushed. "Nein, I going dere to see someone."

"Pretty poor time of year to be visiting America, especially up north. Won't really get pretty for a couple months when it warms up."

Easter is a time of reconciliation, Dee-*eh-tuhr.*

"I am going to California after."

Boy nodded.

"You know the Lord?" asked Boy.

Never having met him, Dieter shook his head. "Nein."

Boy bent over and picked the book from Dieter's lap. "Then why you reading Psalms?"

"I am having purpose." His reply was curt, but Boy Walks-At-Night wasn't fazed.

"My favorite is Psalm 50. You ought to read it someday."

Dieter was too busy trying to translate this man's name into his native tongue: *Junge Geht-bei-Nacht.* It was all too strange for him.

"Bible is myt," said Dieter, confidently, still fascinated by the luminous braids that hung on the sides of Boy's long, chiseled face.

"Now who in the Sam's Adam told you that? You're not one of those liberals, are you? Listen, Detour, the Bible ain't myth. You can go to the bank on that. Jesus Christ is real. He's alive!" (Now he sounded like Molly.)

"You believe in Bible . . . Boy?"

"You better believe I do. I'm a warrior for Christ. On my way to Spokane right now to go to a powwow. Jesus is the Way, the Truth, and the Life. He is my blood brother." He whooped. Dieter wished he wouldn't whoop. "You read that psalm, Detour. I'm gonna pray for you now so the Lord will pour out His grace on you and you will know the truth."

The boy recoiled in alarm as the big Indian clamped onto his hands and thundered his prayer—in the hearing of others on the darkening train, and in the company of two angels who joined their voices in a spectacular chant of praise.

"Heavenly Father, Great Chief, You got the disciples ready for the coming of the Great Spirit through Your son Jesus Christ: Make Detour's heart and mind trustworthy to receive the blessing of the Great Spirit, that he is filled up with the strength of the presence of the Great Spirit through Your son and our blood brother Jesus. Amen."

"Now, you read that psalm I told you about, Detour. And you let Jesus into your life." He gave a war whoop and walked out of the observation car. The angels embraced farewell, glad to have found each other, if only for a short time on a train headed west. Dieter sat in the quiet after the reverberations of Boy's whoop diminished, after it had echoed off every bone in the boy's head, after it settled like dust on every open surface. Molly, Carl, Boy Walks-At-Night: they were all gaining on him. In a fit of defiance, he shoved Brenda's gift into his pack and headed for the passenger car. People were queuing around exit stairs as the quaint ski town of Whitefish lay ahead. Soon the last big batch of Easter travelers would disembark, leaving a copious selection of seats for a student whose confidence in the trustworthiness of his teachers was beginning to weaken; his heart pinched and his armor shuddered.

Returning to the spot he'd manned the night before, Dieter did not sleep. His overhead light would burn late into the night as he continued his study of the book, returning often to Psalm 50.

The mighty God, even the Lord, hath spoken, and called the earth from the rising of the sun unto the going down thereof . . . Now consider this, ye that forget God, lest I tear you in pieces, and there be none to deliver. Whoso offereth praise glorifieth me; and to him that ordereth his conversation aright will I shew the salvation of God.

In Spokane the train split asunder as it uncoupled and coupled up again, jarring sleepy passengers. Seattle or Portland: better be on the right half. Chosen thought of Carl with each bump.

Dieter took a pencil from his pack. Chosen watched as he wrote above Psalm 13 with scrupulous accuracy, his countenance unchanging and clinical as he sat under the beam of a tiny light in the middle of the night.

Wie lange wirst Du mich vergessen, himmlischer Vater? Fur immer? Wie lange wirst Du Dein Antlitz vor
  mir verbergen?

How long wilt thou forget me, O LORD? For ever? How long wilt thou hide thy face from me?

Wie lange muss ich meine eigene Seele beraten? Muss ich dieses Leid in meinem Herzen taeglich ertragen? Wie lange soll mein Feind ueber mich herrschen?

How long shall I take counsel in my soul, having sorrow in my heart daily? How long shall mine enemy be exalted over me?

Erhoere mich, oh mein lieber Gott, oeffne meine Augen, aus Furcht vor dem Schlaf der Toten.

Consider and hear me, O LORD my God; lighten mine eyes, lest I sleep the sleep of death;

Sonst werden meine Gegner und diejenigen, die mich unterdruecken wollen, jubilieren, wenn ich meinen
  Willen, Dir zu folgen, verliere.

lest mine enemy say, I have prevailed against him; and those that trouble me rejoice when I am moved.

Aber ich Vertraue auf Deine Gnade und mein Herz wird durch Deine Erloesung jubilieren.

But I have trusted in thy mercy; my heart shall rejoice in thy salvation.

Mein Lob und Herz gehoert nur zu Dir, weil Du mir andauernd Deine bodenlose Gnade und Muehe
  bewiesen hast.

I will sing unto the LORD, because he hath dealt bountifully with me.

Portland

At ten o'clock the next morning the boy stepped from the train and into sopping cold rain. Wrapped in an army-green poncho, he had the appearance of a hunchback as he and his pack explored urban Portland and hunted for shelter. A coffee shop, emptied from its early morning rush of stockbrokers and merchants and assorted downtown workers, would do nicely. Dieter commandeered a table for four, giving his pack a prominent seat. Chosen sat with the boy, who downed strong coffee and devoured a blueberry muffin. Placing his knife and fork neatly on the empty plate, Dieter pulled the folded paper from his pant pocket and approached a bearded man.

"Bitte, can you tell me where is das?"

The man peeked around his morning news and took the creased paper in hand: 525 Ballard Street.

"Ballard is way over on the west end."

"I am seeking to find Elsa Hofmeier."

"Portland's a big town," laughed the man, beard hairs poking his lips when they moved. The foreigner needed his help, by golly, and he would do his best. "Nick, you got a phone book back there?"

Chosen leaned alongside the man and the boy as a finger ran down "H" in the directory. "Hoffman, Hoffbruner, Hofmeister . . . no Hofmeier." Concern flashed across Dieter's face. He'd come so far. She had to be here. "I will go to Ballard Street; does bus going dere?"

A quick meeting convened, assembling everyone in the coffee shop, and the decision was unanimous: not any longer. The boy ran his hand through his hair, sweeping it off his high forehead, exposing strong, chiseled, Germanic features. "Where can I be renting bicycle?"

The man in the beard chuckled. "Tell you what, I'll drive you over there. Got nothing else to do."

"Bitte, tank you."

The boy, the angel, the backpack, and the man headed across wet pavement to a parking lot where their chariot awaited: a gold Chevy Impala in dire need of a muffler. "Got an appointment to get that fixed next week," yelled the man above the VROOM as they shoved off in a spine-wrenching jolt.

Dieter was surprised by the greenness of the grass. Benefiting from Pacific weather patterns and lots of drizzle, Portland had the greenest grass he'd yet seen, garnished with colorful clusters of primrose and reckless riots of daffodils, tulips, and hyacinth. It warmed him to see—and to be part of— such an aggressive show of spring. Chosen was touched, too, by the new birth as misty rain hovered like a canopy in the air, so like in the beginning . . .

"What's the address?"

The young German pronounced each numeral precisely: five-two-five-one-half.

"There it is," said the bearded man.

The boy's heart began to pound, *thump, thump, thump,* nearly visible— nearly audible!—through his sweater and vest. Worry etched across his brow, his eyes seemed to be thinking from someplace inside his head: he was lost to his thoughts, to the moment, to his fear.

"You all right?" asked the man.

Dieter steeled himself. Yes. He was all right. He would be fine. He grabbed his pack. "Danke, tank you," he said as he backed out of the car and listened to it vroom away, the bearded man checking his rearview mirror to watch the foreigner with a mission.

Dieter took a deep breath, stood tall, and began his walk across the street. And as it is when facing down fear, time shuffled backwards. Somewhere nearby, two dogs battled with backyard bark, overhead an airplane cursed the sky, and on the street, traffic sprayed water against the sides of parked cars. A tired duplex sat heavily in the mist, one walk blocked by a child's Big Wheel, the other by assorted toys. Dieter walked to the door on the right, blue trim still bright against a blistered and peeling beige background. The name "Foster" was scotch-taped above a buzzer. Dieter looked at the creased paper one more time: 525 Ballard Street. He pushed his index finger against the buzzer. No sound. This was not making it easy. He knocked. Fully engaged in this mystery, the angel eagerly watched the blistered door.

A little girl stood shyly in the crease of the door, one hand on its big, high doorknob. Dressed in bib overalls and a Sesame Street sweatshirt, her thin hair flopped onto her face. A woman carrying a baby and heavy with child stood behind the girl, protectively pulling her back when she saw the stranger. Chosen was ecstatic to see the child, who sensed his presence and smiled coyly in his direction. *Verily I say unto you, Whosoever shall not receive the kingdom of God as a little child, he shall not enter therein.*

How the Master loved children! Bashar-el harkened to a sunny afternoon when Peter's son had crawled onto Jesus' lap. The child had put his tiny fingers into the Lord's mouth. Eyes sparkling with the glitter of the cosmos, Jesus had clamped His lips on the toddler's hand and spit it out with a Poof!, the child's guffaw infecting the most intense and somber followers. Poof! And Jesus had laughed. Poof! The child had gazed into the Rabbi's eyes with expectation and trust. Poof!

"Can I help you?" asked the young mother, her foot positioned as a wedge against the door.

"I am looking for Elsa Hofmeier," announced Dieter.

The woman shook her head. "No one here by that name."

The boy showed her the creased paper. She shook her head no. Rain began to intensify; Dieter pushed his body close to the building. The woman backed up, pulling her little girl with her.

"Bitte. Please helping me to find her." He couldn't stop now, not after all of this effort, after all of this planning. He was not coming this far for nothing.

Easter is a time of reconciliation, Dieter.

"Just a minute," said the woman, who hoisted the baby further on her hip and shut the door. Dieter stood in the rain, too late for a poncho of any color.

The next door opened. "Mister!" came the call.

Dieter turned and saw an older woman. She motioned with her hand and he advanced, walking through wet grass that squished like sponge with every step. The plastic sign above her buzzer said "O'Meara." *Where was Hofmeier?*

"Who are you looking for?"

"I am looking for Elsa Hofmeier, please."

This woman shook her head, too, more in thought than rejection. "Someone named Meier used to live next door. I think her name was Elsie. Elsie Meier. Gone now for, oh, I'd say five years. I think she went to the County Home. Can't say for sure. Might have passed on by now."

"Bitte . . . please . . . telling me what you mean 'County Home?'"

Satisfied the boy would not do her harm, the woman invited him in. He stood on a small brown rug just inside her door, his pack a puddle next to him.

"The County Home is where you go when you are too old to take care of yourself and you don't have money to go to a nursing home. You go there to die." Panic flashed across Dieter's face.

"Das is true? To die?"

"Well, you can be sick for a long time before you die. Would you like a towel?"

"Nein. Where is County Home?"

The Encounter

Still full from winter, the Columbia River raced the cab to an old, three-story, brick building. The big building's many windows were covered with dripping iron bars. Honeybee eyes. Shredded wheat. Cages. The building reminded Dieter of the factories of Bonn. Itself too poor to pay for the company of newer, stronger buildings, this one stood alone, a human dump for unwanted people. *Dump closes at 7 P.M.; it is against the law to discard human waste.*

Boy, pack, and angel emerged from the cab in that order. Rain was heavy now, each drop hitting the cement like a pneumatic drill. Dieter raced to the door and squeezed inside.

It was the smell that first assaulted him. And then the sounds. Chosen was immobilized.

The county had done its best: limited staff, decaying building—and dozens of people too poor to be sick, too poor to be alone, too poor to be mentally ill, too poor to be dying. Custodians systematically swept through the building with their chemical arsenal, each one designed to mask the odor of human decay. In spite of their efforts, the smell of urine hung in the air like hazy rain and smote the eyes of the young German student. Two men in pajamas roamed the floor talking to imaginary people. One man fought a foe, the other repeated a mantra: *Silly putty on my face.* Chosen's gut twisted into a knot: *Beethoven with a burr.*

Dieter pushed wet hair from his eyes; hair flat against his head now, he looked like an Angora goat. He approached a tall counter and waited. Screams, cries, calls, whistles, music, yells, and the pneumatic drill of outside rain combined in maddening symphony. A nurse appeared.

"Bitte, please . . ." said Dieter. "I am coming to see Elsa Hofmeier."

Too busy to deal with the drippy boy in her path, she directed Dieter to the administrative wing. The angel followed, hating the Fall, hating the misery, hating the depravity.

"I am coming to see Elsa Hofmeier," announced Dieter, impatient and worried. *She can't be dead. Bitte, bitte Gott . . .*

The nameplate said B. Orzo. B. Orzo turned out to be a cheerful, pleasant advocate with a servant's heart. She checked her files, first offering Dieter a few paper towels and handing him a cup of coffee-flavored muck. No luck.

She checked the dead files. *Please, please it cannot be, not after all of this.* No luck again.

"Bitte . . . please to try Elsie . . . Meier."

"Elsie!" B. Orzo became animated. "You want to see Elsie?!" Others in the office looked at the boy; this was a surprise.

"Elsie isn't doing too well," said another woman.

"Bitte . . . Bitte, I must be seeing her." Dieter became agitated.

Bobbie Orzo recognized the urgency of the boy's plea and left her desk to escort him to Elsie herself. "It's OK. Your pack will be safe here." He trusted her.

Back through the main entrance they went, up the elevator, down a hall. Dieter breathed deeper with each step. Step. Step. Step. Courage. *Tapferkeit.* For two entire years he had planned for this moment, finally submitting to the demanding voice inside of him, a voice demanding . . . reconciliation.

Tell me Dee-eh-tuhr, *just exactly* where *do you think this lofty idea of yours came from, thin air?* First cause, *Dieter, first cause! Goodness and love and kindness do not come out of some primeval swamp!* Molly had wagged her finger.

Chosen glanced through doors into wards where women lay all in a row, waiting, lying and waiting. Lying in wait. He heard their cries, felt their extreme loneliness, smelled death.

"Elsie has her own room, thanks to her savings. Here it is." B. Orzo stood next to a door and motioned to the boy. After all of these years Elsie Meier was receiving her first visitor—now, when she was dying. The administrator would leave the boy and the old woman alone, standing close enough to listen—in case she was needed, of course.

Chosen was first in the room. A bed, a steel stand that swung across the bed . . . a table of sorts . . . no covering on the north-facing window, a chart, a sink. No chair. No color. Just the faded peach tint of the blanket and the paper-white hair that lay on a pillow too high for the dying. One of the woman's arms lay on top of the bedcovers, blue-black veins protruding like mountain ridges in Montana. Chosen saw the tattoo sticking out from under her sleeve and gasped. Now he understood everything.

"Frau Hofmeier, bitte darf ich mit Ihnen sprechen?" Dieter barely whispered.

Once again. *"Frau Hofmeier, ich komme aus Kirchheim."* She kept her eyes on the ceiling. Was she dead? Had he come so far to find her dead?

"Frau Hofmeier!" he pleaded. She turned her head and stared at him through clouded eyes, lashes and eyebrows long gone. Just eyes.

"Ich bin Dieter Stahlberg." Did her eyes change? Did the angel see . . . hatred?

"Don't speak German to me!" she yelled. Where did Elsie get the energy for this outburst? The staff had not heard an outburst from her for weeks.

"I am zuh grandson of Marta; I have traveled to America to ask you . . ."

"Get out of here!" she shrieked, pointing her finger toward the door, her sleeve pulled back completely now: 97437.

"Please, please let me talk wit you." He hadn't expected this. It was not part of his plan. She was supposed to be gracious. It had been a long time since the war. Why wasn't she reasonable?

"Get out!" she hissed. "Get out!" Her yelling caused commotion in the ward down the hall.

Bobbie Orzo took Dieter by the arm and pulled him away. Chosen understood. He was numb with understanding, and although he himself hadn't been there, he knew everything: the torture, the conditions, the human wreckage, the unthinkable horrors, the separation from family. He approached the trembling woman and caressed her brow. She was unresponsive, her heart hardened to flint long ago.

"What did you say to her?" asked the kind woman.

"I did not say it yet," said Dieter plaintively. "I must go back."

"I'm sorry; maybe tomorrow."

A Second Try

Dieter pitched his small tent in the back of the building under a tin overhang. He sat looking at the waterfall of droplets falling to the gravel ground, forlorn but unshaken in determination: he was not leaving. Not yet.

The staff abuzz over Elsie's visitor, Bobbie ordered that the boy be left alone and brought him a tray of food. "It's not much, but it's warm. The night staff will let you use the bathroom, just enter through this side door." She paused. "Are you going to be OK?" Cracks were sprouting everywhere in Dieter's armor. He nodded yes, meaning no. *No!* It wasn't supposed to happen this way! *No!* He should be tramping his way to California right now! *No!* He promised his dying grandmother that he would try. Forgiveness should come easy. It was Easter time, wasn't it? Wasn't it as simple as that?! No.

That is why the Cross, Dieter, said the sympathetic angel. *Man by himself is not capable of forgiving such horrors; man could never pay a high enough ransom or retribution. That is why He paid the price Himself.*

That night, when Dieter closed his eyes to sleep, he had his first conversation with God.

The next morning, his pack safe in the administration office, Dieter traced his way through smells and sounds to a third floor room—the one without a chair. The woman—if this was possible—seemed more frail, making his visit more urgent.

"Elsie," the boy went straight to the point, "I have come asking forgiveness." The woman didn't blink.

"My grandmutter Marta call Gestapo on you, Elsie. Bitte . . . please . . . I am coming all dis way to saying sorry. So, so sorry," he choked. There were tears in his eyes. And in Chosen's.

Elsie continued her forced stare at the ceiling. He was taking her someplace she did not want to go. *One-fourth Jewish blood! One-fourth! "You will come with us."* The beating with the stick when she resisted. Betrayal by her friend next door. Torn from her husband. The loss of her sons! Killed when they were his age, the age of this boy standing in her room in America. America! Land of the free. No. Land of the tormented. Land of the wicked nightmares and appalling memories.

"Please, I have gift for you. It is part of zuh Bible. I have written in German over a prayer to God. It is called psalm."

Elsie spoke. Her voice was thin and bitter. "I stopped talking to God long ago. *Lass mich in Ruhe!*"

"Bitte, Frau Hofmeier . . ." She shot him a wicked glance. "Please . . . Frau Meier, I am asking forgiveness."

"I will never forgive! Get out of here!"

Chosen ached. He ached for the pain buried in this woman's heart; he ached for the rejection filling Dieter's. He prayed fervently for a break in this impasse, for a crack in Elsie's armor. She looked back at the ceiling, now a movie screen for long ago atrocities that plagued her every waking moment. Instant replay. She turned her head and looked out curtainless windows covered with bars.

Tears gathering in the corners of his mouth, Dieter placed Brenda's gift on the steel table that swung back and forth over Elsie's bed, then turned and left.

Chapter
Nine

April 1973, continued

Chosen stood by the window and looked toward the sky, filled with awe at the far-reaching justice and mercy of God. How remarkable that he, even he, an angel who sees more clearly, a being who has danced in the presence of the Holy of Holies, a ministering spirit who could vouch firsthand for the profound depth of agape love, even he could shake his head and flutter his wings at the hugeness of God. The angel could detect a touch of sun breaking through a crack in the clouds. Sort of like a crack in armor. Elsie was dead. Her body carted off a while ago, aides now stripped the bedding off a mattress thick with plastic.

With the swift movements of those who follow the wake of the dead, two aides chatted as they threw sheets and blankets and rubber pads onto a pile. They talked about their children's latest escapades as they collected Elsie's few possessions like so much leftover litter, and they gossiped about other staff as they contemplated what to do with the skinny little book.

Chosen turned and stared at the two women: would it be one of them? Would his next charge be an aide who worked in the County Home to help make ends meet? An aide who bathed and fed the infirmed and indigent and stripped the bedding of worn-out human beings? If it was to be with one of these women, Chosen hoped his time with her would be longer than three hours.

Elsie's Death

The angel's time with Elsie had been just that: three hours, which Chosen spent on his knees; three hours spent in such impassioned intercessory prayer that had he been human, he would have been soaked in sweat. Face cupped in his hands, the angel had pleaded with the farthest reaches of infinite, eternal heaven in a desperate cry for the justice and mercy of God. He had prayed for the woman's immersion in grace and peace. He had prayed for a crack—a hairline sliver—in the crust surrounding her soul. He had prayed for healing of her memories. He had prayed for her forgiveness of a woman named Marta and of a saddened boy who was now halfheartedly tramping his way to California.

Judge nothing before the time, until the Lord come, who both will bring to light the hidden things of darkness, and will make manifest the counsels of the hearts.

The Lord of all the earth knows the intent of the heart. The Shepherd of Israel knows the brokenness and pain, the wretched, wretched pain. How inconceivable the hugeness of the triune God, how vast and incredible for even him, the lowest of the angels.

The message of her memories horribly sketched across the ceiling, Elsie had turned away and stared out the window for a long time after Dieter left. She had lain looking—and thinking—red-rimmed, lashless eyes already glazed with death, her tongue coated with the taste of finality—*they gave Him vinegar to drink mixed with gall and when he had tasted thereof, he would not drink*— her breathing erratic. The power of the angel's supplication had been too great for the frail woman to fight.

The woman had reached into her empty body and groped, feeling for fumes, for droplets of energy evaporating fast in the fever pitch of death, and with supernatural assistance, an arm marked 97437 had struggled toward the metal stand.

Try hard now; you're in a race with the end. Reach, reach, you've survived this long, you can do this; a few more inches; don't give them the final victory. Don't give them your soul. What have you been thinking all these years? You've let them win! You learned the message of the Cross long ago. You must forgive. Defeat them! Go home with your dying breath. Reach. There.

Her limp hand on top the book, fingers barely curled over its hard edge, over the cover declaring *A Resting Place,* and sustained by the prayers of a compassionate being, Elsie Hofmeier had found strength to utter—in German—"Ruhe." I am at peace. It was finished. And the scowling woman who had thrown tantrums and who had had no friends was found with a hint of a smile, her eyes fixed peacefully at the ceiling.

Stay Put

One of the aides studied the book, read Buck's postcards, and began a lengthy complaint about the damp, rainy Northwest, when someplace like Tallahassee might be a lot more hospitable, never mind those hurricanes. The book was summarily tossed onto the cleaning cart and wheeled away. Chosen had no choice but to follow. The answer to his inquiry about the future was concise: *stay put.* And so it was that when Brenda's gift was placed on a book-shelf in the rec room, Chosen became angel-in-residence at the home for the aged and infirm in Multnomah County, Oregon. The next five years would become one of his most treasured and cherished sojourns on earth.

Chosen had been to earth many times before, and along with the other angels had been there when it was uttered forth. *Let there be:* the heaven and the earth, the firmament and the waters, light and night, a division in the day, sun, moon and stars, plants . . . and animals. He had been thrilled with each new animal: the sleek seal, the furry bear, the fuzzy bee. He had soared with eagles and ravens and doves, sang with canaries, and flapped with humming-birds. He had butted heads with billy goats and wrestled with orangutans. He had ridden on the backs of elephants and camels and ponies. He had delighted as one by one the animals had come to the first man, following a command, an instinct that could not be ignored. One by one, Adam had assigned a name. Adam! Eve! How perfect they had been in form. Wise, strong, able, kind: God's greatest creation. *So God created man in his own image, in the image of God created he him; male and female created he them. And God blessed them* . . . How dark and filled with misery was the Fall. . . . *The whole creation groaneth and travaileth in pain together until now.* The horrible change in the animals: eyes suddenly filled with fright, with chase and kill. Oh Lucifer, bright shining one, what havoc you have brought on the world. How your wisdom and beauty has turned to treachery! Oh man, Adam, Adam, if only you had obeyed.

The Home

The staff at the County Home was committed to serve its residents and went to extraordinary means to treat every person with dignity. The one exception was a janitor named Roberto. His cruel comments and behavior toward patients and other staff came to the attention of Bobbie Orzo more than once, and more than once she took him to task.

"Roberto," said the kind woman with the command of a staff sergeant, for that is basically what she was in her role as operations manager, "we must try to respect the people who are here." Roberto respected no one. Bobbie tried everything to change his attitude: happy-face posters where the janitors met for coffee—the long, cluttered table near the boiler; a reward program for anyone demonstrating a cheery and willing spirit; outright insistence that Roberto become more agreeable. Nothing worked. A real dilemma, since Roberto's work was flawless. He was punctual, efficient, and hardworking. He just seemed to hate people.

Chosen zeroed in on Roberto instantly, as if internal antennae brought him to the man. There was a thorn in Roberto's flesh, that was for sure. The angel interceded continuously for him, heaping prayer upon prayer, adding to his already substantial prayer list. Such were the intercessory demands in a county nursing home.

It was at the County Home that Chosen deepened his bonds of sympathy and service. It was there that the ministering angel flew from bedsides to wheelchairs, bringing light and hope and a certain . . . joy . . . to the countenance of those within the caged walls. He helped steady shaking hands as they ferried spoons toward open mouths; he caught bodies as they tumbled off knees no longer willing to bear them; he massaged feet turned black, pushing blood . . . pumping, pumping . . . back into tired veins; he brought courage to those who faced the last enemy; he sang to the broken hearts of those who were alone; he comforted the cries of agony. And he took the hands of wandering men in pajamas, to pass unto them all of the love of heaven. He was nurse, doctor, orderly, psychologist, minister, performer, janitor, and comforter to all, and he praised the Great Comforter for blessing him with this duty. All the while Brenda's gift stood on a shelf in the rec room, stuck between a Zane Grey western and *The Collected Poems of Robert Frost.*

The big angel especially enjoyed visits from outsiders. One particular weekly visitor caused real delight, for she never came empty-handed . . . and usually brought her dogs. Olivia was one of those dear ones with a heart for the poor in spirit, for those that mourn, for the meek. She was a woman filled with amazing grace: *amazing* because Olivia reminded him of Buck in her vivacity, *grace* because she literally left a trail. If Olivia shook your hand (her hand a metronome gone wild), she would leave grace on your palm. When she hugged, you were splattered with grace. It seemed that even Roberto could not resist the magnetic pull of her charm, since he managed to work nearby when Olivia came to visit. Closer scrutiny revealed a cold, hard stare.

Bud

It was Eastertime again, a full year since he'd followed Dieter through the rain, when Chosen saw Olivia standing near Bobbie's desk. Busy with Mr. Silly-Putty-on-my-face, Chosen looked over his shoulder as he led the man toward his room. His eyes scanned the floor near Olivia, expecting to see Jill and Drake, her jet-black Labs who so loved the people in the home. No dogs were in sight. Though disappointed, Chosen hurried with his task so he could join Olivia in the rec room. He was in for a special treat. And so was Bud.

Bud was a woodsman who had spent his life in the dense forests of the Northwest. Bud was forester, conservationist, and outdoorsman personified. Brutalized by a massive stoke, the strong, independent man sat motionless in his wheelchair. Shoulders that had once carried logs now sagged, arms that had once hoisted orphaned fawns now withered, eyes that had once gazed with satisfaction at a backyard filled with bird feeders and larch trees now clouded with stress. Trapped in a body that refused to obey a single command—Talk! Smile! Cry! Move! Think!—Bud sat and stared. That is, until the day one Eastertime when Olivia brought a baby lamb to the County Home—and a big animal-loving angel somersaulted with glee.

The symbolism of a lamb at Easter was so great that the angel yelled in praise. *Halleluia! Almighty God, who is and is to come! The Great One of all ages, He is risen! Lamb of God! Lamb of God! Who took upon Himself the sins of the world!* The little animal was scared witless.

Balking and baaing, the immaculate white creature was gently coaxed toward Bud's chair, for Olivia had plotted and planned how to reach Bud. At the moment, however, things were not going as well as planned. The little lamb would not cooperate. In fact, it protested with a few well-placed head-butts and bucks. Frustrated by her situation, Olivia tried to wrap her body around the lamb to quiet it, causing even more terror in the animal, whose cries were beginning to cause a disturbance. Ready to abandon her great strategy and drag the hapless animal back to her car, the lamb suddenly calmed—as if being commanded by an invisible voice.

Chosen sat on the floor next to the frenzied lamb and surrounded it with his wings. One could hardly spend as much time in Galilee as this angel had without lambs being his specialty! To Olivia's relief, the little critter became still, wagged its tail, and offered a melodic "baa" that lit the room with inquiring grins. One by one, bent-over bodies with drooling, open lips giggled through twisted smiles. Olivia sighed. There was no giggle and no smile coming from Bud. *Baa. Baa. Baa.*

Olivia held the lamb in place, alongside Bud's chair. Chosen cupped the lamb's face in his hands and spoke reassurance. A minute ticked by. Then two. Then three. *So much for my plan,* thought Olivia, who was about to tote the lamb away. She looked across the room at Bobbie giving a shrug that said

I tried. Bobbie looked back with amazement. There stood a sweet, gentle lamb, its eyes on the stony face of an old woodsman. Bud's hand rested on its head.

"Thank you, Jesus!" whispered Olivia, as tears gathered in her eyes, tears that matched the ones now coursing down Bud's stony face.

Thank you, Jesus, whispered Chosen, who wiped away tears of his own. Tearless, unmoved, but secretly watching just the same, Roberto turned and left the room.

Olivia

Because of her vivacity, Olivia's visits were unpredictable. "Wild woman," Bobbie had named her, and breathed heavy sighs when she saw the unconventional woman parade down the sidewalk, for Olivia's visits could sometimes be a mixed blessing. She certainly had a heart for the old: a heart of gold. She was just, as some might say . . . half a bubble off of plumb. False teeth slipped out of place, walkers tipped over, and wheelchairs careened down bumpy sidewalks when Olivia was behind the helm. She breathed life into the dull, monotonous building—and sometimes exhausted the poor souls within.

"Come on, everybody! Let's dance!" came her joyful call one summer's day, when every wheelchair in the rec room became fair game as Olivia boogied with anything with handles. Dolly Parton warbled on the radio, and Olivia pushed a chair to the tempo. Back and forth and sideways, the occupant jerked with the beat.

"Isn't this fun?!" Questions such as this were declarations when they came from the excited woman.

For some it *was* fun. It was a respite from daily routine, from wondering when they'd boogie to the final beat, when their heart would stop and they would face the place that only the faithful didn't fear. Olivia brought back life, the life they left behind, on the other side of the doors—outside, where they used to be young, where they used to be strong, where they used to matter. And where they, too, danced to Dolly Parton and had their own certain charm.

Bobbie stormed into the room. "Olivia!" She switched off the music. Olivia looked up, her hands still gripping the handlebars of a wheelchair, its resident gasping.

"I think they've had enough exercise for the day," said Bobbie diplomatically. "Maybe you could read a nice, quiet book?"

"Sure!"

To insure against further madness, Bobbie walked to the bookshelf to *find* a nice quiet book. What could be more quiet than *A Resting Place: The Book of Psalms?* Guess again.

"'My God, my God, why hast thou forsaken me?!'" It was a time for high drama. Olivia gave it all she had.

"'Why art thou so far from helping me, and from the words of my roaring?!'" She roared.

"'O my God, I cry in the daytime, but thou hearest not!'" The old folks watched her theatrics in dismay.

"'And in the night season and am not silent!' . . . Do *you* cry at night?" she asked her audience.

Bobbie stormed into the room.

"Time to go, Olivia," she said as politely as she could. "Nap time!" Those who could think and rationalize uttered "Amen," as Olivia and her dogs headed out the door to her car, where she found, not one, but two flat tires.

Vandalism

Had Bobbie Orzo been a less trusting soul, had she been a detective, had she noticed the little things and put them all together, she would have seen an emerging picture: since Roberto came to work, there had been an unusual number of mishaps. Neither Bobbie nor the other staff ever connected the small fire in the kitchen, the unplugged refrigerator, the "accidental" switching of medicines, the wobbly wheelchair wheels, the missing items, the broken windows, and the countless other troubles to a man who just seemed to hate people.

Chosen was wise to Roberto and foiled his mischief and vandalism whenever he could. He was aware of demonic influence and knew that

Roberto's torment increased when an angel and the book of Psalms came to stay at the home. Not that there weren't Bibles there already.

Prayer Warriors

The few Bibles at the County Home came as cherished belongings of some residents and were kept at bedsides as extensions of physical bodies themselves, linking them to the home they would one day claim, one day soon.

There were a few prayer warriors in the home, too, who cried to heaven, not for themselves, but for relatives, for every soul in residence, for the country and President Carter, for the world, for missionaries, and for a janitor named Roberto, whose scowl escaped no one, most especially those who claimed the Lord. Two mighty warriors were Viola and Herb, who commandeered a corner of the rec room each morning, Vi shuffling along in her walker, Herb coming under his own steam with the uneven, rocking gait of the arthritic, pain shooting into his joints like a rocket display on the Fourth of July.

Vi and Herb were quite a pair. Because of them, Chosen tended to his daily rounds with enthusiasm and expediency—through his many years at the Home, the angel developed his own daily delivery system of holy aid for every patient in the building—so he could sit alongside the two crippled bodies as stiff fingers expertly turned to Bible passages. Theirs was not a time for study or discussion or fancy exegesis or even for depth of understanding; Vi and Herb simply read the Word and prayed, the period on their paragraph of prayer a plea for Roberto's salvation. Yet in spite of an angel's intercession and those of two prayer warriors, the scowl and the inexplicable mishaps remained.

And in spite of her bad luck with tires—and locking herself out of her car, and running out of gas in the parking lot, and getting stuck in the snow—Olivia continued to barge her way into the lives of the old folks every week, now assigning herself the designation "Reader in Residence."

Halloween

One day Olivia thought it a great idea to dress herself and her dogs as clowns, load a Tupperware container as big as a flying saucer with candy, and head off to the home. It was Halloween, a happy day for most Americans, a hated day for Chosen. The angel did not understand how a day consecrated to Satan could have such popularity. He was aghast and repelled when he saw little innocents dressed in costumes that honored the devil. This curious celebration of Halloween distressed Chosen to tears.

The angel shook his head at the irony of it all: there in the rec room sat a woman in a clown outfit with a big red rubber nose, reading from Psalm 86. *Forbid him not, for he that is not against us is for us.*

"'Bow down thine ear, O Lord, hear me; for I am poor and needy,'" boomed Olivia, her nose bouncing off the floor when she bowed.

"'Preserve my soul; for I am holy; O thou my God, save thy servant that trusteth in thee.'" She picked up her nose: "Do you trust God?" Most stared back; some smiled; one lady clapped, crooked hands missing each other, waving air. Chosen was deeply moved.

"'Be merciful unto me, O Lord; for I cry out to thee daily.'" Roberto pushed against the mop handle with such force that the metal clamp dug a gash into the tiled floor.

"Crea en Dios, Roberto!" *Trust God.* The mop moved furiously down the hall. *Trust God.* Trust Him to let his foreign-born mother die in his arms for lack of medical attention? Trust Him to convince America to care for her? Trust God to heal her? No! Trust Him to care for these gringos, who pushed his mother away? *I spit on this God!* He knew the psalm well, in Spanish, of course: it was his mother's favorite.

Olivia passed out candy, wished everyone a Happy Halloween, and headed out the door with a smile, dogs in tow. By now Drake had wormed his way out of his ridiculous and humiliating outfit. Jill had partially eaten hers. Happily for Olivia, the car started and headed out the parking lot on four sound tires. Tampering with a car would not be enough this time. A button had been pushed that morning, a missile released from its silo, now speeding recklessly through space, heading toward a target more important than a grass-green Volkswagen beetle.

A Final Act of Hatred

November can best be called dull, and the morning after Halloween highlighted that fact. Some days simply feel ominous, heavy, oppressive, and cold, and that is how the month started: cold. Boilers in the basement did their duty, sending steamy heat throughout the building, suffocating the air with a dense, damp blanket that matched the damp, slate-gray air outside. Practiced old bones read the signs and the season, and the halls were quiet as old bones stayed in bed. Chosen made his rounds. Just about everyone was snug as a bug; his realm seemed fine, yet a sense of doom consumed him. He felt the chill of evil. On alert, he was diverted by the sudden cries of a woman in the ward, dementia bringing her to a frightening place that caused terror and alarm. The angel rushed to comfort her, while on the first floor an aluminum walker slowly advanced down a hall, a worn Bible tucked in a bicycle basket on its front. *Shuffle. Shuffle. Shuffle.* The walker worked its way toward the rec room.

A hand reached between Zane Grey and Robert Frost and pulled a skinny book off the shelf. Delighted to be along for the defilement, the demon urged his patsy to hurry with his work. *This book is a sham. It led your mother to her death. Get even! Get even! This must be destroyed. Get it, Roberto, get it! Destroy! Hurry!*

From somewhere deep in his spirit, Roberto heard the taunts. He felt the urgency of the moment, yet hurried only to find a particular page, glancing over his shoulder lest he be caught. He counted through tight, fierce anger . . .

"Ochenta y cuatro, ochenta y cinco, ochenta y seis. *Ochenta y seis.*"

The black marker attacked the page with all the hatred of hell. Psalm 86 would be no more. Just like his mother. Gone. *Trust God, Roberto!* No. Hate God. Hate the gringos. Hate these people dying here with nurses and doctors and clean sheets and stupid women who come to entertain them. Hate the world. Just hate.

"Roberto!" The feeble voice sounded like his mother.

"Roberto!" she would call when she had a surprise for him. "Roberto!" she would call when she made his favorite meal. "Roberto!" she would call when she was pierced by pain that caused each breath to slice her body with razors, her wheezing, desperate plea . . . "Roberto!"

Bashar! Perception hit the angel like a flash of light, a splash in time. He left the wailing, demented woman in the care of a nurse and shot toward the rec room, radar driven. He got there too late, too late by man's time, too late by angel time, but in the troubling time of God, he was right on time.

Vi stood a few feet from Roberto, braced by her walker, her eyes filled with confusion. Caught in the act, Roberto could not think clearly. The demon urged him on. *Deface! Destroy! Defile!*

The woman called again: "Roberto!"

Would he lose his job? Would they realize he was behind so much mischief and vandalism? Would he be arrested? He had to run. *Stay! Destroy!*

Bolting for the door, he shoved Vi with a supernatural strength, a strength that stunned him, that brought him to a momentary stop, a long enough stop to look into the alarmed eyes of a frail woman as her head slammed against the edge of a metal table, just as a ministering angel appeared in the room. Roberto took off at a gallop, a howling demon hovering over his head, egging him on.

"All things work to the glory of God, Bashar," said Zepha, as he arrived with the escort. *"Roberto has much pain and trouble ahead for him, but his mother's prayers will not go unheeded. Nor will yours or the others'. The Holy One knew this would happen. It grieves Him that the man will suffer much because of sin."* Zepha turned to Vi. *"This blessed woman will be in His arms now, her walker gone for good."*

And as Chosen leaned over Vi's body, he heard the tight, arthritic steps of a prayer warrior coming down the hall.

Vi's death saddened the staff deeply. Her broken neck a result of a fall, they held an emergency meeting to discuss policy, worried that others might meet the same fate. Mention was made of the book defacing, but it was easily attributed to one of the mentally unstable. Already on the run and beginning a life of constant fear, Roberto would never learn that his sudden disappearance from work, including his failure to collect his paycheck, was not connected to the unexpected death of one of the County Home's prayer warriors.

The Home Closes

B. Orzo reached for her nameplate and placed it on top of a box filled with years of clutter that only a desk drawer can accumulate: brittle sticks of gum, ballpoint pens long run dry, humorous greeting cards, notepads, coins, slips of paper and business cards from people long forgotten, rubber bands, and dozens of on-the-loose paper clips. The clutter rested atop a plaque for "Twenty-five Years of Service." A job well done. Done. And now it was over. The County Home was closing. She glanced at her watch and looked toward the main door: the man from the auction company was right on time.

Olivia and her dogs arrived on time, too, her brand-spanking-new, red 1978 Subaru safely parked outside. Ever the volunteer, she wandered the empty corridors one last time, as Drake and Jill sniffed and looked around for the people. The dogs slapped their tails furiously when Chosen joined the farewell tour. They all ended in the rec room, where Olivia helped pack what was left on the shelves. Brenda's gift ended in a box with assorted notions, becoming part of "Lot 24" for auction, which included the rec room TV and three stainless steel industrial pots from the kitchen. Not to mention an angel.

In a slump for months while the transition took place, Chosen was bereft, deeply saddened to lose the dozens of people to whom he'd grown attached. Fully aware that his long tenure at the home was coming to a close, he began again to feel homesick—thoughts of home had been pushed aside for years as the angel-in-residence had busied himself with the care of his dear charges, his prayer crusade virtually consuming all time. And now he would have to wait for a bid on Lot 24 and for a gavel to fall before he knew his next assignment.

September 1978

Plywood signs along the highway announced "Auction Today," and attracted others besides those drawn by public announcement to the inventory dispersal at the County Home. Traffic snaked along the Columbia and turned into the parking lot, Olivia's Subaru a prominent red dot protruding from a sea of dusty trucks. The field alongside the Home became center stage as a flatbed trailer was rigged for sound (this being the late seventies, well-equipped auctioneers came with microphones and loud speakers). Inventory to be auctioned sat off to the side, looking ridiculously out of place in the tall grass and wildflowers: desks, chairs, beds, tools, scales, dishes, and more, much more, waited patiently amid daisies and purple knapweed. A sturdy banquet table had been assembled to register the faithful, who wore their numbered cards like scapulars, an auction on such a clear, sunny day nothing less than a religious experience for believers.

Particular people attend auctions, and they were at the County Home in force. They are the people who listen to *Swap News* on daily radio as if it were an allied report from the front, and scan newspapers and telephone poles for the code word: *sale*. Garage sales, rummage sales, and swap meets send the pulse of every diehard devotee into the stratosphere.

Some people came to bid on specific items: the generator, the paper products, the huge assortment of aluminum storm windows (a blunder that Bobbie would like to forget); some came to examine assorted vehicles; some came to bid on the remote-control color TV from the rec room; and some came because they saw a highway sign as they were driving out of town. That is exactly how Bill Stark ended up at the auction—and in direct contention with Olivia for Lot 24.

Chosen sat atop the auctioneer's truck and studied each person before him. Though some people stood, many sat on webbed chairs they had pulled from the backs of pickups or from the trunks of sedans and hauled onto the field. The ardent angel examined every face. Who would it be? Would it be the heavy man in the stained shirt who tested the motor of a Dodge slant-six? The short man with black beard and toothpick? The middle-aged couple sitting neatly on their lawn chairs, way up front . . . or would it be dear Olivia, standing in a corner talking to Bobbie, Jill and Drake at her side? Who would be his next charge? And what would be his mission—or rather—what would be the ministry of the book? The bidding began.

"Lot #1, we have five ten-pound ABC extinguishers, serviced and pressure tested to code last May. We'll start the bidding at $25. Do I have $25 . . . YUP! $30 . . . YUP! $35 . . . Do I have $40? $40? I can see you're gonna be a tough bunch today . . . $40? Last chance! Sold to #18 for $35." Bill Stark was pleased with himself.

"Lot #2 . . . Lot #3 . . . Lot #4" On it went. Tension built in Olivia as the auctioneer came closer to Lot 24. She could sure use a TV with remote control! She looked toward the inventory and saw a man poke through the two boxes next to the TV, one with books, the other straining to hold four big kitchen pots. It was the same man who had bought the fire extinguishers. This worried her: he was there to buy.

Chosen noticed the man, too, as his eyes returned to Brenda's gift again and again. He sighed. Ready to follow the Lord's lead, the obedient angel looked at the big brick building and rested in the comfortable pleasure of having done his best.

"Lot 24." Chosen jumped to his feet. Olivia maneuvered to the front of the crowd. "We have a Zenith remote-control television set, two years old, four stainless steel pots—them would make a lot of chili—and a box of assorted books and bric-a-brac. Do I have $40?" Several cards shot up. The bidding was competitive. At the $100 mark, the field narrowed to the man with the toothpick, #18, and dear Olivia! Chosen held his breath and rooted for his friend.

"$125, come on, $125, come on, YUP! $130, $130, I have $130, YUP! How about $150 takes the whole Maryanne?" Olivia was whipped. She'd quit bidding at her $125 limit, and it was down to the two men. The man with the toothpick closed his eyes and shook his head. He was out. Bill Stark was in. Bill Stark was it. The angel walked next to the man as he headed toward the banquet table to settle his account.

Bill reached into his shirt pocket and dug behind a plastic pocket protector, behind an arsenal of pens and pencils that were as much a part of his dress as was the round snuff can protruding from his dungaree hip pocket. He pulled out a folded blank check marked "M & S Logging," and asked for a receipt. Once he loaded these goods, he'd be on his way. His pocket watch said 11:30 A.M. He'd be in camp by dark.

Time to Go

Bill's truck would best be described as a tool: it was hands-down the hardest-worked vehicle in the parking lot. The three-quarter ton, four-wheel-drive, Ford six-passenger (nicknamed a "crummy") was equipped with a 150-gallon diesel tank. It held three toolboxes and a pile of steel cables. Hanging below the dash were a CB and a company radio, but these, like the truck, were tools and nothing more. There was little time for banter during the workday in Bill's world.

After the "box of assorted books and bric-a-brac" was shoved behind the driver's seat on a cover of heavy plaid, Bill reached for his snuff can. With the sweeping grace of a maestro, he twisted the lid, grabbed a pinch between finger and thumb, and deposited a black mass between lower lip and gum; where it stayed. Chosen cocked his head and stared curiously at the lump under the man's lip as they headed out of the parking lot, and away from Olivia and Jill and Drake and Bobbie Orzo for good.

Glad to be weightless on the squeaky springs, Chosen prayed that his time with Bill would be to the glory of God and for the eternal benefit of the man. He exhorted the Lord for continued blessings and grace on his friends in Portland, smiled as he whispered good-bye to two thumping Labrador tails, and wondered if Bill had a dog. There was certainly no sign of one in the large cab, so full of mail and papers and manuals and tools. Not to mention the smell of diesel, oil, tobacco, and sawdust.

They drove for hours before Bill fiddled with a radio knob to hear the five o'clock news. The voice of an old bearded cleric cracked through broken reception: "All Western governments are just thieves. Nothing but evil comes from them." The nightly news was reporting more and more about an exiled Iranian called Ayatollah Ruholla Khomeini.

Bill cussed, taking the Lord's name in vain as he rolled down his window and spat. The angel's head whipped sideways and gawked. Bill, obviously, was not a devout believer. *Bless His holy name,* uttered Chosen, remembering a couple of friends in a rib joint in Kansas City. *Bless His holy name.*

A deer darted across the highway in the dusk of day. Inertia from the truck's forward movement defied the brake pedal and sent a magazine sliding from under the front seat, landing, as it were, under Chosen's feet. The angel looked down as the truck was worked back into a lather. *Lord, God!* called the angel. There on the cover of the magazine was a naked man and woman, and the scene was far from Edenic.

Through heavy static, Chosen could hear the familiar sound of Johnny Cash, his voice straining from far, far away. *Understand your man,* he sang. Another man. Another soul. How critical the role of prayer in all their lives! Chosen pressed himself into service. He prayed for Carl and his mother—for Brenda and her baby, for Patty and Ed Harwood, for Joshua and Mattie, for Nancy and Buck (oh, Buckaroo!), for Dieter, for Olivia and Bobbie—and everyone else he'd encountered during this latest sojourn on earth. He prayed for the people who had attended the revival in Alabama, he prayed for the Vietnamese, he prayed for Monroe X. He prayed and prayed and prayed, and now he prayed some more. *Know ye not that the unrighteous shall not inherit the kingdom of God? Be not deceived: neither fornicators, nor idolaters, nor adulterers, nor effeminate, nor abusers of themselves.*

The Camp

Bill Stark was a gyppo logger. Too much renegade in him to work as an employee, Bill worked best as his own boss. And as boss to his highly seasoned crew, he maintained loose authority. His foreman, Stubby, took care of daily drudge, freeing Bill to bid jobs, administer sales, and govern his small company by radio and regular visits to camp.

Sick of static interference, Bill switched off the radio as he turned from the "Scenic Highway" and disappeared into a dense wall of lodgepole pine. The nearly primitive road he found himself on bothered Bill: rain or snow on this road would make access difficult for the huge logging trucks that would be hauling timber like worker bees within a month. This was an urgent matter for Stubby: blade the road. If it was this bad down here, it would get worse up above. And "up above" he climbed, following the rutted road *up, up, up* toward a steep drainage that would be thinned and logged by his crackerjack crew.

Chosen welcomed the passing scenery, which reminded him of the lush, fragrant forests of Lebanon. How good to be in the midst of Creation, away from the mark of man and reveling in the pure, undefiled gift of the earth bringing forth grass and herb and tree! A cow elk and her yearling crossed in front of the truck at a switchback, marmots seemed to be everywhere, scattering as the Ford bumped closer to the logging camp. Stars were beginning to reveal themselves in the slice of sky that could be seen from the road. Squeaking springs and steel cables shifting in the truck's bed were the only sound, the truck's high beams the only light. Man was of little significance here in the natural force of Creation. The mountain was the power throne of God.

Honey was first to greet the Ford as it pulled into camp, and Chosen swiveled to attention as the chubby golden retriever ran alongside the truck and barked the comfy bark of dogs who know you well. Five miles from the job site, and along Cilly Creek, the camp was pitched on a level expanse of ground. Men were busy setting up campers, trailers, tarps, and tents, pushing ahead fastidiously in the dark. Everything about this job would be a push: September was not the best time to begin. Their three-month contract brought them perilously close to weather that could shut them down . . . and prove dangerous.

Just back from R & R with their families, the men on this job were ready for work; two week's clean underwear, ample supplies of chewing tobacco or snuff, goodies from home, pictures of wives and kids adorning their cramped campers, their first night's meal a bucket of chicken bought way back in Eugene and smoked salmon, compliments of Butch. Cookie and Burl were still organizing the thirty-foot cook trailer. At that moment, however, Cookie was in his private camper *behind* the cook trailer, stashing his contraband Jim Beam, for the men themselves had agreed that booze and chain saws and Skagits and loaders didn't mix. The dangerous work these men performed required clear heads. Saturday night at the nearby hole-in-the-wall bar would be soon enough for drinking.

Cookie emerged from his camper as Bill pulled alongside the cook trailer.

"Got you some pans."

Cookie had the appearance of someone who spent more time with the jug than worrying about personal improvement; a better moniker for him might have been "Slim" or even "Emaciated." But could he whip up a batch of beans! Cookie hefted a pot for its weight.

"Here's a box of books and stuff that came along with the lot. Think there's a radio in there."

Summary inspection of the second box followed, a raised eyebrow from Cookie as he examined the books. The small box was hauled into the cook trailer and shoved under a bench.

Stubby appeared. Bill greeted him. The men talked business and unloaded fire extinguishers.

"That road needs grading."

"I know."

"Anybody from the Forest Service been up here yet?"

"Not today," said Stubby. "I expect tomorrow. What you gonna do with that TV?"

"Give it to my old lady," said Bill, with an impressive sweep of his hand to deposit more snuff.

Bill swung into the Ford and parked. The aluminum paint on his small, homemade travel trailer cast a glow against his headlights. He reached across the cab and grabbed a magazine before heading inside.

This was a fine kettle of fish for Chosen. The book was under a bench in what appeared to be a huge covered wagon. He had seen these wagons while on the road with Carl. Bill was in a similar, though smaller, contraption across the clearing. Standing on a carpet of moss and pine needles and patches of weeds, Chosen considered his situation while a golden retriever in sorry need of a bath sniffed the ground around him. Several other such wagons were there, most now dark as men prepared their bodies—and minds—for the challenge that lay ahead, the challenge of a timber sale on a dangerous slope of mountain called Packsaddle. The skyline operator, the choker setters, the sawyers, the mechanic, the knot bumper, the loader operator, the cook and his helper, the foreman, and a dirty golden dog were all primed for the next morning, when work would begin. One lone light burned late into the night as the owner of M & S Logging looked at pictures in a magazine.

So . . . where do I go, Lord? came the angel's plea.

I will lead, Bashar, I will lead. Many in this place will come to me. For now I am preparing one man's heart.

Alone after Cookie beckoned Honey to his camper, Chosen sat on a tree stump and added prayers for the men in the logging camp to his ever-growing list of souls. After a night of prayer in his wonderful new surroundings, Chosen clearly understood that a young man named Tony would be his next charge.

Tony

If it is possible for an angel to gasp, that is exactly the reaction Chosen had when he first set his eyes on Tony Sullivan, for he was looking into the face of David. Chosen guessed the young man was about the age when David was first called by Samuel. A beauty of countenance—a rugged, warrior beauty—radiated from the logger: facial features carved from marble, a nose perfectly aligned with cheeks and lips, clean-shaven and blemish free, eyes black as the darkest night, distant shining stars beneath full lashes and sturdy brows. Tony sat at the mess table that next morning, curly black hair licking his ears, a spitting image of the king, though smaller in size. Tony was dwarfed by his older brother, too, a fine-looking man, but not a match for him. There was a wedding ring on Tony's finger.

Tony had married young. It was the way of his family, the entire clan clustered in assorted mobile homes on family land in Grady, Oregon. Donna had grown up with Tony, within the ranks, and knew the system well: she would handle home and kids and see him every now and then. Once this job began, that had meant alternating weekends when the men quit work at noon on Friday for their furlough home. They would go to the local café when Tony was home, take a trip to Medford or the ocean, spend Saturday night at the town bar, and sleep late on Sunday. Otherwise, Donna was home alone, as were many other women, who watched soap operas and met for coffee and hung the wash on lines strung between pine trees. It was an agreeable life for Donna, who had gone from child to teen to adult within her little community and expected the day would come when kids were grown and she and Tony could go to the bar every night, just like the others whose footsteps she followed. It was a passage. But it wasn't all that agreeable for Tony.

Since the day he had watched a short film about Peru, Tony had wanted out. During his long trip home on the school bus, the fourth grader had promised himself he would bust loose of Grady some day—and go into the world. It was a secret dream he soon tucked into the same archives that everyone stuffs with wishes and plans for when they grow older and answer the urgent call of responsibility: married at 18, first child soon after, second after that, third on the way. The calls muffled his small inside voice with so much noise, the young man joined rank and file at the altar of community agenda: child, teen, adult-by-virtue-of-marriage-and-fatherhood, get a job in the woods. Do what you learned to do by osmosis, by living with and around sturdy lumbermen for so long that gene pool and environment coalesced into a force that became not second, but first, nature. Firsthand. Go to the woods. Follow your destiny. Follow your brother. It was a passage.

Chosen acquainted himself with the men at the breakfast table. He saw Cookie and Bill and Stubby, and Cookie's helper, an old man called Burl. There were the sawyers: Butch and Barney and Skip, Lenny and Fender and Cyril, and an apprentice named Jamie. The mechanic's name was Fred. The choker setters clustered together: Tony and his brother Tweed, and Paul and Walt and Ramon. And the skyline operators and loaders: John and Art and Spud. Not to mention sweet Honey, who had free reign of all the camp, yet managed to plop in places where she could only be a bother: in doorways, narrow trailer halls, in front of a bulldozer. "Honey, move it!" was a common cry in this logging camp, as the fat golden dog languidly got up and walked deliberately to another spot and plopped.

After breakfast, Tony followed the others out to Tweed's crummy. The choker setters filled a cab that smelled like diesel, oil, tobacco, and sawdust, and zigzagged five miles up the mountain to their new job. The angel rode atop a pile of steel cables in the back of the truck, waving happily at a fat dog as she barked and chased them out of camp.

Logging Packsaddle Mountain

Bill stayed much of that first day before he mounted his faithful Ford and turned it toward the scenic highway, taking a remote-control color television home to his wife. He wanted to be sure the crew got off to a good start, for this was an unusually steep job, even for them.

Steep-slope logging was left to the experienced, to the gyppos, to the crazies, to the men who took whatever work they could get. It was tough, dangerous, intense, serious business, and the crew of M & S Logging was ready for the challenge. They were dressed for the occasion too.

Men in "Can't Bust 'em" black pants with stagged-off pant legs; suspendered men wearing JCPenney striped shirts that zipped in front; men with red hankies—if you wore white you'd get shot, mistaken for a deer—and wide-brimmed aluminum hard hats and hobnailed boots; men with worn leather gloves and pocket watches; men in clothes that over time had become tools . . . these were the hombres who tackled the mountain.

These men, the crew of M & S Logging, demonstrated their skill and experience as they constructed the slackline yarder (tradename: Skagit) and cleared a corridor at the western boundary of the timber sale: erecting the Skagit and setting line took much of a day.

With a bottom much like an army tank, ninety feet of steel beams jutted out of the Skagit yarder like an Eiffel Tower. Guy lines as thick as wrists anchored the derrick into the mountainside behind. Tall girders hung lopsided like a gigantic duck beak, looking like a swimmer poised for the starter gun. Anchored to sturdy trees at the foot of each cleared corridor, the skyline cable became a highway, a route, a channel through which the logs moved, way up in the air. It was off the cable strung from the tower that most of the men would work; a clothesline with clothespins the size of telephone poles. Every day was wash day.

Sawyers downed trees close to the skyline corridor; men called choker setters surrounded each tree with massive cables connected to the main cable. Horns would blast and loggers would scatter as load after load of limbed trunks were skidded and hoisted up, to dangle off the skyline like so many fish caught on a lazy afternoon.

This was the A team. And Stubby was coach and cheerleader. Paid by the piece and by volume, one slip-up, one broken machine, one absent man would slow down the job, could put the crew out of business, and would certainly affect the size of their paychecks. These men were doing what they did best, what only they knew, the only thing they knew. Most had been raised in the forests, had been weaned on thick tree sap that flowed through their bodies like blood. They were men who would rather be on a forested mountain slope than any place on earth. To most, the forests even prevailed over the comfort of home and family. Not that they weren't devoted to their families. But for many of them their life in the woods was more than a job; it was identity. It was who they were, and they couldn't—wouldn't—be any different. Except for the one among them who once dreamed of busting loose.

Each workday, the most daring of the bunch, and always—always—proving his superiority over his younger brother, Tweed stuck one foot in a choker cinch and rode the skyline cable down the mountain. Leaving Ramon and Walt to unhook chokers at the landing, Tony and Paul walked down, ignoring the crazy man zipping eighty feet in the air.

Hour after hour. A mass of cables and choker bells swung from their carriage on the skyline; cables were attached to felled trees; trees were dragged and snugged up tight till they hung in the air all the way up to the landing; cables were then unhooked and sent down by carriage for the next load. Over and over. The sound of chain saws, the sound of skyscraper-high giants as they hit the ground with thud and groan, and the future houses of America, and lately of Russia and Japan, dangled like spaghetti off a fork tine. Again and again. Horns would blare when a drag of logs was ready to begin its ascent, and men would scoot like BBs on a linoleum floor.

Hour after hour, over and over, again and again. It would be three weeks before the men would have enough timber on deck for the trucks to come. By then the road would be graded, and by then the men would have had their first weekend furlough home.

Grady

Tony and Butch jumped into Tweed's truck for the ride home, laundry bags piled in the back next to a new plastic cooler with a hinged top that opened with the push of a red button. The first stop for the men was at a bar called Liquid Lizzie's for a six-pack of Coors for the long ride home. Grady was seven hours away.

It is hard to explain a town like Grady. Hard, that is, unless you are from the mountainous West, where a wide spot in the road became a makeshift town when people with a pioneering spirit once settled, got stuck, were trapped, ended staying, would-never-go-anyplace-else till death do they part. A place like Grady is usually within a couple hours of a real town—the kind you find on a map—and might have a bar, a café, a combination gas station/store, and sometimes . . . sometimes . . . when a missionary met up with the spirit of God, sometimes even a church. Mail arrived addressed to Rural Route, fire and police protection were community responsibilities, and schools were miles away. Electricity coursed through rural cooperatives, phones tagged behind, and satellite dishes popped up on homesites like wild mushrooms.

During hunting season every garage or shop or barn in a place like Grady sported a deer or two hanging by hind legs to cure; dogs that weren't shot for chasing deer were tethered to a stake with chain.

Children's toys and bicycles cluttered yards, abandoned cars stood like lawn ornaments, and well-worn paths connected homes and trailers like a giant connect-the-dot game in a children's puzzle book. In Grady, the path between Tony's trailer and his brother Tweed's was packed solid, a route followed by adults and children for generations.

Tony's two boys played on a dirt pile. Toby, the two-year-old, filled his diaper with scoops of sand. Jason, older by a year, pushed a purple plastic truck over a mound. *Whirrrrr. Whirrrr.* He made truck sounds with vibrating lips. Popsicle sticks loaded, Jason guided his truck down toward flat, hard ground. Shirttails sticking from under light coats, the little boys followed the paths in the dirt pile left by little boys and men before them as they ignored the chill of late September and learned about the elements from an outside post—almost as if by osmosis.

Donna checked the boys regularly, her kitchen window just above the dirt pile. Uncomfortable in her pants, she knew this was her last gasp with these jeans. Her third baby was beginning to show. She checked her makeup one more time. Trying for that same glow she saw on the soaps, she smeared a concoction of Vaseline and lipstick on her cheeks.

Tony knocked on the trailer door with his foot, one son under each arm. Chosen watched the scene and saw David with Absalom and Solomon, the boys miniature replicas of the strength and warrior beauty that held them.

"Open up in the name of the law!" he yelled. Donna held the door and looked into the distant shining stars in her husband's eyes. There was no man on earth as handsome as Tony.

"Toby has a little present for you."

"You mean his diaper? It's his new trick. Welcome home!" Boys deposited on the floor, the man and woman kissed, Tony's hand going straight to his wife's stomach. Donna blushed.

"Another boy!" he exclaimed.

"Don't be so sure! Aunt Jenny says if a needle on a thread goes in a circle, it's a girl."

"You said that with Toby. Hey! Close your eyes!" Tony reached into his pocket. "Here."

Donna opened a small box to find an ankle chain with a red stone.

"We stopped at K-Mart in Eugene. Tweed helped me pick it out. It's your birthstone. You like it?"

"I love it!" she exclaimed, with the teeniest hint of uncertainty, and wished she could bend over. "I'll let you put it on later."

The children instantly sensed Chosen's presence. Toby stumbled in the angel's direction, pointing. "Flashlight!" Jason sensed the angel, too, and was drawn to him, and that night slept soundly for the first time in months, to his mother's relief.

Saturday Night

"Where the heck is your mother? Tweed and Darla are gonna be here any minute."

"Tony," said Donna, finally getting courage to make her announcement, "I told Mom not to baby-sit tonight. I thought it would be nice if you and I just stayed home together and, you know . . ."

"For crying out loud, Donna, there's time for that tomorrow!"

"Tony, I'm just not feeling well with this one." Pregnancy the perfect excuse. "You go by yourself, I don't mind."

"You sure?" Tony's question was more for good measure than intent, because it was simply something one did on Saturday night: you went to the bar. He'd been meeting friends and family there since he was young, since at a bar in a place called Grady, children were more than welcome. After all, the bar was as much a meeting place as a place to drink. A community well. A watering hole. Where every able-bodied man and woman and child assembled as they always had on Saturday night in a show of solidarity, esprit de corps.

"Of course I'm sure," said a somewhat nervous wife.

Back at Camp

Indian summer smiled on M & S Logging. The crew worked during bluebird days, larch needles changed from green to yellow, and the few deciduous trees and bushes in Oregon forests added vibrant color to excite the senses of every woodsman on duty. Cookie and Burl had a celebratory cookout after Bill delivered thick T-bones and cheesecake in gratitude for the excellent work and high volume the men had produced. Now that the timber was moving and on its way to the mill, paychecks would reflect production, and K-Mart would have more visitors on the alternating Friday nights that men returned home.

After his second trip home, Tony moped in the backseat of Tweed's crummy. Once again, Donna had refused to accompany him to Saturday night doings, this time even refusing to join Tweed and Darla for breakfast at the café on Sunday, a rite the two couples had performed since they were teens.

"Tony, what do you think about going to church?" Donna had asked early that Sunday morning. "There's a new family in town, and he's a pastor and he's starting up a church in Jette's old cabin. He and his wife have come by to see me a couple of times."

"You go ahead if you want to go; I never been and I ain't gonna start now. What's coming over you anyway? How come you don't want to go out with Tweed and Darla?"

She seemed jittery. "It's just my hormones."

More like horrible-moans, if you ask me, thought Tony as he pouted in his big brother's backseat. All the more reason to decline Tweed's offer for a ride home the next Saturday afternoon and join the fellows at Liquid Lizzie's. "For crying out loud, Tweed, you'll barely get there and have to turn around to come back!"

Liquid Lizzie's

Chosen didn't like Saturday nights. At all. In Grady or in camp. Following the men down Packsaddle to a bar was a heavy time for him. He found solace in the few men who stayed in camp, among them Spud, a recovering alcoholic, and Paul, a quiet man who loved the Lord.

The angel frowned as each man filled basins from kettles of hot water for his go-to-town sponge-bath. All over camp, trailer doors opened and wash water splashed onto the ground, a clean shave the closest to "godliness" some of these fellows ever got. It simply irked Chosen that these men gussied up for a night of drunkenness *in spite of* his supplications. Not that he had made no progress at camp. Far from it! Even though it took a little creative sabotage at times (for instance, knocking cold coffee onto a certain man's magazine), Chosen was probably the reason the camp worked with such efficiency that fall. Many accidents had been averted by the angel's quick intervention, errant trees with a mind of their own nonetheless fell perfectly into a lateral line to make the choker's job easier, and temperaments among the radically individualist and independent men melded into an A-plus team.

In camp for that particular Saturday night, Bill offered a ride to several men, a spit-and-polished Tony among them. The young man was overdue a good time; punishment, in a way, for Donna's strange behavior during his past two visits. Chosen steamed in the backseat of Bill's crummy as it bumped toward the backwood's watering hole, a community well that took its drinking much more seriously than the one in Grady.

Liquid Lizzie's was a simple wooden structure begging for paint. A crude sign over the door proclaimed "Free haircuts for hippies"—the now famous rumor of chain-saw haircuts gave each man a sense of regional pride as he swaggered through the door. Chosen hated Liquid Lizzie's. He hated it for the damp whiskey smell that assaulted him when he entered; he hated it for its lack of light, for whether it was sunlight or moonlight outside, it was dark inside the bar; and he hated it for the demons that inhabited its nooks and crannies. He hated that people came to a place like this for fellowship. Fellowship! If only they could experience the fellowship of believers, the certainty of membership in the kingdom of God, the joy of corporate worship! But here, here they came together in a very different community indeed.

The horseshoe bar was to the right of the door, liquor bottles lined against tired plywood painted black. A large clock—*Miller Time!*—occupied the center of the plywood wall. Dozens of photographs, notes, IOUs, and lurid jokes were stuck to the plywood with tape and tacks, sometimes anchored between the cracks. A jar of pickled eggs, a jar of pigs' feet, and a jar of hot peppers kept company with metallic blue or green aluminum ashtrays that looked like cereal bowls. Leather cups with dice were strategically placed along the bar; a black iron dinner bell hung from the ceiling. *Listen up, everybody! The house is buying a round! Yay . . .* Stools were crammed in clusters, leaving the mark of romantic interludes, of loud dice games, of lonely hearts, and of rowdy bunches of locals who'd been to Lizzie's earlier. Tony took a seat next to a jar of pigs' feet.

A jukebox played background noise, the groundswell of shouts and beer-bravado building until its music was incidental. Chairs were skidded across the floor to tables too small to manage the gathering crowd. The sharp sound of pool balls slamming into each other came in staccato bursts from the corner. Laughs and shouts of defeat pierced the room with each dart thrown, and the unmistakable sound of girlish giggles added to the bray. It would be a good time in the old bar tonight. Tony ordered a red beer: tomato juice and Coors—a strange concoction to anyone who has never ventured into a bar inhabited by loggers, or by those who choose to live tucked away from the beaten path.

Chosen stared at every face, expecting to find misery, expecting to find despair, prepared to pray for the critical needs of each individual soul. Instead he saw gaiety. He saw happy faces and laughter and teasing play. Was it only surface? Were they all dying underneath, down below the skin where private thoughts and pain and hell reside? How could they be separated from the Holy One and be happy?!

Chosen remembered the night at Matthew's house, how the Pharisees attacked the Master for eating with sinners. What did Jesus say? The angel remembered well: *They that be whole need not a physician, but they that are sick. . . . I am come not to call the righteous, but sinners to repentance.* How often the Lord would attend banquets given by those who chose to live tucked away from acceptable protocol and behavior! Could he, an angel invisible and undetected, minister in prayer and supplication with the same spirit as the Master? Could he, an angel who hated sin because of its wicked curse on humanity, rise above judgment and do his job in a squalid backwoods bar called Liquid Lizzie's? Could he have any effect on this happy, drunken brawl? Could he fight against the dark forces that resided here and battle demonic influence? He would try. He would try. In obedience he would try, and praying all ways with all prayer and supplication in the Spirit, Chosen valiantly stayed in the fray.

Temptation

Tony played darts with Skip, Jamie, and a young woman with long, straight hair and curly bangs. Acting coy and cozy toward the handsome logger, she brushed her body next to his at every chance and begged his help throwing darts. *Above all, taking the shield of faith, wherewith ye shall be able to quench all the fiery darts of the wicked.*

Oh, no, you don't! yelled the big angel, who ran block against her moves. Tony never felt a thing.

Wanting to put a stop to the tease, and therefore the game, Chosen knocked Tony's darts off target and brought Skip's into the middle of the board with stunning accuracy. Bull's-eye! Bull's-eye! Skip couldn't miss. Tony slinked back to the bar a loser. More red beer. More music, louder now that someone found the volume control; more noise; more laughter. And now dancing. Long-hair was back. She took Tony's hand, and he followed. His wedding ring meant nothing to her. Or to him, apparently.

No! yelled the angel again as he shot toward the slow-moving couple like a bear protecting her cub.

"Ow!" the girl grimaced. "Ouch!" Tony, who had learned to dance at the community hall when he was five, was mashing her toes with every chord and banging her shins as the seductive movements of a slow dance were successfully sabotaged by a foot-smushing angel. Dance over, she took Tony's hand and led him to a table.

No, Tony! Don't do this! cried Chosen as red beer began to fog the young man's senses and other senses took over.

"Bashar, Bashar, you pray in vain. He will yield to the temptation. We need to do little; his flesh is weak." Chosen swung his mighty sword. *"The Lord rebuke you!"*

Laughter.

Chosen watched the young man and girl huddle at the table. This called for drastic measures. Ramon and Art, who could barely stand, were trying to play pool in the corner. Ramon pulled his elbow back, thrust the pool cue with all his might, and hit the white ball just right.

"Watch it!" yelled Ramon as he looked at his pool stick in surprise. The hard ball sailed through the air like a bomb aimed for Tony's table. Everyone ducked. But the ball seemed to be caught midair and stopped. It dropped to the floor with a thud. More laughter. *"Do you really think you can stop them with your foolish tricks, Mighty Angel?"*

Bill approached Tony and the girl, a buxom woman with bleary eyes hanging on his arm. Both couples left the bar and drove off in the crummy, a despondent angel trailing behind. If only Tweed were here, this wouldn't be happening!

The Accident

Tony had never been unfaithful before. The emotional fallout from his tryst with the girl was more than his sensitive spirit was prepared for. Word spread throughout the camp that Tony was among the few men that night who ended up in the arms of local women. There followed a mix of ribbing from partners in crime, looks of disapproval from the likes of Paul—and others who considered marital vows sacrosanct—plus an odd silence from his big brother, who had certainly been privy to the gossip. The reactions of his workmates, however, was trite compared to the guilt Tony heaped upon his own head, and though he presented his normal self to the men in camp, he was embroiled in turmoil within . . . not to mention his fear that Donna might one day learn of his infidelity.

The rain clouds that came midweek suited Tony's inner disposition perfectly. It needn't physically rain: when you are high atop Packsaddle Mountain, you don't look *up* at clouds, you are in them; the air was thick enough with water to make going miserable for the men who donned their "tin" pants and coats—oil-treated, canvas wet-weather gear.

Tony and Paul were working at the bottom of the line. Their hobnailed boots did double duty as the men coursed the slick hillside and scrambled over massive trunks to set their chokers. The job had been going smoothly. Around midmorning, however, the loggers' worst fears were realized. The tower up on the hill wobbled against the weight of the logs inching toward the choker carriage when an immense tree at the base, to which the skyline was anchored, uprooted. Slack suddenly snapped the entire cargo like the end of a bullwhip, and the skyline shuddered and roared with earthquake intensity as white-eyed men outran each other to safety.

Paul screamed. "Tony!"

A partially chokered tree whipped sideways and came at Tony like a flyswatter on a gnat. The young logger was dead center in the path of the charging tree. His face frozen with the certainty of collision, Tony tried to fling his body out of the way. A powerful angel tackled him and formed his wings into a shield, the errant log breaking loose of the choker cable as it glanced over the flattened man and came to rest ten feet away. Scrambling to his feet too soon, Tony's shoulder caught the full fury of the wayward cable as it vibrated like a downed electric wire in an ice storm. The end of the choker ripped his arm open just above the elbow. Knocked off his feet, he clawed at the sloppy hillside with ferocity until his boots found traction and he was swept fast in the strong arms of a ministering spirit: past the lump in his throat, past his frantic heart, past flailing logs that thundered to the ground as the skyline went limp.

Leaning against trees, against stumps, against each other, the men held aching sides and opened mouths wide to fill empty lungs after their race with death. Every man's body heaved with physical exhaustion. Tony felt warm blood run down his arm and drip between his fingers. Chosen held his hand against the wound to stop the flow as Tweed raced to Tony's side. It would be Tweed who took his brother to the emergency room in Bend that afternoon while the men mopped up the mess and reset the line. Work would go on, and the doc would have Tony patched up and back on the line in no time, wasn't that right? Part right.

After Cookie dressed Tony's wound, he was loaded into Tweed's crummy for the trip to Bend. In pain and frightened—had he broken a bone?—Tony sat stoically in the front, determined, as ever, to demonstrate his courage to a brother he adored. As they drove in silence, Tony's fear turned to a matter more worrisome than a broken bone: would his brother confront him about Saturday night? Had Tweed lost respect or trust for him? *Why wasn't he saying anything?*

Chosen was not surprised that Tony was allowed to be hurt, in spite of the angel's heroics. A tad presumptuous for him to assume *exactly* what was happening in the young man's life, Chosen knew that once the Lord had singled out a soul, He often used pain, suffering—and even tragedy—to gain attention.

How troubled the apostles had been by the hard words of Jesus that one afternoon! "Rabbi, who sinned, this man or his parents that he was born blind?"

"Neither this man nor his parents sinned," said Jesus, "but this happened so the work of God might be displayed in his life."

Tony had been singled out; would the work of God be displayed in his life? Would this accident play a role in his redemption? Chosen fretted over his young charge, who was pale now from blood loss and shock, and was glad when the crummy turned toward "Emergency Entrance Only" of the Bend hospital.

All three were relieved when X-rays proved Tony to be as strong in bone as he was in grit while the doctor sewed him up. Trying still to impress Tweed, Tony swallowed hard when the wound was cleaned and flaps of flesh on his upper arm were joined again. The doctor gave him an injection for pain and handed Tweed some pills. "The shot will knock him out. May also make him loonier than a pet coon."

"He can lay down in the backseat," said Tweed, who bunched an old, woolen Woolrich shirt to form a pillow and used an oiled canvas coat as a blanket.

"Doc says you should take it easy for a week or so," said Tweed as he headed toward the logging camp on Packsaddle Mountain.

Discovery

Tony fought the drug as he lay in the backseat, its first rush reminding him of the effects of red beer. His mind, heart, and soul all went back to his little scandal, the accusation of infidelity charging at him like a runaway tree trunk as the faces of Donna and Jason and Toby paraded through his thoughts. His head pounded out of sync with the sound of tires on the highway in the otherwise quiet cab as Tweed headed home. No! Not home! Not yet! What would he say to Donna? Would he have to hide this awful secret forever? He tried to move to his back but his wound would have none of it; he shook his head back and forth, eyes closed, eyes opened . . . they had pledged fidelity to each other long before they were married.

"You are the only one for me, Donna."

"Tony, there will never ever be another man, even if you left me. Tony, I swear to God. You are it."

You are it.

They had played games when they were kids, all of them. Tweed and Darla and Donna and Tony. "I'm it!" Donna would yell. And Tony would run and hide.

Tony's hand hung down onto the truck floor and throbbed. He braced his fingers against the rubber mat, trying to push the pain away. He was losing his battle with the medicine. Merciful sleep could put an end to this misery. As he braced his arm in a burst of pain, his fingers brushed a small length of chain on the floor of Tweed's truck. Tony felt a bump in the chain and lifted it to see, his eyes struggling to focus, his shoulder screaming in protest. And as Tweed turned into a dense wall of lodgepole pine that would swallow his truck whole, Tony clenched his fist around an ankle bracelet with a ruby-colored stone and fell asleep.

The Ten Commandments

Roger Wilcox and his wife, Leila, sat across from Donna while Toby and Jason napped in their bedroom. The three held coffee mugs and chatted about the new church down the road. Their new church. The community was in sorry need for some sort of church, after all, and Pastor Wilcox had felt a call to rural America. With pledges of support from his home church, the newly ordained Christian Missionary Alliance pastor felt a "burden" for people in America. "We would probably never come face-to-face with a Zulu, but we could minister in our own backyard, don't you think?" Donna didn't quite grasp his message but nodded in agreement when his kitchen table homily was over. She really liked Roger (*Pastor* Roger) and Leila. Not to mention how desperate she was to go to church this past Sunday, both children in tow.

Acutely aware of a need for child care since Sunday morning, the good pastor and his wife set out to visit every person in attendance, bearing gifts: a loaf of bread, Leila's homemade jam, and a brand-new Bible.

"Have you ever belonged to a church before?" asked Pastor Wilcox.

"I've been to a couple of weddings and funerals, up in Roseberg, over to Coos Bay, even was in a Catholic church down in Grant's Pass. But no, we never got into religion here much. Nobody ever bothered. Seen some on TV. My grandmother used to watch a guy called Oral Roberts—right before *Highway Patrol* on Sundays. I never much understood him. I did read the Ten Commandments, though! Saw them in the county courthouse when I went to buy plates for the truck."

"What did you think of them, Donna?"

"They made sense to me. Except I didn't know then what a couple of words meant." She averted her eyes. "I do now."

"Which words?"

"Doesn't matter."

Yes it did matter. It mattered very, very much.

The Fifty-First Psalm

Paul lingered in the cook trailer the night after Tony's accident. It was Thursday of the alternating week, but because of the accident and the weather forecast, the men would work through the entire weekend. Tweed and Butch stuck around to play rummy after the tables were cleared.

"Burl, where's that box of books that was under this bench?" asked Paul.

"Cookie finally got tired of them and put them out back this afternoon."

"Didn't there used to be a religious book in with them?"

"Beats me."

Paul grabbed a flashlight, donned his tin coat, and doffed his ball cap before stepping into the miserable, dark mist swirling around the trailer. Smells from tonight's pot roast drifted into the cover of trees. He wandered behind the trailer and shined his light. Little did he know of the light standing nearby, a light that had pushed the box under a wheel well to keep the contents dry; ever vigilant, Chosen had checked the book regularly and had flown in frustrating circles around Cookie as he plopped the books behind the trailer.

"Brings me all this junk and 'spects me to play nursemaid to a bunch a grown men half the time; who the heck's gonna read a book a poetry; who's gonna read po-eh-tree, for cryin' out loud; tell him to keep his junk to himself . . ." on and on Cookie muttered. Honey wagged her tail, barked like a puppy, and sniffed the ground near Chosen.

Once Chosen had protected the box from the elements, he flew back to a camper shared by two brothers. He fretted over the younger one inside and beseeched heaven for his relief from physical, emotional, *and* spiritual pain.

It was the worst day of Tony's life. He'd never felt anguish before, never felt betrayed, never felt such guilt, and never ever felt such physical pain as the searing poker prodding his shoulder and his arm. As soon as Tweed left for the day, the young man had taken a double dose of pain medication and lay back on his bed as best he could without disturbing his wound. But which wound?

Ah! The wound on his arm. No! The wound in his heart. Or . . . the wound in his soul, in the place called *conscience*.

His awe and fear of Tweed made quick resolution of his first, angry thoughts of confrontation. Besides, maybe Donna had just gone for a ride with Tweed and Darla. He closed his eyes and breathed heavy spurts of air through his nose. He knew better; it was no secret that Tweed had been stuck on Donna before he got Darla pregnant. Truth be known, Tony felt he'd aced his big brother when he and Donna got married. It was his claim to equality, a certification of authenticity: Tony is all grown-up now and has a wife and kids, just like his brother; he works a job just as well as his brother, and he brings home the pay. Why, he even cheats on his wife like his brother.

Tony gave the wall a right hook with his good arm, sending shock waves through his body. The pain hurt! And she even wanted to go to church! She's pregnant with my kid! A thought shot through Tony's mind like a dart, too horrible to stay; he banished it with all his might: Jason, Toby, the baby. This is too much! His arm sent signals to his brain: more pain! Coming right up! Just like logs on the haul-back line. *Beeeep. Beeeep.* Pain coming! Out of the way! Pain crashing down on the ground. He heard the words of the girl in the bar, whispered into his ear, her soft lips brushing against his face: "Hold me. Touch me. Take me." He fought back vomit. Chosen saw the battle, and his prayers became more urgent.

The camper door opened following a knock. It was Paul—and he was carrying Brenda's gift. Chosen smiled and offered praise. *So this is your messenger, Father!*

"Thought I'd drop off a little reading material for you."

"Thanks."

"Look, um, Tony, I was up a lot during the night . . . now listen to me before you get a notion to kick me out . . . when it happens that I can't sleep it means one thing: that God is gonna talk to me."

God?

"Anyway, it was you who kept coming in my mind, Tony." He cleared his throat. "Now don't go thinking I'm one of those religious kooks. You know I don't go pushing religion on nobody around here. You got to admit that."

Tony nodded, pride wanting Paul to go, his insides screaming at Paul to stay. The angel lay flat on the skinny floor in the camper and sent up worship by the truckload.

"Tony," Paul cleared his throat again, "you coulda been killed yesterday. I seen that cable come at you, Tony. It came right to your head. So help me.

And just when it was going to hit, it moved down to your shoulder, like a big hand swatted it away. So help me, Tony. You woulda been dead."

Tony stared hard at Paul, who stood firm, courage building and speaking clearly. "Tony, I believe that God saved you. I know He saved you. And when God saves someone, it's because He has a special plan for him. It's true, Tony, I hear about this kind of thing all the time. He's got a purpose in store for you, and I don't think it's in a logging camp."

He *really* had Tony's attention.

"I prayed for you last night, Tony; got to admit I never prayed for you ever before, but I prayed last night, and Psalm 51 kept coming into my mind. Just wouldn't go away. That's when I knew God was talking to me. That's how He does it." There was an embarrassed pause. Paul cleared his throat and went on. "I know what you did last Saturday . . ."

Normally Tony would be swinging or yelling epithets if another man dared to confront him, especially with something as fresh and awful as this. "That don't matter," said the guilty man, as he averted his eyes.

"What matters, Tony, is that God knows what you did last Saturday, too. And here's the message He wants me to give you. Now don't go thinking I'm some kind of nut, OK?"

Tony nodded.

"He wants to forgive you, Tony. Except you gotta ask Him to." Deep breath. "And then you gotta ask Him to come into your heart."

"God?"

"Yep. God."

Paul laid the book of Psalms on Tony's bed and turned to go. The blockade by the door stopped him cold. He turned back.

"I . . . um . . . I'd be mighty honored if you would let me pray for you right now, Tony."

To Tony, this was practically akin to a homosexual advance: a man, a rugged man from camp, a man he'd known for years, was next to his bed and wanting to pray.

"OK."

Paul knelt next to the bed (Tony's hands were tucked safely out of sight) and prayed a simple prayer:

"God, I know You got special plans for this man. But he's got to know You first before he can figure out what You got for him to do. I know that Your Bible is the Word of truth, and I thank You for the miracle of having this little book of Psalms here in camp on account of what You put in my mind last night. Tony—he's got to recognize that he's a sinner . . . maybe that won't be so hard for him right now . . . and he's got to realize that there ain't no way he can be reunited with You but through Your son, Jesus Christ. Please be good and fair to Tony, forgive him for what he done on Saturday, and bless him. Lead him to salvation on account of Jesus. I pray this in Jesus' name. Amen."

With that, a very red-faced Paul smiled uncertainly and backed out of the camper, into a miserable, damp mist.

Tony picked up the book. Many feelings leapfrogged inside of him— but not the bursts of pain, not the guilt, not the anger and turmoil; all of that was pushed into a heap and out of the way, like dust in a dustpan. Wave upon wave of peace flooded the young man, a euphoric peace the likes of which he'd never felt in his life. All he knew was that nothing could ever matter to him but that peace that burst its way into his soul. Tony turned to Psalm 51 and read it over and over again.

> *Have mercy upon me, O God, according to thy lovingkindness; accord-*
> *ing to the multitude of thy tender mercies, blot out my transgressions.*
> *Wash me from mine iniquity, and cleanse me from my sin. For I*
> *acknowledge my transgressions; and my sin is ever before me. Against*
> *thee, thee only, have I sinned, and done this evil in thy sight. . . . Make*
> *me to hear joy and gladness; that the bones which thou hast broken may*
> *rejoice . . . . Create in me a new heart, O God. . . . Then will I teach*
> *transgressors thy ways; and sinners shall be converted unto thee. . . .*
> *LORD, open thou my lips; and my mouth shall shew forth thy praise.*

To that he added: *Please come into my heart, Jesus.*

Before long, the words became Tony's prayer, and he read them with purpose of heart. And more peace came. He prayed the prayer for his wife. And more peace came. He prayed the prayer for his children. And more peace came. And while Tweed headed toward the camper from a night of cards with Butch, Tony prayed the prayer for his big brother. The floodgates of heaven were opened and an angel was soaked through to the bone in joyful tears.

Sometimes it happens this fast, thought Chosen. Sometimes the Lord prepares the heart for years, for months, for weeks, for days, until His grace and mercy become irresistible to one of his Beloved children and he surrenders. Little did Tony or Chosen know that a similar scene was taking place in Grady, Oregon, as a penitent wife sobbed, a brand-new Bible opened to Psalm 51 on her lap.

Chapter

Ten

May 1984

Weeds and grass filled a rectangular patch of ground next to a well-worked dirt pile. Bleached from sun, a cotton clothesline flopped against a tree, clothespins making a portable staircase for butterfly and bug. A well-worn path was hard to find through the branch and bramble closing in from the sides. A purple plastic truck, with no wheels. lay in the yard. The population of Grady had diminished by five. Someone had busted loose.

New Life

"Did too!"
"Did not!"
"Did! . . . Mommmmiiiieeeee!!!!"
Donna stormed into the living room. Her face had the sunny, healthy

glow of coastal California, where she'd lived the past five years. Her disposition was not quite as sunny.

"Toby, I told you to keep an eye on him!"

She was cross: Tony's preoccupation with finals, their upcoming move to Nebraska, and three rambunctious boys had all pushed her buttons. It had been a long haul for her—for all of them—beginning with selling their trailer and moving to Oakland, home for the five years it took Tony to graduate from Simpson College. A cramped flat on the second floor of a cramped house on a cramped street in a cramped neighborhood was all they could afford. And now it was filled with assorted boxes that Donna had lugged home for their upcoming move. Yes, indeedy, it had been quite a haul.

All their struggles! The baby-sitting jobs, Tony's off-hours mechanic work, living hand-to-mouth while her husband followed his dream, and now they were down to the wire. The congregation in Nebraska that had "adopted" their family would house them and pay a small wage as Tony began his two-year stint with a home church before going to language school . . . and the mission field. Donna supported her husband totally. It was really *their* dream, to become career missionaries. She was as eager to serve the Lord as her husband.

What a dramatic change in plans, mused Donna whenever she thought back to life in Grady—another time, another life, a life to remember but not to dwell on. Folks from Grady would be down in force for Tony's graduation with a B.A. in Biblical Studies. A first for Grady, something for them to shake their heads over when they met on Saturday nights. "That Sullivan kid went off and got religion. Gonna be a missionary to South America. Prob'ly end up in a pot!" But they'd be there just the same: Tony's parents, Donna's parents, Tweed and Darla, and Butch and Paul. Rumor had it that Bill Stark was planning to come. *Lord, that was sure a miracle of redemption!* thought Donna. At the moment, however, other thoughts occupied her mind.

"He wouldn't listen, Mommy! I even told him Jesus was watching." Eight-year-old Toby looked at his brother with high-ranking superiority and savored the upcoming execution: Pauly would get it now!

The guilty party sat staring at his mother, crayon in hand, a pile of books in his lap. He held up Brenda's book, one page decorated elaborately with circles and lines and stick men and squiggles.

"I did this for you, Mommy!" He was working awfully hard to wiggle out of his mess.

"Pauly! That is your father's favorite book!" She grabbed the book and scanned other pages. "You know better than to draw in a book!"

"I made pictures of you and Daddy and flowers," said the frightened little boy. "It's a picture of heaven, Mommy!"

Donna counted to ten—not the loud, threatening count she used on her three scalawags, but the count she used for herself before she erupted in anger and frustration. Pauly was crying. Her sensitive one, whom she had to discipline with care.

"Mommy and Daddy are sad when you color in our books. Next time use a piece of paper, OK?" She held the boy to her chest as Toby stomped out of the room.

"Let Mommy give you some paper so you can draw a picture for Uncle Paul, OK?"

"Is Uncle Paul coming?" A few sniffles for good measure.

"Yep, he is. Next week. Everybody is coming to see Daddy graduate. We will get all dressed up and be very, very quiet."

"Just like in church?"

"Just like in church."

Finals

At that moment, Tony wished he were in church. The final exam in Systematic Theology cramped his fingers. He looked at his wristwatch and ran his hand through his hair. *Please elaborate upon the following statement: The church is not coterminal with the interregnum.* Why did they make it so hard? Why couldn't it be as easy as coming to Christ and answering a call to missions? What happened to the days when men just headed out and witnessed to the unreached? *That,* Tony had learned, was the stuff of fourth-grade imagination. The Church made it hard because it was equipping the saints. It was determined to send quality men and women who not only had a heart for missions, but a head. The church wanted missionaries with a heart commitment who were willing to dedicate their lives to go into the world to preach and to demonstrate the good news.

Right now the good news for Tony was the last stroke of his pen; it was his hand rubbing neck muscles that felt like a slash burn in the Oregon woods, his hand rubbing eyes puffy from study, his hand slapping the backs of students younger than he. All the while a proud angel monitored every syllable, every comma, and every struggle during Tony's five years at Bible college, an angel who loved and protected a young logger who looked like King David.

It seemed absurd to Chosen that Tony and so many others like him had to sacrifice so much to serve the Lord. Not that sacrifice wasn't part of a Christian's calling, but the early Church had handled things so differently. Everyone had pitched in; everyone had helped the needy; everyone had supported missions. A shudder passed through the angel when he thought of Ananias and Sapphira, of how upset Peter had been that day. What sorrow! The first recorded sin in the Church . . . the love of money.

Tony reached into his pants pocket for car keys, anxious to go home and celebrate. He did it. He DID it! No more homework until language school, no more tests, no more classes. "All praise and glory to you, Lord God!" he proclaimed out loud as he headed toward the parking lot. An ankle bracelet with a ruby-colored stone hung from his key chain, a reminder of another time, another life, an inconceivable time when he had lived a life apart from Christ.

The contrast between then and now was too glaring, too impossible for words. Tony *had* to tell others about the difference in his life, that all the jargon about death to life is real; all the comparisons between turmoil and peace are real. He *had* to shout about the peace and certain security that came and stayed when he accepted the Lord. Tony had been born again. Not of flesh and blood, but of Spirit. He was lifted from the very pit of despair and brought to the very height of hope in a camper on Packsaddle Mountain. He *had* to tell others about Jesus. He had to become a missionary.

Tony drove his old station wagon through the cramped streets of Oakland. He drove through his neighborhood, waving at everyone he met. In the midst of a basketball game at the school down the block, Jason waved back as his father turned a corner for home. In a few short weeks his family would leave this place and head toward Omaha, Nebraska.

Law and Grace

Armed with the mail and with a box bulging with the contents of his locker, Tony banged on the door with his foot. True to his pledge of monthly support, the mail brought a familiar envelope from Paul, his third son's namesake, his trusted friend, and now his dear brother in Christ.

"Open up in the name of grace!" he yelled.

"Grace isn't home today!" Donna answered wryly as she opened the door.

"Uh-oh, who got in trouble?"

Pauly was hiding between the couch and the wall. "I did, Daddy," came the penitent cry.

Tony winked at Donna. "And what did you do, son of mine?" he asked with a deep, threatening voice, a dead giveaway that this would be a game. Breathing prayers behind the couch, Pauly responded: "I drew you a picture of heaven, Daddy!"

"And what, son of mine, does heaven look like?"

"Well," said Donna, "we know it's orange and green."

Tony stared at the damage to Brenda's book. Pauly stood next to him, studying his father's face; Toby pouted on the couch. "Well," said the man who had finished five years of college a mere hour earlier, "it's just one page. Don't be writing in books again, Pauly. Promise?"

"I promise."

"Tony," said Donna, "speaking of books . . . don't you think we should pare down this load before we head east? I remember hearing a little something about missionaries not hauling too much around."

"I agree."

Donna did a double take. Was this her hoarder husband?

"I think we should cut down on everything, Donna, go with bare necessities. Matter of fact, I was hoping to just pull a little trailer when we go; the house we're getting is furnished."

Finished with school, Tony switched gears and was now able to focus on his true purpose, his course, his call. Lord willing, in three years they would be packing for their first mission. No amount of books could slow him down. And, besides his Bible, the only book that really mattered to him was a book of Psalms.

Cathy

Jason and Toby raced their Stingrays down the sidewalk. His prized possession, Jason's brilliant blue bicycle was a present from a man who sometimes heard from God in the middle of the night. A neighborhood pal rode double with Jason on his long banana seat. The boys brought the bikes to a smooth stop and hit the ground in one fluid movement, momentum carrying them upstairs to a refrigerator door. As usual, their friend Kyle would stay for dinner and TV until he headed home to his empty apartment. As usual, Kyle's mother, Cathy, was working until nine.

The Sullivans were a safety net for the fatherless boy and welcomed Kyle into their home. With his dark eyes and hair, eight-year-old Kyle fit comfortably into the family picture. *There is still a son of Jonathan. . . . So Mephibosheth ate at David's table like one of the king's sons.*

Their move to Nebraska would leave Kyle high and dry, a great worry for Donna, who prayed fervently that she could develop a friendship with the boy's mother. With no less than three part-time jobs, Kyle's mother had no time for friendships and barely time for her son.

Cathy Powers was as deeply troubled as she was devoted to her only child. Since her husband abandoned them last year, she was dominated by three brutal commands: struggle to survive, struggle to hold back fear, struggle to care for Kyle. And the best she could do at the moment was hope and pray that Kyle was cared for. As a matter of fact, it was at one of her jobs that she prayed for Kyle. As housekeeper in a decrepit motel across town, Cathy got to her knees in Room 7 and uttered a simple prayer each morning, a prayer to that thing called "God"—for lack of a better term. Her prayer had no beginning (Dear God) and no end (In Jesus' name, Amen). Because Cathy's understanding of God was confined to "higher power," her prayers were more personal projections than pleas to the One who is holy and sovereign over all. Cathy's prayer just had a middle: *Please bless my sweet babe and keep him safe.*

The Rest Eazy Motel seemed more like a cement bunker than a motel, flamingo-pink color fading from its facade, streaks of rust and green algae trickled on every seam. It was a damp, murky place, a motel that saw its heyday in the twenties, when tourists sat in white wooden chairs on its lawn. Now it served as a flophouse for the poor, for the indigent, for two-bit drug dealers, and for prostitutes. It also served as a part-time job for a single mother who braced for the stench of mildew when she entered each room and swallowed hard as she approached the sheets on each bed. When she prayed, Cathy asked nothing for herself. Though the world might think otherwise because of her absence, her child was her life. Thrown into the role of provider, each day she battled rising terror that gripped her by the throat and shook her like a rag as she cleaned toilets and made beds before she drove to a warehouse to sweep floors. In the evening, she waitressed.

The facade of a life of ease and plenty crashed down on Cathy and Kyle when her husband disappeared. At first it was a relief—for a man who is morally unfit is bankrupt in many more ways than just financially. Then the reality of her situation crept up on the young woman like the rising bank of a river on a sunny spring day: in the midst of initial feelings of freedom and determination to set out on a new, safe life, the floods suddenly came as creditors began to knock on doors and call. Without higher education or credentials to land her a career job, Cathy was stuck in menial positions. Their home lost to foreclosure, Cathy found cheap rent on a cramped street in Oakland, and Kyle found a safety net. He also found two friends in Jason and Toby Sullivan, who pinch-hit for the siblings he never had.

That afternoon, the boys ate pretzels and covered the table with a board game called Risk. Hot dogs, macaroni, and corn would be served soon, Donna warned, so they'd better not get too involved. Kyle was in the process of capturing North America when the phone rang.

"Jason, get that, honey," called Donna, her hands full with margarine and milk.

Jason walked to his mother and whispered. "Mom, you better come into the bathroom with me."

Donna looked at her eldest son's face, turned down a burner, and followed him into the closest private room. "What is it?"

"Mom, that was Kyle's mother on the phone, and she said something weird. She was crying, and she told me to ask you to take care of her sweet babe—that's what she calls him, Mom—and to always, always tell him that she loved—she said *loved*, Mom—that she loved him more than she could ever, ever say." Jason looked to his mother for answers. "What did she mean, Mom?"

Donna feared she knew exactly what a desperate, troubled, single mother meant.

The Crisis

Cathy wasn't in her right mind. She had lost all coping abilities. Her overwhelming dilemma turned to crisis and then to hopelessness; she lost her balance; she lost her grip. She. Just. Could. Not. Go. On. For her to be driven to such action was proof she had snapped. To leave her child, her precious child, in the hands of strangers—even good strangers—was utterly outside the realm of sane thinking.

Cathy drove aimlessly. There was no voice egging her along, no note left behind, no premeditation, but only a hollow spot from the top of her head, traveling down to her heart. She was siphoned dry. Empty space in place of feeling, in place of memory, in place of future. Zombie. She drove her old, broken car over the Golden Gate Bridge and stopped on the other side. The vast parking area for the overlook was empty. Just like Cathy. She looked at the lights of San Francisco, looked at the vast expanse of the bay area, and studied her gaze on Alcatraz. The famous prison was now . . . empty. No one could escape; many had tried. *Sometimes there is no escape, no matter how much you try.* She looked at the bridge. Would a fall to the water feel like freedom, or would it feel like fear? Would she land feetfirst or flat? Would she shatter on impact or sink *deep, deep, deep* into the cold, black pool below? Would the water feel like satin or fire? And what if she landed just right—she was a champion diver, after all—and came back to the surface, breaking water with gasp and splash—what would she do then? She was too strong a swimmer to just lie there.

Her rusted Ford Pinto crept along the bridge, back toward the city. It slowed near the highest point, Cathy's foot shaking violently against the gas pedal. The car inched along in jerks, hiccuping its way toward the middle of the bridge.

On a cramped street in Oakland, four little boys in sleeping bags cluttered a living room floor, a nine-year-old sleeping the fitful sleep of one who sits perilously on the cusp of tomorrow, of finding himself privy to more and more adult language, more and more adult behavior, more and more adult responsibility. Too young to grasp the full potential of the situation, too old to let it go, Jason prayed extra prayers for his buddy Kyle that night and for Kyle's mother, Mrs. Powers.

Chosen prayed fervently for Kyle's mother as well, as did Tony and Donna, whose muted voices in their bedroom alerted the boys that something was going on.

Donna called Kyle's home for the hundredth time. No answer.

Tony rubbed his mouth and his jaw with his hand. As soon as his boys finished school, he and his family would be on their way to Omaha. Yet the Lord had placed this child in his home for a reason. He could not ignore the situation. Just what did the phone call mean? Was the woman out on a date? Did Jason get the message mixed? Should Tony call the police? Why didn't Kyle's mother answer her phone at two in the morning?

At two in the morning Cathy lay on the floor in Room 7 of the Rest Eazy Motel. She was tired, as if she had been awake for her entire thirty-two years and was finally, *finally,* getting sleep. She was cold, the linoleum on cement like lying in a cellar, in a hole dug underneath the living that goes on up above. Upstairs. She was lost in the basement. Everything there ever was, is, and was to come spun in a vortex that pinned her to the floor, then whirled in dizzy spirals farther and farther away. She was crying but could not cry. She was yelling but could not speak. She was dying but would not die. She was leaving but would not go. And unknown to Cathy, that night she was gently nursed and protected by a heavenly host of very concerned angels.

Ministry

Four boys sat amid a forest of cereal boxes.

"I want you to start using up this cereal!" came the sharp command from Donna, mother of three and extremely worried guardian of a fourth. "Kyle, you wear some of Toby's clothes today. Pauly, don't put sugar on that cereal. Jason, go ask your father for lunch money for the four of you."

Toby and Kyle cheered with approval when school lunch became an option because Friday was pizza day, and Jason slipped from the table after sharing a worried glance with his mother.

"Kyle, you come here to our house after school today; your mom needs to . . . to work extra, so we said you could . . . spend the weekend here."

More cheers. Soon hair cowlicks would be wetted and smoothed, shirts would be tucked, sneaks would be tied, and four boys would be on their way to the school down the block, lunch money in hand.

"Pauly, Daddy will come pick you up from kindergarten."

Donna put the receiver against her ear and dialed, the long cord stretching the width and breadth of her kitchen duties. "Dear God!" she whispered in alarm as she heard the recorded message: *We're sorry, the number you have reached has been disconnected. Please consult an operator for further assistance.* Mrs. Powers had not paid her phone bill for a long, long time.

A tentative knock at the door. "Just a minute!" She put the phone in its cradle and looked through a peephole. "Tony!" her call was insistent. "Come out here right away!"

Mrs. Powers seemed in a daze, as if in shock. She looked into Donna's eyes with such a pitiful, confused look that a lump was caught between Donna's throat and chest. The woman was exhausted from her battle, her retreat, her defeat. Tony guided her to the sofa. Cathy huddled in a corner, legs folded against her body in a fetal position, and rocked. Spit dripped from her open mouth.

"*Thank you, Lord, that the children are not here to see this!*" prayed Donna.

"*Dear Lord God, guide us now,*" prayed Tony. His classes on pastoral care had not prepared him for this.

"*I give You praise and glory for the work You are doing in this woman's life, Lord on High,*" prayed Chosen.

"Mrs. Powers, would you like to talk?"

She stared.

"Mrs. Powers."

She was Mrs. Powers, wasn't she? Whatever happened to Miss Harris? Where did *she* go? She got married—buried. Made dead. She didn't need a bridge. Mr. Powers hurt so bad. And now he hurt some more. Mr. Powers was the beginning of hurt. Mr. Powers was the beginning of trouble. Mr. Powers was the beginning of sorrow.

"Mrs. Powers . . ." Donna reached to touch the woman's tight clutch as she gathered her legs up close, "we were very worried about you. Do you want us to call your doctor?"

And tell him the bruise came from a fall . . . beg him again to help you to cope, give you a pill. The doctor! The doctor didn't care. The doctor and Mr. Powers, quite a pair.

Tony offered the woman some tea. He bent over to look in her eyes. "I want you to drink this," he said with rather surprising authority. (Chosen was prying apart the woman's death grip.) She yielded and held the cup with both hands. This was a start.

"Mrs. Powers, is there anything we can do for you?"

Pay my bills, take away the hurt, make it all go away, wave a magic wand, make everything OK. It's all empty inside, see? Look for yourself! Nothing here but skin and bones. Inside is all cleared out. Just space.

"Mrs. Powers, look, you must talk to us," declared Tony, pushing his luck. "Mrs. Powers! Mrs. Powers!"

"Don't call me that!," she snapped. Victory! The angel fluttered his wings and caught his breath.

"We don't know your first name."

"Cathy."

Tony and Donna released a little tension and dug in more deeply. They both knew—instinctively—that they must get this woman talking; they must break through the thick barrier that stood between them and her.

"Cathy! You know, I've spoken to you on the phone so many times, and we've never really met! I am Donna, and this is my husband, Tony."

"Hi. And, thank you."

"Cathy, you need help. We will help you. You just have to tell us how."

Cathy almost spoke, her body crept forward, her jaw jutted just a bit, she was poised to speak . . . right . . . there . . . and the line went blank again. *This is a recording. The number you have reached is not in service.* Tony breathed in loudly through his nose and bit his lip.

"Cathy, you need to talk to us for your son's sake. Kyle needs you."

Cathy's head nodded imperceptibly, up and down, up and down. More feeble tremor than affirmation, she nodded, nodded, and followed thoughts as they ran away from her, far inside, she chased them, pursuing frantically, clutching. Kyle! Her beloved child. Love so deep it had no bottom, reaching into forever. She almost left him. She. Almost. Left. Him. She grabbed hold of a fleeing memory and flung it back into the present: *Tell me about your day . . .* they talked every night lying on blue Batman sheets, a pile of toys next to Kyle's bed. His sweet smell, his sweet words as they recounted each day, his silly jokes: the two of them. Her sweet babe. Every night. Every day. How close she had come to throwing that away. Her son! She would die for her son! She grabbed a chunk of broken heart and ripped it from the clutch of despair: her mother's heart pieced together grab by grab, Cathy put her feet on the floor and cleared her throat.

"I'm scared," she said, and began to cry, the company of heaven weeping. *Rejoice with those who rejoice; mourn with those who mourn.*

The Move

Now it was two families trying to liquidate belongings: a logger-turned-missionary-in-training with wife and kids, and a single mom with son who was squeezing belongings into her old car for a trip to Texas.

"You ought to make it to your brother's. I think we should pray some serious prayers over this thing before you leave, though!" Tony let the hood of the little compact drop before he pushed down and heard its *click!* Every belt replaced, the oil changed, new filters, new tires . . . Tony gave Cathy and Kyle a better than fair chance to make the trip in three days. He wished she wasn't traveling so far alone; if only she had a man on board. Or an angel.

Jason and Toby rode up to the loaded car on their bikes. After weeks of protest, Tony had consented to hire a larger U-haul so the trusty Stingrays and a few other important toys and belongings—*Mommmmm . . . that's my favorite! Tony, I'd be lost without this Crock Pot!*—would not suffer the fate of the dreaded garage sale. Yowls and howls had continued until personal possessions had been pared down to lean, and that went for Tony's books as well. No problem, since his most prized possession took very little room.

It had been four days since Cathy had sat in their flat, four days since they had huddled together and decided Cathy should go to her brother's in Texas. Money they'd saved for their trip would go to Cathy. "Don't think anything of it, Cathy. It is our gift to you." Tony and Donna would trust the Lord to find them cheap motels and prevent blowouts from their own worn tires.

Cathy had soaked up every drop of love the Sullivans could muster in those four days and now seemed stable enough to make the daunting trip. (Until she succumbed to the demons of despair, Cathy was a strong, intelligent woman.)

None the worse for wear, and completely oblivious to his mother's close brush, Kyle hugged Donna, shook Tony's hand, and said good-bye to his buddies. Bereft of Kleenex, Cathy used the back of her sleeve to hold off sniffles as she stepped back from a long clutch with Donna.

"You remember what I told you about Jesus," Donna whispered. "Promise me you will."

"I promise."

Cathy hugged Tony and the boys and joined Kyle in the car. Chosen prayed for her safe travel: *"Heavenly Father, whose presence is wherever we go, preserve this mother and child, surround them with Your loving care, protect them from every danger, and bring them in safety to their journey's end. And please, Holy One, send one of my own to follow and protect this woman and child."* Okey-dokey.

"Wait!" came Jason's call as he wheeled his prized Stingray toward the open passenger window.

"I want you to have my bike," said the nine-year-old, who had learned to follow the path of a man who walked in Galilee long ago.

Kyle was out of the car in a flash. Donna's entire body went into meltdown, choked with pride over this selfless act of her son. Pegged to be the heavy, though he, too, was touched by this grand gesture, Tony declared the gift impossible: there was no way to transport the bike.

"Yes there is, Dad. I figured we could cut pieces from a cardboard box so it doesn't scratch the car, and you have a bunch of rope near the spare tire in the station wagon." He'd thought this through. Kyle looked at Tony with pleading eyes. Tony snorted through his nose and jogged up the street to get the rope. And something else.

Shamed by his son's show of love for his friend, and bothered by his lackluster witness to Cathy over the past few days, Tony reached for his prized possession. Within a half hour, a rusty white Pinto with a shiny blue Stingray bike on its top and arms waving out its windows headed toward Texas.

The Sullivans stood in a cluster, waving back. Soon they would pile into their car and head toward Nebraska. Tears streaming down his face, Chosen opened his wings wide and held the family inside his embrace. He sniffled, and through trembling lips said his good-bye. He then turned and raced to catch up with a devoted mother, a loving son, and a skinny little book of Psalms.

Texas

The angel was certainly getting around! For two days he sailed through the Southwest, keeping Kyle's bicycle on top of the car his full-time job. Had it not been for Chosen, the bike would have tumbled off the Pinto several times. From time to time the Southwest reminded him of Samaria and Judea. For a mother and her son, it was like driving through an oven. They sang songs to occupy time: camp songs Cathy had learned as a Girl Scout, itsy-bitsy spider songs that made the eight-year-old-and-therefore-very-grown-up scream in protest, and "100 Bottles of Pop on the Wall," which was good for several miles of parched desert highway. When they hit the Texas border, it was love at first sight. For the angel, that is. To a mere mortal it was as if driving to the very edge of the world and staring at a new, strange geography of wide, barren space. It was another planet. But it was home to Chosen. The vast, arid, endless land with swale and gulch—how much it reminded him of the land where Jesus walked!

Cathy drove with one eye on her temperature gauge. As she'd promised Tony, she carried a gallon container of water, just in case. And "just in case" happened, interrupting an angel's reverie. The Pinto jerked to a stop, steam hissing under its hood. And there was not a person, a tree, a building, a road sign, a bush in sight.

Cathy forced herself to remember Tony's instructions. "Don't open the radiator cap too fast, use a rag, the steam will burn you, let it all cool down, fill it slowly or it will boil up."

The pavement was griddle hot, heat undulating upward in visible layers, and she wondered if her all-season radials would melt right on the spot. Kyle chased a lizard through the scrub. Cathy fiddled with the hood latch until it yielded to her pressure, the blast of steam and heat from underneath hitting her like a sauna. Unable to open the radiator cap, Cathy was close to tears—and burned herself just as Tony had predicted. Not only that, her water jug had leaked through its poor seal and soaked the backseat floor. She was in a predicament. Concerned about the predicament, Chosen rose high into the sky to have a look. Far in the distance, a Winnebago traced its way along a line of road drawn in the sand.

"OK, Jesus," Cathy said with uncertainty, "I need help."

Way down the road, as if sniffing along their trail, came the motor home. Cathy and Kyle sat in the shade of their car and waited.

Joe and Flo

Joe and Flo carried on active conversation as they tooled down the road. They'd been down thousands of roads in their sixty years together, yet still filled every waking moment with chatter. Today they were talking about Flo's cousin Harriet and her good-for-nothing husband.

"He could mow that grass with his teeth, that lawn is so small. I never seen such a lazy bum in my life."

"I know," said Flo in a singsong sort of way, "he's never going to change. Looks like Harriet will end up cutting the grass, just like always. Where are we now?"

"Looks like we're twelve miles out of Wildorado. Uh-oh."

"What?"

"Looks like someone's broke down, Grandma. We better see if we can help." Joe parked the motor home behind the Pinto and rolled down his window.

"Looks like you need some help," said Joe.

"Looks like you need to get out of that heat," said Flo. The two highway veterans opened their motor home and ushered a distraught mother and child into the welcome relief of air conditioning and lemonade.

"Looks like you got a whole house in that little car!" said Joe.

"Looks like you might be hungry," said Flo.

That is how it went. The kind couple, who could have been angels for their caring spirit, followed Cathy as she inched her crippled car to the nearest town. Kyle commandeered Flo's up-front seat and talked nonstop with the chatterbox couple.

A powwow with the mechanic revealed what Joe suspected: the radiator needed rebuilding.

"Where you headed, anyway?" he asked Cathy.

"Wylie. My brother lives there."

"Looks like we get to go to Wylie, Grandma," said Joe.

"Looks like we get to talk to Kyle for another day," said Flo. And they were off: a Winnebago pulling an old Ford Pinto with a Stingray bike on top, an angel the only one remembering a distraught mother's plea. *Thank you, Lord Jesus,* he said.

Neil

A day later the troupe pulled into the huge parking lot of the Covered Wagon Restaurant. A sign in the restaurant's window said: *Best grub this side of Dallas,* and meant it. The Covered Wagon was an institution, large enough to host people by the busload, cheap enough for a man to bring his family, and good enough to satisfy the appetite of the tallest, hungriest Texan in the state. The door to the motor home opened, and Kyle darted out. He'd been to the Covered Wagon once before and knew he would find his uncle near the till, supervising staff and collecting money.

Older than Cathy by ten years, Neil had swapped his chef hat for that of cowboy-in-chief when his boss retired from the restaurant business. A big, tan Stetson his trademark now, Neil was a fixture at the front of his eatery, glad-handing everyone who came through the door. Divorced and childless, he lived alone in a three-bedroom house behind the restaurant. *It will work out fine, Sis. You just get out here, and I'll take care of the rest. You need some cash to travel?*

Kyle walked back across the parking lot with a John Wayne swagger and a Stetson that stopped at his nose. "Howdy, partner," he said to Joe and Flo. "I was wonderin' if you'd all like to have some grub." And then, excitedly, "Mom! Uncle Neil said to come in with our friends and eat before we get settled!"

"Looks like we might as well stay around for a while, Grandma" said Joe.

"Looks like we're going to have a nice dinner," said Flo.

In keeping with the restaurant's tradition of Sunday closing, the next day Neil and Joe and Flo and Cathy and Kyle rested and barbecued, conversation as thick as the sauce on Neil's famous ribs. Cathy felt safe for the first time in years. It felt to her as if it had always been; it felt as if the two strangers in the Winnebago were family; it felt as if Neil had never left home to go into the service when she was ten; it felt as if she and Kyle had spent their lives in the back two bedrooms of Neil's comfortable ranch house. Cathy was surprised by Neil's sparkling personality and open heart. After all, with the exception of one visit while she and Cliff were married, she had had no contact with Neil as an adult. Other than obligatory holiday cards, that is.

Promising to send cards at Christmas, Joe and Flo waved good-bye to Cathy and Kyle as the two veteran travelers wheeled out of the parking lot on Monday morning.

Wylie

Life in Wylie would be idyllic for the mother and child. Expected only to "keep house, and heck, I'm never here to mess it anyway!" Cathy asked for a waitress job at the restaurant. After all, she explained, a woman needs her own "walking around money." She started on the busy lunch shift a week after she arrived, once she felt her son was acclimating to his new environment.

Worried about Kyle on a bike near the busy highway in front of the restaurant, Cathy explored the neighborhoods behind Neil's house and acquainted her son with safe passage into housing developments that held promise for friends. Chosen scouted the area with them and was first to find the stray kitten in their path.

"Mom! A cat!" Kyle pounced and the cat blasted up a tree. Hair spiked like porcupine quills on its humped back as the emaciated gray kitten hissed.

"It might be feral, Kyle, be careful."

"What's *feral*?"

"Wild."

Chosen flew into the tree and stroked the cat until it purred. He pushed the reluctant animal backwards, forcing its little claws to loosen and clutch, loosen and clutch, until it was in Kyle's hands. "Look, Mom, he's backing up! Can we keep him?"

Cathy had a soft spot for animals as big as . . . well, as big as the angel who was peering down from the tree. "If it's OK with Uncle Neil."

"He's smart, Mom! Did you see how he came down that tree? And look how he's sticking his head in my pocket. I bet he's hungry." Hungry was not the word.

After a trip to the store in Neil's Lincoln, a litter box was installed in the laundry room of the ranch house, and Sagacious (for smart) Clapsaddle (Neil's idea), aka Sage, became the light of a little boy's life. And, needless to say, of an angel's.

The hot, miserable, dusty, dry, wonderful, happy, safe, snug summer passed. Neil became surrogate father for his nephew, Cathy developed confidence in herself, Kyle found new friends, the cat ruled the house, and an angel became impatient over the lack of attention to spiritual matters. Cathy didn't even pray to "for lack of a better term" anymore, and the book rested in the glove compartment of a rusty Pinto, permanently ensconced behind Neil's garage.

"That thing is starting to grow weeds. I still think you should junk it, Cath."

"Not until I save enough to get another car."

"You can use the Lincoln anytime you want."

"Not the same. Besides, it's not hurting anyone stuck back there."

It's not helping anyone, either, pouted the angel.

The Abduction

Kyle was enrolled in a nearby school, transported by the black Lincoln each morning until he convinced his mother that a back route would be safe on his bike. Cathy stealthily followed him the first few mornings, strategically maneuvering the Lincoln through neighborhoods as she watched her young son with pride and assurance. Chosen followed Kyle to school and returned at the end of class, delighting in the mob of children when they scattered from the building like buckshot. Every day he flew alongside the boy on his bike, steadying the front wheel as Kyle raced over bumps on the trail. It would be a chilly day in late November that the angel waited by Kyle's Stingray as kids poured out from school, and he would wait in vain.

Earlier in the day a tall man with a mustache—that was the description given the police—had arrived at Page Elementary School in Wylie, Texas. A well-presented man, and filled with charm, he gave his name: Clifford Powers. He was there to pick up his son for Thanksgiving holiday.

Chosen saw Kyle's buddies leave the building one by one: Robert, Timmy, Colby . . . he craned his neck to see Kyle. No Kyle. He waited. And waited. After a time the school emptied of all its children as administrators and teachers finished work and custodians regained custody of the building. Custody. The familiar black Lincoln pulled up to the curb. Cathy approached the bike. A split-second thought charged through her mind, a sudden strike of lightning; she shook it off: it couldn't be possible. Kyle was probably in the school yakking with one of the janitors. He was probably at one of his friend's homes playing a game. Agh! He probably took the bus and was in the restaurant having a treat with Neil. For heaven's sake, he was probably already back home throwing a ball of aluminum foil for

Sage. Cathy's chest began to heave as her breathing took on the pace of fear.

Chosen searched the entire school building, raced to friend's homes, to the restaurant, found Sage sound asleep on Kyle's bed. Where was Kyle? *"Lord, God! Almighty Father! Please lead me to the boy!"* The angel was in a frenzy. *"My ways are not your ways. It will all work to My glory, Bashar. It will be hard. Comfort the woman."* Obedience. Obedience. He had sworn before the throne of God to obey. He did not have a human mind; he was not subject to human limitations; he knew—he knew that all things work to the glory of God—but still he questioned. *"Why?! After all she's been through! She has finally found rest!"*

"She has not found me."

Hell on Earth

There was no consoling Cathy. His restaurant left to the care of able managers, Neil would not leave his sister's side. The two of them became obsessed and tortured and frightened and furious. Cathy's anguish was overruled by one driving force: she would find her son; she would get him back. Nothing. Nothing! Do you hear me?! NOTHING! could separate her from her boy, the memory of a night near the Golden Gate sending her into spasms of revulsion. She would fight to the death; she would die—she would kill—nothing would stop her from finding her son. But where to look?

Neil approached his sister. Cathy was standing in the doorway to Kyle's room, choking on the devastating fear and sorrow that consumed her. Her knees buckled, and she sunk to the floor. Neil grabbed her shoulders and pulled her away, away from the torment of the quiet, empty space. Empty.

"Cath, look, the police are doing everything possible. I've got friends in the department. They will get him back. You have *got* to get some sleep."

"We have to go looking for him, Neil, please," she was begging him, begging the older brother who gave her shelter, gave her safety, gave her back a family. Older brothers are supposed to make everything all right. "Please, Neil." Her words were barely coherent through the anguish. "Please, we have to go and find him."

Neil held his sister's head next to his chest, the chest that held a heart as broken as hers, for he'd come to love the little boy with more than an uncle's love. Kyle was his blood, his flesh, his little buddy who snuck into the kitchen when he came home late at night—pie buddies, they called themselves, hushing giggles from Cathy's hearing. This boy, this nephew, was more like a son. "We will find him, Cath. I promise." But his promise was empty. He didn't know where to look. It had been three days.

Smells of turkey wafted from the Covered Wagon as pilgrims came by the carload to their traditional feast at Neil's restaurant. Since Kyle's abduction, it had been one long, continuous day. The idea of Thanksgiving dinner was repugnant to the owner of the popular restaurant.

Chosen begged. *Mighty One, the torment is too great for her! Please hear my cry!*

The angel knew the book played a role in this unfolding drama, but he could not resolve how to get Cathy to remember it, let alone retrieve it from its little tomb in a rusty, white Pinto. The phone rang. It was Donna, calling from Omaha—after all this time!—to wish her friends a happy Thanksgiving.

Donna turned ashen and gathered her boys to pray after she handed the phone to her husband, currently serving as Supervisor of Religious Instruction at their large church. Tony talked and prayed with Cathy for nearly an hour. Prayed! She hadn't prayed in so long: not even a word of thanks! Was this punishment?

"NO!" Tony nearly bellowed. "He bore all the punishment, Cathy. He didn't program your ex-husband to kidnap Kyle and cause this tragedy. But we do know He didn't stop Him. Cathy, you must believe that all things will work to His glory, and you must believe that He is not in the business of separating mothers from their children. Turn to Him, Cathy. Give this over to Him, put it in His arms. But Cathy . . ."

"Wh . . . wh . . . what," she mumbled through tear-dribbled lips.

"*You* have to crawl into His arms first."

"You mean J . . . J . . . Jesus?"

"Yes, Cathy, I mean Jesus."

There is no Bible in this house! Mention the book! Tell her to read the book! Tell her to read Psalm 5! Chosen paced impatiently. He wanted the boy back too.

Cathy lay on her bed after the call. There was no wrestle, no fight, just awkward silence as she desperately tried to remember Tony's words so she could get this matter over . . . she had to crawl into His arms first . . . then she would hurry and turn this over to God. But she didn't know what to do! In an awkward fit, she bolted upright on the bed and talked to the ceiling.

"Whoever you are, whatever you are, HELP ME." Nothing happened. The ground didn't rumble; the sky didn't fall. The ceiling stared back. "HELP ME! Don't you hear me?! Help me!" She was screaming now. Neil ran into the room. "Why is God letting this happen to me?!" Cathy shrieked and ran from the house. She ran because she had to get away, but went nowhere. She ran because the agony of her heart was pushing her to action. The house was holding her back, stopping her. See, if she was in the house, she couldn't find her son. Because he wasn't home. He was out there. She stood in the yard between the house and the garage. Now what?! Not to worry, the angel had a plan.

How Sage managed to get inside the Pinto will always remain a mystery, but as Cathy stood in the yard, she heard his urgent meow. The cat's cry frantic, she followed his call. Seeing his mistress, Sage rubbed his body against the seat. Rather than dart out when Cathy opened the door, the cat backed toward the passenger side (well, the cat was *pushed* toward the passenger side), where (surprise, surprise) the glove compartment was sprung open, a skinny book occupying a rather prominent spot. Cathy reached into the car for the cat. Sage rubbed his face on the corner edge of the compartment lid. Cathy saw the book. *Cathy, this is my treasured possession. It was given to me by a friend when I felt my life was over for the shambles it was in. I want you to have it. Read it. I promise you, Cathy, as the Lord God has promised, the words in this book will not return void.*

Hope surged through Cathy as she raced back to the house. A confidence swept over her now: she'd found the key to unlock the treasure, a clue to solve the problem. She'd uncovered the code word to open the closed door, the door marked Enter Here to Find Son.

In the privacy of her bedroom Cathy opened the book. Or rather, because Buck's postcards and Will's crude confession were bunched in one spot, the book nearly opened itself. Way up toward the front. Cathy stared at the words of Psalm 5. And with each reading she became more confident, more convinced that Tony might be right.

Under other circumstances Cathy would have scoffed at the notion of trusting anything—anyone—so suddenly, but she was desperate enough to put her trust in Jesus. And so when she repeated the words of the psalm, she replaced every reference to the Lord with the name of Jesus until she proclaimed his name with conviction.

"'Give ear to my words, Jesus, consider my meditation.
Hearken unto the voice of my cry, my Jesus, for unto you do I pray.
My voice shalt thou hear in the morning, Jesus, in the morning will I direct my prayer unto thee, and will look up. For thou art not a God that hath pleasure in wickedness'. . . ."

He didn't program your ex-husband to kidnap Kyle and cause this tragedy. All things will work to His glory. He is not in the business of separating mothers from their children. Give this over to Him, put it in His arms.
"'. . . let all those that put their trust in thee rejoice, let them ever shout for joy, because thou defendest them' . . . thou defendest them. Jesus! Defend my boy, bring him home to me, please, please I beg you!"

And I beg you, too, Holy One, bring him home, whispered Chosen as he tenderly touched the shoulder of a heartsick mother as she knelt by her bed.

The Phone Call

Sooner or later, sleep will claim its victims. Struggle as she did to stay alert, Cathy fell asleep on the couch. Neil remained posted next to the phone. His head nodded, nodded, until it finally submitted and hung in front of his chest, pulling neck muscles like taffy in a souvenir shop window. The phone was Neil's command post. From the phone he had spoken to friends on the force, networked with the Missing Person's Bureau. It was theoretically too soon to call Kyle missing, and the Missing Children's Act would not be legislated for another year. Neil also had consulted with a private detective firm in Dallas. A tall man in a mustache with a boy. At Thanksgiving time. Were they in a car? What did it look like? Which state plates? Was it a rental? How about a plane? A train? They could be on another continent by now. Neil protected Cathy from the phone and bore the pain of possibility himself. When it rang, it startled the dozing man. Cathy stirred in her sleep.

Neil shook his sister's arm. "Cathy! Quick! It's Kyle!"

Feet wrapped in an afghan, Cathy tripped face first onto the living room floor, the swift move of an angel bringing her to her feet and to the phone. Oh, God!!! Kyle!

Kyle spoke in spurts of broken sentences through heaving sobs. "Mommy! Mommy . . . my . . . whole . . . body . . . is . . . mad! Mommy, tell Uncle Neil . . . to come . . . and get me!"

"Where are you, Kyle?! Kyle, listen to Mommy, slow down"—*Slow down, Cathy*—"Is your father with you?"

"No, he's . . . sleeping."

"Kyle, *where are you?*"

"I'm at a . . . telephone . . . on the street."

"*Where?!*"

"I think it's a . . . place called . . . New Orleans. Come . . . and get me!"

"Kyle, are there people nearby?"

"There's people . . . all over the place. I don't . . . like it here. I want . . . to come home."

"Kyle, is there a street sign near you?"

"No."

"What about stores?"

"There's a lot . . . of bars . . . and restaurants . . . and a lot . . . of noise."

"Tell me the name of one of the restaurants," Neil barked into the phone, for he was sharing the receiver with his sister.

"It . . . looks . . . like Bren, Bren . . . something."

"Brennans?" Chosen was off in a flash.

"Yes . . . Uncle Neil . . . come . . . and get me."

"Kyle, son, listen to me. I want you to find a policeman and tell him to bring you to his headquarters. There should be cops all over the place down there. Do you see one?"

"I saw . . . one go by . . . in a car."

"Kyle, do *not* go with anyone no matter how nice they are. Is there a number on the phone?"

"No."

"Stay where you are, and the next time the policeman comes by, you stop him. I'm going to run to the restaurant and call the police. You stay on the phone with your mother."

Neil raced off, fingers trembling as he fumbled for the right key. He blasted to the wall phone in the chef's cubby.

Cathy gulped back fear . . . *slow down, Cathy* . . . and calmed her voice for her son.

"He said . . . we were all going on a trip . . . for Thanksgiving, that you . . . were coming here . . . then he said . . . you were bad . . . Mommy, I'm scared!"

"Kyle, listen to me. I talked to Tony today, and he told me to pray to Jesus and I did. Kyle, I want you to do the same thing."

"I don't . . . know how."

"Mommy will pray with you."

Chosen shot through the French Quarter like a guided missile: he was looking for his boy. Past open doors where lasciviousness spilled onto the sidewalks, through clusters of moral deviants and drunken tourists, the angel searched for a little boy on a phone. Police were on their way, as well, but all were too late. Someone else was searching too.

"Dad!" came the scream on the phone before it went dead.

Cathy shrieked into the phone. She had him—they were connected, the two of them, like they'd always been. She would not lose him again. "Jesus!" Cathy pleaded, "defend my little boy!" At that moment that is exactly what He was doing, through an angel called Chosen.

As a man's strong arm reached into the phone booth, a passing reveler threw him off balance, giving the boy the chance to slam the door. Push with all his might, the tall man with a mustache was no match for an eight-year-old boy with angel backup. The man cursed and kicked, but a mighty fortress was the phone booth.

What an outrage this was to Chosen! How can man's rebellion lead to this, that a son must be protected by all of heaven against a rampaging father?

The man kicked hard, shattering a plastic panel out of place. Under the hold of fierce fury, he reached through the panel to grab the boy's legs. A phantom force came down hard on his arm and pinned it to the phone booth floor— just as a police car pulled next to the curb.

* * *

It took several months to settle legal matters between Cathy and Clifford Powers, whose sudden interest in his son merely added to the confusion and heartbreak. His motive nothing more than punishment for Cathy, Cliff caused trouble at first. When Cathy once and for all stood her ground and hired a knowledgeable attorney, Cliff faded into a past that Cathy would rather forget—were it not for the fact that she had given her life to Christ during the turmoil. Not to mention, it was when she met Chuck.

Without a formal divorce (after all, Cliff abandoned his wife and child and seemed to just disappear), custody became a sticky wicket, but thanks to Chuck, Cathy prevailed. Ensuing restraining orders were put in place for added protection, yet until the boy was older there would be an edge to their lives, a guard that would not come down.

Peace at Last

Sundays had once meant sleeping late, barbecue, and conversation. Now the family of three—soon to be four, as Cathy's romance with her lawyer had blossomed into a marriage proposal—gussied up for church. As always, Neil wrestled with homework from his Sunday school class. As always, Cathy laughed and kissed him on his bald spot, prime reason for the Stetson.

Kyle swept his dresser of loose change for the mission's collection and brushed a hair off his pants. The very grown-up ten-year-old was eager to get going: youth workers were taking the children to a local water slide after church.

Cathy adjusted her makeup one more time. Chuck would meet them at church.

Hard as it was, Cathy forced herself to pray for Cliff. She prayed that her unregenerate ex-husband would someday know the Lord as she did—and her prayers now had a beginning and an end.

It was during her quiet prayer time lately that she had a nagging notion to return Brenda's gift to its rightful owner. She, too, had come to think of the book as a treasure. But she had a brand-new study Bible to fill her needs. And then there was the matter of the still, small voice of God, this time corroborated by the prod of a gentle angel, for Chosen was already in prayer over his next assignment.

After church Cathy bought a package of manila envelopes, and while Neil and Chuck visited in the living room, she sat at the table and printed an address.

Chapter

Eleven

June 1987

There was no farewell salute, no party, no gold watch, no celebration. With the exception of one colleague who took pity on the man, there would have been no notice of the empty office, emptied of its volumes of literature so exquisite that they could only be called classic, emptied of its clandestine stash of booze. No longer would *The Sonnets of William Shakespeare* hide the scotch; the sonnets were gone. No longer would the bottom desk drawer hide a pint of vodka; the drawer was empty. No longer would the deep pocket of a raincoat that hung in the corner conceal little bottles of gin; the coat was rolled into a bundle and stuck on top of a box of belongings. It was time for the man to retire, time for him to leave. Finally. And good riddance. Tenure holding him to his position until now, others on the staff shared relief or repulsion, depending on their moral barometer, when the man retired.

He was a broken man. Broken in outward appearance from the withering blight of alcohol: body thin from forgetfulness to eat, whites of eyes yellow from a protesting liver, face and hands red-streaked with spider veins gone berserk. Personal hygiene gone, too, the man's graying hair was slick with grease that comes from grime, dandruff covered his shoulders like a shroud, clothes were stained and wrinkled, fingernails dirty. And that was just the outside.

If it were possible to look at another person's soul, if there were such a thing as a machine that scanned our inside places until it found the dust of the ground commingled with the breath of life in that composition called soul—*Smile for the camera!*—then a picture would be worth many, many sorrowful words. For the man's soul was black. Black like the board he used all those years, black with not even a trace of chalk dust left. The picture would break the heart of anyone who could see what lay inside.

The man left work for the last time. His car slithered from the faculty lot like a rat scurrying from the light of day. It was headed to a bar on the seamy side of town that held the stench of darkness, where he would pay to stay. The sedan's backseat filled with boxes, there was nary a demon in sight. Spiritual forces of evil had gone on to other souls, souls with still the slightest dust of white.

Full Circle

It was later than usual when the man returned home, for this was a special day, this retirement day, and it deserved special observance. Chosen watched as the car pulled into the driveway, his eyes widening in unbelief as the man got out of his car. *Father, God!* he cried.

The man ignored his mailbox, hardly worth checking, for not even his sister wrote any longer—and that because of mere outward appearance! Mail just brought bills. Or those confounded catalogs, a nuisance to the man who pitched them on a growing mound on top of a flower-patterned living room rug. And so a book returned to its rightful owner sat in the mailbox, in a manila envelope addressed to William Harwood at his home in a suburb of Chicago.

Chosen followed Professor Edward P. Harwood into his filthy home and summoned all the stamina and grit he had, for this would be a formidable duty. *How marvelous are Your mercies, O God, Your mercies endure forever!* The angel fluttered his wings.

Ed pulled himself upstairs with the railing, walked by Will's door as if it were wall, flopped on his bed, and was immediately asleep. Chosen stared at the man for a long while. Here lay the absolute depravity of living a life apart from God. This is how it can go. Ed rejected it all: light, grace, peace, life, even the moral sensibilities in which he was raised. What moral memory there might have been was lost in a fog of booze. And the angel wasn't looking at the outside.

While Ed slept, Chosen explored the home. He went straight to Will's room. Surprisingly—*very* surprisingly—it was exactly as he'd last seen it. Hangers in the closet once again in their neat row, the boy's wooden box of treasures hidden way back on the closet shelf. There were the dog tags, Brenda's unopened letter, carnival trinkets, and coins. The angel slipped from the shrine, the little grotto, a once-upon-a-time resting place for a mother gone mad. *Where was Patty?*

The angel searched the house for signs of Patty, but none were there. No clothes, no personal belongings, no makeup or perfume, no Old Gold cigarettes. No Patty. Just grimy drapes shut tight against day and night in a living room where junk mail piled on top of the shapes of roses that never connected.

Patty had been dead for seventeen years. Driven past delusion, past pain, past caring, past life, Patty deteriorated physically and emotionally after Will's death. During the winter of 1970 she wandered off one night in search of her little boy. (This happened just when Ed was looking into a mental institution for his demented wife.) Her obituary was short and succinct: *Wife of Local Scholar Dies: Patricia Harwood, née Smith, was found dead yesterday from exposure. There will be no services, the family requests that no cards or flowers be sent.* Listen to that! A local "scholar" no less! Exposure! She froze to death near a swingset on a playground three blocks from home! The family requests! What family?! Her family, the one back in Charlottesville, Virginia? They didn't even know! Ed?! He was glad his ordeal was over. Now he could get on with life, become the man he was destined to be, now that he was rid of that sorry mess. His plebeian wife and idiot son. To *think* he could have had another imbecile under foot!

The Abortion

Soon after young Will's limitations became clear, soon after the good professor began to turn his own insecurities and lack of personal responsibility into virulent attacks on his wife and son, whom he blamed for holding him back, soon after he became particularly dependent on the jug, Patty announced she was pregnant again. Not again! Not over his dead body! Bad enough he had one half-wit. He *knew* better than to marry beneath his class—he would not beget another idiot.

All of Patty's pleadings fell upon deaf ears and upon a soul that was beginning its journey toward solid, scratch-resistant enamel black. Patty loved Will, wanted children, could not—*under any circumstance, do you hear me?!*—allow this to happen to her baby. Destroy the life inside her?! She was wild with fight. How could he think such thoughts . . . where did this thinking come from?! *Hurry, run, go someplace, you can't do this to my baby! No! Stop!*

He nearly dragged her up the steps to the third floor of the tenement. The steps were divided by several landings, landings where they could rest before turning to follow more steps and rest again. There was a small, filmy window at each landing, covered with clumps of dust and spiderwebs that looked like pockets on a pool table. Patty pleaded at each turn. *Please! Stop! I'll go away! I'll take the children and go someplace else, please, oh my God, please, I can't . . .*

Two women greeted the couple. Their apartment was dark; that was all Patty could remember. It was dark and had one long, lush, tufted couch along a wall. And one of those wall hangings that look like black velvet rugs. A bloody bullfight. The women were not kind. They weren't particularly mean, either. They, well, they were in business—black-market, illegal, but, hey, business is business—and treated the couple as another transaction. Patty was led into a bedroom with a large bed and ordered to lie down. She protested. One woman pushed her. Not a mean push, you see, just part of the transaction to get the business day over with. Patty begged, whimpered, and clutched the chenille bedspread as she was approached by a woman who brandished a meat baster filled with lye soap and turpentine. And then she was degraded, dehumanized, raped, bludgeoned, set on fire, martyred, tromped upon, and brutally violated as one woman held her knees apart and another squeezed a rubber bulb. That afternoon, in a tenement in Chicago, Patty snapped, Ed was rid of a potential liability, and a baby died.

So in the winter of 1970 when Patty died, she died only a physical death, a death of outward appearance, for she had been dead inside for a very long time.

Preparation

Chosen recognized the urgent need to prepare for this mission with fervent prayer, for the angel would be facing extreme challenge in the weeks to come, when—so his prayers implored—God's mercy would triumph over His justice in this hopeless situation. Chosen *must* hope. For the angel, there could be no other way, no other thought than one that led to hope. He had seen the most unregenerate souls come to repentance and regeneration . . . and redemption. He could not abandon hope, as certainly as the Ancient of Days was not abandoning Ed, and a book lay stuffed in a mailbox outside.

If it knew the story behind the living room drapes, the world would not hope and pray for mercy. It would demand punishment for Ed. It would scream for justice. But angels held a higher understanding of justice, of justice that could redeem, an understanding of justice that brought it under the supremacy of mercy. *I will have mercy on whom I have mercy, saith the Lord.* The world wouldn't understand; the angel could. Bashar-el knew with all of his being that God's justice could be swept away through His mercy—even though Ed Harwood deserved the punishment of hell.

I will give him another chance, Bashar. I stand at the door of his heart, but he must decide to let Me in. My knock will become louder. Chosen thought a battering ram might be more effective as he watched the sleeping man.

Thursday

It wasn't necessary for Ed to leave home. It didn't matter that the sun was shining and that birds were calling to each other on tree branches in his unkempt backyard. The unsightly mess in the Harwood's backyard provoked one neighbor to erect a high, solid fence. Lucky for all his neighbors, though, that Ed had hired a young man to trim the two patches of lawn in his front yard.

Everyone in the neighborhood referred to the Harwood home as if it sat behind a shadowy screen of obscurity. *Step right up to the House of Mystery! Pay your quarter and have a peek through the drapes! Surprise! Nobody home!*

Benjamin was a hard worker. He pushed his lawn mower through the neighborhood, rake over his shoulder, a plastic gasoline jug swinging from the handle, heavy-duty trash bags shoved in his back pocket. Strong, athletic legs bulged from dungaree cutoffs; thick wool socks cushioned feet from ankle-high hikers. Benjamin liked the wacky professor. And the wacky professor liked Benjamin, in spite of the cross the teen wore prominently around his neck.

The roar of the mower broke the silence of the house. A muscular young man under earphones—the music in his Walkman turned up louder than the mower (a point of issue between the good boy and his parents)—pushed the machine in neat rows, back and forth. Ed poked his head out the door. He was sporting a three-day growth. Benjamin waved and turned off the motor.

"Saw your car, Professor. Finished school for the year?"

"Finished school for good," answered Ed.

Benjamin stared at the unkempt man, a pinch of sorrow for his condition. The gregarious boy jumped right into the middle of an embarrassed silence.

"What are you going to do now? Travel?"

Ed's head jerked. It was a queer kind of movement, the kind of reaction you have when suddenly you are faced with a thought that has never passed through your brain before. Why, he hadn't even thought about "what," let alone travel.

"I will probably catch up on some reading," he liked the boy enough to try to impress him. "And I may try to clean up this place."

"Hey! I could help you on Saturday!"

Whoa. He didn't mean right away! But he would be glad to be around Benjamin some more; he *needed* to be around the boy. Truth be known, Benjamin was the first person in a long time to treat him in that wonderful, insipid, casual way that people treat other people whom they consider normal. There were no strange stares, no rude comments, none of the avoidances he'd grown accustomed to, no polite protocol, no "ahems" or pauses in embarrassed silence. Benjamin just talked to him as a regular guy. He didn't feel like the "wacky professor" around Benjamin.

Chosen liked the boy at once. It felt wonderful to be in the company of a believer, to be in the boy's bright light after days in the oppressive dark of Ed's boozy tomb. Besides, maybe Chosen could use this boy . . . hmmmm. The angel looked at the mailbox and back to the boy and Ed.

"Say, Professor, maybe you could help me plan my schedule for my senior year!" said Benjamin, glad the old duffer was talking to him.

"Yes, probably," grumbled the cranky man as he headed inside, glad that the boy was talking to him.

Benjamin reached for the starter cord and gave it a yank. The pulley offered no resistance, sending the boy backwards into the mailbox, which opened and spilled mail onto the ground. "Ow!" said the boy. *Yay!* said the angel.

"Hey, Professor," came a knock at the door, "here's your mail."

To Ed, the color of manila meant magazine sweepstakes. Poised to toss the envelope onto his mountain, he felt the certain feel of a book. When he saw the name of his long dead son, his head jerked once again.

Brenda's gift slapped against the dull, cluttered Formica table. There was a nod inside the place where memory is kept, barely perceptible, mind you, but a nod of recognition. The book lay on the table staring at Ed. He stared back. The angel stared at both and hoped and prayed. And nothing happened. The note that fluttered to the floor stayed there. In the meantime, Ed reached for a bottle to quench his thirst, to throw *another* bucket of water on a fire long, long dead, to be absolutely certain no embers were left. We wouldn't want a fire, would we?

Chosen prayed until he was weak. Sin had taken such a strong hold of this man, he feared that God would give him over to a reprobate mind. He shuddered when he recounted the words of Peter, words superintended by God the Holy Spirit: *"The Lord knows how to rescue godly men from trials and to hold the unrighteous for the day of judgment while continuing their punishment. This is especially true of those who follow the corrupt desire of the sinful nature and despise authority."*

Yet mercy prevailed. That is why he was there, on a mission of mercy so great as to seem absurd, contrived, happily-ever-after-Amen. *Go to the man, Bashar, and minister to him throughout. I will knock. I will be heard. But the choice must remain his.*

Choose this day whom you will serve. Self or God. Can't be any clearer.

Saturday

Ed was drunk when Benjamin arrived on Saturday, and the boy knew it. He'd been praying for the wacky professor since Thursday, and in the idealistic, romantic, and yes—innocent—way of teens . . . *Lord, God, help me reach Professor Harwood for Jesus!* . . . he considered the man a personal ministry.

"What are you listening to under that thing?" Ed asked as he brought Benjamin into his backyard jungle.

"It's a group called Petra. Sort of like Christian rock."

Ed snorted and returned to his tomb. Sounded like an oxymoron to him: Christian rock. He sat at the kitchen table and stared at the book. A sharp pain in his chest came, again, like it had been coming for years. He'd grown accustomed to the jab, long since abandoning medical attention to avoid a predictable scolding from his doctor. Ed knew he was an alcoholic: he'd known for years. He didn't have to "admit" it to anyone. Now that school was over for good he didn't have to hide it anymore, either. He could come and go and stay and sit and drink and sleep and care or not as he pleased. He answered to nobody. Never did. Ed chose self. It couldn't be any clearer.

A knock came at the door. Benjamin needed a drink of water.

"Use the faucet outside."

"It's all rusted shut; I can't open it."

Ed stepped aside, and the boy entered the kitchen. The room stank. Not so much of garbage, but ... well, sort of like the smell of decaying flesh, of body odor, like a tight closet smells when it needs airing. Benjamin was mighty embarrassed when he saw the dirty dishes on the counter. Ed was embarrassed too. The boy panicked at the thought of using a glass for his water and was in a bit of a dither. He wanted to run outside, fresh air certainly trumping his thirst. Ed wiped a glass and handed it to him.

"I don't suppose you do dishes," said the man, half-trying to joke, for his embarrassment was great. For some inexplicable reason, it mattered what the boy thought of him.

Benjamin hesitated, but remembered his prayers. "I do dishes all the time for my mom," he declared in a way that said: *Sure, I do, and I'd hire out to do yours if you'd like.* He sipped at his water. "I could come after school on Monday. Maybe then you could help me with that schedule. I have to turn it in this week."

This was a fine howdy-do. Ed didn't really *intend* for the boy to help him. But, you know, it might be a good idea. "How much?" he asked.

"Tell you what! We'll trade. You help me plan my senior year" (he'd already *planned* his senior year with his parents) "and I'll do your dishes. Deal?"

"Deal."

Benjamin-the-Missionary was headed out the door when an angel toe pushed a piece of paper under his foot. "This was on the floor," he announced as he stuck the note in Ed's hands and headed to the backyard.

It might as well have been flypaper. Ed really did not want to read the note, but he just ... could ... not ... get himself to put it down. He leaned against the kitchen counter and held it close to failing eyes.

> *Dear Mr. Harwood,*
> *My name is Cathy Powers. A few years ago, a friend gave me this book. He said it came to his rescue, and I sure can say it came to mine! I've felt the urge during my prayer time to return it to you, for it must have been as much a treasure to you as it was to me. Thank you so much for*

the "loan" of this book . . . and please give my regards to Brenda, if you
still are acquainted with her. May God's rich grace and mercy shine upon
you all your days.
       Cathy Powers

Ed crumpled the note, threw it on the floor, and stormed from the
house. He did not look at nor touch Brenda's gift, to an angel's relief, for
Chosen remembered well the last time Ed stormed from the house, book in
hand!

The Evil Spirit

"I kind of like the old guy, Dad, but he intimidates me a lot."

"There is a lot of bad history in that house, Benjamin. He may be very
bitter."

"I don't know if I like you going inside that house," added his mother.

Benjamin gave his mother the look of *Excuse me, but I am seventeen years*
old, I can bench-press two-hundred-fifty pounds, and I will be off on my own in a year.
She smiled, mindful of the change in their relationship as her son began to
reach for independent status.

Benjamin was at the Harwood house by 6:30 Monday evening. What
he saw was alarming.

The screen door was unlocked, the main door open (on purpose?), and
the boy tentatively stepped in when calls went unanswered. Ed Harwood sat
on a yellow Naugahyde chair next to the kitchen table. The man sat slumped,
blood from his nose dried on his lip, down his chin, on the back of the hand
he'd used as a wipe, and on various piles of paper as if he'd leaned over the
table and bled while searching for something. A big blotch had landed on the
edge of the book and slid down its side, the edge of its pages soaking the
blood like a blotter. Benjamin shook the man's shoulders.

"Professor!"

Ed looked into the boy's face, not three inches from his. His breath
blasted the foul smell of liquor and gum disease. "Oh, it's you . . ."

Chosen looked with pity on the man. It had been quite a battle.

* * *

Whether it was because of the angel's presence—or most likely, the presence of the Word of God—Ed was to be haunted by demons once again. Chosen was prepared for the onslaught, for he was certain they'd appear at the slightest prospect of losing a soul: to keep souls eternally separated from God and defeat the children of God on earth was the overriding mission of the fallen ones.

Long ago consigned to the lost, Ed Harwood had not been of interest to them for years. But now that even a *single* book of the Bible, of the eternal Logos, was present, they came.

Chosen had been in special prayer and preparation for the inevitable; the battle over this man's soul would wage for weeks. Why someone like Ed Harwood would matter to the demonic realm might puzzle those with mortal minds and human limitations, but it was of no surprise to those who existed on the spiritual plane. One soul submitted to the Holy of Holies was another reminder of their defeat in the culmination of time, another reminder of their doom. The Master spoke of their coming destruction in a parable. Chosen drifted back to the hard words of Jesus on the Mount of Olives, when the Lord had spoken of false prophets, of His return, of preparation, of stewardship, of charity. *When the Son of Man comes in all his glory, and all the angels with him* . . . How the heavenly host yearns for that day! The Master spoke of the wicked. *Then he will say to those on his left, Depart from me, you who are cursed, into the eternal fire prepared for the devil and his angels.*

Oh, how you have fallen from heaven, O morning star, son of the dawn. Such were the thoughts that mingled with supplication on behalf of the angel and his charge.

Other than a few forays to the store for more booze, frozen pizza, milk, and shredded wheat, Ed stayed housebound. His forays into the kitchen became more numerous as he was drawn to the book on the table. Chosen did his best to make the book as evident as possible. Curiosity, and an angel's prayers, were getting the best of Ed. Round the table he would walk, until he'd scuffed a path in the dirty floor. *On the seventh day, march around the city seven times . . . the wall of the city will collapse.* Like a caged tiger paces back and forth, Ed went round and round. And during his journey the faint nod of memory brought him back to his son.

His son! Why couldn't he have been like Benjamin! Why couldn't he have been like so many other sons he'd taught through the years. Why?

Chosen paced around the table with the man. He discerned great evil.

"And so the ministering angel returns to save the soul of the drunken man. This man has been given up to a reprobate mind, Bashar." It was a bluff.

Bashar-el was ready. *"You come because you fear you will lose him. You fear your hold will weaken. And you are right. You cannot withstand the power of the Word. This man is being drawn by grace. Be gone! The Lord rebuke you!"*

"I will not go anywhere."

Ed began to curse. Foul words came from his mouth, words that could come only from hell. Chosen brandished the Word of truth and steadied the man who stumbled in a circle, a bottle of whiskey in his hand. The man swung at imaginary people. "Hahaha! I am Professor Harwood from the Harwoods of Richmond! I am their distinguished son. Hahaha!" (He swatted the air: *Get outta my way!*) "I could be president! Did you know that?" (He spoke to the chair.) "Know what I wanted? I wanted to be like Faulkner. Yes, yes, that's true, I did! And . . . shshhhh . . . you want to know a very BIG secret? I wanted to be the father of many sons! Hahaha!" (He talked to the book.) "But then I got you! You little moron. I got you! Hahaha!"

Chosen prayed: *"It is written: the prince of this world stands condemned! Great is the Lord and most worthy of praise!"*

The demon egged the professor on. "Here is what I think of you!" he said as he held the whiskey bottle over the book and poured. Chosen pushed the man off balance and the whiskey hit the floor. "Hahaha! You just wait! You'll get yours! Oh, hahaha, you already got yours, didn't you? Your mother did too. God's rich grace and mercy shine on the *both* of you, my dearly departed family! Grace and mercy on you, too, God! You need all the help you can get! Hahaha!"

"You see how he curses God, Bashar? He deserves hell. He does not deserve redemption. God is just, is He not? Do you hope for a cute conversion? That is the stuff of fluffy novels! This is real, Bashar; he is real. Watch what I do with him!"

Ed felt the pain in his chest again. This time it caught his breath and wrung it tight. He flopped into a chair and gasped. He felt hot. His nose began to bleed.

He took the Lord's name in vain over and over and over. He dragged the Name through the sewer, through mud, over dung heaps, into rat-infested cellars, down into the stench of hell. He cursed, the demon laughed, and the angel stood undeterred. *Salvation is found in no one else, for there is no other name under heaven given to men by which we must be saved!*

Ed groped for the book, bent on destruction. In spite of the vise in his chest, and incited by the bottle, Ed stood, using both hands to lean over the table, unable to find the book. He didn't need his son barging into his life right now. Blood dripped in huge splats. Splat, splat, splat. Overconfident from his power over the man, the demon went too far.

Aha! There it is! As he reached for the book, Ed slumped back in the chair, a grand-slam blast to his heart screamed for attention. The angel grabbed him with arms and wings and held him tightly. *Merciful Father! Look with pity on this man. Comfort him with Your goodness. Giver of health and salvation! Drive all sickness and oppression from him. In the name of Jesus!* Chosen held the stuperous man for hours, until a young man stopped by to wash dishes.

* * *

Benjamin wanted to call the ambulance. Ed would have nothing of it. "Come back and do the dishes tomorrow."

Tuesday

Benjamin went back the next day at dinnertime, carrying a casserole. His father found an excuse to stop by ... *Thought you'd like to know your friend Kelly called* ... It was a ruse, a reason to size up the professor; a nod hello to Ed, the kind of nod that men allow when they are on their guard. Ed didn't bother to nod back. His head was splitting and that darned pain in his chest was getting worse. Maybe he *should* go to the doctor.

"Your father was checking me out," said the professor.

Benjamin protested, arms up to his elbows in soapsuds.

"No, it's a good thing. It means he cares about you. Consider yourself lucky."

"I do, Professor Harwood. Say, didn't you have a son?"

Ed would not reply, and Benjamin went on washing. When he had said he did dishes at home, he *meant* he loaded the dishwasher.

"I'm glad that you're better today," the boy declared, trying to sound casual, trying to show concern, trying to be cautious: the three C's. Sort of like the three R's. Reading was OK for Benjamin, 'riting was his life's dream, but 'rithmatic! Forget it.

"My mom says I should take creative writing next year. I want to go to college for a degree in English Lit." Ed's head didn't move, yet his eyes looked up. "My dad says I should continue Latin, says if I learn Latin well, I will enhance my writing skills tremendously. He says I should study the classics."

"Listen to your father," said Ed, the teacher in him trumping any determination not to get close.

"What did you teach, Professor?"

"English Literature, with an emphasis on the classics. I can help you with Latin if you'd like." Benjamin nearly dropped a plate. *Dad! It's just like the Lord, isn't it? So then he says to me . . . "with an emphasis on the classics!"*

And they were off. Plate after crusty plate, glass after murky glass, the sink was emptied and filled three times before kitchen cupboards were once again stocked with dishes with blue willow trim. Chosen was brighter than the landing lights on a 747—and just about as high in the sky.

Friends

Benjamin became somewhat a fixture in the Harwood kitchen. Ed was drunk much of the time, yet the boy tried to weasel his way into the man's life, tried to witness, waited for the right time to share Jesus. The angel battled against the fury of hell, and the book sat on the table. During one of his visits, Ed was particularly mean-spirited.

"Why do you wear that cross?" It wasn't a question; it was an indictment, a sneer.

"I'm proud of it!" It wasn't an answer; it was a proclamation, a smile.

"Stick it under your shirt and keep it to yourself."

"No, sir."

"I don't believe in blind faith." Whoa! Where did *that* come from?!

"Neither do I, Professor. That's why I'm a Christian!"

Way to go, Benjamin! Good job! crowed the angel.

Benjamin sensed the book played some sort of role in this man's life, but got the message—*Leave it where it is!!*—that he must not touch it. If there was any way to consort, the angel and the boy would have been in cahoots, for they both prayed and schemed to prompt Ed to pick up Brenda's gift. What to do. What to do.

Benjamin's Latin was improving. His aptitude excited Ed. Now this, *this,* was the real thing! This was what it should have been like! To have such an excellent young man, a young man of character, good physical form, propriety, and an outright lust for the subjects Ed loved most—never mind that computer nonsense that was ruining good minds nowadays!—this was food to the starved man.

The Plan

Benjamin turned on his side and punched his pillow for good measure, a Cheshire smile from ear to ear: Benjamin had a plan. When he arrived at Ed's home a few days later, Chosen laughed and praised the Lord. *Of course! Jerome!* Now why hadn't he thought of that?

Benjamin had had to call the Roman Catholic Diocese to obtain a copy of the Latin Vulgate. He nonchalantly plopped it on the table and bantered with Ed before he got down to business.

"Wow! What a find! I didn't know the Bible was written in Latin!" Benjamin lied. Did lies count when he was trying to save a man's soul?

"Jerome. Under Pope Damascus." Ed had taught "The Bible As Literature" at least a dozen times during his tenure. It was all quite surgical, pedantic. Just facts about a book. No big deal. Could have just as easily been Ovid or Milton. "Actually, Jerome revised an older manuscript of the Old Testament that had already been translated into Latin."

"Wow! I didn't know that." Another lie; Benjamin had spent hours preparing for this moment.

"In revising the text of the Old Testament, Jerome began with Psalms. In 392 he completed the Gallican Psalter, using Origen's hexaplaric text of the Septuagint."

"What's the Septuagint?" Not a lie.

"Greek translation of the Old Testament. It's probably what your Jesus referred to when He quoted from so-called sacred texts."

"I practiced reading one of those psalms last night. Let me show you!"

Chosen cocked his head and wondered what the boy was up to. Benjamin opened to Psalm 1. It was perfectly logical for the boy to open to the first Psalm. After all, it was the beginning of the book. Not to mention that he prayed over this matter: *"Lord, I'm trusting you to help me with the professor. I keep ending up with the first psalm. I mean, there's 150 of them Lord, shouldn't I just pick one out of the middle?"* He started to read:

"beatus vir qui non abiit inconsilio impiorum et in via peccatorum non stetit in cathedra derisorum non sedit, sed in lege Domini voluntas eius et in lege eius meditabitur die ac nocte . . . "

And then Benjamin deliberately stumbled in his translation. "Blessed is the man who does not walk in the counsel of the godly—"

"That is not correct. Try again."

"Blessed is the man who does not walk in the . . . counsel . . . of the . . . godly."

"Benjamin, think about what you are saying. Read again. Read!"

"I don't get it."

"Read it again."

Sigh. (A sigh lie.) "Blessed is the man who . . . does not walk . . . in the counsel . . . of the godly!"

Ed shook his head. His protégé was disappointing him.

Big breath. For angel and boy. "Professor, can I peek?"

Ed shoved Brenda's gift toward Benjamin, who immediately opened it to a rather grimy Psalm One. "Oh!" Benjamin laughed a nervous laugh. (A laugh lie.) "How did I miss that?!" And he left the book open on the table. *"God,"* the boy prayed to himself, *"You promised Your Word would not return void. This guy really needs You!"*

Funny, Chosen was praying the very same thing . . . but in the tongue of angels.

Evil tried to infiltrate the professor's house that night, but a full contingent of armed guards surrounded the building. There was an important showdown taking place inside, and a merciful God was stacking the odds in the favor of a bleary-eyed professor who loved no one but himself.

The Showdown

Ed poured himself a scotch and water, just a touch of water, mind you . . . turn the faucet on and quickly turn it off . . . it was an art, knowing how much water to put in your scotch. Less and less and less. He paced around the table again, stopping to sip and stare. Sip and stare. That stupid book! He'd finally remembered the day it came, remembered that he had thrown it in the trash at the Pleasant Valley Pub. How on earth had that book found its way back here? How long had it been? Just about twenty years. He had to shake his head. Shake, sip, stare. What was there about the Bible that caused such dedication? He paced some more. He remembered student faces through the years . . . the ones who had taken him to task for deriding their stupid book . . . and the looks on faces when he marked papers callously low because of their sophomoric attempts to "reach" him. Imbeciles.

His heart was pumping particularly fast. He was in a race: round and round he went. He sat heavily in a chair. Chosen joined his voice with a full company of heaven—a battalion—all there to give this man another chance. *Just read it, Ed! Read the words. Go to the back cover!* Ed tilted back his head and downed the scotch in one giant gulp. The glass nearly shattered as it hit the table. He reached over and pulled the book toward him. Chosen was frozen with apprehension. Ed read the beginning of Psalm One:

Blessed is the man that walketh not in the counsel of the ungodly, nor standeth in the way of sinners, nor sitteth in the seat of the scornful.

Hah!

But his delight is in the law of the LORD; and in his law doth he meditate day and night.

Hah! His eyes fell on the last verse.

For the LORD knoweth the way of the righteous; but the way of the ungodly shall perish.

A sharp spear stabbed his chest. He cried in pain and held his hand over his heart. The pain traveled into his arm. Perspiration. He held the side of the table and caught his breath. And when the pain finally subsided, as it always did, he read the book of Psalms. All of it.

A multitude continued to chant in prayer and praise; an angel renewed his pledge to erase some black from the lost man's soul.

Surprisingly alert after the drinking, the reading, and the pain—rusty as he was, Ed had spent his life reading late into the night—Ed finished the last psalm and closed the book. But a funny thing happened. The back cover stayed open, long enough for writing to catch the eye of the father of a boy who hadn't been as lucky as Benjamin.

I want to be a gud son. I pray fore my mom and dad. Jesus is my rok.

Ed stared at Will's inscription until the dawn began to change outside from dark to light. If only that could happen on the inside! If only it was as easy as the shift of a planet on its axis, the orbit of moon and stars, so predictable. Sit here, sir, and in twelve hours or so, you will see the light.

As morning broke, Ed pulled himself up the stairs, needing sleep. When he came to Will's room, he stopped. That the door was open was a perplexity, but Ed would have stopped regardless. *I want to be a gud son. You needed to have a gud father, first, William. One that knew the way of the righteous.* He walked into the room and sat on the bed. So this was his son's room. He was surprised by its normalcy. He touched toy cars on the dresser, polished to perfection by a mother long dead. He tossed a baseball in his hand. He opened the closet door, the hangers reminding him of Patty's pitiful state before she died. A wooden cigar box was prominently on the shelf, perched in such a manner that it would have fallen on him if not retrieved.

Contents scattered on the bed, Ed opened and read Brenda's letter to Patty, postmarked February 19, 1968.

Mrs. Harwood, Will was never understood. He was a sweet boy who was a loyal friend. I just know his torment is over now and he is with the Lord. I want you to believe that too. I will pray for you and your husband during this most difficult time. Brenda Martin

Ed opened the cellophane packet with the dog chains. He stared at his son's name. Harwood, William, PFC. His son a Marine. The Harwood name carried into battle. History would record Ed's death clinically: *And Edward P. Harwood had one son, William, who was killed in action in Vietnam*. Literature would handle it quite differently: *Edward P. Harwood had one son who was probably dyslexic, and Edward Harwood was a fiend to the poor boy, who was banished from the house and ended up dying in a bullet-riddled, bug-infested hole called Vietnam*. That was enough for one night, one long night that turned to day as a man of letters slipped his son's dog tags into his pant's pocket and headed out the room.

Benjamin brought the Vulgate with him over his next three visits, played dumb (all right—lied) about his translations of texts, and left Brenda's book open. It was during his third visit that Ed made an announcement.

"Benjamin, I am going on a trip. I'd like you to keep the lawn neat and collect my mail until I return."

"Where you going, Professor?"

"Home."

Back East

Trying to limit his consumption (for his need to consume consumed the frail man), Ed traveled to Virginia. Fallen from grace, a Harwood was coming home. He visited his only sister, stayed at the family estate, and re-visited his life. Ed was examining his conscience.

He drove down to Charlottesville, back to a place where life had held promise. Maybe if he traced back his life he might find where he had abandoned the strain of nobility and honor that once coursed through one of the first families of Virginia. He the torchbearer, the torch a flicker by the time it was passed to him by a father already embroiled in the tension between character and self-aggrandizement. He walked the grounds of the University of Virginia and saw the ghost of Edward Harwood walking ahead of him, a young man who had never accepted personal responsibility. A cocky, self-absorbed young man who had believed the world belonged to him. He remembered the blame he had placed on professors for their incompetence when grading his work. He remembered his haughty arrogance with the girls he had dated and how educated, modern girls would have little to do with his chauvinistic manner. He remembered the attention given him by a waitress at an all-night diner.

It was during a walk on the grounds that Ed felt a crushing pain in his chest. His knees buckled, and he reached out to the imposing statue of Thomas Jefferson for support. Hidden somewhat by bushes, the man lay in a heap at the feet of the third President of the United States, the one who gets the glory or the grief over separation of church and state. Not the most favorable place to be with an exploding heart. Ed decided to see a doctor then and there—and he would. There was something he had to do first. As his hand came up to hold his chest, it hit the solid cover of Brenda's gift, which he carried in his sports-jacket inside pocket, close to his heart.

Chosen was terribly distressed over Ed's physical condition, distressed because even though the man seemed headed toward heaven and guided by grace, he hadn't yet come to the Lord. The angel closed his eyes and thought of the thousands—millions!—who all seemed headed and guided, who *intended* to come to Christ, who actually *planned* to turn to the Lord on their deathbeds: *There is time enough for religion. I'll live my life first.* Fools! There was no convincing them that deathbeds come in many different forms: car wrecks, bullets, during sleep, from heart attacks. *Ed! Get to a doctor!*

Ed went to Washington.

Father Meets Son

The line was long. Not surprising, since the Vietnam Memorial had turned into the hottest spot in D.C. People queued on the mall, the tourists, the curious, the patriotic, the ones left behind. Downward, downward, they inched toward a grave that held thousands upon thousands. Downward toward the mountain of names stuck into the sod. That's where they all are now, you know, in the sod . . . or missing. Downward sloped the walk, bringing a penitent father to a list of those who died, and of one, in particular, who was dead.

Ed felt trembly. Trembly because he was facing his son in an urgent pilgrimage that had summoned him since he first held Will's dog tags, which were now around his neck—on the outside of his shirt. Trembly also because he was determined to be sober when he visited the memorial. The black granite slate stretched for miles, eons, *years* before him. People gathered in clusters, men and women held children on shoulders to touch the cool stone. The Vietnam Memorial had become a resting place, a national shrine, a wailing wall. Ed caught his breath. The professor was experiencing what happens when a heart long dead begins to feel love.

Ed had come to Will, and when he found him, everyone and everything around him became surreal. He was alone in the universe, he, his finger, and the etched tribute to a son who bore his name. Rumbling from his feet, gathering momentum as it coursed up through his loins, up into his chest, up came the proclamation as Edward P. Harwood clutched at the flat, black board. "William!" he cried, "Forgive me! I am so, so sorry! Please, please, forgive me," he wailed as he dropped to his knees and pressed his face against the granite. "What have I done?" he wailed. "Oh, God, I'm sorry," he said as a lightning bolt struck his heart with such force that he fell backwards. "Je . . . ," he uttered, just as he collapsed.

Ed's younger sister drove home to Virginia after making arrangements for his body to be sent to Richmond for burial. His clothes were in a white bag with a strong plastic handle in the backseat of her Mercedes. Dazed and worn from his time with Ed, Chosen sat next to the bag and prayed for Mrs. Alexandra Harwood-Jones.

Chapter

Twelve

September 1987

Alexandra Harwood-Jones thought it curious her brother had a book of Psalms in his coat pocket, but added the strange discovery to a long list of idiosyncrasies that included his refusal to visit or to respond to her letters. It was troublesome to Alexandra that her only sibling had estranged himself from the rest of the family (and they from him), but when she saw him a few weeks earlier she had immediately recognized the signs of alcohol abuse that undoubtedly helped him sever ties. Alexandra was proficient in recognizing the signs, what with her father and long-gone ex-husband.

It was no secret to the Harwood family that Edward had gone astray. They politely avoided mention of him and became properly practiced at diverting dialogue when the matter of son—or grandson—entered conversation. At first delighted to have a grandson, and then appalled, Ed's parents validated the adage that an acorn does not fall far from the tree ... Ed came by his disposition quite naturally. If it be known, the Harwoods never recovered from Edward and Patty's wedding reception in the church hall. So . . . pedestrian. No matter, now that they were all dead, all except for the childless and divorced Alexandra, who spent her perfect days in perfect clothes, perfectly coifed and manicured, chatting over lunch with perfect friends in a perfectly phony world. If she had any idea that there was now a big, kindhearted angel watching her every move she would faint dead away.

Quite satisfied with her huge, gilt-edged Imperial Family Bible—which would be collecting spiderwebs were it not for the maid's diligence with a feather duster—and practically burning incense to her engraved prayerbook, Alexandra had no interest in a messy little book of Psalms. Brenda's gift was summarily tossed into a box in the butler's pantry, joining other contributions to the American Association of University Women's annual book sale, to be held, as usual, on the first Saturday of October at a local (good heavens!) mall. Before she put the book in the box, she threw all notes, cards, and bookmarks in the trash. Had she looked closely and read inside the back cover she would have seen a recent entry, dated 8/27/87: "I wish I had been a gud dad. Edward P. Harwood."

Chosen Goes to Church

Chosen followed Mrs. Harwood-Jones as she attended functions necessary for social protocol. The angel despaired over the woman's lack of attention to spiritual matters. Her brother may have been hostile to matters "religious," but this woman's ambivalence toward God—and satisfaction with a life apart from intimate relationship with Him—saddened Chosen. Her spirit life was flat, without sign of pulse or heartbeat. How wise Paul's words to Timothy, *to command those who are rich in this world not to be arrogant nor to put their hope in wealth, but to put their hope in God*. Certainly without thought to such weighty matters, Alexandra developed a superficial relationship with her waiting Lord through strict church attendance, for it would be unthinkable for those in Alexandra's crowd to abandon the tradition and institution of the grand church on the hill. And what a church!

There was a hint of Temple splendor in the big, beautiful church. Its interior seemed carved from a single piece of mahogany. Robed clergy spoke the majestic words of liturgy as the comforting moan of an organ filled the cavernous sanctuary like unction. The words of the communal prayers were rich with wonder, worship, penitence, and supplication, and the words of hymns joined the gentle organ sound that carried them like scent across forever. And so Alexandra Harwood-Jones and her friends prayed. And sang. And communed. But their spirits were flat.

Where was the awe that reduced God's own to childlike wonder at the mystery and magnificence of Creation? Where was the depth of worship of the Great I AM, the Ancient of Days, the God of All Comfort and Grace, the Most High over All the Earth who orders the universe in a single command? Where was the heartbreak and the wrenching sorrow over sins of omission and commission, the stark terror of life apart from the Stronghold of their life? Where were pleas for mercy and grace? In the words, indeed! But not in the hearts. The chilling indictment in the Apocalypse ran through Chosen's mind:

To the angel of the church in Sardis write:

These are the words of him who holds the seven spirits of God and the seven stars. I know your deeds; you have a reputation of being alive, but you are dead. Wake up! . . . If you do not wake up, I will come like a thief, and you will not know at what time I will come to you.

The sorrow of it all, to have such a form of godliness and know Him not. Chosen studied the faces. *Seek Him! He is not far! Reach!* They politely shook hands with each other during the Peace. *Say His name! He seeks your love! Why do you come here to speak words that do not connect to heart?!*

The people in this particular church didn't *need* Jesus; they needed tradition, institution, prestige, red carpet, mahogany pews, nonthreatening homilies, lovely hymns, coffee hour, and the latest trends in tax-deductible giving. Chosen had been in many churches with mahogany and red carpet that *had* a heart for God, that sought Him, and though the angel had heard of such churches as this, he wept over its reality. How the Master had wept over such ambivalence! Chosen remembered the pain in the Lord's face as He spoke to a crowd one day: *Oh Jerusalem, Jerusalem, you who kill the prophets and stone those sent to you, how often I have longed to gather your children together as a hen gathers her chicks under her wings, but you were not willing. Look—your house is left to you desolate.*

Chosen cared deeply for Mrs. Harwood-Jones and tried to find a hairline crack in her perfect world, but—other than the performance of the Dow Jones Industrial Average, of course—she was without a care in the world. Knowing his time with her was short, Chosen spent their last night together kneeling next to Alexandra's bed in supplication. *There is so much more, dear one, than pretense and preoccupation with pride. Listen to the counsel of Scripture: Be careful that you do not forget the Lord your God . . . when you eat and are satisfied, when you build fine houses and settle down, and when your herds and flocks grow large and your silver and gold increase and all you have is multiplied, then your heart will become proud and you will forget the Lord your God.*

The Book Sale

Crowds flocked to the Gateway Mall on Saturday morning. The annual book sale was a huge moneymaker, proceeds dumped into a scholarship fund for promising young women. The sale followed traditional protocol: fifty cents per inch of books purchased until Saturday noon, when the price was reduced to twenty-five cents per inch. On Sunday, leftover books sold for one dollar per grocery bag. It was on Sunday that a pudgy woman named Clara examined the long display tables, filled her bag at the table marked "Metaphysical," and paused long enough at "Religion" to pitch Brenda's gift in her sack.

Clara forced her heavy legs into a shuffle toward her old Chrysler New Yorker, barely able to see above the bag of books she hefted. Arthritis tightened her walk on one leg, giving Clara the appearance of shuffle/limp. Her lips resolutely shut, painted white with gloss, Clara hummed. A mole painted black just under her right eye, long gray hair pulled back on her head like a schoolgirl, she limped and hummed, and landed on the car seat in a dusty thump before she searched her messy pocketbook for keys. In dire need of paint—a sort of battleship gray—the sedan hummed like Clara as it headed toward Virginia's east shore. The car was cluttered with bags of

books, most of them primers on the New Age and occult practice now
sweeping the country: *The Search for Omm Sety, How to Discover Past Lives,
Shakti Hymns to a Divine Mother, The Course in Miracles.* Chosen followed
along. He immediately sensed the presence of another spirit: it was Clara's
spirit guide, Dede—one of her many past-life personalities, she would tell
you breathlessly.

"What have you to do here, Bashar? You cannot minister to this wretch!"

*"She is loved of God, who wishes her to have eternal peace and salvation through
His Son."*

"You and your God waste your time."

*"To all who receive Him, to those who believe in His name, He gave the right
to become children of God."*

"She left Him long ago."

"The Word of God shall not return void."

"Watch what I do with your precious Word!"

The Long-Forgotten Neighborhood

Clara pulled her long car into a makeshift parking spot next to a ram-
shackle bungalow. The small house was in a neighborhood long forgotten, one
certainly overlooked by progress—but not by time: homes, sheds, garages, and
assorted outbuildings were in various stages of decay and deterioration.

The neighborhood was a big loop of tarred road, homes screened from
the outside world by overgrowth and trees gone mad. Clara's bungalow was
exactly at the center of the loop, where it curved to swing back to join itself
at the mouth of the road, where it spilled into another road, that led to
another, that led to places not forgotten, where lawns were trimmed and trees
were pruned and the sun was welcomed in.

Vinyl sun screens hung cockeyed over two front windows of Clara's
bungalow and framed a door boarded shut, giving the appearance of a
home long abandoned. The brown vinyl was faded to a strange sort of pink
hue and frayed on its ends. Trash littered the ground. Not the kind of trash
you find alongside a road or next to an overturned barrel, this was junkyard
trash that came with the house when Clara bought it years ago. *Amenities:*

honest-to-goodness junk pile. Tires, tools, old motor parts, upside-down three-legged sawhorses, an old-fashioned washing machine, even an RCA television. It was a junkyard graveyard; machines once heralded as the latest techno-gadgets now adorned the path alongside the bungalow as Clara hummed and carried a bag of books toward her back door. Up the steps (one missing), into a dark porch (some floorboards missing), through a screen door, and into a kitchen (quite a bit like kitchen missing). It was a room that mimicked the outside perfectly, but held a more delicate melange of trash: mail and magazines, empty jugs and jars, permanently wrinkled clumps of clothing, boxes of newspapers piled to the point of tipping sideways, a menacing threat to anyone who would dare to disturb it. Dishes helter-skelter near the sink, the stove held dirty pots. Water dripped from the leaky faucet, the stain of orange rust and the smell of sulfur strong. Clara shuffled into the living room.

Other than her comfy reading chair—and an obvious altar in one corner—the living room matched the kitchen for hoarding. As did the two bedrooms and bathroom. Clara's small home was negotiable only by way of a well-worn trail. The trail wove its way through the hodgepodge and stopped at certain spots: a small table with one chair in the kitchen, a recliner in the living room, the toilet, and a single bed. *Happy trails to you.* If a room had a faucet, it leaked, as did the roof. Buckets were strategically placed to catch water that pushed its way through plywood ceilings and Sheetrock walls, making the home thick with the smell of mold and mildew. The phone next to Clara's reading chair sounded.

"How did you do?"

"There was only one, and it's just the Psalms. I should have gone yesterday."

"You were *supposed* to go yesterday, Clara!"

Clara hummed.

"Listen, Clara, it won't suit our needs . . . turn it into one of your little projects. I'll see you later."

Oppression

Chosen felt as if he'd been body-slammed by the oppressive forces that permeated the home, as if he'd slipped between the pages of a book marked "hell," the covers screwed down tight. Girding his loins with the strength and power of the Word of God, the angel prepared himself for any siege that might come his way. How wise he was to do so!

Clara donned a long, white bathrobe with hood. The terry cloth had long lost any wicking ability and lay against the woman's bumpy body like silk, its belt still reminiscent of the original lush texture. She walked to her low corner altar, lit several candles, and knelt to stare into the flame of one as black as the farthest reaches of her soul.

"Step aside, tender Bashar!" came the command. "I have work to do!"

Clara stared intently at the flame, made brighter and more powerful by demon breath. And then she began to chant. "Olarrrr . . . olarrrr . . . olarrrr . . . " She hummed and chanted until she achieved a state of altered consciousness. "Olarrrr . . . hummm . . . olarrrr . . . hummm." Her normally startling eyes—Clara's eyes were startlingly, strangely, troublingly blue—widened into a dull glare as Dede took over.

"Beloved mistress, do not be frightened. I am here to answer to the lord god of your being. I have come from the brotherhood of light. I have come to bring wisdom of peace and love."

"Teach me, Dede."

"Within this earth plane there are glorious masters. Many have come forth, all are termed love. Their vibrations are of that which is termed light. That which is termed hatred or abuse or anger or jealousy there is not. All that is, my beloved mistress, are incarnated beings, and that which is termed earth, the mother."

"Teach."

"That which is termed your earth plane is not. The sun is nothing like the radiation that issues forth from your RA. You must relearn that which is termed truth. Repeat, beloved mistress, repeat: 'In the beginning I am.'"

No! screamed the angel. In the beginning was the Word!

"In the beginning I am."

"The earth is my mother, I call down the moon to bring that which is termed wisdom.*"*

The fear of the Lord is the beginning of wisdom! The knowledge of the Holy One is understanding!

"The earth is my mother, I call down the moon to bring that which is termed wisdom."

"The serpent is myth."

No! Christ has crushed the serpent's head!

"The serpent is myth."

"I need no one to die for me."

No! The Son of Man came to seek and to save what was lost!

"I need no one to die for me."

"Beloved mistress, that which is termed light is within you. You are keeper of the light. You must destroy darkness. Darkness has come into your house."

"Darkness has come into my house."

"Destroy!"

Clara reached for Brenda's gift and for the hatchet that lay on the altar, the closest she could come to a ceremonial dagger. She raised the hatchet and swung. A mighty angel pushed his way through the demon's resistance and smacked the hatchet sideways into a cluster of candles. Wax splattered on Clara's hand, bringing her back to reality.

Destroy! the command still echoed in her subconscious. Confused, the woman grabbed the book and slammed it against the altar. Chosen knocked over the black candle. Commotion reeled in Clara's mind; all bets—and chants and hums—were off. It was fire-prevention time.

"You fool! You waste your time!" screamed the demon. And like the snuffed-out flame on Clara's candle, Dede was gone.

Chosen watched Clara with repulsion—not toward the woman, but toward the work of the enemy, that someone would be so shackled. Clara extinguished the candles, put the book next to her reading chair, underneath a fat volume of spells and rituals called *Liber Spiritaum,* took off her robe, and vanished into the wood behind her bungalow. After a long hike she met "fellow friends" for sacramental rites around another fire. This one much bigger than the flame on a black candle.

Bonfire

Time—as humans count time—had changed, but the ceremony Chosen watched was identical to pagan ritual he'd seen before: encircling the fire, hand in hand, side by side, swaying, walking, chanting, invoking the spirit of the earth, of harmony, of the inner god . . .

"Father, stop them! They worship and serve created things!"

"My way is a refuge for the righteous, Bashar, but it is the ruin of those who do evil."

The climax of the evening was one of mirth as people danced in trance while the fire blazed more brightly—and with greater ferocity—as each book was tossed into its demanding blaze. Bible upon Bible was flipped into the inferno with cheers and applause, as people stuck colorful leaves in their hair and wandered in couples and threesomes toward the cover of bush. Chosen lay facedown in utter agony at the horrific sight of the fire and of the looks of glee on the faces of housewives, accountants, teachers, salesmen, and even some ordained to preach the gospel of Christ.

Drone filled the wood as Chosen followed Clara on her long hike home. It was a drone that only he could hear, one that overpowered the hum of a woman who believed she was a goddess. At least in this incarnation.

Blasphemy

Clara spent days at a time in her reading chair, leaving her broken-down bungalow for visits to the store (she was partial to gingersnaps and milk), to browse a book sale, or to wander back in the wood behind her home. Utterly exhausted from constant attack by Dede and his cohorts, Chosen stayed the course.

The angel stared long and hard at the snoring woman in her easy chair. *She is so deceived!* Brenda's gift sat under the heavy volume, under the weight of foul, malignant evil. Clara's evening ritual of candles, chant, and invoking her spirit guide became a time of impassioned pleading by the angel. Yet after two weeks of desperate appeal, he had made no headway. *Why, O God, are You forsaking me? Why am I here if not to serve this woman?* he asked in frustration, but he knew. He knew. In obedience he knew. *She has eyes to see but does not see, ears to hear but does not hear.*

Can any good come from this?! cried the disconsolate ministering spirit as the robed woman approached her little altar.

Candles lit, the humming and chanting began in earnest. Frustrated by the continued presence of the angel and the book, Dede had had enough. *"I will be rid of you, Bashar, for good!"*

"Greetings to you beloved mistress goddess, you who was and are and will be to come. There is an urgent matter for you today."

"Tell me, Dede."

"That which is termed the Word of God is in your house. Get it."

"I have it."

"Take your pencil, great mistress goddess, and write as I say, for that which is termed truth is a lie. We must set the people free."

Chosen was wild. *"The Lord rebuke you!"* screamed the angel over and over as he was restrained by powers from the dark world.

"If you desire me to leave, Bashar, command me by the god of your being."

"Blasphemy!" yelled the angel, who watched with horror as Dede dictated and Clara wrote.

"Turn to the page that is termed Psalm 31, beloved goddess. Where it is written 'In thee, O LORD, do I put my trust,' you shall write: 'Has not the Christ said, "Go away, I never knew you?"'"

Clara wrote automatically.

"Turn to the page that is termed Psalm 38, beloved goddess. Where it is written: 'For mine iniquities are gone over my head,' you shall write: 'Has not the Christ said, "Be ye perfect as a God?"'

"Turn to the page that is termed Psalm 133, beloved goddess. Where it is written: 'Behold how good and how pleasant it is for brethren to dwell together in unity,' you shall write: 'Christ has taught there is nothing in man that entitles him to say, "I am this and you are that, through all eternity. We are one."'"

Dede waited while Clara's pudgy fingers formed the words. And then he struck.

"Turn to the page that is termed Psalm 62, beloved goddess. Where it is written: 'Truly my soul waiteth upon God, from him cometh my salvation,' you shall write:

Jesus the Christ said, "You search the Scripture because you think in them you have eternal life."'"

Clara balked. Chosen saw a glimmer of cognition in her eyes. He bellowed the Psalm: *He only is my rock and my salvation! He is my defense! In God is my salvation and my glory! The rock of my strength and my refuge!—Trust in Him at all times, Clara!* Before he could continue his voice was silenced by a suffocating grip.

Dede prodded. *"Write, beloved goddess!"*

Clara stared at the words on the page that was termed Psalm 62.

"Stupid woman, write what I command!" Clara shook her head and closed the book. She placed it underneath *Liber Spiritaum* and headed to the kitchen for gingersnaps and milk.

Another Halloween

The excitement was palpable. Her usual Friday gathering in the woods postponed until the next night—the big night that would happen on Saturday this year—when fellow friends would call down the waning moon and invite all who have gone before to come and to make merry. Always a time of nightmarish wildness for Clara and her friends, the high holiday even caused a stir in the all-business Dede, whose careless behavior almost cost him a soul. Clara lugged her robe down the path in the back woods, for what was Halloween, anyway, if not a dress-up affair. It was a night of supreme importance, the night the Mother Goddess went to sleep and her consort the Horned God took over. It was a night of great celebration, a time to cast spells, a time to commune with the Lord of Death.

Outnumbered by powers and dominions, the angel watched the merry-making and debauchery from a grove of trees. He was helpless in the midst of such force and could only wait until dawn when Clara shuffled through fading bushes and ferns that lined her path. When she finally left for home, she was alone. Dede and his cohorts were occupied goading others on to perversity. *Therefore God gave them over in the sinful desires of their hearts to sexual impurity for the degrading of their bodies with one another.*

This his chance, Chosen sprang to action. Shielding the woman with his wings, he tried to penetrate her thoughts with the Word of God. *Clara!*

Listen! Please listen! The Lord is not slow in keeping His promise. He is patient with you, not wanting anyone to perish, but everyone to come to repentance!

Clara stumbled face first on the steps to her bungalow when she stepped on the hem of her robe. Exhausted from a night of dance, revelry, and physical encounter, she followed the trail that led to her bed. Oddly, she bypassed her bedroom and slumped with a thump into her easy chair. There, on *top* of *Liber Spiritaum* sat a skinny little book, opened to Psalm 62.

Clara flashed back to a little girl in Sunday school, who loved Psalm 62, a little girl who would grow up to enthusiastically embrace the nonjudgmental message of the New Age and reject the judgment and hypocrisy of Christianity as sham. It became Mother Earth to Clara, not Father God. It became love and harmony, not judgment and hell. It became the divine spark that is in all of us, not the God "out there." The little girl, long lost, was once free and filled with love and harmony, the very love she now pursued under cover of bush and bramble and in the secret places in the wood. *Have mercy on her, O God!*

Where had the little girl gone? Would she have reveled with the others as Clara did tonight? Would she have called down the moon and stars and danced provocatively in the shadow of hell?

Also unto thee, O Lord, belongeth mercy!

Chosen felt a blow to his back as a pair of strong wings slapped him across the room. The demon was enraged, the composite ugliness of evil engorged his face with ferocity. His words whipped into fury and froth. *"She belongs to me!"*

"She belongs to God!"

With a roar that reverberated throughout the heavens, the demon charged. And while Clara dozed in her chair, book in hand, a spiritual battle was fought as far away as heavenly places, as near as her lap.

Defeat

Clara slept through most of the next day. Chosen lay on the floor, chest heaving, and battered. Dede was not in sight. The battle was a draw. Fight as he may, protect her all he could, the final skirmish would be Clara's. Would she let the Word penetrate her heart, travel down into the place called soul, and wash her fresh in the hope and true love of her Creator God? It must be her choice. Always, it must. In the mercy and love and justice of God, He gave His Creation—and Clara—the gift of choice.

Chosen watched the waking woman. He'd had so little time to reach her. Yet with God time is of no import. The angel closed his eyes in desperation. *Jesus, Lord Almighty, please do not let this woman slip from You.* Clara stretched and thought back to the night before with toothy grin. After pouring a glass of milk and filling her robe pocket with gingersnaps, she slumped again into her recliner. She reached for Brenda's gift. Chosen held his breath. And then Clara grabbed a pencil and began work on her project in earnest, starting with Psalm 62.

The Book Leaves

It was one of Clara's pet projects, to "correct" a sacred book and place it in a fitting spot so it could "enlighten" a poor, misled soul. Stealth project. It gave her an indescribable thrill to slip her adulterated works into a church, and if she smuggled one inside a pew rack, she was overjoyed. Her trip to her aging mother's home for Thanksgiving would fit perfectly with this latest endeavor: the book would be left in a church somewhere in Tulsa, Oklahoma.

Chapter
Thirteen

September 1988

Clara did her job. On Thanksgiving Day, Brenda's gift was covertly placed in a rack on the backside of a pew at the Easthaven Baptist Church in Tulsa, Oklahoma. It was the best Clara could do, as she perched on a chair against the sanctuary wall. She would never know her plan failed. The pew she selected, you see, was pulled from the wall only on special days and holidays, when every pew was pushed forward to make room for a long row of folding chairs. Efficient ushers returned the church to normalcy the minute overflow crowds dispersed. And so it happened that Brenda's gift remained wedged against a wall for several years before it was discovered under the harshest circumstance.

It was a bittersweet moment for Chosen when Clara deposited the book, for though he was thrilled to be called home, his heart ached as Clara shuffled/limped out the church in search of her next special project. The angel would not return to Easthaven until late summer.

Easthaven Baptist Church

Not a thing about the church had changed since Chosen's brief visit. Nothing, that is, besides the church body's decision to call a young man to join the staff as youth pastor; pastoral care was becoming too much a load for Pastor Reiner.

A venerable old congregation in Tulsa, Easthaven had grown exponentially in past years due to urban sprawl; part and parcel with renewed interest in things spiritual, families with children had expanded membership considerably. And youngsters who were once content with videos and pizza were now restless and troubled in an increasingly hostile environment. The entire church took its responsibility to children very seriously, thanks to Pastor Reiner, who pounded the pulpit with alarm over eroding cultural values, violent trends, and outright rejection of biblical conduct. At his prodding, and after much prayer, twenty-eight-year-old Daniel Ross and his wife, Ellen, were moving to Tulsa on September 5, just in time for the annual Labor Day picnic. It would be a perfect chance for the young couple to meet church members. They would lock it into memory as the day they met Frosty and Leah Trippett; the day an angel named Chosen returned to his mission.

The Trippetts

Every organization has a Frosty or a Leah. Easthaven, however, was favored with one of each. The Trippetts were a couple who found identity in their beloved Baptist church and who dedicated all of their time to service. Among their many talents, they both played organ and wormed their way to the top of the organist list, a position they held come sickness or death; rain, sleet, or snow; power outage; or flu epidemic: Frosty and Leah literally flung their bodies over the instrument and dared any pretenders to advance. They were opinionated, talked nonstop about everything and everyone, and knew each member's name, birthday, and zip code by heart. They were also garage sale maniacs and wore the strangest clothing combinations this side of Greenwich Village. The rock-bottom line was that

Frosty and Leah were easily classified as busybodies . . . who took their right and duty in the government of Easthaven quite seriously, and who were certain the church could not function without their guidance. Needless to say, Pastor Reiner's copy of *How to Get Along with Difficult People* was well traveled, dog-eared, and discreetly kept in his desk drawer for quick reference!

Ellen and Dan were tense as they drove to Frosty and Leah's massive backyard, which featured a red-brick outdoor grill and horseshoe pit. It was not like the young couple to bicker, but nerves were frazzled.

"She asked me why we didn't have children yet, Daniel! I mean, I barely met her after church yesterday and the first words out of her mouth weren't 'Welcome to Easthaven' or 'We hope you enjoy your stay here' but 'Are you planning on having children soon?'" This was a painful matter to Ellen, who'd suffered three miscarriages since their wedding four years earlier.

"Every church has a busybody, El, just try to avoid them. I'll get us out early if you get too uncomfortable. But we have to buck up and meet these folks, El; they are our family now."

"I know, I know! I'm just tired." She *was* tired. The disbanding of Dan's class at Southwestern Baptist Theological Seminary, the good-byes-until-we-meet-again, and the physical move from Fort Worth had been particularly hard. Truth be known, Ellen was a little scared. What would this congregation expect from a pastor's wife? Could she measure up? And how much would they meddle into her life? Determined not to be a "typical pastor's wife," Ellen saw herself in a joint role with her husband.

"Know what my mom always says, El? Give them ownership! Just because Leah asked you questions that were so invasive doesn't mean she was mean-spirited, it just means she's nosy. You're going to run into a lot of nosy people now that you're away from the safety net of seminary. Make her your friend, Ellen."

Ellen chortled. The thought of that busybody becoming her friend seemed ludicrous. But Daniel was right. They were finally starting out on a first call. No more practice, no more probationary internship, no more tests. This was it. And they were in "it" together.

All through school Dan had insisted the ministry must be their joint decision. And it really had been. Ellen would get the hang of it, with God's grace. She pushed her straight, strawberry blonde hair behind one ear and squeezed her husband's hand. He held on tight until he pulled onto a street already lined with cars. As they walked up a black macadam driveway, hand-in-hand, they passed under a banner that said: Welcome Pastor Ross and Ellen!

Pastor Reiner was first to greet them, backed up by Frosty and Leah, who instantly abandoned their conversation with a woman near the lemonade stand.

"It's about time you got here!" yelled a flushed Leah, who barged through clusters of picnickers and grabbed Ellen's hand. "Come with me, my dear. There are so many people I want you to meet." With a look of chagrin on Ellen's face, she was ripped from her husband's grasp and ushered toward her first inquisition under an oak tree. "We have lots of questions to ask you!" said Leah as she pulled Ellen toward a bank of friendly and interested faces, lined in a row, waiting for the new pastor's wife to make girl talk. She was about to be formally inducted as " . . . and Ellen," "the youth pastor's wife," or "Hi-is-your-husband-home?"

Chosen liked her at once and was thrilled for Dan. Reserved, private, and quiet, Ellen had many skirmishes ahead of her as she developed a dual persona: one reserved for the public (for in the fishbowl called "ministry," she had to learn to swim—or sink), and one for home. Curiously, a third, reclusive, personality was to develop that spanned both worlds, for though Ellen learned to protect her privacy with the likes of Leah, at home she was completely free and open with Dan. Personal solitude was savored during her special time each day, her quiet time, when she studied and meditated and prayed on the Word of God. Ellen had a hunger in her heart for God, a feature her husband found irresistible.

Frosty had commandeered the young pastor and considered it his bounden duty to officiate over each introduction. "Earl, this is Pastor Ross. Say, I bet he'd like to go fishing with you some day. How about next Saturday? Good! It's a date! . . . Stanley, this is Pastor Ross. You ever have any leftover pizza at your restaurant, you give it to him for the youth group. Say, you got a big freezer down there, Stanley?"

Daniel held up well. He was the outgoing personality in the marriage. Intense, driven, happy-go-lucky when time would allow, Dan had a knack for mingling with others and a tender heart that would never, ever be stopped. The product of a strong Christian family, Dan and his siblings were reared to consider others more important than themselves—a far cry from the "Love yourself first" mantra that now dominated popular culture. From birth, Dan had been taught to model Christ, and counted it his privilege to be guided by His Lord. *The path of a righteous man is guided by the Lord,* his mother had said over and over, until it was drummed into the boy's very brain—and soul.

Chosen was so beside himself to be with Dan, he begged to take human form just to hug him in greeting. For when Bashar-el was informed of this next charge, he somersaulted through the heavens and skipped on tips of galaxies.

Love

Days pushed into themselves, tripped over weeks that became months, every day filled with counseling, planning, meetings, and strict adherence to Dan and Ellen's vow to share dinner together, come what may. This would be an inviolate rule when they had children, a rule that would create much difficulty and some dissension, yet a rule that evoked the healthy respect of all around them. Frosty and Leah had complained *once*—and caught a stern lecture from Pastor Reiner—about Ellen's calico-lined basket filled with dinner whenever Dan worked late, their madras tablecloth spread across a pew that was only pulled forward for special occasions.

"Why on earth do they insist on eating in the sanctuary?" muttered Frosty. "It's downright disrespectful." *It's downright an honor,* thought the youth pastor and his wife.

"Ownership, Ellie." Dan would smile.

"Leah and Frosty, would you like to share our meal tonight?" The invitation came through gritted teeth. In time, the Trippetts accepted. In time, invitations came both ways.

"You sure will make pretty children," said Leah one day as Frosty practiced hymns for Sunday. *Ownership, Ellen* . . . "Do you and Frosty have children, Leah?" asked Ellen. "No!" came the quick response as the subject was summarily switched.

Ellen slipped into bed next to her husband. "I think I hit a nerve with Leah today."

"Let's not talk about Leah, El," said Dan as he gathered her in his arms. "Let's give *her* something new to talk about."

Chosen left the couple in the privacy of their bedroom and sang praise for the mystery and beauty of union in a marriage bed that would forever remain undefiled. How great the gift of intimacy between husband and wife, a gift this young couple received with gratitude and celebration.

The song of Solomon played majestically in the angel's head: *Place me like a seal over your heart, like a seal on your arm; for love is as strong as death, its jealousy unyielding as the grave. It burns like blazing fire, like a mighty flame. Many waters cannot quench love; rivers cannot wash it away.*

Pregnant

Well talk Leah did! Within three months Leah figured out the sudden change in Ellen's demeanor, read all the signs well, and confronted the poor young woman with a question that Ellen had tried to evade for weeks. Hard to do now that she was starting to show. The pastor and his wife were going to have a baby! This put Leah and Frosty into overdrive, Ellen's pregnancy energizing the couple into buying sprees at every garage sale that advertised children's clothing, long visits to the library to learn the latest in child care, and prolonged stops at a local Christian bookstore where they bought every possible resource to give the new mom. The new mom, by the way, who was desperately trying to trust her holy God to see this pregnancy through. Ellen was not in the mood for such attention, nor did she want anyone to carry on about a child that might not live. *Please, Jesus! Please let this baby live!*

Dan remained outwardly stalwart. Inside he lived a private pain and implored his Lord with the same supplication as his wife. Yes . . . he wanted children, but he braced himself long ago for news that never came, that Ellen could not bear children. This pregnancy was a gift. But, oh! how he loved his wife! After God, Ellen was Daniel's universe. Her sorrow from previous miscarriages took all the support of friends at seminary to get him through, for in times of such profound sorrow, it is much too clinical and cold to turn to theological texts or finger-wagging. It is during times of profound sorrow when the fellowship of believers works best. Dan and Ellen's parents and siblings also provided comfort that was invaluable, the death of their three babies a crushing blow to all.

Ellen approached her sixth month with trepidation. What would the doctor say? Quite frankly, he would say: "How do you feel, Mrs. Ross?" And she would say, "I feel really fine." And he would say, "Everything looks like it is supposed to, Mrs. Ross. Judging from what I can tell, you'd better prepare for a bruiser. This is going to be a big baby!" Ellen and Dan and Chosen— and Leah and Frosty (there was no getting rid of the two now that Ellen faced her last trimester)—were on air. Casseroles were delivered, the house was vacuumed, trips to the store were manned by the indefatigable duo until the day came, the blessed day that brought out banners all through the church. *Unto us a child is born,* wrote Frosty with fat-tipped markers, *and her name is Hannah. And she is an angel.*

Chosen could not have said it better. Her parents' outright sobs of joy joined in crazy harmony with the nine-pound baby girl as she burst onto the scene. Dan held his wife's face in his hands and gazed with every conceivable positive emotion he could conjure—respect, pride, joy, ecstasy, relief—all giggled out of his lips as tears danced a jig on his chin. There was no question that her name would be Hannah, and after the baby was cleaned and rolled to the nursery, after his wife was brought to her room, Pastor Ross sought the silence of the hospital chapel where he knelt and pulled a small Bible from his shirt pocket, a Bible that never ever left his side, that had been given him at birth. It was a little book that he carried next to his heart, his link to a mother named Brenda. He read from the first book of Samuel as he'd read since his adoptive mother first told him of Brenda and gave him the Bible.

"This is a gift from your mother, as you were a gift to us. There is a great woman in Scripture, Danny, who offered her beloved son to serve the Lord.

Read Hannah's prayer often, and remember the sacrifice of your birth mother."

Hannah was flawless. A Gerber baby. Members of the church came to look through the nursery window, Leah and Frosty leading the parade. The Trippetts became a bit petulant when Dan and Ellen's extended family began to arrive in carloads, for the young parents had both come from close, supportive homes. No matter: Leah and Frosty bade their time until relatives left. After all, this was *their* baby; *they* were the ones who lived here and would baby-sit, and push the carriage, and change the diapers, and get on the floor and coo and sing, and play the organ, and knit booties! They would do it all, they would, because they never could with one of their own, you know . . .

Hannah

"If she's a girl, she will be a tomboy," was Pastor Ross's constant comment to his youth group during Ellen's pregnancy, and though the girls presented the baby with her first "Barbie," Dan's prophetic utterance held sway. Hannah lifted her head, rolled over, hoisted herself, crawled, walked, teethed, and maneuvered her walker more like a miniature Evel Knievel than a diminutive little lady. This was much to Ellen's dismay, who would dress her daughter in the adorable outfits that crammed the closet—thanks to the garage sale maniacs—only to face rips, grass stains, and dirt.

"Hannah-anna!" called Dan whenever he saw his daughter.

"Daddy-dear!" giggled the toddler.

"Introducing the first female to leap tall buildings in a single bound!" declared Dan. "The first girl to swim the Atlantic Ocean! The first girl to fly to Mars! Yaaayyy, Hannah-anna!" And Hannah would fling herself from the back of the couch in complete trust of her father's catch and yell, "Daddy, more!" as he swung her in circles, a big angel hanging on tight and swinging along for the ride.

It was during dinner one night, and a month before Hannah's fourth birthday, that Ellen made her announcement. Chosen and Leah had already figured it out. She was pregnant again. And old fears returned.

"How can you look at this child and be scared, El? You're going to be fine! I promise. Did you make an appointment with the doc?"

"A week from tomorrow."

"Next Thursday? I will never understand why it takes so long to get in!" came Dan's reply, as he unconsciously touched the Bible in his shirt pocket, an automatic gesture whenever he felt insecure, uncertain, or afraid. Chosen prayed that Ellen's body would be strong to bear this new child. He, too, was frustrated that a visit to the doctor would take so long. A lot could happen in a week. A lot.

Dan slept fitfully during the next week, waking often in the night to pray over his wife's still body, placing his hand fully and tenderly on her stomach, feeling it rise and fall with each breath. Could it be that a child now grew—a son, another daughter—under his hand? Could he protect the child in any way? No, no way but to pray. And to trust.

Dan would rise from bed carefully and go to another room to lay his hands on the irrepressibly impish Hannah, whose little body seemed animated even in sleep. Could he love something—*anything?*—more than he loved his wife and child? He knelt by Hannah's bed and prayed the prayer of a father greatly blessed.

The doctor's appointment inched closer. Two separate home pregnancy tests said "yes you are" and "no you're not." Ellen felt worse and worse. Chosen felt uneasy.

The angel approached the throne: *"Father?"*

"They will need you, Bashar. There will be great weeping and then there will be blessing. The man will be a mighty voice for the kingdom one day. First, his faith must be challenged. He must learn to rejoice in suffering before he can do the good works prepared for him in advance."

Chosen could not shake the evil sneer he heard in a maternity ward so many, many years ago in Albany, New York: *It is the child we want, Bashar!*

Thursday finally came, and it held only promise. Flowers of every color waved cheerfully at the sun as it rose in the east like a blazing daffodil. Birds sang, Danny whistled, Hannah appeared in the kitchen with her sneakers on the wrong feet, and Ellen felt healthy for the first time in days.

"Hannah-anna guess what? *You* get to go to work with Daddy today—"

"Daddy-*dear*!" scolded the bright-eyed Hannah.

"Daddy-dear!" said Dan as he tickled his daughter into loud snorts and guffaws. "Aunt Leah and Uncle Frosty are going to take you to McDonald's!"

"Happy Meal!" squealed Hannah. "Hangaburger with cheese!"

Ellen shook her head at the impossible feat of keeping her child *away* from Happy Meals—and soda—but all of her pleading would never override the Trippetts when they had their "doll," the one and only Hannah Felicity Ross. It was lollipops and ice cream—and a cranky child at night.

Hannah jumped off her chair into her father's arms. Danny gave his wife a long kiss.

"Call me the *minute* you find out," and the two were off, a little girl pushing her sticky finger into her father's ear.

"Daddy-dear," she whispered. "I went to heaven!"

"Oh, you did, did you? And when did you go?"

"When you prayed," she whispered.

Danny buckled her into her car seat.

"And what did heaven look like, my dear Hannah-anna?"

The little girl pointed to the sun.

The angel looked at the sun—and the sky—with concern.

Dr. Weeks

Dr. Weeks watched the same sun. It reminded her of home. She stared at the sky and wondered how the hospital staff was getting along without doctors, content that able nurses and aides could manage while she and her husband took a long, overdue furlough to the States. Funny, she thought, that she would consider West Africa home. But she did.

A final seminar on head trauma at the Tulsa Medical Center would wrap up continuing education requirements, and with their support raised for another three years, the medical missionaries would return home to Niger, where the same sun would not be shining, but burning; where no flowers would be waving; and where no birds would be singing.

"Dr. Weeks? The session is about to start."

The woman nodded and turned to join her husband down the hall, the husband handpicked by her roommate long ago, the husband who had sacrificially given up fatherhood when he married a young woman who could never bear children because of emergency surgery to stem the flow of blood, the husband who had put her through medical school and said, "We will take care of God's children; our hearts will never be empty."

Stephen was right, of course. The career medical missionaries, who now spoke fluent French and Hausa, fell in love with the people of West Africa—young and old—and treated them as if they were their own. And in a few short days, Stephen and Brenda Weeks would happily board a plane that would bring them home.

Tornado

"Dan?" Ellen's voice sounded weak and distant as she forced optimism. "I guess I should say 'Daddy.'"

"You are?!" In spite of his concern, Dan could not control his joy. "What did the doc say?"

"He wants me to get a lot of rest. He says the next two months will be guarded. He gave me a prescription . . . where's Hannah?"

"She's learning how to play Happy Birthday on the organ, compliments of Frosty. They're going to McDonald's as soon as Leah finishes the bulletin."

"Dan, I'm worried." Dan was worried too. Chosen, on the other hand, was *very* worried as he felt a drop in barometric pressure and the sun began to dim.

"Ellen, stop by and we'll go to lunch."

"Honey, I'm tired. Let me just go home and take a nap. Pray for the baby, Danny!"

Danny prayed on the spot. The sun vanished from sight.

Hannah bounded into her father's office.

"Daddy! I'm almost this much!" She held up four fingers. Frosty appeared behind her.

"She's going to be a talented musician; she has a natural rhythm." That was this week. Last week she was going to win an Oscar; before that, be president of the United States, ambassador, professor of economics, a Pulitzer Prize winner. Their little doll was a genius, after all.

Dan thought the better of telling Frosty that Hannah's "rhythm" was the bounce he put into her with all that sugar. He was preoccupied with Ellen's call. The sky turned black and blue, with just a hint of yellow bruise. Frosty took it upon himself to police the parking lot for open windows; a downpour could start any second. And it did. Hail the size of peach pits pelted car hoods and rooftops and sidewalks. "Daddy! Look at the ice cubes!" The hailstorm was over as quickly as it began, followed by urgent sirens that warned folks to look up and to run for cover. Out from the cover of the building, Frosty ignored the sirens and went about his duty, until a peculiar whistling sound pinched the air, when Frosty Trippett took the siren seriously.

A lifetime of tornadoes had taught Frosty two things: ninety-nine times out of a hundred nothing happens, but that one time when something does happen, dive for cover. The sky, the hail, the peculiar sound: Frosty scanned the horizon, and there it was, heading straight toward him. What it was, was an F-4 tornado, the kind that maims and murders everything in its path. It was the force of an atomic bomb punching its way through a cold cap of air until it cried uncle and fell fast toward the ground while warm air shot upward like a corkscrew. It was the roar of hundreds of locomotives, thousands of cannon, billions of bees, and it sent Frosty into the church at breakneck speed.

"Tornado!" he screamed. "It's coming! Run for cover!"

Danny grabbed Hannah and shoved her under his desk. Growing up in the Midwest, he'd been through drills like this a dozen times: in school, at home, in Boy Scouts. He'd never personally experienced a tornado, but the abrupt blackness and sudden roar that headed his way convinced him this was not a drill. Within seconds, arctic and tropical winds would duke it out in an impromptu battle of strength right smack over the Easthaven Baptist Church.

Chosen shielded Dan's desk with his entire body as windows began to vibrate and debris hit the outside wall. Everyone was praying: Danny, who pleaded for his California-born wife's savvy during this storm; the Trippetts; and an angel.

"Jesus! . . . Father God, protect this church and all inside . . . Yahweh Elohim, thy mercy endure forever!"

The sound was maddening. Hannah cried. Danny shielded his daughter as the most dangerous force known to man descended on the church. The roof over Dan's office ripped away, his desk shuddered but remarkably held its ground. Pews in the sanctuary were sucked into the vortex like last week's dust in a powerful Kirby, lumber and shards of glass were flung about like popped corn. A scream pierced the air, shrill and filled with fright. It was Leah, trapped under a beam, the weight of Frosty's lifeless body weighing her down and keeping her from the suction.

"Help!" her scream was filled with all the power of fear. The column of wind spiraled away and back, away and back. Up and down like a malevolent yo-yo. Leah's pleas became more desperate.

Hymnals and Bibles flew like angry wasps from an upturned nest. The back pew shot straight into the whirlwind like a pogo stick, books flying every which way. An angel hand snatched Brenda's gift from the violent spiral and anchored it under a pile of rubble before racing to Leah's call. Someone else was racing too.

With fierce, strict, I-mean-this orders to Hannah to stay under his desk, Dan ran through the maelstrom to help his friends. Confident the worst was over, he left the love of his life for just a second—he could not ignore Leah's call. He found the woman flung halfway into the parking lot, a twisted wreck of beams pinning her dead husband to her chest. She was wild with shock.

Glass shards pelted the young pastor as he pulled with all his might to free the woman as a second satellite tornado slammed the church.

"Daddy!" The shriek cut through the air and suspended time. The universe froze into a moment of sound that would be permanently etched on the man's body, mind, and soul, branded into his skin, joined now with his bone, with his blood—a moment in time—he would forever wait for the moment to explode and to leave him in little pieces like the glass and wood that exploded in a final act of demolition before the world became still.

The entire event took less than three minutes. In three minutes, Frosty lay dead, Leah lay dying, and an irrepressible little imp of a girl was hurtled against a tree in a neighboring yard.

Danny was found walking on shoeless, bleeding feet, carrying the still body of his beloved daughter through the wreckage. Ambulance personnel rushed Hannah to the trauma unit of Tulsa Medical Center. Danny refused attention and summoned the strength to call his wife, assured by others that his neighborhood was spared. He reached for his small Bible. It was gone. He fell on a chair in the hospital and wept as his little girl was hurried into the care of several surgeons, among them a husband and wife team visiting from West Africa.

Chosen Bargains

"Life for life!" yelled the emotional angel as doctors crowded around Hannah's battered little body. *"I will give you my position in eternity in exchange for the child's life! Banish me now that the girl may live! I bear the responsibility for her injuries. Oh, Most High God, send me to the pit, let me rot as dung, let me be payment for Hannah, for Danny, for Ellen, for Leah"* . . . the angel's list included the names of all he'd loved and served during his mission on earth. He pleaded. He bargained. He choked with remorse and obligation and cries of incompetence. Utterly bereft, the angel was willing to forfeit his place in the kingdom in exchange for healing, for resurrection, for redemption. Deep in his heart he knew everything was working to God's glory, but the angel yielded to the pain he felt for the fallenness of the world. And in an instant he was face-to-face with God.

"Bashar, I have done that already. It is finished. I Am that I Am. You are chosen for a reason and have done well, faithful servant. Go back and remember that I will be God. It will all work to my glory."

The Vigil

A sharp pain brought Ellen to her knees. It was followed by the ripping sensation she'd felt three times before. Her face grave with dread, she replaced the receiver and crawled to the bathroom. Pastor Reiner and his wife were rushing home from a regional meeting; a deacon would bring her to the hospital to join Danny.

Church members began to arrive to pray, to support, to be there: for Hannah, for Leah as she stubbornly clung to life, for the dozen other people who were pulled from wreck and ruin along the tornado's violent rumble.

Kind, loving friends wanted to dress Dan's cuts, but he would have none of it. How could he accept comfort, aid, help, when Hannah fought to live? Tears streaked through dried blood in channels alongside his nose. Ellen collapsed in his arms.

"Danny," her face had the look, the color, the pain he'd seen three times before, now multiplied by infinitude. She was so pale, so fragile. Her husband knew at once.

"No!!" screamed the young pastor, the murmur of the packed waiting room becoming deathly still. Sitting her down, Danny put his head into Ellen's lap and sobbed.

Prayers of Hannah's parents, prayers of the faith community, prayers of the worldwide Baptist convention, prayers of the country, and prayers of a suffering angel joined in supplication for a tough little girl during her five-hour ordeal under the competent hands of gifted doctors—and of her grandmother.

Danny allowed Ellen to clean his wounds, protesting that he should be caring for *her*. But Ellen had grit. She would see the doctor as soon as she knew her daughter was going to pull through, was going to make it . . . was going to live. The news of Leah's death caused the room to shudder, as friends and strangers held on to each other for fear of losing even more, of losing themselves to that devastating, unforgiving enemy. Ellen felt as if razor blades were systematically slicing through her stomach: the aftermath of her miscarriage, the aftermath of the tornado, the aftermath of a promising day when the sun shone like a daffodil.

Pastor Reiner charged into the room and came to the side of his assistant. The two men looked into each other's eyes. Danny's eyes begged him to make it all go away, to bring down the company of heaven, to move the mountain—Christ said we could!—oh, the retching pain that filled the heart of a man named Dan. *I tell you the truth, if you have faith as small as a mustard seed, you can say to this mountain, "Move from here to there," and it will move. Nothing will be impossible for you.*

"I've called both your parents," Pastor Reiner told the stunned couple. "They are all on their way."

Dan Ross wanted his parents at that moment. He wanted his mother to tell him as she had so many times that everything works to the glory of God. He wanted her to shore him up, to keep him going, to promise him that everything would work out fine. And his dad! To feel his arms around him, to feel his strength. How could he *ever* be the father his dad was! He would have never left Dan under a desk all alone. He would have protected him with his life. A tear fell slowly down Dan's cheek, a tear that managed to wring itself out of his body after all the others had fled.

"Dan, your mother told me to tell you that you must dig deep now and keep your focus on the Lord no matter what."

Appraisal

Three doctors approached the crowd. Daniel and Ellen Ross knew they were coming for them. They grabbed each other's hand and held on for dear life: *Stay away from us!* Dan closed his arm around his wife's shoulder. *Go away! No! Come! Tell us!* Ellen's knees buckled. Danny looked into the grim faces of the doctors and bit back the anguish and fury that clashed like hot and cold air that threatened to blast his body to smithereens. The head surgeon, Dr. Vrainish, was first to speak.

"Pastor Ross, your daughter is in extremely critical condition. We have her on life support. Her spleen has been removed. The problem is with the swelling in her brain. We are faced with a waiting game here." He hesitated, but felt it his duty . . . "The consensus is that life support is the only reason she . . ." Dan frantically searched his face. *No! No, do you hear me, NO! My child* will *live!* He wanted to grab the doctor by the throat, to strangle him, to stop the words that came too easily for the man. *This was . . . my God! . . . this was Hannah-anna!*

Pastor Reiner saw the mounting tension and stepped into the middle. He moved the surgeon to the side for hushed conversation. The woman doctor took over.

"Come and sit down," she said as she led Dan and Ellen to chairs. The doctor was overwhelmed with emotion at the sight of the distraught parents, overwhelmed from the battle she'd just fought in the operating room, overwhelmed with the certainty that the child would not make it through the night. But she would not take away the tiniest shred of hope, not the tiniest crumb. And so, the woman doctor who under other circumstances would have borne noticeable resemblance to a little girl named Hannah—and to the young pastor she was comforting—gave the parents hope.

"Pastor Ross, you must dig deeply now and keep your focus on the Lord. It is time to pray for a miracle. My husband and I would like to pray for you and your daughter right now." Danny nodded. Ellen nodded. And Stephen Weeks began to pray, and Brenda Weeks joined in, taking Dan's hands in both of hers, and telling him that everything would work out fine.

"I have to see her!" the pitiful cry came from Ellen.

"Mrs. Ross, I want you to be prepared. Her head is shaved, there is swelling, there are tubes . . ."

"We will go to our daughter." The terse statement came from Brenda's son.

They could have never, *ever,* been duly prepared for what they saw. What they *didn't* see, however, was that surrounding their mangled and swollen child was a multitude of heavenly hosts, led by Chosen, who sang continuous lullaby and eased her suffering with gentle touch. It was a bittersweet moment for Chosen when he saw Danny enter the room, led by the hand of his mother.

Hannah Hangs On

The night passed. And then another. Little Hannah showed no sign of progress, but beating all odds, she clung tenaciously to life. If it is so that a child can be willed to life by her parents and grandparents, that was the case with Hannah, for her family left her side only when pressured by staff. Hannah Felicity Ross became a symbol of hope and trust for everyone in the hospital and beyond. Supplications by the planeload were delivered to the throne of God. Prayers came from every person who knew of Hannah's condition, yet came less and less from one who found himself more and more drawn to despair and distrust as he tried to reconcile the immensity of his loss with the faithfulness of God. It had all been easy until now. Dan had faced a couple of difficult moments in his life, but he'd been spared a more monumental test of faith. *And he is tested with the life of his child? This is a loving God?!*

Dan's mother saw the change in her son, the gradual shift toward a hard crust of anger that comes at crucial times in life and sometimes never leaves. She let him be: this was not a time for advice, for lectures, for counsel. It was a time to pray and to believe and to . . . simply . . . take the test. But why? Danny's mother sat in the hospital chapel and shook her head. "I don't know why You allowed this Lord, but somehow You always turn our tears into dancing."

Danny's adoptive mother, Hannah-anna's grandmother, stood heavily, walked with bowed head from the hospital chapel, and held the door for another mother. For Brenda, also, was drawn to the little chapel near intensive care. Today she sank into a small pew in desperation and distress. She feared that little Hannah Ross might be blind.

Scheduled to leave for Niger the next day, Brenda was drawn to the child, unable to concentrate on duties elsewhere. "There is something special about that little girl, Stephen. I can't get her out of my mind."

"That's what makes you such a good doctor, Bren. What is the prognosis?"

"Still poor."

An Empty House

With both sets of grandparents at Hannah's bedside, Dan and Ellen left to attend Leah and Frosty's funeral. It was their first time home since the tornado. Church members had mercifully cleaned the house and discreetly placed Hannah's toys in her room. To no avail. The house could have been swept clear of every mention, every reminder of their little girl, and it would still miss its energetic Hannah. Could they have hidden the couch, whose back she would climb and fling herself off of and into Dan's arms? Could they have removed the kitchen floor where she twirled and danced "like an angel, Mommy!" Could they have replaced the bed where the child was conceived . . . and where, once she learned to walk, she would crawl between her parents for snugs? The house brought manifold sorrow to Ellen, but nudged Dan closer to the rage that was simmering in his gut.

"Daniel," said his weak wife, "are you OK?"

OK?! What the heck was that supposed to mean? Am I OK?! Are you crazy? Where have you been the past three days? Outer space? Don't you know that my child is in a coma, my wife miscarried a baby, my church has been flattened by a tornado, two people I grew to love are dead, AND I FAILED AS A FATHER?! Am I OK?! Dan grabbed Ellen and held her close. "Oh, El," he cried, "I will never be OK again!" And he ran outside. He had to get out of the house, to run full force into the blame that filled all of time, that laced the air he breathed, that pelted him with an overwhelming sense of failure wherever he turned. Ellen slumped onto the sofa.

Danny ran for blocks, his feet bleeding again when the wounds opened, his chest heaving. He picked up a rock and flung it at the sun. "How *dare* You!" he screamed at the top of his lungs. "How *dare* You!" And he fell to his knees holding his head, stopping the sound of a billion bees.

The Funeral

The funeral was, fittingly, a celebration. All of their past annoyances turned inside out, one person after another stood and told tales about Leah and Frosty. They spoke with real affection, and to a person recognized that just maybe the irascible couple was the asset to the church they fancied themselves to be. Dan and Ellen sat passive and numbed, anxiety body-slamming them every time they saw a person approach or heard a phone ring. Chosen attended the funeral, too, leaving Hannah's bedside long enough to honor two saints who had passed on to eternity. The big angel wished he could take his turn in front of the congregation, to tell them that Leah and Frosty were sublimely—ecstatically—happy now. And probably taking over every organ and learning everybody's names! Not to mention adding a touch of color with their outlandish outfits.

A Meeting in the Night

It was early the next morning, the time of day called night, when people sleep and dream—when some people fight with demons of despair, demons of sleeplessness, demons of outrage—that Stephen and Brenda Weeks were packed and ready to go. An early flight to New York before they caught the plane that would bring them to Niger, a courtesy van was called. Brenda could not leave without one last visit to the Ross child. She hurried through the medical complex, crossed the street, and entered the hospital through the emergency room. Up she went to Hannah's room, where she found an exhausted mother on a cot and a father slumped against the wall.

"Pastor Ross?" Dan looked up at Brenda. Chosen fluttered his wings with gladness and wished there was a way to let them know. He remembered her prayer when she held him so many years ago, and now here she was, drawn to the child she lost.

"Hello, Dr. Weeks."

"My husband and I are leaving for Africa. I wanted to see Hannah before I left."

Dan nodded. Ellen stirred slightly, the weight of sleep pulling her against her will into deep slumber.

Brenda checked Hannah's charts, checked her reflexes, sighed in secret, and joined Dan on the floor. She sat close enough to hug him. Tears fell off Chosen's face like a waterfall.

"You know, Pastor, I've seen many miracles over the years, and I cannot shake the belief that one will happen now." She looked him square in the eye. A jolt of recognition shot through her, but the kind you have when you meet someone you cannot place, not the kind of recognition that you have when you meet the child you handed to another woman thirty-three years ago.

Surprising himself with his candor, Dan blurted, "I don't believe in miracles anymore, Dr. Weeks."

Brenda wasn't fazed. Chosen was bouncing off the wall. *One is happening right now, Daniel! This is your mother!*

"I think I know how you feel."

"No one can know how I feel."

"It says in Psalms: 'When I felt secure, I said, "I will never be shaken. O LORD, when you favored me, you made my mountain stand firm; but when you hid your face I was dismayed."' It also says: 'He raises the poor from the dust and lifts the needy from the ash heap.'"

"What does it say about Him *creating* the ash heap?"

"Pastor, it is now that your faith has a face."

"That sounds so cliché."

"It is the very cliché that separates the wheat from the chaff, Pastor. Tell me, what would you be counseling a church member now? To abandon hope? To abandon God? No, I suspect you might quote Romans: 'For neither death nor life, neither angels nor demons, neither the present nor the future, nor any powers, neither height nor depth, nor anything else in all creation, will be able to separate us from the love of God that is in Christ Jesus our Lord.'"

"You sound like my mother," chuckled Danny. It was his first chuckle since Hannah held four fingers in the air.

"Listen to your mother, Pastor. My husband and I will continue to pray for Hannah. We will keep tabs on her progress through our colleagues here. But please, please believe me when I say that there is a peace in my spirit about your child. She is in God's hands."

And that is exactly the problem, thought Danny as he accepted a quick hug from the doctor before she left, a hug that sent a jolt of emotion through him that he barely noticed, and would never understand if he had.

Brenda's Gift

Dr. Vrainish brought the weary parents and grandparents into a small conference room. Pastor Reiner had been invited to the meeting as well. It was time to give Hannah's parents the hard facts about their daughter, who showed no sign of progress and was kept alive by machines that hummed and did their jobs magnificently—every machine tended, it is worth noting, by a doting angel.

The doctor stared at anxious faces and was grateful the young couple had such strong family support. He was a grandfather himself and related instantly to Dan and Ellen's fathers, who remained standing, arms crossed, two sentinels prepared to do battle to protect their own from further harm. *What a wicked position to be in,* thought the surgeon. To be so helpless, when without so much as a blink of an eye they would lay down their life. All these two men could do was stand, arms braced, prepared to carry the load, the pain, the ugly news they sensed was coming their way. Dan and Ellen's fingers joined, their eyes studied the face of the doctor for a trace of smile. The grandmothers never, *ever,* stopped whispering prayer.

"The swelling is starting to go down," the doctor began. *Well, THAT was good news, wasn't it?!* "But there seems to be little . . ." (he meant no) ". . . progress. Every day that goes by is good, but our tests show that the optical nerve has been . . ." (how could he say *destroyed?)* ". . . compromised."

Ellen's hand closed on Dan's like a bear trap snapping shut.

Dan's father spoke. "Do you mean she will need glasses?"

Listen to that! thought the doctor. *Glasses! No! I mean she won't see at all. I mean that if she even survives this ordeal that she will be blind! Why are you making this hard for me? Stop trying to make everything I say all sunbeams and flowers. The child will probably not live, and if she does she will be blind! Can't you understand?!*

"The prognosis for severely impaired eyesight is certain," Dr. Vrainish stammered and cleared his throat.

"Are you telling us she is blind?" There! Dan said it. He said it like a curse. He accused the doctor with his words, words that slapped everyone in the face. Ellen's grip loosened. She needed both hands to hold her head. She could not take any more. The grandmothers held her, Dan stormed out of the room, and the grandfathers did what they do best. They cornered the doctor and began to make plans—pipe dreams, it didn't matter—to restore their beloved Hannah to perfection. "Is there a specialist? We'll fly him in. Are there drugs, tools, equipment, people, *tell us what.* We will move heaven and earth."

Dan stormed past his daughter's room and headed toward his car. A big angel kept pace. Chosen knew the young pastor was headed for a showdown.

"How *dare* You!" It came again, and again as he gunned the accelerator and headed recklessly into emptiness. He drove through tears; he drove through fear; he drove straight into consuming, blinding rage. Blinding. The angel moved the steering wheel for him, the car on autopilot, Dan too absorbed with fury to pay attention to direction.

The sight of his leveled church shocked Dan back into the moment. It was his first time back since the killer storm, his first time to see what others spoke of in hushed tones, his first time to see the freakish mess left by an insane giant who left flowers alongside the sidewalk unscathed. He picked his way through the twisted metal and lumber and glass. Fat, yellow tape surrounded the rubble with warning: *Danger Police Line*. Here was his office, no . . . there. The organ gone, the steeple, his desk. His desk! Chosen led the disconsolate man toward a certain spot. *Come a little closer, Daniel, right . . . here.* The toe of Dan's shoe caught an edge of Brenda's book. He leaned over and pulled it from underneath jagged tin and lumber laced with nails. He blew the dust of debris off its cover: *A Resting Place: The Book of Psalms*. He opened the book (the book quite frankly opened on its own) to Psalm 139, a psalm that was spared Clara's pencil.

> *Whither shall I go from thy spirit? Or whither shall I flee from thy presence?*
>
> *If I ascend up to heaven, thou art there: if I make my bed in hell, behold, thou art there.*
>
> *If I take the wings of the morning and dwell in the uttermost parts of the sea;*
>
> *Even there shall thy hand lead me, and thy right hand shall hold me . . .*
>
> *How precious also are thy thoughts unto me, O God! How great is the sum of them!*
>
> *If I should count them, they are more in number than the sand: when I awake I am still with thee.*

Dan's spirit came home. He tried to run, but where could he go? No power on earth or in hell—not even the power of a tornado—could conquer the Spirit of God that lived in his heart. He yielded all of his anger and fear and hurt into the nail-scarred hands of its rightful owner. The Cross would always be for Dan the center of time and eternity. He dug deep and steadied his focus. *When I awake I am still with thee. When I awake from this nightmare, from this ordeal, from the striving of my soul to hate You, blame You . . . when I awake to a new ray of sunlight that looks like heaven . . . I find You there.* Dan fell to his knees. "All praise and glory to You, Lord God. I trust in You, O Lord, my times are in Your hands. And Father, into Your hands I place my daughter. Thy will be done."

The Angels Dance

Dan drove back to the hospital. Chosen blasted ahead to return to Hannah's side, for he had just received special permission, as it were, to interfere to his big old angel-heart's delight. So as Dan was turning into the hospital parking lot, Chosen was laying hands on a child in intensive care, while grandfathers manned telephones down the hall and grandmothers and mother prayed. "Dear Jesus, Great Physician, restore this child to health! Master, I beseech You!" Hannah stirred and moaned.

"Get the doctor!" yelled Ellen, who was leaning over her daughter's limp body and restraining the frenzy in her voice. "Hannah, Mommy loves you! Hannah! Oh, Hannah!" Ellen wanted to scream but kept calm, as nurses gently pulled her aside to make way for Dr. Vrainish. Orders were barked, machines and tubes and people went into high gear with hope, the hope of faith—more mighty than the most powerful force man could ever imagine. Chosen beamed the beam of grandfathers, grandmothers, parents, angelic beings, the Baptist convention—the collective beam of thousands whose petition had been heard. Dan shot into the room. Hannah opened her eyes.

"Daddy-dear," she peeped through blurry vision, as every heart in the room—in the universe—pushed its way past protocol and shouted, "Thank You, Jesus! Thank You!"

Some were bold to call it a "miracle," some just shook their heads. But they knew. They knew.

There would be many more vigils at the Tulsa Medical Center, many more breakthroughs for little Hannah, whose room was soon decorated with birthday balloons as Dr. Vrainish ceremonially removed her last tube. Dan and Ellen maintained a vigil at their daughter's bedside while Easthaven Baptist Church hastily assembled a rebuilding committee and accepted the gracious hospitality of an Assemblies of God church to convene in their Fellowship Hall. It would be a long journey back for Hannah and for her loving congregation, a journey all the poorer for the loss of the Trippetts, a journey that began with the purchase of an eraser at a local Wal-Mart. For Dan had grown quite fond of a skinny little book of Psalms—especially since someone named "Brenda" signed the inside cover—and set out to eradicate the vile comments and heresy infused within. So while Hannah-anna grew stronger and became a living terror for her nurses, Pastor Daniel Ross took it upon himself to rehabilitate Brenda's gift—his mother's gift—which would become the seed book in the library of a brand-new Easthaven Baptist Church in Tulsa, Oklahoma. A church now big enough to handle overflow crowds.

Chapter
Fourteen

April 1996

How Brenda's book ended up in The Second Time Around Thrift Store is so strange a story it could only be real: it all started with Leah and Frosty Trippett.

It so happened that having no heirs, the Trippett's will held a big surprise for Easthaven Baptist Church. It gave an endowment large enough to rebuild the entire church were that necessary, and the money came with a hitch: it was to be used to build a combination gym/auditorium, and scholarships were provided to any child showing interest in performing arts as ministry.

Completed in 1993, the Trippett Wing—how they would have loved that!—was dedicated to children everywhere, and Assistant Pastor Dan Ross soon needed his *own* assistant to keep pace with an ever-expanding youth program. The building was used for afternoon and late-night sports as basketballs slapped against the gym floor, for the customary mayhem of

Wednesday night youth group, and for presentations of dramatic skits written
and produced by the kids themselves, always with an eye toward evangelism.
Dan and Ellen personally spearheaded the drama team, and the congregation
at Easthaven was often ministered to on Sunday morning as teens presented
mime, song, dance, and drama in the name of Jesus. Much to her chagrin,
eight-year-old Hannah merely qualified as team mascot and could only
dream of the day she would be old enough to join in. At least she got to tag
along. That is, when she wasn't assigned to supervise her twin sisters who
were just learning to walk.

"Bradley! Do you have the props?"

"I already put them in the van, Pastor. We still need a cigar, an alarm
clock, and a book."

"Run over to the church library and grab a book. You can use my alarm
clock. I'll buy a cigar when we get to St. Louis." Dan could just imagine what
his prankish teens would do with a cigar during the seven-hour road trip. He
called home.

"You sure you'll be OK, El?"

"Daniel, we will be fine! I have all the help I need from church. You go
and win that trophy. We'll be praying for you!"

"Let me speak to Hannah."

"Da . . . ad."

"No, Hannah."

Sigh. How long did it take to grow up anyway? "Bye, Daddy. I love
you."

"I love you too, Hannah-anna. You help your mom with the girls. I'll
bring you back something special from St. Louis, OK?"

"OK . . ."

"Kisses?"

Hannah blew kisses into the phone, and Dan headed out the door. He
and his ace drama team were going to compete in a regional match. Bradley
jumped into the van with a skinny little book and put it in a box before Dan
could see to object. The others hopped aboard, a prayer was prayed, and the
six were off, an angel cruising alongside.

St. Louis

Easthaven Baptist Church vanquished all competitors at the drama festival, thanks to a mime presentation of a song called "Lazarus" that brought down the house.

The weather, the sights, and the elation of their victory all combined to make the team's visit to St. Louis a premier event. Even Dan cut loose more than usual. A trip to the Zoo, Gateway Arch, and to Busch Stadium to see the Cardinals/Cubs baseball game added to their exhaustion. When their stay was over, the euphoric group loaded into the van and promptly fell asleep as a gratified youth pastor began the drive to Tulsa. And so it was that hurry-up, excitement, and absentmindedness contributed to the reason their props were left behind. The skinny little book of Psalms, Brenda's gift so long ago to a boy named Will, a book that had seen many miles and many more tears, would only months later be missed.

The folks at Easthaven Baptist Church in Tulsa, Oklahoma, however, would never know that *they* were missed by a ministering angel, a servant of the most high God, a heavenly host who stood on a St. Louis sidewalk and watched their van disappear from sight. It was time for the book's final journey, one that would begin at a thrift store in downtown St. Louis, Missouri.

All props and belongings left behind—for absentmindedness was a universal characteristic of youth groups—were boxed by the America's Center custodial staff and sent to a store run on behalf of the developmentally disabled. Chosen followed the box and became angel in residence when *A Resting Place* was tossed onto a heap of old textbooks and corny romance novels. He was not to be in residence long. Within a few days of his arrival, an attractive woman with short, auburn hair walked through the door. She was a regular at the thrift store, following in the footsteps of a frugal grandmother who had taught her to develop a good eye for quality and to prowl these shops for "finds." *I had quite a* find *today,* Gram would say.

The woman's face reminded Chosen of a bird. Her features were angular and tight, the casual hairstyle almost too much a contrast as it framed such sharp features. Her chin, her nose, her brows: all of her face looked as if chiseled into cut glass. Most who came to the thrift store seemed mellow; this determined woman with green eyes and perfect teeth appeared purposeful. Chosen knew at once that she was the one.

A little careful maneuvering of racks, a little strategy blocking an aisle with piles of clothes . . . and there! . . . enough detours and the woman found herself in the used book section. And now a little prodding, a bit of extra light, a few angelic hymns and prayers, and Brenda's gift, which now sported a sticker marked "29 cents," was stuffed in a grocery bag with two plastic flowerpots and a purple sweater. The birdlike woman actually bought the book in spite of herself, for she rejected religion outright. But "a resting place" . . . the title intrigued her. What the heck.

Chosen followed the woman into her blue Honda Accord, the one with the "I Vote Pro-Choice" bumper sticker and a plastic silver fish affixed to the trunk, a fish with feet and the word *Darwin* inside. Chosen's stay with Wendy Hunt was about to begin.

Wendy

Wendy pushed the button on her answering machine.

"Tonight is off, have to head out of town. Call you when I get back."

Geoff's call didn't surprise her. After a year, their relationship had deteriorated to little more than sexual gratification and Wendy's companionship when the stockbroker needed a date for one of his many "client" functions. She was a concubine and a prop.

Geoff's treatment of Wendy was no different from the other men she'd dated, others that started with the excitement and mystery of romance and fizzled to excuses, cancellations, and disappointment. She felt used, relationships littering her past like so many derailed trains. After work, after golf, after going out with "the guys," after visiting their kids (at Wendy's age just about every suitor had once been married and had a couple of adolescents going through their latest snit), after their personal business—whatever that meant—after their exhaustion, even after their daily dog runs, Wendy fit in someplace. And it wasn't a comfortable fit. Truth be known, she hated it. Wasn't there someone out there who would put her on a pedestal? She poked through her mail and banished that thought to the trash with the latest pleas for donations. The last thing she would ever, *ever*—do you hear her?—EVER do was go back to the way it used to be. On a pedestal over her dead body! What was she thinking? Women were submissive, obedient little slaves back then. Stepford Wives. Not this lady. With the exception of her love life, Wendy was thoroughly satisfied with career and friends. She'd carved a place for herself in the publishing world, had material comfort, rallied with like-minded activists for various causes, took proper care of her body. No fat, lots of water, and appropriate exercise were mandatory protocol for the woman who fancied her body to be her temple.

Chosen surveyed Wendy's condo. Icy colors cooled the interior. Prints hung framed in chrome; furniture, a white leather; the carpet, hospital white. A large-screen TV dominated one wall, the couch facing it like a pew faces an altar. A multicolored afghan put color into the otherwise monochromatic room. Wendy might not feel completely happy inside, but she would at least cover herself with a splash of cheerfulness and hide beneath the smell of her grandmother who crocheted it for her. *Gram* was never lonely like this.

Chosen wandered through the sterile kitchen, countertops clear of any clutter. Actually, countertops clear of any*thing*. A Siamese cat jumped on the counter, arched its back, and hissed when the angel's presence was felt. Wendy attempted to push the cat off the counter and it swatted her with its claws.

"Edgar!" Even the cat rejected her.

Great. The puncture in her thumb was right at the spot where she tapped her advance bar on the keyboard. Her subcontractor job as copy editor for several book publishers was going to be a bit tender for the next few days.

Chosen followed Wendy as she headed into an extra-bedroom-turned-office. At least she had work. But burying herself in work was getting old. She was growing weary of her predictable romantic rut, tired of Geoff, tired of how alone fierce independence had made her. She heard a big truck.

The empty condo next door had finally sold, and a woman about her age was moving in. She'd watched her from a bedroom window and eaves-dropped when the realtor walked the new neighbor through a small backyard.

"Each yard is separated by a high privacy fence. This is a quiet place. You should be able to garden to your heart's content back here. I'm told the woman next door pretty much sticks to herself."

Ouch. It pinched, but it was true. Wendy wasn't practiced at the coffee klatch routine; besides, she'd rejected that notion as nostalgic nonsense. Coffee klatch indeed. What on earth would she talk about? How degraded women are in a society that expects them to rear children and keep their mouths shut? Forget it. She didn't need that. So what did she need? To be cherished, to come first, to matter . . . her yearnings collided with her resolve to remain independent and liberated. Just then she wanted to be liberated from her cat, who had followed her into the office on an attack mission.

"Edgar! What is going on? EDGAR!" The cat was clawing at her leg. It wanted no part of a heavenly host who was on his knees, snapping his fingers and calling *Kitty, kitty.*

Neighbors

The pounding, hauling, scraping, bumping, and laughing coming from the condo next door was getting on Wendy's nerves, and if it lasted one more day she would complain. Michelle never gave her a chance. The doorbell rang.

"Hi!" A perky redhead, all five-feet-two of her, stood in front of Wendy holding a bakery bag. "I figured I'd better come meet you before you call the police! My name's Michelle. And I promise the noise will stop as soon as I can get my crazy boyfriend to quit trying to put up shelves. Anyway, here's a bag of Gooey Butter Cakes from McArthur's Bakery, sort of a peace offering. What's your name?"

"Wendy Hunt."

"Maybe we can get together for coffee one of these days!"

Yeah, right, thought Wendy as she shut the door.

Chosen felt grace ooze from Michelle and could not resist following her home for a peek. He immediately noticed the fish on her car—the one that said "Jesus"—and instantly saw *My Utmost for His Highest* on top of a well-traveled Bible next to Michelle's single bed.

During the next few weeks Michelle's attempts to socialize with Wendy were met with excuses. Wendy's loneliness persisted, but a full life kept her occupied until the nighttime hours, when crawling into her queen-sized bed alone squared her strong beliefs against emotional turmoil. She was woman! Woman who most nights found herself wrapped in an afghan watching TV while the distant hint of laughter seeped through adjoining walls.

Geoff's occasional visits left Chosen in despair. How different the contrast between lust and physical indulgence, and the intimate sexual expression shared by Danny and Ellen. And the angel despaired over Geoff's self-absorbed attitude: Wendy was definitely not cherished, nor did she come first, nor did she matter. She *was* used.

"There is an important party coming up on Friday. Wear that tight, red dress of yours. You may have to meet me there, depending on work."

Chosen wished the woman would read Brenda's gift. Wendy wondered why she'd even bought it. Consigning the twenty-nine-cent purchase to impulsive whim, she'd shoved it inside an end table drawer next to the bed. Chosen grew more and more frustrated. It was one bright day in May when the angel began to plan . . .

Sabotage

Michelle spent much time in her backyard garden. Edgar had become a regular visitor—or nuisance, for such is the way of Siamese—and would perch precariously on top of the fence to watch Michelle plant and weed, sometimes carrying on full conversation.

"Meeoorrwww."

"You don't say, Edgar! Now you stay out of this bed, you little scoundrel."

It was Tuesday when Wendy heard her cat sing along with that blasted radio Michelle always had playing. Tuned to a Christian station and blaring, Michelle sang along freely. Not to be outdone, Wendy propped her boom box on a flower box and broadcast National Public Radio, overtly outpacing her neighbor's decibel level. All she got for her effort was: "Hi, Wendy!" thrown over the fence like a comfortable old blanket. "Hope you don't mind that Edgar is helping me garden! I put in, and he digs out! We make quite a pair!" Curiosity getting the better of her, Wendy went down on all fours to peek underneath the fence, only to have her nose whacked by her cat's paw. The injured woman went inside and surveyed the rip in a mirror. *Oh, swell. So exactly how do you put a Band-Aid on a nose? This ought to look good on Friday.*

The next morning Wendy awoke with a start, thanks to a conniving angel. Expecting to hear the early edition of the news, Wendy lay in a fog until she detected something drastically wrong. It seemed the local Christian station and NPR were so close on the dial they were practically on top of each other. She heard a familiar voice, but it wasn't the usual NPR commentator. It was the voice she had heard on Michelle's radio!

"Good morning, Gentle Listener! The Psalms say: 'My lips shall praise you. Thus I will bless you while I live.' Dear ones, can there be a better time to praise God than right now?"

Her eyes widened, and her hand slammed the wake button. A persistent phone was ringing in the background.

"It's about time you answered!"

"Geoff?" She felt her nose. It didn't feel good.

"I'm going to drop some papers off tonight. I need you to clean them up for me—important letters, Wendy. And you need to run by and pick up my tux for Friday night. Are you going to get your hair done?"

She felt her nose again. "I made an appointment with Trevor."

"Good! See you later!"

The mirror did not hold promise. Edgar's swipe had been particularly deep, and now the entire tip of Wendy's nose was bright red. Just like the dress she planned on wearing. She hurried to her medicine cabinet to find a salve. Nothing. Ever frugal, she'd combine her trip to the pharmacy with a stop at the cleaners.

Backing out of her garage the same time as Michelle, she steamed as she followed "Jesus" down the street. She switched on her radio. Chosen could barely stifle his chuckle. "What is going on?!" Wendy growled as she heard the voice again—a man's voice.

"'God so loved the world that He gave His only begotten Son, that whoever believes in Him should not perish but have everlasting life. Blessed are those who hear the Word and don't see, but believe.'"

"Agh!!!"

Geoff threw a fit when he saw Wendy's nose, which put her in contention for Grand Poobah of the local clown fraternity. She could direct traffic just by nodding her head.

"Can't you put makeup on that thing? It better be OK by the party!"

Wendy ignored the comments and pushed her body next to his. "You're not in a hurry to go, are you?" She just couldn't face the sofa again tonight.

"I can't stay long . . ."

Chosen would see to it that he didn't.

If the angel timed it right, if he waited just for the moment when the couple would leave the couch and head for the bedroom, then he could . . . now! Geoff's car alarm sounded. *That should break the mood!* thought the angel. He was right. Geoff shouted as he grabbed his suit coat and ran out the door. "I've got to prepare for my meeting tomorrow morning! I'll pick you up on Friday at seven! And do something about that nose!"

The phone rang. It was Michelle.

"Is everything OK?"

"Yes. Thank you for calling."

"Wait! Listen, some friends of mine are coming over tomorrow night, and I wondered if you'd like to join in—"

"I already have plans, thank you."

The Plot Thickens

It happened again. Deep in sleep, she woke again to the man's voice.

"Good morning, Gentle Listener. I want you to remember that nothing can happen to you today that you and God can't handle."

What on earth?! There must be some sort of magnetic field. She punched the button. It went off. It went on. She punched it again. It went off again. It went on again.

"When Jesus comes into a life, He changes everything."

She pulled the plug from the wall.

Coffee in hand, Wendy decided to enjoy the early sun in her backyard and to confer with herself about the pus that was now dripping off her nose.

Apparently Michelle liked the early sun as well . . .

"Wasn't that a powerful song? Can't you just imagine what it will be like in heaven? Man, I get a rush just thinking about it," waxed the radio announcer.

Wendy tromped back into her condo and slid her patio door shut. She called her doctor. Three-thirty would be fine.

Well, it wasn't fine at all; at four-thirty Wendy headed back to her car with a fat length of adhesive tape from one cheek to the other, bridging her freshly lanced and cleaned infection. There would be no party for her, and nothing but insult from Geoff. On Friday night she sat on her couch and listened to the distant hint of laughter. If she had listened hard, she would have heard the sound of the man who woke her from her sleep.

The Meeting

Wendy backed her car into the driveway and began to assemble buckets and hose. Washing her own car was a Saturday—and frugal—thing to do. Michelle and her steady, Tom, were apparently like-minded.

"Hey, Wendy, want some help?"

"No thanks."

Tom and Michelle looked at each other in secret smile, and without so much as a word began to pray for the woman next door. They were in the habit of praying for the "unsaved" and the next-door, pro-choice evolutionist was at the top of their list. To break the ice and develop a friendship was their most recent supplication.

Wendy slathered the Honda with a big, soapy sponge. A Jeep pulled next to the curb—next to Michelle's curb. Wendy hunkered down next to a tire and watched as an extremely appealing man in faded jeans and a black turtleneck headed up the walk. She squinted to see if he wore a wedding band, a habit she would never break. He didn't. Sleeves pushed back, he joined Michelle and Tom. Chosen was quite pleased with the arrangement. He stepped on Wendy's hose. This created quite a dilemma. Because in spite of a face that looks like you banged into a truck, and in spite of the fact that you would rather not get involved with some Jesus freak who lives next door, when your car is completely lathered in suds in the blazing sun and you have no water coming from your hose, you swallow hard and promise yourself you will be nice this *one* time.

"Michelle . . ." The three friends looked at the bandaged woman.

"Whoa, Wendy! You look like you slammed into a wall! What happened?"

"I developed an infection." *Actually, Michelle, my very own cat swiped me across the nose when I was lying down in the grass and trying to peek under the fence to see what you were doing next door.*

"I can't get any water to come out of my hose."

"Hey, let me take care of it!"

Wendy almost dropped on the spot. It was the voice! Chosen glowed: one "Jesus freak" coming up! Just for fun, the angel kept his foot on the hose until the right moment . . . sort of like an angelic ice pick.

Screams came from Wendy's driveway. Tom and Michelle gaped. Wendy and a voice belonging to a man named Mick were standing with wet heads and looks of surprise. Ice broken, Chosen prayed that the dripping woman would allow the three dear saints to minister to her.

"Guess I'm not the plumber my old man was!" laughed Mick as he stripped off his wet shirt and Wendy stared. "You go change your T-shirt," said Mick, diverting his eyes. "I'll finish your car."

Ice cubes neatly stacked on top of each other again, Wendy would later decline an offer for burgers in Michelle's backyard. For one thing, she didn't want to miss Geoff's call; it was such a glorious weekend, surely they would spend some time together. His call came late. She could tell he'd been drinking. He wanted to come over to see her. No, he wanted to come over to use her. She wanted him there too. Anything to feel needed, or close.

They Meet Again

Geoff was leaving the next morning when Tom drove up. Tom saw Wendy in her doorway, waved hello, and rang Michelle's bell. Wendy stared through a crack in the door and watched him escort Michelle to his car, stealing a quick kiss before he opened her door. She was carrying a Bible covered with flower print fabric and lace. He was wearing a sport jacket. Wendy reached for her fat Sunday paper and headed for the coffeepot. An article in the "Living" section of the paper caught her eye at once. There was a picture of the man who washed her car! She put her mug on the table and held the paper with both hands.

"Mick Cochrane, popular Christian DJ, serves meals at a battered woman's shelter." *There's a contradiction in terms,* thought Wendy, who read on. "Mick in the Morning can be heard weekdays from 6 A.M. until 10 A.M. at 101 on the FM dial. For information on booking concerts, call the Station. . . ." She put the paper in the recycle bin. And faced a lovely Sunday afternoon alone.

Testing the dial before she pulled her car from the driveway, Wendy settled back to listen to NPR as she headed to Forest Park with her new pair of rollerblades. Taking up the better part of a bench, she tugged on the straps of her skates.

"I'd know that nose anywhere!" came the voice as a man in bike shorts skidded to a half-circle stop. It was Mick Cochrane. Wendy looked up.

"Do you need help?" Without so much as a pause in his words, Mick was on one knee in front of the woman, tightening her straps. She felt his strength as he cinched them around her ankles. "These look brand-new."

"They are."

"Where's your helmet?"

Helmet! She'd forgotten a helmet!

"Here, take mine." She protested, but two firm hands were already shortening the chin strap. "There. With that bandage you'll look like a real veteran out there." She didn't budge. "I'll pick it up next time I stop at Michelle's." And he was off in a dash . . . showing off just a little, his smile as wide across as the famous St. Louis Arch.

Wendy raised her eyebrows and smiled. Chosen lowered his eyebrows and frowned. The electric charge that arced between the man and woman worried the angel, whose singular prayer was for redemption—not romance.

Geoff

At thirty-seven, Geoff Newgard was heading toward the pinnacle of his career. Nothing could stop him. Trim, driven, smart, and unattached best described the man who eyed full partnership in the brokerage firm where he worked. And it was within reach. Totally consumed by goals, Geoff was more than content to be on a single track—mark that: *single*—as long as it was fast. What little thought he gave to a wife and children was backburnered for some time off in the future. The distant future. For now he was free and would so remain until he found the perfect match. It might be Wendy, one never knew. There were others before her, others who suddenly announced an ultimatum, others who were driven by the goal of a diamond on their ring finger. At least it was a perfect match for now; Wendy had her own life, was not a clinging whiner, and followed her own career. Lately, though, he'd detected a little smothering, a sure and certain tack that would push him away.

Birthday

Wendy called Geoff at work and left a message. "I'm going to give a little dinner party on Friday night. Be here at seven." She invited two other couples: one from her reading group, one from yoga class. And she flew into happy frenzy. After all, she was planning her birthday party.

Having a task besides work was therapeutic for Wendy, who put her heart and soul, and rare extravagance with her pocketbook, into the affair. Jumbo shrimp, pâté, fine champagne, an assortment of varietals, leg of lamb, and chocolate decadence for dessert. Every detail was thought through as she lay in bed each night with pencil and pad: perfectly pressed linens, flowers, Gram's china, after-dinner aperitif, freshly roasted coffee beans—water-processed decaf, of course—and candles. Lots of candles.

The phone began to ring on Friday afternoon. The couple from yoga shared a splitting headache—some flu going round, they suspected. Not to worry. Two settings were removed from the table. The phone rang again. "We are just overbooked and cannot possibly face an evening out tonight, Wendy, you'll have to excuse us." Her little party was going down the drain. *Well,* she decided, as she removed the next two settings, *we'll have a romantic evening together, just the two of us.* She headed to her bedroom to don a certain red dress.

Wendy strategically lit candles as the magic hour arrived, slipped a CD called *In the Mood* into her machine, lowered the dimmer switch, and checked her face one more time. Her nose had healed nicely, and thanks to the flickering candles and Max Factor foundation, she looked stunning. She stuck Edgar in the garage in spite of his protests, and waited. And waited. At 7:30 she had Geoff paged. She left messages on his recorder. Wendy padded around in her stocking feet, stopping to read the birthday cards from her mom and Gram, before finally depositing them under soggy tea bags in the trash. At 8:30 she blew out the candles and turned up the light. Edgar came in and went straight to the counter. She let him munch on the shrimp and wrapped the lamb in foil. She was furious and hurt. "Happy Birthday, Edgar," she said bitterly as the doorbell rang. Geoff! He'd certainly have some explaining to do! She swung the door open with the ferocity of a woman-at-arms. "Where have you been?!" she screeched.

"Well, let's see . . . first I went to work, then I went to the store, then I went home and had some leftover pizza, and then I watched some TV and then I decided to stop and see Michelle and maybe pick up my helmet, and now I'm here." It was Mick. "Can I come in?"

Immediately conscious of her provocative appearance, Wendy stepped aside and held her hand against her cleavage. "Nice dress!" he said as he waltzed into her life, the smell of extinguished candles still strong. Surveying the circumstance and noticing mascara-smeared eyes, Mick came to the rescue. "I'm starved!"

"I'm a little chilly," said Wendy. "I think I'll go slip on a sweater."

What a grand meal they had! Mick had a way about him, was able to say just the right thing, able to smile and laugh. How long had it been since she laughed? He regaled her with stories from radio, about growing up in St. Louis, and even snitched on his sis who lived next door.

"Michelle is your sister?"

"Yep. Now she's engaged to one of my best friends. I tell you, there is no justice! I lost my buddy! Got no one to pal around with now that he's gaga over her. She lived with me until she could find this place. Moved here from Florida after her husband died. Just too weird it happened to both of us . . ." His voice trailed off.

What? What happened to both of you? You mean you both lost a spouse? Wendy felt it too invasive to ask.

Mick insisted she sit while he cleaned the table. "You cooked; I'll clean!" He noticed the birthday cards in the garbage and read them secretly. "Be right back!" came the call as he ran to his Jeep.

"Here," said Mick, as he handed a brown store bag to Wendy. "Happy Birthday."

"How did you know?"

"My guardian angel told me!" Mick laughed. Chosen grimaced. "Sorry it's not wrapped." Inside was a brand-new helmet and a pair of knee pads. "I circled around and watched you skate the other day, Wendy. I'm including a skating lesson as part of your present. Followed by a kosher hotdog and a milk shake!"

She blushed. And *almost* cried. But certainly didn't. Nosiree.

Mick thanked her for the evening, held her hand in a sort of a handshake, hand-holding kind of way, the old-fashioned way that sent shivers up her arm. "How about having that lesson next Saturday?" She nodded. In spite of herself.

It wasn't until 11:30 when the phone rang. Wendy was asleep under her afghan on the couch. "Wendy? Sorry I missed dinner. Look, can I come over?"

"Not tonight," she said, and put the phone back on the receiver.

Apologies

Realizing he'd gone too far this time, Geoff did try to compensate. He swung by Wendy's on Sunday and took her with him to the driving range where he slugged at bucket after bucket of golf balls. She brought work along and sat in the sun with a diet soda. Afterwards they ate at the clubhouse where Geoff talked shop with everyone he met. Wendy began to drift and caught herself thinking about next Saturday.

"One of my clients has a cabin on the lake that we can use next weekend. I told him we'd love to take him up on it. This is a major breakthrough, Wendy, when they start offering *their* place. You're free, right?"

Wendy hesitated. Their relationship was hanging by a thread, and they both knew it. What would it be, rollerblading and hot dogs, or a cabin retreat with this arrogant, selfish glory-hound? "Yes," she announced. "It sounds like fun."

"Great!" Geoff had his prop for the weekend.

That night when the couple began to consummate their revitalized dedication toward each other, an angel would have none of it. As Geoff was about to make his move, a Siamese cat landed on his shoulders, all claws extended. *And let that be that,* said Chosen as he rubbed his hands in victory.

The next morning Wendy called her neighbor.

"Michelle, would you please give your brother a message? Tell him something has come up and I can't make it on Saturday. Thank you."

Betrayal

Wendy let her answering machine take a message while she struggled through a tough manuscript. As she heard the message unfold, she pushed herself away from her computer and stared at the machine in disgust.

"Wendy, afraid I can't make it this weekend after all. Going to have to call it off. Maybe we can get together for a movie. I'll be in touch."

The phone rang again. Her machine gave its instructions and beeped, the message began: "Wendy, a couple of us are getting together for a little Bible study tomorrow night. Thought you might like to come. Anyway, it's at 7:30. No need to bring a Bible, we have plenty."

No one had ever, *ever,* asked her to a Bible study! And speaking of Bibles, where was that book she had bought? She marked "7:30 next door" on the patch of her desk blotter marked "Thursday" and went back to work, thinking if she saw Mick again she could reinstate her skating lesson.

Mick wasn't there. It was all women at Michelle's Bible study, and the skinny book she'd rescued from her nightstand was of no use to her: they were studying something called Beatitudes. Annoyed that she was trapped with a bunch of Jesus freaks, Wendy prepared to make a quick getaway but found herself having fun. Whatever she expected, this wasn't it. Maybe part of her loneliness was the loss of female fellowship, of a vital connection with other women. Wendy hadn't realized how parched she was for this kind of relationship, and soaked it up like the blotter on her desk. She agreed to meet with them next Thursday. What could it hurt?

After she left, the women held hands and prayed that the Lord would send a company of angels to watch over her and that He would bring her to a saving relationship with Himself. Chosen blushed when they prayed for an angel to attend her and stepped through the wall to do just that.

Though it remained unopened, Brenda's gift was placed on top of the nightstand next to Wendy's bed, and she moved her radio dial just a bit to the right before she went to sleep. Mick's voice greeted her the next morning.

"You know what? Sometimes we get so wrapped up in ourselves that we forget to be kind and loving to others. Why don't you go out of your way today to turn your attention outward for a little while, and reach out to those you love. Better yet, reach out to the unlovable. That's what Jesus did—and does!"

Wendy thought about Mick's words all day. She had become self-absorbed: perhaps she *should* turn her attention outwards. That afternoon she packed a lovely basket of food, snuck out front to pluck a flower from Michelle's yard, enclosed a cute note, and jumped into her car. Across town she drove, as Bach blared busily in the background. She pulled into a huge parking garage, took an elevator, entered a skyscraper, and headed toward the brokerage firm where Geoff would certainly be working late. She met one of the secretaries just outside the door.

"What are you doing here?" she was perplexed.

"I'm here to see Geoff."

"He's on his way to pick you up. I heard him tell you he'd be there in a few minutes. He just left. Oh, I get it. You have one of those new cell phones, don't you?"

"No. I don't. What makes you so sure he was talking to me?"

"Had to be you," she laughed, "unless he's going to the lake with some-one else!"

* * *

Wendy rang the doorbell. Michelle opened her door and stood stunned.

"May I come in?" Wendy asked. Though a game of Scrabble was in progress, Tom immediately recognized that Michelle's neighbor was not there for word games; this visit was a most unusual event. He folded the board and declared himself Champion Scrabble Player of All Time before he hugged Michelle good-bye. "I'll be over at Mick's," he announced, a flutter kick of electricity shooting through Wendy.

"I didn't mean to break up your date, Michelle."

"What are neighbors for?" she laughed, and then turned serious. "What's going on?"

"I've been driving around. I just . . . you know . . . there's just something missing, that's all. I look at you, and you look so happy, you've got Tom . . ." she pursed her lips. "This is stupid. I don't know why I'm here."

"I do." Michelle shot back.

"You do?"

"Sure!"

Oh my goodness, is it that obvious? Does she think I'm after her brother?

"You're here because this is where the Lord wants you to be. And if this is where He wants you, I'm going to pour us some tea!"

They talked late into the night and began to build a "friend next door" relationship. Wendy preached feminism, Michelle listened, and they forged a certain security that comes from sisterhood. How much more special it would be if they *both* claimed God as their Father.

The next day Wendy headed for the asphalt trail in Forest Park. She jerked along on her rollerblades, glad to have her new knee pads and helmet when she crashed into a park bench. A stiff, mechanical doll, the big angel held her steady against her awkward attempts to skate.

Two arms suddenly held her from behind and pushed her gracefully along the path. "I almost didn't recognize you without your nose wrap or your red dress!" he whispered into her ear as they glided along the trail. "My sister told me you were home this weekend. I hoped you'd be here today."

"You did?"

"Yep. Now how about that kosher hot dog?"

Chosen flew alongside, becoming increasingly concerned. He doubted Mick was thinking of evangelism as his strong hands held Wendy's shoulders close to his.

The Turn

Wendy waited for Mick's words on Monday morning.

"Good morning, St. Louis! Scripture reminds us to: 'Give unto the Lord the glory due His name, Worship the Lord, Let the heavens rejoice and let the earth be glad; let the sea roar, Let the field be joyful, and all that is therein, then shall all the trees of the wood rejoice.'"

Was there a particular lilt to his voice? Did he sound happier to his listeners? Could they tell he spent most of Saturday laughing and talking with a woman named Wendy? Wendy could. And before she got out of bed that morning, she reached for the book of Psalms. If her new man was "into" this stuff, why she'd learn something about it herself. Doesn't hurt to hedge your bet. Mick was funny, bright, full of life, and certainly appealing. He just might be the one to bump Geoff and become Wendy's new lover. She was already dreaming of their first sexual encounter.

Knowing that it took the power of God the Holy Spirit to reveal the Word to anyone, Chosen turned to most ambitious prayer. Even Edgar did his part as he jumped off the headboard and settled into a tight ball on top of Wendy's legs. The morning, the day, the week, all of life, looked rosy for Wendy as *she* curled into a comfortable ball herself and listened some more to a voice that was beginning to resonate in her heart. *Pay attention to the book, Wendy, not the radio!* Chosen was troubled enough to tap the dial back to NPR.

And so it went for the next few weeks: Wendy listened in the morning, happily took Mick's calls, walked hand-in-hand, read from Brenda's gift, went to Thursday night get-togethers next door, and began to fall in love.

Mick, who was childless and had lost his first wife to breast cancer, showered Wendy with attention. He E-mailed whimsical notes: *My sufficiency has been fully sufensified. Any more would be a superfuency.* And affirming notes: *I really admire your smarts, lady!* They biked and rollerbladed and hiked down trails. They challenged Tom and Michelle to Scrabble, watched videos, and went bowling. Wendy even went along when Mick did his weekly stint at a homeless shelter.

As Mick felt himself more and more attracted to Wendy, he struggled with revitalized emotions that begged to be felt again and the clear command of Scripture. He began to compromise, to convince himself that their relationship would never become serious—and if it did, why, he'd certainly save her soul for Christ. Yes, he would. Yesiree. Wendy held a guarded respect for Mick's beliefs, beliefs she knew she would never ever share. She worried that some day the "shoe would drop" and he would preach to her. But she compromised, convincing herself that if he ever brought up religion, she would resist his Jesus. Yes, she would. Yesiree.

It was late July when the shoe did drop and landed heavily on Wendy's foot. The question was: Would it send her limping for a while, or would it permanently cripple the woman? It was a Thursday afternoon. Wendy brought work with her into the backyard and spread out on a chaise lounge, pencil in hand. The sun warmed her, and in no time the manuscript was abandoned to dreamy sleep. In her dream she heard Tom talking to Mick:

"You cannot let the relationship continue, Mick. She is not a believer."

"It just hasn't been right for me to talk with her yet, Tom. I have every intention of witnessing to her."

"You're playing with fire, Mick. Every time you are with Wendy you are unequally yoked. It will not work. God's Word is clear about that." *Do not be yoked together with unbelievers. For what do righteousness and wickedness have in common? Or what fellowship can light have with darkness?*

"I know. But I care for her, Tom. And I intend to share the gospel."

"When? On your honeymoon? Mick, I'm telling you, break it off before it's too late."

Wendy sat stunned. It wasn't a dream. It was a real-life, honest-to-goodness conversation going on less than five feet from where she lay. The sneers came all at once.

You see, Wendy? Christians are all the same. They believe they are the only ones who have exclusive claims to God, that theirs is the only way. They show you all this highfalutin love and acceptance and plot behind your back. To them you are nothing more than a heathen who needs saving, a notch on their belt. You almost fell for it, didn't you, Wendy? Aren't you lucky you saw them for the phonies they are! You never did feel totally comfortable with them, did you? That's because they are so high and mighty. The whispers came like snarls. Wendy detonated. She went into her condo and paced. She reached for the most logical thing she could to vent her wrath, and hurled Brenda's book against the wall, leaving a smudgy dent.

Chosen found himself neck deep in wicked laughter and snide, filthy comments from Wendy and her many invisible consorts. Even Edgar joined in. "Meowwrrrr." Noise on the spirit level was deafening, loud enough to drown all vestige of hope, to stomp silent the salvation message that was working in the woman's heart. But it couldn't. The angel was smug in his confidence that the enemy with all his demonic legions, with all his power, with all his guile and deception, was as a flea before God. *"I will take over from here, Bashar. Step aside . . ."*

Rebound

Wendy went straight to Geoff. Skipping her Thursday Bible study, she dressed for seduction and drove to the downtown parking garage. Geoff couldn't possibly refuse an invitation to dinner at an upscale "be there/be seen" restaurant. They would talk. They'd get back on track. He was as arrogant as ever.

Needless to say, dinner was a disaster. Geoff talked nonstop about his latest slams in the market, how close he was to full partnership, how important he was to the firm. He ordered expensive wine and blew cigar smoke into Wendy's face. After her subtle maneuvering and not-so-subtle innuendo, he agreed to spend the night with her . . . if she put the cat in the garage. Wendy hurried home to prepare her bedroom for romance. She shoved the book back into her nightstand, burying it under the latest copy of *Cosmo*.

Geoff's Porsche and a Jeep pulled to the curb at the same time. Geoff glanced at the man in jeans and sneakers, his French loafers mirror clean as he walked the sidewalk to Wendy's condo and disappeared inside. Soon after, the Jeep started and drove down the street . . . the man in jeans might be gone, but he'd not be forgotten.

"It's seven o'clock. Remember! Jesus loves you!"

Mick's strong morning greeting surprised Geoff. "What is that?"

"Oh," covered Wendy as she pulled the plug, "that station keeps bleeding in on NPR. It has something to do with the airwaves."

"Bunch of idiots listen to that junk." He grabbed her and pulled her toward him. Chosen was repulsed. "I've missed you," he said.

Edgar screamed in the garage. He screamed again and again.

"Geoff . . ."

Geoff rolled out of bed in a huff. "You should take that cat to the shelter. I can't stand him."

Mick brought catnip toys for Edgar. "I'll give you a call in a few days." At that moment Mick was taking calls from little old ladies who adored him. Geoff left a parting shot: "Maybe we can get together next weekend." What was wrong with *this* weekend? She and Mick had planned a long bike ride.

"Oh my gosh . . . Mick!" Wendy called the radio station.

"May I have Mick Cochrane's voice mail, please?"

"Mick? This is Wendy. I don't want to see you anymore. I want you and your phony, hypocritical religion to drop dead. Just leave me alone. And I hope you crash on your bike ride!" That was rather childish, but she had to get back somehow.

And back she went. Back to the way it was before, the way it had always been. Lonely evenings in front of the TV, a distant hint of laughter coming through the walls, steadfastly avoiding her neighbor, making it clear despite Mick's protestations that she would have none of him. None. Just his E-mail. She read that. It was her one concession. She would not listen to his voice. She would not buy into all that Christianity. She would just read what he wrote—every day—and wait for Geoff to call.

"How come you're screening all your calls lately?" he asked one day.

"I got tired of phone solicitation."

"I hate talking to your machine."

"I hate talking to a machine, too, Geoff . . ." the rest of her sentence was better left unsaid.

One day she didn't talk to a machine, when she called Geoff at home and another woman answered. "Is this his mother?" she asked Wendy. "He should be home at noon. Do you want him to call you?" And the thin thread that held their relationship together snapped like the G-string on a guitar.

October

Wendy collected the Friday paper and hurried inside. Hoping the cold October morning was not a harbinger for winter to come, she poured herself a big mug of coffee before settling on the couch. Enjoying a few days' reprieve before starting a new project, she stretched and pulled Gram's afghan over her legs. It was one of those wonderful mornings when the entire paper was read with lazy interest: every classified ad, right down to Homes for Sale, the Personal Ads . . . she secretly wished to find an ad from Geoff: "To the Woman of My Dreams, will you forgive me, you are the only one for me, please call." She could not help her smile. It would be so like Geoff to ask *her* to call for his apology, probably a taped message on his machine. No doubt someone else was getting his phone calls now.

Friday's paper carried a religion page, one she deliberately avoided. Not this time. There, again, was a picture of Mick. She stared at it long and hard. If Wendy was of the persuasion that it was all right for women to have such feelings, she would admit that she missed him. She would admit she felt special when she was around him. She would admit that even though he'd only kissed her, she dreamed of the day when they would do more, much more, to establish their rightful relationship. She would even admit that she peeked when he pulled up next to Michelle's curb. But Wendy would not allow herself such feelings in the first place. Nosiree.

Mick was host at a "Community Praise Celebration" that evening, heralded as an event that would draw thousands. Thousands minus one, thank you. The doorbell rang. Wendy turned the afghan into a makeshift robe and scuffed to the door. Chosen laid down the red carpet. It was Michelle, carrying a tray crowded with teapot, teacups, scones, and lemon curd. "I slaved over this all morning," she announced. Wendy stepped aside and let the woman in, thinking the better of it.

"Am I interrupting your work?" asked Michelle as she set up an impromptu tea party.

"I'm taking a few days off."

"I made Earl Grey especially for you—you take sugar don't you?"

Wendy nodded, surprised that Michelle remembered her preference in tea. She hadn't been to that many Thursday night get-togethers.

"You know," said Michelle, "I was thinking about writing a cook-book . . . what do you think about that?" Michelle was as talented in conversation as her brother, and was particularly chatty that morning.

A bit guarded at first, Michelle covered as many "safe and neutral" subjects with her neighbor as she could think of: films, the Olympics—I'm an Olympic junkie, you know!—writing, her failed attempt to trek the Appalachian Trail, the chance the Cardinals had at the pennant. There was nary a mention of Mick—or Jesus. Wendy did notice the engagement ring on Michelle's finger, but chose not to comment. *OK, get through your stupid warm-up,* thought Wendy. *The shoe is going to drop any minute.* When it did, it felt more like a fuzzy houseslipper than a heavy boot.

Michelle collected her tea party, insisted on leaving the scones, and headed toward the door. She paused and turned to Wendy with . . . well, with rather pleading eyes.

"Wendy, there is a praise concert tonight . . ."

I knew it, I knew it!

"I'm going to give my testimony." She seemed genuinely nervous. "I've never done something like this before . . . you know . . . told my story in public like this. Anyway, it would mean a lot to me if you would come and sort of be, like, moral support."

"I'm sorry, I have plans."

"Oh. Well, it was nice seeing you again."

Wendy's plans consisted of watching television on her couch, probably with a container of Chinese takeout. Chosen smiled and stepped aside.

Wendy picked up the paper and put it in the recycle bin, accidentally locking Edgar in the garage. She spent much of the day catching up on her dreaded filing, paying bills, tending to much-needed cleaning in her office, NPR playing softly in the background. Vacuum attachment in hand, she went after dusty book tops with a vengeance, pausing when she noticed the skinny old book stuck between two Michener novels. *That's weird,* she thought, having not the slightest recollection of placing it there. Something tugged at her heart. She reached for the book and turned off the vacuum. What a surprise when she heard Mick's voice! "Make a joyful noise unto the Lord all the earth, make a loud noise and rejoice, and sing praise!" Those scrambled airwaves again! She switched off the radio, sat on the floor, and—in spite of herself—scanned several psalms. "Light is sown for the righteous, and gladness for the upright in heart." What an interesting word: *gladness.* She scanned Psalm 98. "Make a joyful noise unto the LORD." That's what Mick just said . . . Wendy heard her cat screech and a loud noise.

Quite perturbed over his incarceration, Edgar had shredded and bitten her neat pile of newspapers and swung determinedly on straps until rollerblades crashed to the floor.

"Edgar! What a mess!" The rollerblades were lying directly on top of Mick's picture, which, by the way, had been spared the wrath of a recalcitrant Siamese. Wendy picked the paper from the floor and stared at Mick. *Go tonight,* came into her subconscious like a command. It was. And it didn't come from an ardent angel.

Bundling the papers with string, Wendy set out for the recycling center and the Chinese restaurant. A taped promo played for the Praise Celebration as Mick's voice boomed over her car radio, flustering her enough to back into her trash can, left in the driveway by the St. Louis Sanitation Department. Glad it was sturdy rubber, she moved it to the side and headed down the street, the two tiny feet on her fish falling off as she drove. *Go tonight.* Chosen prayed the woman through her battle . . . and had fun with the radio until Wendy was so fed up she turned it off completely.

Carrying a bag with fried rice, wonton soup, and Kung Pai chicken, Wendy reached for the door of the Chinese restaurant and was eye to eye with a poster: "Community Praise Celebration with Mick Cochrane." *Go tonight.* She barged past incoming customers. Once back in her garage, she slipped slightly on a section of paper that somehow had been left behind, the section marked "Religion." *Go tonight.* A woman from Bible study had left a message on her machine. "You know, we are trying to round up as many people as we can to support Michelle tonight. We hope you can join us. We'll be looking for you." She was afraid to check her E-mail.

The message on her computer came from an address she'd never heard of before, certainly from a stranger someplace far away. Maybe an editor. The message was brief and to the point: *I've missed you. Won't you meet me tonight?* She looked back at the address. Was the message from Mick? It was impossible.

She changed into her pajamas immediately and made certain every lock was double-checked, every window shut, every curtain, every drape closed. Remote in hand, she switched on TV, only to find a black screen with block letters: "We are sorry for the inconvenience. The channel you have selected is not available at this time." Every single channel. She turned on radio, but those airwaves again! She turned to her CDs. *In the Mood* stared up at her from her music collection; she plopped Brahams into the player and headed to her bookcase. There on the floor sat Brenda's gift, waiting patiently. She grabbed the book with destruction in mind.

Testimony

Michelle sat up front so she could access the stage easily. She was extremely nervous.

"Just tell them the truth, kiddo. I'm real proud of you."

"Mickey, I'm shaking so much I don't know how I will get through this!"

"Grace, little sister, grace and mercy."

Mick was a hit. In his trademark black turtleneck, plus gray flannel slacks and loafers, he pushed back his sleeves and joined with musicians as they each took their turn. He laughed with his friend who played guitar and sang country. He sang along with two women with long, blonde hair. He led the clapping, in perfect rhythm, when a black choir blasted into the rafters. He quoted Scripture with the ease of one who held it in his heart; he joked, he cried.

And a sea of people raised their hands and swayed and shouted *Amen* and *Halleluia* in a show of community praise.

"Isn't it great to worship the Lord this way?" he whooped into the mike.

Yays, and claps, and "Go on, Brother" came in unison.

"To be together like this in community, to be sharing our love of Jesus in public: let me ask you, is it even possible to be sad when you are worshiping your King? Is there a lonely or unhappy person to be found in this entire building?"

NO!!!! And there wasn't.

It was time for Michelle's testimony. What she said left the crowd staggering for breath, and a woman way in the back shamed, for she had selfishly determined Michelle's little tea party that morning a ruse; she'd not taken her eyes off herself long enough to consider her neighbor might have really needed her support. Until now.

Michelle told of growing up in a loving home, of moving away to college for a degree in Genetic Engineering, *Huh?!* of selling out totally to the liberal mantra of radical feminism. *Michelle?* She told of her marriage to a man who adored her, of the power she felt: she was woman, she would roar. She told of her two children. It was here that she bit her lip and looked at her brother, who was already crying for what was to come.

"I was free, you see. Free to explore my life according to my own standards. No one had a right to push their morality on me. I was infuriated every time I heard some Christian do-gooder on television talk about family values, family this and that. And then I lost mine." The room held its breath.

"I thought nothing of having an affair. I'd had more than one, actually, and my latest lover had gotten me into cocaine. I used the cover of job demands to supposedly work late or attend conferences, and left my husband with the kids so often we just stopped fooling each other after a while. Our marriage was in shambles, and he was getting increasingly hostile, but it was my life, my sexuality, my body, my freedom." She took a long pause.

"One night . . ." her voice began to shake, and Mick gave her a thumbs-up. "It was Valentine's Day. I tried to figure how I could meet my lover and still keep things balanced at home." She began to cry. "My children had made little cards for me out of white paper doilies." *Of course! The doilies that are framed on her wall!* "I don't know what my husband was thinking. I guess he'd had enough, wanted to confront me. I don't know. He put the kids in the car. It was icy. A drunk driver." Michelle began to swoon, but steadied herself.

"I was in a motel, high on drugs. It wasn't until I went home at three in the morning that I found out." *Sweet Michelle? The neighbor with the frilly Bible cover who talks about Jesus all the time?* My *neighbor?!*

"I cannot even attempt to tell you the guilt and pain I carried. I became suicidal, had to be put in a hospital for my own protection, had to take drugs just to stay sane. You've heard people say that things happened to them that made life not worth living. Well, let me tell you, when they say it, they mean it. And I'm also here to tell you that when people say that Jesus Christ is the Way, the Truth, and the Life, they aren't being narrow-minded, hypocritical phonies. Because if it wasn't for Jesus Christ and His forgiveness, His death, His promise of eternal life, *I would not be here today!* Some of you may be thinking I don't deserve to be here today." Her voice drifted. "Mickey and others came to me, stuck by me, but it was Jesus who rescued me, who propped me up and told me that I, even I, deserved His death and redemption. The enormity of that realization was at first harder to bear than the death of my family. Do I still feel guilt and pain? Oh yes, yes I do. I will always bear the scar, the consequence of my sin. Until I gave my life to Christ, it was the loneliest, most horrible place to ever be. *Don't you see?*" She was impassioned now, tears falling as freely as all the other tears in the building. *"Everything people say to you about Jesus is true! Everything!"*

Mick jumped on stage and held Michelle to the sound of tentative, then thunderous, applause. Every musician surrounded them, singing "Jesus Paid It All."

Weak from emotion, hoarse from song, Mick took the microphone.

"Jesus paid it all. All to Him I owe. Sin had left a crimson stain . . . He washed it white as snow." He caught his breath and began to pray.

"Father God, we are here tonight to worship You, to give You praise, to give to You all glory, Lord. Jesus came into the world to restore our relationship with You. His suffering and death takes away the guilt of our sin. His sacrifice brings redemptive healing. We know no one comes to You but by Him." And then he dropped the shoe . . .

"Father, we pray tonight if there is anyone here who does not know You through Your Son, give that person neither rest nor peace until he or she finds You."

Mick turned to the crowd as the keyboard began to play soft music. "If there is anyone here tonight who is tired of living apart from God, we are inviting you to come forward right now. You may not have as dramatic a story as what you've just heard, but you know in your heart that He is calling you."

Go tonight.

"He wants to have a close, personal relationship with you. He stands at the door of your heart and knocks. He whispers in your ear. He talks to you through testimonies like Michelle's. He causes your heart to soar when you join in song to His glory."

Yeah, and he uses a Siamese cat and a radio, too . . .

"However He calls to you, won't you come up here and meet Him tonight?"

I've missed you. Won't you meet me tonight?

The crowds separated as one by one people walked forward, some struggling under the weight of depression, sin, loneliness, and separation for the last time, feeling it lift from them as new life breathed into trembling, smiling lips that were parted to offer praise, to ask forgiveness, to beg for mercy. Among the crowd was a woman with features like a bird, whose heart felt full and right for the first time in her life, and who would never be lonely again.

Epilogue

Mick felt the one-year anniversary of Wendy's acceptance of Christ a fitting time to pop the question. In spite of his certainty that Wendy would say "yes"—she needed him, after all, for all the sporting equipment they shared—Mick had a lump in his throat when he went on the air that morning. Wendy knew her man well by now, and caught her breath when she awoke to his words: "Gentle listeners, I may have big news for you tomorrow!" She closed her eyes, hugged her pillow, and pet Edgar. She imagined what it would be like to roll over and touch Mick in the morning, to go to sleep with him each night. A blush warmed her face with pink glow.

* * *

"Why on earth you agreed to live in his place is beyond me! It might be the family home, but it will take years to clean out his junk !" Michelle lugged yet another box and headed for the Honda, the outline of a bumper sticker nearly gone, a plastic fish in the place of Darwin.

"OK, yard sale or home?" Tom held a heavy box of books.

"That stays here. I should have my head examined for having a yard sale a week before my wedding!"

"You should have your head examined for not having a yard sale at Mick's first. At least this stuff has value!" Michelle reached for another box, before Tom stepped in.

"You shouldn't be lifting, Shelly!"

"That's an old wives' tale, Tom!" she laughed, "This baby is going to be strong like a bull."

"But I want his mother to be safe like a little lamb, so put it down!" Michelle obliged.

"We'll be over bright and early to help you set up for the sale, Wen."

* * *

Cars suddenly appeared. Lots of cars. People felt, examined, man-handled, tested, tugged, read, and bargained over every item on three long tables. Following the advice in *The Trash to Treasure Handbook,* Michelle and Wendy put a lot of planning into their effort and it was proving to be lucrative.

"Maybe I'll retire from broadcasting and let you support us with yard sales!" laughed Mick.

"You could keep her in profits for years," quipped his bulging sister.

The four sat on lawn chairs and offered assistance when needed, their main job to collect quarters, dimes, and dollars. They each noticed the man as he approached them from the street. Had they been watching carefully, they would have noticed he didn't arrive by car.

He was an extraordinary man, with bearing that must be called regal. His skin was the color of burnished copper, his hair jet black and shoulder length. His eyes were like chunks of coal with diamond chips sparkling under thick black lashes and brow.

"This guy must work at the gym!" whispered Tom, who felt puny in his white plastic lawn chair.

The man wore a casual white shirt, unbuttoned at the neck, tucked into khaki trousers as if an artist drew it into place. He wore sandals on his feet. None of the four could take their eyes off of him. He returned their looks with such affection that they squirmed. All of time stopped and seemed replaced by a moment without end as the four gaped at the amazing man, fighting an urge to . . . to worship. They would say later that they felt embarrassed, self-conscious, vulnerable . . . almost naked when he looked at them, but when Mick declared, "Naked in a good, peaceful way," they all nodded.

The man picked Brenda's gift from the stack of books. "This book is priceless, you know."

Unable to speak, they nodded back, the women troubled into thinking where they'd seen him. Edgar shot out from behind a bush and pressed his arched back against the man's leg.

"Just push him away," Wendy managed to squeak.

"Oh, Edgar's my buddy," laughed the man. Later they would wonder how he knew the cat's name.

"It is time for me to take this book home," said the incredible man who stood before them. They nodded some more, the women suddenly conscious of bare knees, the men feeling curious and uneasy . . . in a good, peaceful way.

"No charge," Wendy squeaked some more. "Please, just take it."

"Why thank you, Wendy," said the man, who gazed at each one with the eyes of his Master. "It has been so very, very good to be with you."

And with that, an angel named Chosen, Bashar-el, whose job it was to follow the book, headed home, Brenda's gift in hand.

SDG
Soli Deo Gloria

About the Author

Cynthia and her husband live in Montana's Rocky Mountains. A popular radio personality, motivational speaker, and humor columnist, she has written several books and articles. This is her first novel. She is an eager beginning gardener and positively swoons at the notion of exploring a distant land or trying a new recipe.